Morning Glory Girl

MARIA ANNE LENIHAN

Scan QR code for Content Warnings, Map, & Bonus Scenes

Or visit www.marialenihanauthor.com/my-books/morning-glory-girl

MORNING GLORY GIRL

ISBN: 979-8-9988028-0-5 (Paperback edition - first run)

ISBN: 979-8-9988028-2-9 (Paperback edition)

ISBN: 979-8-9988028-1-2 (Ebook edition)

First Edition: June 2025

Editing: Victoria Hayes (Victoria Jane Editorial); Allie Samberts; Sara Sudol (Write Way Edits)

Cover Design: Ink and Laurel

Chapter image & scene break images: Author via Canva.com

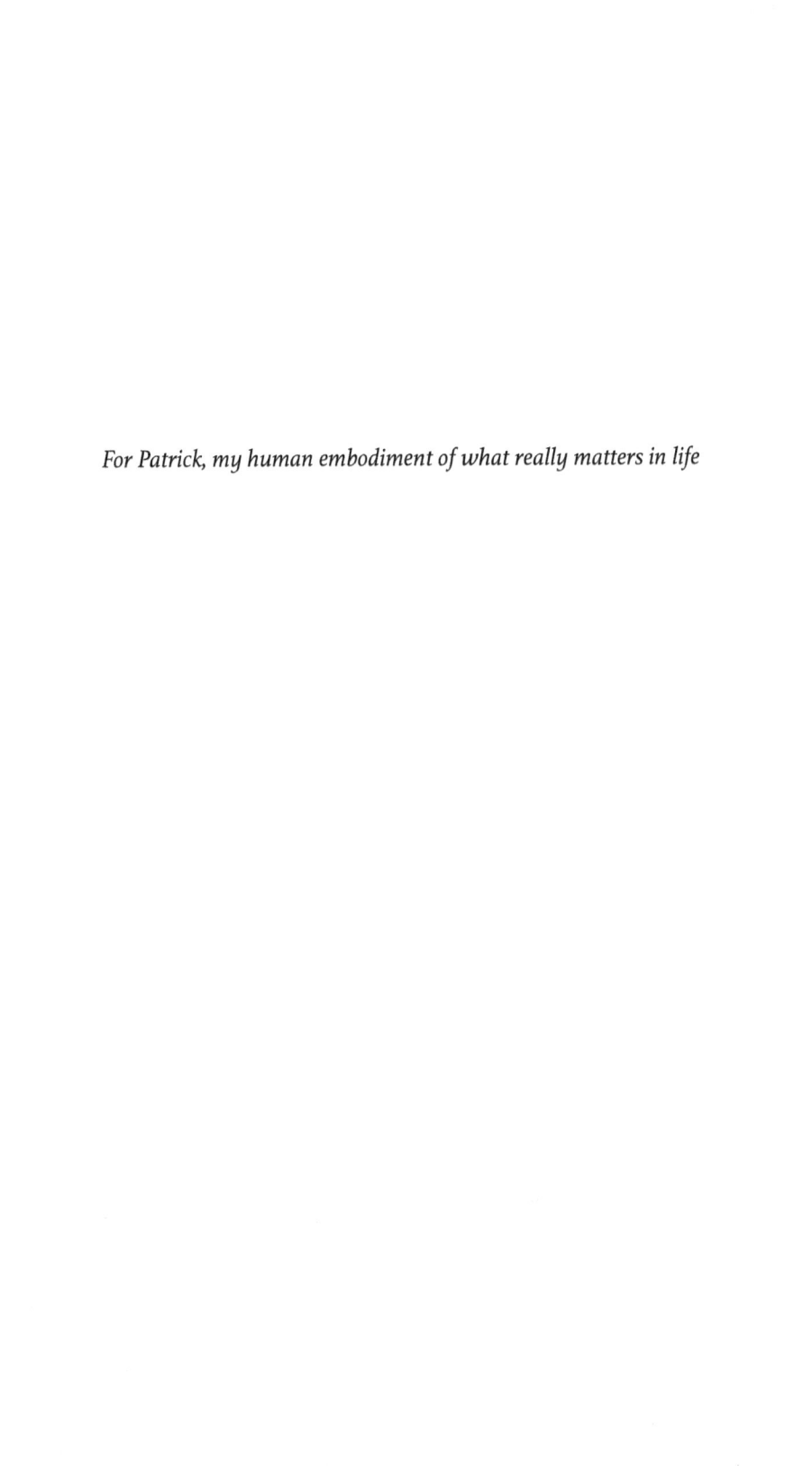

For Patrick, my human embodiment of what really matters in life

1

On a Thursday in March, I made a fortunate mistake. It would take me a long time to see it that way, though.

By the time I looked up from the contract on my desk, it was dark outside my office window and my reflection stared back at me from the glass. My honey brown hair was piled in a bun on top of my head, and the puffy bags under my eyes were a shade darker than usual from last night's all-nighter.

I straightened the stack of papers and slipped them into my bag. My hand trembled as I closed my laptop. *Probably hunger.* On cue, my stomach grumbled, and I considered where to stop for takeout on my way back to my apartment.

When I stepped out of my small associate's office, the light was still on in the corner office down the hall. *Great, I'll quickly let John know I'm almost done reviewing this vendor contract and ask if he got any updates from our client today.*

I knocked on the threshold of the office belonging to the head partner of my firm's private equity department.

"Val, I'm glad you stopped by," John said. "I've been wanting to talk to you about this Brower Capital deal. Give me one second to finish this email."

My stomach sank. I had a feeling I was about to regret my decision to drop by. As he typed away, my gaze snagged on a picture of his son in a football uniform on his desk. He was probably watching the Thursday night NFL game alone while his dad was still at work.

John spun in his desk chair and barely made eye contact with me before he started speaking. "You need to work on producing contract drafts and other work product faster. I've noticed on this tech investment that things are taking us longer than they should."

What?

My brows furrowed in confusion as I wracked my brain for examples of times we'd missed any deadlines we promised to this particular client and came up blank. In fact, I could count on one hand the number of times I'd missed *any* deadline in the last six years. And even when I had, it was always an internal deadline— telling the partner I'd need a few more hours to finish a draft or a diligence summary. Client deadlines, however, were sacred.

I'd missed my brother's PhD graduation ceremony but never a client deadline.

John looked at me through his round, black glasses. His full head of gray hair was still coiffed even at this time in the evening, his pleated khakis and navy-blue blazer barely wrinkled. He probably got back from a client dinner not long ago.

"Definitely noted, John. I'll do my best to make sure we're getting work product to the client as fast as possible every time. I'm not aware that we missed any deadlines we promised though, right? I've gotten the impression Brower has been happy with our services on this deal."

"No, we haven't *missed* any deadlines, but that's not the point." The word 'missed' came out as a hiss. "You often indicate to me that more time is necessary for deliverables than it should be. Devon would have gotten the first purchase agreement to the client in less than forty-eight hours. That's what you need to be doing, too."

Shock landed like a blow to the chest, immobilizing me in the doorway with my bag slung over my shoulder.

My junior associates hadn't slept in weeks, and neither had I. We had turned things around as quickly as humanly possible without sacrificing the quality of our work, which was important to me, too. *We've been doing a great job on this deal,* my brain insisted. Our client, the lead in-house lawyer at Brower Capital, regularly thanked me and the team and complimented our performance. How could John have anything to critique?

Devon was another seventh-year associate in the private equity group—my practice group. He was well-respected by the partners, feared by junior legal associates, and definitely going to make partner in a few years. I'd only ever been compared with him in a positive light: we were peers, colleagues, and both considered the go-to senior associates for the highest profile deals for our most important clients. Apparently, he got things done faster than me, and John had taken notice. *Crap.*

How was I supposed to make partner in three years if John didn't think I completed my work fast enough?

My heart rate climbed, and I wiped my damp palms on my pants.

I tried again to defend myself. "I understand. I'll work on improving turnaround times and make sure the juniors understand the urgency. I do think quality of work product is important to Brower, too—you know Jasmine actually reads everything. And I'm confident we've provided really high-quality representation on this deal, and she has noticed that."

I held my breath and hoped John would agree, at least on the point of quality.

But he didn't. Still seated, he used the stern but unfazed tone he normally reserved for negotiations to say, "You're missing the point, Val. We need that quality, *and* we need to get things to them even faster. That's what your peers are doing, and that's what our peer law firms are doing."

I opened my mouth to reply, but nothing came out. My heart rate had accelerated so much that now I felt winded. *Calm down, Val,* I said to myself. *Take a deep breath.*

I tried, but I couldn't get the air to move past my throat and into my lungs. And then a cloudiness built at the top of my spine. *Oh no.*

John went on to say something about helping me out and seeing my potential, but I could barely hear him. *I need to get out of here. Fast.* Despite my attempts to breathe deeply, my heart wasn't slowing down. It was picking up. A prickle climbed my neck toward the back of my skull. The panic attack was coming, and experience had taught me that my body won't stay conscious long enough to ride it out. I needed to run back to my office, drop to the ground, and put my head between my knees because if I let that cloudy, prickly feeling crest over the top of my head and start sinking down toward my eyebrows, I was done for.

I made something up. "Thanks for the feedback, John. I actually have to run, I have a call later I need to get home for." I turned on my heel, ready to make a break for the nearest empty office.

It was too late.

The last thing I heard was John's voice saying, "Val, are you okay?" from a mile away as the world turned sideways.

I came to a few seconds later and blinked. The hallway ceiling came into view, and then John's concerned face, kneeling beside me on the carpeted floor, his hand gripping my elbow.

Oh my god.

"Are you okay? I caught you before you hit your head."

No! I am mortified.

"Yes," I lied, sucking in a deep breath. "Um, thank you."

"Do you need anything? I hope it wasn't what I was saying."

I shook my head. "No, I just probably haven't eaten enough today." *And I didn't sleep at all last night, as you well know,* I refrained from adding. I straightened my shirt and pushed myself up.

John hovered nearby, apparently worried I might collapse again.

"I'm going to head home." I was disoriented, but after several gulps of air, the cloudiness cleared. More than anything, I wanted to leave the building. "I'll get you my comments on that vendor contract by tomorrow."

"Okay, thank you." A line formed between his brows. "Take care of yourself."

"Will do." I walked as quickly as my wobbly legs could carry me to the elevator bank.

When I got back to my one-bedroom apartment in the Hudson Yards neighborhood of Manhattan half an hour later, I turned on the light with a shaking hand, and then sat on my couch and stared at the wall above my television.

What is wrong with me? I'm so bad at receiving constructive criticism that I fainted at work?

I groaned. *Fuck.* Six years of killing myself to rise through the ranks and now I'd had this moment of humiliating weakness that would probably follow me. Tears started flowing unbidden.

"You're missing the point, Val." John's stern, all-knowing tone played on a loop in my head.

I'd sacrificed all of my plans and most of my sleep these past weeks for the deal in question, all so that we would be on track to sign the purchase agreement next week like the client requested. I thought I'd been doing so well. I could tell the client liked me. I still didn't understand where the negative feedback came from.

Not bothering to get my breathing under control first, I took out my cell phone and called my mom.

"I fainted at work."

"Oh, honey. That hasn't happened to you since college. Are you okay? Are you sick? Have you been eating?"

"I don't think it's that. I was just stopping by John's office on my way home and he told me that I haven't been producing my work fast enough on this tech deal."

"He can't be serious." My mom knew this deal had taken over my life lately—consistent sixteen-hour days, no time for even a phone call to catch up.

"Oh, he was. He said Devon would have gotten the agreement done faster, and I basically need to match his speed. But I know our client is happy with our work on this deal, and I tried to tell him that, but he really dug in. Said I'm missing the point, and I panicked and fainted right there in the hallway." I sped through the summary, hands shaking, voice trembling, cheeks heating by the second. I still couldn't fully believe it happened.

"That's completely unacceptable, Val. He had no right to ambush you like that."

"I should be better at taking constructive criticism by now," I muttered. "I might be too sensitive for this job."

"I don't see what part of that was constructive. You can't find more hours in the day. I'm sure the quality of the work this male associate he's so fond of is producing isn't as good as yours, either, if he's doing it so fast."

I sighed, helpless.

"You're too hard on yourself, honey."

"Probably," I relented. "Please don't tell Drew."

"Valerie, he's your brother, he cares about you."

"I know, but I'm embarrassed. I've shown this sign of weakness, hypersensitivity..." Drew had always been successful. It came naturally for him. If he found out, he would probably ask me how this episode was going to negatively impact my success at the firm and then try to help me come up with ways to mitigate it. I couldn't take that right now.

"I don't agree with that at all," Mom insisted. "Did you ever miss a client deadline or an internal deadline?"

"No."

"So, it sounds to me like the feedback was completely unwarranted and this partner is a jerk."

"I don't *get* to feel like he's a jerk, Mom. He's head of the group. My only chance of making partner is if *he* thinks I deserve it."

My mother didn't speak for a moment.

"I know that's your goal, honey, and I support you. I'm just frustrated on your behalf that it seems like they keep moving the goalposts. You work so hard..."

My mom paused but my throat was too tight to fill the silence. My head hurt, and the comedown from the intense distress of earlier had left me wrung out. Still, the anxiety over what this lapse might cost me hummed in my fingertips.

"I'm really proud of you, Val," she added finally. "Please eat something and get some sleep tonight? *Please* tell me you don't have to do more work."

"A few emails and then I'll get in bed. Promise."

"Okay. I'm bringing you some groceries this weekend when we visit, too. No objections," she added before we hung up.

Crap. I'd completely forgotten they were visiting me this weekend for my dad's birthday. But we probably wouldn't get the contract back from the counterparty until Sunday or Monday at the earliest, so I should have time to hang out with my parents while they're here.

As I watched the little tray of frozen mac and cheese spinning in my microwave, I mulled over my mom's choice of words: *"I know that's your goal."* Wasn't making partner what she and Dad wanted for me, too?

My parents had always encouraged Drew and me to work hard, and to go to schools and go into fields where we'd have financial security. It wasn't as easy for them, they'd say.

"I don't think anyone in high school expected me to succeed," my dad had told us over dinner one Sunday when Drew and I were still in grade school. "No one was more surprised than your mother when I came home in my Navy uniform, flight-school bound... Well, except for maybe your grandmother." He chuckled, but pride shone clear in his blue eyes.

"I wasn't *that* surprised," Mom had insisted.

"We've done well for ourselves as a team." He tapped her thigh and scanned the kitchen of the newer, nicer house we'd moved into on the other side of town the year prior. "And the sky's the limit for you two." He pointed his raised fork at Drew and me in turn. "Got way more opportunities than I had, and you're much smarter than me, too. Got your mother's brains to thank for that."

My dad's stories always inspired me, stoking flames of motivation in my belly. They all had the same refrain: prioritize striving and achieving and work tirelessly toward success and financial security for you and your family. So, for my whole life, that was the objective: work hard, excel in school, get a prestigious, lucrative job, succeed at it, and attain even more than my parents had out of respect for their hard work and the opportunities we had that they didn't.

All of that had been going pretty well for me before today.

After one scorching bite of macaroni, my phone buzzed on my coffee table. I groaned and answered.

"Mom told me what happened." Drew's confident, slightly accusatory voice emanated from my phone speaker. "Why'd you tell her not to tell me?"

"I'm embarrassed, and I don't know, Drew, I didn't think you'd understand. You've never fainted at work. And you're not, like, the most sympathetic person." I wasn't sure how slinging insults at my brother was supposed to make me feel better. It didn't. I braced myself for his defense, for the conversation to devolve into a spat like it almost always did with us.

"I know. I'm sorry."

My jaw fell down to my chest. Was he really just apologizing and letting that comment go?

"Okay," I said quietly, frozen in shock.

"But in any event, fuck him."

"What?"

"Fuck him. The partner that criticized you. He sounds like a sexist, small-dick asshole who needed to knock his all-star female associate down a peg to make himself feel important."

I couldn't help the smile that tugged on my lips. Not that Drew could see it.

"Drew," I said, low and admonishing.

"What? You know I'm right."

I sighed in defeat.

Fun fact: Drew was always right.

As early as elementary school, I'd noticed how much easier school subjects came to Drew than they did to me. He'd spend twenty minutes studying and come home with perfect scores on all his exams. Based on his standardized test scores, he was placed into all the accelerated programs. *"Drew is so smart,"* everyone would say to him, to my parents. *"You must be so proud."* They used words like 'advanced,' 'gifted,' and 'genius.'

I'm smart, too! my little eight-year-old self wanted to say. But to get the same results, I had to toil at our kitchen table for hours, growing frustrated when things didn't click. Sometimes my mom would ask Drew to help me. He'd sit next to me, solve the homework question quicker than I could read it, and then say something like, "See? It's easy." When I didn't get the hang of it after a few tries, he'd grow frustrated with me, too. "I don't understand, Val. How do you *not* get this?" he'd ask me. We'd fight. Sometimes I'd cry. I wanted to be like Drew. I wanted to be told I was smart and gifted. But seeing firsthand how much easier it all was for him, feeling his judgment and condescension, made me feel stupid.

Eventually, Mom stopped asking Drew to help me and would sit with me at the table herself. *All the better*, I thought at the time. She was kinder and more patient than an eleven-year-old boy. And I wanted to do it without his help, anyway.

"You still there?"

"Yeah," I muttered. I appreciated him taking my side, but it was still hard for me to talk to him about things like this.

"Mom said he's the head of your group so you have to, like, play the game and pretend to roll with it, but that doesn't change the truth. I know how these firms work, how they leverage the associate workforce to the hilt so the partners can take on several deals at once and maximize profits. He'd be *nowhere* without you. What an unbelievable prick." Drew's vitriol radiated through the phone.

"Thanks, Drew." His loyalty was actually touching. Sometimes he wielded his blunt, ruthless tongue for good, I supposed.

"Anytime. You're okay though?"

"Yeah, I'll be okay. Sending a couple emails and taking the rest of tonight off."

"Good."

Once my emails were sent, I was as exhausted as I had ever been, but I still couldn't fall asleep. The chorus of car horns and voices from twenty stories below didn't faze me. It was the self-doubt swirling in my mind that kept me up. I stared at the ceiling as my subconscious poked and prodded at my resolve, asking—for what felt like the tenth time this month—if this success I was striving for was worth everything I'd given up to attain it.

2

Two Weeks Earlier

"**D**o you think you can get us a draft of the purchase agreement by Monday?" Jasmine stared at us from her little video conference square on Thursday night. She'd just explained the details of their opportunity to acquire 51 percent of a hot new tech company.

I shot John a look that I intended to say: *They cannot be serious.* We only learned about the deal that morning when Jasmine sent us a two-sentence email with an angry red exclamation point marking it as *high importance.*

John acknowledged my look with a slight shake of his head, but to the client he said, "We can do that."

I controlled my facial expression until the call was over, but after we hung up, I dropped my forehead to my desk. *Another weekend, ruined.* I stopped keeping track a long time ago. And unlike most weekends, this weekend I actually had plans. *I'm so tired of this.*

After a minute I turned my head to the side and focused my

gaze on the plain white wall of my little office and the UPenn and Michigan Law diplomas I had hung there. I usually felt a surge of pride when I looked at them, but today my brain decided to fixate on the diploma that wasn't there. The first one I ever really wanted.

Franconia Academy was nestled unassumingly in a small town in New Hampshire not far from where we grew up. I was in sixth grade when Drew got in. The school looked like an idyllic small college with brick buildings, a state-of-the-art athletic facility, and a collegiate-level theater program. Almost every student that went there gained admission to a prestigious college.

I wanted to go there desperately, too. *I'd study and do theater and make friends and get into a great college,* my younger self thought. Whatever natural ability I lacked that Drew had, I would make up for by working harder than everyone else. After that—I'd been told by my parents and teachers and society—I'd be on the fast track to success. I'd be respected and admired by everyone I met, and my parents would be just as proud of me as they were of my brother.

Drew was home for spring break when my letter from Franconia arrived a few years later. I ran to the mailbox as soon as the mail truck pulled away. Back inside, I sat on the couch and tore open the letter, ready to read the word *'Congratulations.'*

My stomach plummeted when instead it said: *We regret to inform you...* Hot tears built behind my eyelids. Thirteen years old, and I felt like the universe was telling me I wasn't good enough. *You don't get to be as successful as your brother and his classmates.* The thought burrowed into my psyche and set up a permanent residence.

Drew found me in the living room of our childhood home, holding the letter in my clammy hands, staring at that first line but unable to read the rest of it. He read it over my shoulder.

"I'm sorry, Val. That stinks. But some people find it really challenging there, you know. Maybe you'll like public high school better."

Whether he meant to or not, his suggestion that I'd find Franconia to be too challenging made the rejection sting even more.

"Please leave me alone." Humiliation laced my tone with venom.

Drew slipped out of the room silently, and next thing I knew, my parents sandwiched me on the couch.

"I'm sorry, honey," my mom said. "I know how badly you wanted to go there."

My dad patted me on the back. "Going to that school isn't the only way to succeed. Their loss. Stay the course, Val. Keep working hard and it will pay off."

So that was what I did. I spent high school and college and law school grinding to get the best grades I could, and it all culminated with the rare, highly sought after job offer from Peters & Dowling, one of the top law firms in New York City, and the world. In just three years, I would be eligible for the promotion to Peters & Dowling partner. If I got it, I would make millions of dollars, and make a career of negotiating the most high profile, highest dollar-value deals.

The definition of success and financial security.

I pushed myself up from my desk and concocted a plan for how I'd make it to the birthday party I'd committed to that weekend *and* meet this client deadline.

Stay the course, Val, I said to myself.

It will be worth it.

Right?

The sun was far from up when my alarm sounded on Saturday morning. I fumbled through the top drawer of my dresser and pulled out a well-worn, full-coverage, tan bra. It used to be comfortable, but now it was too small. I'd gained enough weight that I needed to buy new bras, but part of me held out hope that

I'd find time to exercise again soon, so I didn't want to replace them all just yet. I clasped it behind my back and pulled each strap up to rest on my shoulders.

Besides, it didn't matter that it was ill-fitting, I'd just be sitting at the desk in my living room. Alone.

My law school friends, Tyler and Erica, were having a birthday party that afternoon for their two-year old daughter, which was mostly an excuse for them to invite all of their adult friends over to their new house for food and cake and drinks. I'd been looking forward to it for weeks.

I hadn't seen them in months.

I refused to let Jasmine's request for a contract draft by Monday prevent me from going, so here I was, at 4:30 a.m. on a Saturday morning, firing up my computer and making a cup of coffee. I had about six hours to read and revise every line of the 150-page document before sending it to John. Then I could get ready for the party.

But six hours later, I was still hung up on the indemnity section, agonizing over which representations and warranties should be considered 'fundamental,' and therefore result in enhanced damages for my client if they were breached by the tech company.

Eventually my drooping eyelids compelled me into the kitchen to make another cup of coffee from my little single-serve machine. The time on the stove glared at me. I was hoping to be in the shower by now, but I had another thirty pages to revise.

Should I text Tyler and Erica and tell them I can't make it?

No. I clenched my fist. *I need to show up for them.*

Glass of water in one hand and boiling cup of coffee in the other, I only spilled a little as I ambled back to my desk. My trembling hands landed back on my keyboard. I rolled my shoulders and began reading the next section.

By 12:30 the document was in John's inbox, and I was sprinting into my bedroom. I skipped my shower, left on the ill-fitting bra, and threw on a pair of jeans and a blouse that used to look good on me, but now were a little too snug around my waist and hips. My makeup routine got bypassed, too, replaced with few swipes of mascara and some tinted lip balm so I didn't miss the train to the suburbs. When I walked out of my apartment fifteen minutes later, I felt thoroughly disgusting, and not much in the mood to socialize.

Hopefully Chris doesn't come to this party.

Enjoy it, the voice in my mind said as my boot-clad feet carried me up the walkway to Tyler and Erica's front door. *You love your friends, and you haven't seen them in so long.* Despite repeating these things to myself as my hand hovered over the door handle, I already knew what would happen once I went in. I'd be surrounded by people I cared about, people I genuinely wanted to see and talk to, but at the same time, in a very real way, I'd be completely alone with the stress inside my own head.

Half-present. Pretending.

Erica spotted me the moment I entered their kitchen. "Val, I'm so glad you could make it!"

I rushed over to give her a hug.

"Wouldn't miss it! It's so good to see you. And look at this house!" Their white kitchen cabinets extended all the way to the ceiling, and the wide-planked hardwood floors gleamed.

"Thank you! It needs a few updates, but I'm so glad we found something with enough bedrooms and not so far outside of the city."

"I think it's beautiful."

Erica smiled.

Tyler was talking to a few people I didn't recognize on the other end of the kitchen. I decided not to interrupt.

"Help yourself to a drink." Erica gestured to a bar cart in the living room. "And there's a raw bar in the dining room."

"A raw bar? Incredible."

Erica rolled her eyes. "Please eat at least five oysters."

"You don't need to tell me twice," I assured her, instantly glad I came. They clearly spent a lot of time and money on this party. *It matters to show up,* I told myself. *Even if you're exhausted and don't feel like your full self right now.*

I headed toward the living room and took out my phone, holding my breath while my inbox refreshed, that familiar little kernel of dread flaring in my belly. It dissipated when no new emails popped up.

I exited my inbox and texted Natalie to ask what time she was getting here before navigating around an L-shaped leather couch and several clusters of balloons to get to the bar cart. As I poured myself a glass of chilled rosé, my phone vibrated.

NATALIE

Walking up the steps now!

Thank god. Natalie was my first friend in law school. We did our first group project for Civil Procedure together, decided we liked each other, and then did almost everything together after that: events, parties, classes, and study groups for every class we had in common. Natalie had tight black ringlets (a stark contrast to my golden brown, pin-straight hair), a heart-shaped face, and a round, button nose. She was single, like me, so we had more time for each other than our coupled-off friends like Tyler and Erica. She was Jewish and holding out for the right Jewish man to come into her life.

I was single for other reasons.

I pulled open the front door and Natalie immediately wrapped her arms around my neck, artfully avoiding the glass of wine in my hand. "I need one of those," she said instead of hello.

"Follow me!" I guided us back to bar cart in the living room, uncorked the wine, poured it into a stemless glass, and slid it toward my friend.

She knocked her glass into mine with a *clink.* "I'm glad you made it! I know it's been hell lately."

"I woke up at 4:30 this morning to draft a purchase agreement."

"Shit," Natalie breathed, shaking her head.

I sighed and took a sip of my wine, already relishing its numbing effect on my nervous system.

I glanced over my shoulder. "I need to find little Mina and say happy birthday," I said. We meandered from the living room to the playroom attached to the kitchen.

Natalie broke off to say hi to Erica.

I dropped down on the carpeted floor in front of where Mina was playing. "Happy birthday!" I said. The little girl stared at me for a second but didn't react. "What's the name of your doll?" I gestured to the infant-sized baby doll in her hands. She mumbled something I didn't understand, handed it to me, and toddled over to a bin on the other side of the room, the tulle skirt of her princess-like pink dress rustling with each step. She returned a moment later, handed me another doll, and murmured its name. She reminded me a little of a toddler I used to babysit for when I was a teenager. When Natalie found me again, I was still on the floor, *ooh*-ing and *ahh*-ing over the dress on the fifth doll Mina had brought to me.

"Hi, Mina! Happy birthday!" Natalie sang. Mina gave us a bewildered look, her adorable chubby cheeks pulling upward in an almost-smile, before running away, this time back to her grandparents, the doll show abandoned.

"Oysters?" Natalie said. "I've been instructed to eat at least five."

I laughed, sure of two things: the raw bar was definitely Tyler's idea, and Erica was dreading having leftover oysters at the end of the day.

"Yes." I pushed myself up from the floor. Natalie and I made a plate of three oysters each and found seats in the dining room. We sipped our rosé and caught up on the first dates she'd gone on recently.

"At least this one didn't mind when I wanted to take a picture of our cocktails." She rolled her eyes. As she described the latest guy, I tried to calculate how long it'd been since I went on a date. Could it be two years?

Natalie left her law firm three years ago to take a position on the in-house legal team at a hospital. The new job came with a lower paycheck but a more predictable schedule and more control over her time, in part because she could hire law firms for the hospital's bigger, more complicated deals. She'd been imploring me to do the same for years, and this was her primary reason: I'd actually have time to date. "I haven't found my person yet, but at least now I have time to try," she'd always say. She wasn't wrong.

But I still wanted to see if I could do it—make partner, make millions, show I could succeed even in such a competitive environment. Even though it had been particularly rough lately, I still felt that need to prove to everyone that I was smart and hardworking enough to be a Peters & Dowling partner.

When Natalie got up to refill our wine glasses, I checked my phone again. *Lord knows why I haven't gotten an Apple watch.* This time I had an email from John. *Dammit.* My pulse thrummed. I brought my laptop with me so I could slip into another room to work or hop on a quick call with John if I needed to, but I'd been hoping I wouldn't have to do that this time. My mind's eye flashed to images of me in my childhood bedroom on a conference call on Christmas Eve morning, and then me in the guest bedroom of Tyler's old apartment, typing away while my friends watched the Super Bowl.

My hand shook slightly as I tapped the message with my thumb. Luckily, it was just a discrete question about one section of the agreement. I fired off a reply, hoping it wouldn't prompt a lengthy exchange.

When John responded two minutes later with, Fair point. Let's try it, my shoulders relaxed. I grabbed two more oysters, complete with lemon and hot sauce, and returned to my seat.

That small burst of relief was short-lived, however. If he was already reviewing the liability cap section, he'd be sending me his comments soon.

I didn't notice Natalie had returned until she pushed a glass with a heavy pour of rosé right under my nose. Love her.

"You okay?" she asked.

"Oh yeah, I'm fine. Just a quick work email." I smiled and took a sip, holding the bright, tart liquid on my tongue for a moment before swallowing it.

"No, I mean...Chris is here," she whispered, her lips barely moving.

My stomach dropped. I twisted to look over my shoulder and sure enough, there he was. Chris LaMont. Tyler's old roommate, and my ex-boyfriend.

"Come on. He never comes to things like this, and today he decides to show up?" I hissed to Natalie under my breath.

"I thought you saw him. Sorry. Let's leave." She took a big gulp of her wine and rose from her chair.

"No, we can't leave. He'll know I left because of him. Besides, I don't want to." I forced a deep breath into my chest. *I can handle this.*

I knew Chris would be invited to this party, but the anxiety tearing through my stomach told me I hadn't believed he'd show up. I frowned at my little plate of oysters with their perfect dollops of hot sauce, and my stomach lurched again. *Dammit.* I hated myself for letting his presence make me lose my appetite. *I don't know why I even care after five whole years.*

But our breakup took a toll on me, which Natalie knew.

I looked up at her. Sympathy covered her face. She glanced down at her watch and said, "We'll stay until they do the cake, and then slip out and go back to your apartment. Sound good?"

"Yes, perfect." Gratitude for my loyal best friend settled my stomach, if only slightly.

"How's work going?" Tyler asked, placing an overflowing plate of food in front of the empty chair next to Natalie.

"It's going well! Nothing terribly exciting to report," Natalie said. I knew she wasn't lying about things going well like I so often did.

"What about you, Val? Has it been nuts as usual? I heard the private equity business is going off." This was how 'BigLaw' lawyers spoke to each other. *"How are you?"* was replaced with *"How's work going?"* Since, for us, they were the same thing. The litmus test for our sanity was how many hours we billed last week.

"I'm...surviving," I responded to Tyler, forcing a closed-lip smile.

"Hang in there. Hopefully it slows down soon."

I nodded, even though I didn't think it would. "How's the break going? You find a dads' softball league out here in the 'burbs yet?" Tyler had left his law firm job a few months ago to stay home with Mina for a bit.

"Not yet, but that's a great idea. I'd love to crush some other dads on the softball field. Maybe I can find a spring league."

"I'm sure whoever's team you end up on will be very grateful," I said.

Tyler shrugged. During law school we'd learned he was a great softball player, but he was humble.

"And then you have coaching all of Mina's sports to look forward to," Natalie added, looking over into the playroom at the gaggle of babies. I followed her gaze to where Mina was banging a toy pot on the counter of a toddler-sized kitchen.

"I'm counting down the days. Can't wait to get her on the golf course, the tennis court, the tee ball field." Tyler looked over at his daughter. "You guys, I'm obsessed. She's the coolest little kid. I would be so happy being a stay-at-home dad." His eyes gleamed with pride and love. Happiness and envy warred inside me.

What was it like to love someone so much that nothing else compared or mattered? It must feel great. My younger self assumed I would know what that felt like by this time in my life—thirty-one years old. But that hadn't been my path. Not since Chris let me walk out the door and never called me again.

I bit the inside of my cheek and refocused on our conversation, all the while attempting to put a lid on the void yawning open inside of me. "I don't doubt it," I said. "I knew since the moment I met you—this guy has major dad vibes."

Tyler laughed, a full-bellied guffaw that traveled into the next room where a few of the adults looked up. "I'm not sure how I feel about that, Val!"

Natalie and I broke out laughing, too. "It's true!" I defended.

"Yeah, we both agree, we even talked about it at the time, after our first grad school softball game," Natalie said, wiping away a tear of laughter with her manicured fingertips.

Tyler shook his head and took another big bite of his burger, eyes still alight. He swallowed before adding, "Unfortunately, I'll need to start looking for an in-house job for the fall. We just took on quite the mortgage."

"You'll find something with a better balance," Natalie assured him.

He clinked his beer can against her wine glass.

I walked into the kitchen a few minutes later to grab us some waters from the cooler, but Chris stood right next to it, talking to a girl I didn't recognize. *Probably a new girlfriend.* He was never one to suffer long relationship gaps. I spun around before he could look up, my stomach flipping over, and slinked back into the dining room.

"Can you actually grab the waters?" I whispered to Natalie.

She tilted her head to see through the arched entry separating the dining room from the kitchen, immediately clocking my obstacle. "Absolutely," she said with resolve before pushing back in her chair.

"Hey, Nat," Chris said when she reached the cooler.

The stilted, sharp, "hi," she gave him in return could cut glass, and I smirked to myself.

I twisted the cap off the water bottle after she handed it to me and sipped it slowly. Why did Chris have to be here and remind me how easy I was to drop? It made me feel even worse about my appearance and mental state today. Luckily, I managed to avoid speaking with him using similar tactics for the rest of the party. He never approached me, either. Probably because I didn't give him any openings to do so.

If he even wanted to.

One hour and a loud, off-tune rendition of "Happy Birthday" later, Natalie and I left together to head back to my apartment.

3

We took seats opposite each other on the train, and Natalie dove into her social media feed on her phone. Since moving to an in-house job, she'd started a page about her favorite New York restaurants. She was always our go-to person for restaurant recommendations, so it was fun seeing her turn her foodie hobby into an actual side business.

While she scrolled and tapped away, I looked out the window and ruminated about why this party—and seeing Chris—had made me feel so *off*. Even though I was glad I went, for some reason, it spurred an uneasy feeling in my bones—a disquieting, uncomfortable doubt, like I thought I knew where I was going, but somehow, I got lost.

Chris and I broke up for the last time right before I started my first year at the firm. Even in school, it was always on-again, off-again. Chris alternated between showering me with love and praise and withholding it. Every time he withheld, I would eventually get fed up, we'd break up, then after not enough time had passed for me to get over him, he'd come back, say he still loved me, and pull me back in.

But when we moved to New York, where he was from, after law school graduation, it became clear he only wanted me to be a part of his law school life. He was always going out with his friends—men and women—and never invited me. It didn't feel right to me. I was his girlfriend, the woman he was supposed to love, why wouldn't he want me around? I got so upset one time we fought that I asked him if he still even loved me. It took him so long to answer that I stormed out, saying I was leaving for good. Even then I hoped he'd stop me, hoped he'd apologize and do better. But he didn't. I never heard from him again.

It wasn't just losing him that hurt, it was losing the future I'd pictured for us: moving in together, getting married, starting a family. Seeing him while being surrounded by friends and acquaintances our age that *had* gotten married and started families was a brutal combination. I still wanted those things, but I hadn't had a boyfriend—or even connected with anyone in a meaningful way—in over five years. It was hard to picture a future that included those milestones when I didn't have anyone to picture doing them with. I didn't have time to go on dates with any regularity because of my job. And who would want to date a stressed-out workaholic like me, anyway?

I'd come to terms with the fact that Chris wasn't *the one.* But the depth of the rejection I felt when he ended our relationship was so overwhelming that some part of me still wasn't over that feeling. He made me feel like I wasn't good enough.

So, like every other time I'd felt like I wasn't good enough, I coped by working harder. In reality, I could attribute some of my high performance at Peters & Dowling to Chris. After the breakup, I threw myself into work. I had the highest billable hours in my associate class for the first two years, and got a reputation as a go-to associate, some partners telling me I was partner material as early as my fourth year. The validation I felt each time I received praise for my work and my hours helped me build back a bit of my self-confidence, even though it wasn't quite the same.

And for a while, I found the work interesting enough, thrilling enough—analyzing companies, figuring out what they had to offer, locating the skeletons in the corporate closet, thinking through how to solve them. I liked negotiating, and loved the feeling when we got our way on a particular point and the client was happy.

I'd worked on early investments in dozens of companies that went on to become household names. I'd negotiated mergers between major corporations for hundreds of millions, sometimes billions, of dollars. Each time I would send the closing announcement press releases to my parents and Drew, they were enthusiastic.

This is amazing, congrats! Mom and Dad would say.

Very impressive, Drew would say.

I did it, I would think every time another big deal closed or another partner expressed enthusiasm about my future at the firm. I proved everyone wrong that had ever doubted me. I was smart, talented, and accomplished. I made great money. After just six years, I'd paid off all my law school debt. And in three more years, I could be a big law firm partner with a million-dollar paycheck. The success I had wanted—needed—since the day I got my rejection letter from Franconia Academy was within reach. Mine for the taking.

But in six years, I hadn't stopped to ask myself: Once I got that promotion to partner, would I finally feel content?

When would it be enough?

And what was I missing out on to get there?

In answer, the image of the unadulterated smile on Tyler's face as he watched his daughter play at her second birthday party flashed through my mind.

"Eek! The literal chef of the restaurant I featured on my page last week commented on my post!"

My gaze whipped from the cloudy train window to my friend.

She was wiggling in her seat, grinning ear-to-ear like she won a trip to Bermuda.

My cheeks tugged upward. "That's awesome, Nat."

"Now I have to decide what to say." She wiggled again and settled back into her phone.

My hand reached for my own phone in my bag, but I stopped myself. Checking it didn't bring any joy. I didn't have a passion or a hobby like Natalie did. And if I was being honest with myself, I didn't love my work anymore. I wasn't sure if I ever had.

I think I just loved the validation.

Watching Natalie, I felt a pull to do something I loved, too. But what? Did I have anything in my life that I genuinely, truly loved to do?

No.

When we got to my apartment, I caved and checked my email. A jolt of terror shot through me when I saw John had emailed thirty minutes ago with an attachment containing his comments on the purchase agreement.

John Adler: Here are my comments. Please incorporate and send to the client ASAP.

Natalie noticed the consternation on my face.

"Work? Do you need to handle it now? Because I can head home..."

I thought for a moment. It was already 8:00 p.m., and even if his comments were light, it would still take me several hours to get the full draft polished and ready to go to the client. It was Saturday night, I was with my best friend, and I was inebriated. He said ASAP but I chose to believe he meant ASAP, tomorrow.

"Nope, I'm going to handle it tomorrow morning." I forced a smile, already partially doubting my decision. But the client asked for the draft by Monday, and at this rate, I would have it to them by Sunday afternoon, well ahead of the deadline. That should be more than fine.

I replied to John: Received, will do!

"Remember that snowstorm party in law school?" Natalie asked. "We all went to Tyler's house and sang along to music videos on the TV, dancing on the couch, yell-singing into our beer bottles like they were microphones. We were so loud that someone called the cops with a noise complaint." We were sprawled on my couch and had already finished another bottle of wine since getting back from Mina's birthday party.

"Probably because it was a Tuesday!" I said.

Natalie giggled. "The cops show up thinking they're busting an undergrad party, only to find out we're all in our mid-twenties and we're just maniacs that sing so loudly someone called the cops on us."

We devolved into uncontrollable laughter at the memory.

"We were such goofs," I said.

"We were happy," Natalie said.

"We were drunk!"

"That's true, too."

"Oh, you know what we should do?" I asked.

"Put on the *Hamilton* soundtrack?"

"Yes! Mind reader." I furrowed my brows, feigning concern that she'd read my mind, even though this sort of thing happened with us often.

She laughed as I stood to turn on my speaker. We *were* happy back then, during school. When was the last time I felt like I did that night? Totally unencumbered, so in the moment. This came close—wine drunk on the couch with my best friend. But it was different. Deep down, I was worried about that stupid email and all the work I had to do tomorrow, likely with a hangover.

I frowned to myself, my body angled away from Natalie as I called up the *Hamilton* soundtrack on my phone.

You don't have to keep doing this, my own voice slurred inside my head as the familiar notes wound their way into my tiny living room.

Don't I, though?

I'd come this far. What would people think if I gave up now?

4

I woke up with a headache and a racing pulse. Natalie had taken a car home just before midnight. I fired up my coffee machine and then immediately started incorporating John's comments into the purchase agreement. Three cups of coffee and four and a half billable hours later, I sent the draft to our client.

John replied within five minutes:

> Thanks for sending it out. Thought you might be able to get it over to them sooner but it's fine. Please send a calendar invite for first thing tomorrow morning but tell them we can hop on the phone later today if they would like.

I frowned at my computer screen as my body filled with a helpless resignation that made my limbs feel heavy. I wanted to take a nap or go for a walk or call my mom or do literally anything else besides spend my Sunday evening on the phone with the client. But John didn't ask me what worked for me. It wasn't acceptable to have personal plans that conflicted with your work at a firm like Peters & Dowling, anyway. I sent the email and prayed the client wouldn't take us up on the offer to speak today.

But of course, they did.

We went through the agreement section by section, Jasmine sharing her reactions and answering the questions we had for them about their risk tolerance and how aggressive they wanted to be on certain positions.

"Can you send it back to us by noon tomorrow?"

But it's already 9:00 p.m.

I sent John a private instant message asking if we could suggest 5:00 p.m. instead, hoping he'd see it before he answered her.

"Noon might be a little tight but we'll get it to you by end of business," John said.

"That works," she replied with a smile.

Phew!

I'd still need to start working on it tonight, but at least I could get some sleep and finish it up tomorrow.

"And the virtual data room will open tomorrow. We'll need your diligence report by next Monday," Jasmine added.

"Will do," John said.

I sent an email to the team of three associates I'd staffed earlier this afternoon to warn them.

After working all day the following day to get the revised purchase agreement to our client and then sent over to the tech company's counsel to review, the data room—a massive shared digital folder containing all of the tech company's important contracts, patents, certifications, financial information, employee information, and more—became accessible at 9:00 p.m. I did a video call with my team of junior associates: Claire, Will, and Jared.

"Val, did you see there are 1,500 documents in the legal folder?" Will asked, wide-eyed, his mouse clicking in the background.

"Yes," I said. "It's going to be a stretch. If you need me to take the first review of any of the contracts, send them my way, okay? We'll get it done." Maintaining the appearance of optimism was a challenge as my own stomach sank to the floor. We'd usually have at least two weeks to do this level of diligence, not less than one.

We were on and off calls with Jasmine and her team at Brower

Capital several times a day over the next few days. At night, I stayed up late with my associate team, reviewing contracts and their summaries and talking through their questions.

On Friday morning, we woke up to a notification that another 400 documents had been added to the data room. At least this week, I knew better than to make any weekend plans. Still, my chest tightened when I saw that email.

I sent a note to John letting him know about all the new documents and asking if we could ask Brower for an additional day to finish up the final diligence report. Clients usually understood that more time was needed when the target company did a data room dump like this. But John said no.

I spent all weekend in my apartment, alternating between drafting the supplementary contracts we'd need for the deal and chatting with the junior team about their diligence progress. I picked up the review of several of the agreements in the data room myself. If I hadn't, there'd have been no chance of making the Monday deadline, despite my associate team working through the weekend, too.

On Monday night (technically Tuesday morning at 1:30 a.m.), I finally finished revising the fifty-page diligence report and sent it to Jasmine. I told Claire, Will, and Jared to go to bed once they sent me their reports, but Will stayed online until I sent it out. For moral support, I supposed.

After I pressed Send, I scanned the unread emails in my inbox. A deal for a different client that had gone on pause in February was coming back to life—the client had emailed to say they'd started talking to the target company again. *As long as it doesn't pick back up until the end of next week, it'll be okay,* I thought as my eyes filled with moisture.

I pushed back from my desk. Cortisol (or adrenaline, or whatever other stress hormones induce heart palpitations) coursed through my bloodstream like a river in springtime. Despite the hour, I wouldn't be able to fall asleep right away, so I ambled into my kitchen and opened a bottle of wine.

Even though the stemless glass was only half full, my hand was shaking so badly that I spilled some on the way to my couch. *What is wrong with me?* I'd experienced stress before, obviously, but never uncontrollable hand shaking.

I set the glass on my coffee table, leaned back, and rubbed my eyes. *I think this is the worst deal I've ever worked on.*

And it was nowhere near over.

I rolled over after four hours of sleep, awoken by a pit of dread in my stomach just before my alarm, like I had every day for the past week. On autopilot, my hand reached for my phone on the nightstand. Jasmine had replied to the email with the diligence report at 6:00 a.m.—saying Thank you so much!—and telling us the tech company would be sending us their draft of the purchase agreement by sometime today, along with the disclosure letter. I swallowed as my eyes burned before willing myself out of bed and into the shower.

You can do this, I said to myself as I rubbed shampoo into my scalp with the pads of my fingers. *Just keep going.* I lost my footing for a second and my shoulder slammed into the shower wall. Using both hands to push myself upright, I dipped my head back and let the hot water run down my face and through my sudsy hair. I might have been crying. If I was, the water washed the tears away surreptitiously.

But when I got out and toweled off, they didn't stop.

Despite my shower pep talk, my motivation was getting harder and harder to call upon with each passing day. *Didn't I want to make partner? Didn't I want to make that kind of money?* The prestige, the recognition of my talent and intellect, the admiration of clients and other attorneys and my family and my brother. It wasn't just me that had sacrificed; my parents worked so hard to give me these opportunities.

I have to be successful.

I'd just have to get through this deal and then take a couple of days off to catch my breath. Like every other demanding deal I'd worked on in the last six years.

I pulled on a pair of black jeans, a T-shirt, and a blazer, and then I piled my wet hair on top of my head, securing it with a hair tie before walking out the door.

No one in the office would be able to tell if the puffiness under my eyes was caused by tears or exhaustion, anyway.

On our daily 10:00 a.m. call with the Brower team, Jasmine said, "The other side said they'll send us the purchase agreement and related documents back by 9:00 p.m. tonight. Can you guys review it, propose revisions, and send us updated versions by 7:00 a.m., and then we can talk about it at 8:00 a.m.?" Her tone was businesslike, almost casual, like she hadn't just asked this entire team to pull an all-nighter.

Besides that birthday party, I hadn't had a night or even a weekend afternoon off in nearly two weeks, and neither had any of my junior associates. For the hundredth time that week I considered telling John that, despite Jasmine's consistent gratitude and positive feedback, her timing expectations were unreasonable, and the pace of this deal was unsustainable. But I worried he'd think I wasn't willing to work hard if I said something like that, so I refrained.

John didn't bother messaging me to ask if we could meet that timing before he nodded and told Jasmine, "Will do."

I sucked in a breath through my nose and willed myself not to cry right there on the video call. It would take at least five hours to review and revise all the documents, which meant the associates and I would be going into that client call with four hours of sleep, if we were lucky. In her little video square, Claire's face crumpled momentarily, like she was about to cry, too. When the call ended, I asked her to swing by my office.

"You okay? I know that deadline Jasmine requested is insane."

"Yes, I'm okay. We'll get through it." Her glassy eyes and wobbling lip told me she was lying.

"Please tell me. Do you have something important coming up that you're worried about?"

Her lip wobbled more. "It's my anniversary. My husband made us a reservation at this nice place. I know he'll understand that we need to postpone now. I just feel bad."

"Go to dinner. The rest of us will handle the documents."

"But Val, I'm running point on the material contract disclosures. I don't think Will or Jared will have time to pick that up on top of the parts they're handling."

"I'll do them myself after I finish the purchase agreement. I'm up to speed." I schooled my face into a smile to reassure her.

"But won't John—"

"Don't worry about John; I won't mention it to him. He only cares that we get it done by 7:00 a.m. like the client asked."

She still seemed reluctant, but some light returned to her eyes. "Are you sure?"

"Yes. Please enjoy your anniversary. I feel bad enough that you might fall asleep before dessert, but at least you'll be there." The encouraging smile I gave her belied the roaring stress in my gut.

"Thank you so much!"

"Thank *you* for all your hard work. It doesn't go unnoticed."

Claire left my office with a tad more spring in her step. Once she was out of sight, I let my mask fall, closing my eyes and dropping my head back on my desk chair. *Deep breaths*, I told myself. But it was futile.

A few minutes later, I rose from my chair to go to the kitchen and make another cup of coffee.

I wouldn't be sleeping at all tonight.

Sitting in my office that evening, I'd just decided to do this all-nighter at home when a text came in from Natalie saying she got last-minute tickets to a Broadway show we were both interested in. Technically, I could go and be back at my apartment a little after

9:00 p.m. when the contracts were supposed to come in, but I declined.

I was so stressed out that I wouldn't be focused on the show, and I wouldn't enjoy it. I used to be able to compartmentalize, but one too many times getting home from dinner to twenty-seven missed emails had robbed me of my ability to put my phone away and enjoy myself.

Warning bells sounded in my head after I messaged Natalie saying I couldn't make it. *It's bad if I can't enjoy the things I used to enjoy, right?*

Later that night, as I stared at my inbox waiting for the contract to come in, Natalie told me she went to the show by herself.

"The revisions look great," Jasmine said on our 8:00 a.m. call. "Thank you so much for getting it done so quickly."

The documents had come in around 10:00 p.m. the night before. John sent me an email with his thoughts on the purchase agreement around 11:00 p.m. and left the rest to us. Will, Jared, and I worked until almost 4:00 a.m. reviewing and revising everything. Then I sent them to bed and finished the material contracts disclosure review for Claire—sending it all to Brower by 7:10 a.m.—before collapsing on top of my comforter in my clothes for half an hour. I remembered at the last second to throw on a different shirt before this video call.

Jasmine told us a handful of things she wanted us to change and then said to go ahead and send it to the counterparty when we were done.

After the call ended, I stared at my screen. The edges blurred and my arms tingled. Despite being seated, I struggled to breathe. It felt like the air was only reaching the top half of my lungs. I inhaled deeply—audibly—five times, lifting my chest up with each breath. It helped, but only for a minute or two, and then I needed to do it again. I repeated the exercise until I finished the revisions and sent all the documents to the counterparty an hour later.

I was so exhausted I felt physically sick. Coffee seemed to be making it worse at this point. I stumbled into my bedroom and fell asleep for an hour. When I woke up, I mentally went through my to-do list: check in with the juniors about the recent data room uploads, respond to a backlog of emails from a different client, and finally sit down and review the key vendor contract that Brower wanted the tech company to renegotiate.

Even though I wasn't looking at my phone for once, I nearly collided with the person exiting the bakery next to my building as I entered. Gripping a paper bag containing a muffin I wasn't sure I even wanted, I trudged into the office, barely feeling the chill spring wind on my cheeks and questioning how much longer my body could operate on adrenaline and coffee fumes.

At least we were well on our way to getting this deal signed and the client was happy.

By later that evening, I'd somehow managed to finish most of my tasks and review seventy-five pages of the 120-page vendor agreement.

That was when I made the fateful decision to stop by John's office on my way home.

5

The Day After the Fainting Incident

I hunched over my desk and read the three-page email of diligence updates from Claire while holding back tears. I'd just told her to go ahead and send the note directly to our client when a knock on my glass office door jolted my system like a jump-scare straight out of a horror movie. My heart rate settled slightly when I saw it was Mallory and not John. I waved her in.

Please don't have a new deal for me.

Mallory was a partner I enjoyed working with and often sought out for advice. She was one of only a few female partners in the private equity group. She had a daughter, made partner three years ago, and was a great mentor.

"Hey, Val. Just checking in. You've seemed more stressed than usual lately, and I wanted to see if you're okay?"

Is it that obvious?

The concern on her face was genuine. It made me want to cry.

And then, a burst of anxiety. *Does she know I fainted last night?*

"I'm okay." I willed down the emotion in my voice. "It's just that this Brower Capital deal has been super intense. But I'll get through it." Even as I said it, I wasn't sure I believed that anymore.

She nodded, her dark bob bouncing slightly, but she looked skeptical. "It's supposed to sign by the end of next week, right? Will you get a breather after that?"

"Yes, and I hope so. There's another deal I'm on with Carl that's percolating, but I hope it doesn't take off for another couple of weeks."

She reached for the hand I had splayed on top of that printed vendor contract and gave it a brief squeeze. "Hang in there, okay? Let me know if there is anything I can do to help."

I nodded as hot tears burned right behind my eyes, hoping Mallory would turn before they fell.

What is wrong with you? I chided myself as she closed the door behind her. *Nearly crying in front of a partner.*

It wasn't until I sent my comments on the Brower vendor agreement to John two hours later that I let myself feel a glimmer of temporary relief. I started packing up my things in a hurry. Not that I had any Friday evening plans. I was just excited to sleep before I saw my parents tomorrow.

My hand was reaching to pull the cord out of my laptop when my office phone rang—a piercing, awful sound. *No, no, no.*

I inhaled, blew out a shaky breath through pursed lips, and answered. "Hi, Carl."

"Val, great news. The Choice Partners deal is back on, full steam. The client is sending us those two key agreements they need to renegotiate within the hour. Can you take the first pass and send me your comments by Sunday night?" With each statement, he sounded farther away, drowned out by the tidal wave of stress collapsing on top of me.

It was Friday. The time on the corner of my computer screen said 4:00 p.m. I was going to throw up.

I opened my mouth to ask for more time, but then I heard John's voice in my head. *"You need to work on producing work product faster."*

"Okay," I said instead.

"And the data room will open back up this weekend, too."

I swallowed the growing lump in my throat.

"Actually, Carl. Do you think there's another senior associate that could tag into this deal? I'm stretched pretty thin on the Brower Capital deal right now. It's supposed to sign next week." It was a really bad look for me to even ask, but I physically couldn't do it.

"You already have all the background on this one. We can't bill the client for the time it would take to get another senior associate up to speed. Plus, the guys at Choice love working with you. Can you just staff some extra junior associates, delegate most of it to them until you free up?"

But I still have to instruct them and review their work. It used to be an enjoyable part of the job: training the junior associates. But not this month. Not when my nerves were as fried as the charred remains of a July Fourth sparkler.

I pinched the bridge of my nose and closed my eyes. He phrased it like a question, but it really wasn't one. "Yeah, let me call staffing right now and line up the team."

"Thanks, Val."

The line dropped with a click, and tears erupted from my eyes, pouring down my cheeks until they spilled off my chin. I should have worked from home today. I felt so exposed, visible to anyone walking past my clear glass office door.

And what the fuck is up with all this crying? I'd never been like this before. I clenched my fists, frustrated and helpless. My job had always been onerous, but it rarely brought me to tears.

Every other time I'd gone through a rough patch as an associate I'd convinced myself I could get through it, and there'd be some benefit in the end: client loyalty, high billable hours, a big annual bonus, my eligibility for partner improving for closing another high-profile deal successfully.

I closed my eyes again now and tried to picture a way through. But when I did, it was like a big, iron gate slammed down in my mental path. *STOP!* my body insisted. *How many more times do I need to show you? You can't go on like this.*

But don't I care? I asked myself.

Didn't I want to make partner?

My drive to succeed had been an unflappable part of my personality for as long as I could remember. I dug deep, clawed to find it, but it wasn't there anymore. At some point in this last month of hell, it had vanished.

And that was what scared me most of all.

Guilt clung to me like a weighted blanket, pressing on every pore, every appendage, as I took out my phone on my walk home to call my mom and cancel our plans for this weekend.

I trudged down the sidewalk, braced against the raw, March chill in the air, and waited for her response.

"Oh, it's okay, honey. We won't bother you. You can do your work, and we'll occupy ourselves on Saturday, and then we'll come by for a quick lunch on Sunday before we head home, okay? You have to eat anyway, right? I still want to bring you some groceries, too."

I felt like I couldn't even manage that, but I reluctantly agreed.

When my parents arrived on Sunday afternoon, I barely knew who I was anymore.

I hadn't left my apartment since Friday night, when Jasmine emailed to say that we'd be getting the contracts back from the tech company on Saturday morning, earlier than expected, and asking us to keep an eye on our inboxes.

Just like that, the whole weekend became reviewing documents and hopping on and off phone calls with my client, my team, John, and the counterparty. We'd just sent the agreements back to the tech company, and I'd only looked at the two contracts Carl asked me to review long enough to see they were sixty and eighty pages long, respectively.

When my parents called to say they were on their way, I wished they weren't coming. And then I hated myself for wishing that.

What kind of daughter can't spare an hour to have lunch with her dad on his birthday?

This isn't who I am.

This isn't who I want to be.

My hand shook violently as I reached for the door. *I know!* I wanted to yell at it. *I know I've pushed myself so far beyond my breaking point that I'm a shell of who I used to be.*

When I opened the door and saw their tentative smiles, I immediately burst into tears.

They dropped the boxes of takeout and bags of groceries on my kitchen counter and guided me to my couch like a histrionic child.

"I'm overweight and exhausted and—and miserable. I don't have time to do anything for myself, let alone my friends or family. I haven't gone to the gym in months. And even when I do have time to see my friends or do anything that's not work, I don't enjoy it. I couldn't do anything with you guys this weekend after you traveled all this way," I blabbered through heaving sobs.

And then I whispered, "I don't care about making partner anymore." And after another shaky breath, "I don't know what I want, but it's not *this*." My hands gestured to myself, my messy apartment, my desk in the corner.

My mom nodded, a look of pure sympathy on her face, like she was despondent, too. She rubbed circles on my back.

My parents sandwiched me on the couch just like they did when I was thirteen. The glassy-eyed disappointment I felt then paled in comparison to the hysterics I displayed now. Maybe that was why instead of telling me to stay the course, my dad said, "Quit."

I whipped my head around to look at him. He had never told me to quit anything in my life.

"They don't own you, Val. You don't need to be this miserable."

At thirty-one years old, I didn't need my father's permission to quit my job, but his support meant a lot to me.

They finally get it.

In their defense, I spent years convincing myself and everyone around me, including my family, that I was doing great. "I love my job. It's interesting and challenging, and I'm getting great performance reviews," I would say. I would send them those press releases about the splashy deals I'd worked on and tell them about the big bonuses I'd get at the end of each year. I felt accomplished, and the personal sacrifices—sleep, extracurriculars, dating, workouts, plans, events—seemed worth it.

But I wasn't so sure it was anymore.

I looked back and forth between my parents' heavy expressions. They waited patiently for me to respond to my dad's suggestion.

I didn't want to miss important family events like my brother's graduation. I didn't want to show up exhausted to weddings and parties and other gatherings with my friends. I didn't want to *not* make plans for fear of having to cancel them when something flared up with work. And I didn't want to spend holidays up in my bedroom crouched over my laptop instead of downstairs with my parents, my grandmother, and my brother and sister-in-law.

More than all of that, I wanted to enjoy things again. Relentless crashing waves of cortisol had broken down whatever mental barriers I used to have between work and leisure that allowed me to enjoy things like dates and musicals, birthday parties and wine nights with my girlfriends. I needed to build them back.

Between this tech company deal from hell and the regular cataloging of all the things I'd given up over the last six years that it had inspired, something had snapped inside me. I didn't care about success, prestige, money, or being the best corporate lawyer anymore.

I have to get out.

The warning had already been rattling through my head, almost every second of every day, like a ringing in my ears I couldn't shake. It had manifested itself in tears and shakes and panic attacks and musings about what my life might look like if I didn't spend every second working.

I'd been ignoring it, but not anymore. Hearing my father tell me to quit was the last push I needed to finally listen.

6

On Monday, after three hours of sleep, I walked into my office in a trance. I'd only finished one of the two contracts for Carl last night. The godforsaken Brower tech company deal was supposed to sign this week, but I wasn't sure I could make it to Friday. I headed toward Mallory's office.

"Val, come in!" she said after I knocked on the threshold of her open office door, putting down the printed contract she'd been reading. Apart from the bags under her eyes, Mallory looked like her typical sunny, put-together self in a black, cap-sleeve business casual dress and leopard print high heels. Meanwhile, I was in my usual T-shirt and blazer combo, looking as defeated as I felt.

"Can I close the door?"

"Of course."

I removed the tasteful throw pillow and sat down in the chair across from her desk.

"How are things going? Any better since last week?"

I opened my mouth to answer but my eyes filled with tears. Instead of speaking, I shook my head.

"I knew it was bad. You haven't caught a break in weeks. I assume this weekend wasn't any better?"

I swallowed over the lump in my throat. "Nope."

"How can I help? Maybe we can get one of your peers to tag into that deal, so you can take a few days to recoup."

"I think I need more than a few days." I refused to close my eyes and let tears roll down my cheeks. My hoarse voice was telling enough.

"Do you need a leave?"

"If I'm being honest, I think I need to quit. I've hit the wall. I'm miserable, I'm not *me* anymore." My lungs drew in an unsteady breath.

"I'm sorry, Val. I didn't realize it had gotten to this point."

"I haven't exactly been telling people. I reached my breaking point this weekend."

She nodded, her look sympathetic. "But don't quit, okay?"

I bristled. *Please don't try to convince me to stay. I can't.*

"Take a medical leave," she said. "Get a doctor's note saying you're suffering with mental health issues and need a leave from work to recover. Take a couple months off, fully paid, and then decide what you want to do with a clearer head. I don't want you to have to worry about money while you're going through so much already, okay?"

I nodded, not sure what to say. I'd heard of a person here and there taking a medical leave of absence from Peters & Dowling, but it was always very hush-hush. Gratitude and relief washed through me. A tear slipped down my cheek before my hand shot up to wipe it away. "Okay," I said. "What do I need to do?"

For the next twenty minutes, Mallory walked me through all the steps of setting up the medical leave. First, contact HR and ask for the paperwork for my doctor; second, talk to the firm's insurance company; and third, go see my doctor and have them put a mental health diagnosis code, a medical leave start date, and proposed return-to-work date into a form for the insurance company, and sign it.

"And legally, your job is protected. It will be waiting for you at the end of the leave, okay?"

"Thank you, Mallory. Seriously."

"Of course. You're smart and talented, Val. But you're also human. Take care of yourself."

I smiled at her on my way out and kept my head down until I reached the privacy of my office. I emailed HR immediately.

By Friday morning, I had transitioned all of my deals to colleagues and submitted glowing performance reviews for my junior associates, and HR had informed all of the partners I'd be on a leave of absence effective Saturday. The guilt I felt for saddling other associates with my work was suffocating, but I couldn't change my mind. I thought maybe John would reach out after HR notified him, but he didn't. It was a relief, I supposed.

On Friday afternoon, I set up an auto-reply message to send every time I got an email and packed up every personal item from my office to take home with me, even though I told myself it wasn't necessary. I'd be back here after I got my strength back. And thanks to the anxiety diagnosis from my doctor and the paperwork she filled out, I had three and a half months to do just that.

Later that evening, I walked to my apartment with a backpack and three tote bags hanging from my body and cortisol coursing through my veins, feeling like a complete failure.

That night I crawled into bed at 8:00 and didn't stir until 8:00 the next morning. The next few nights were the same: twelve or thirteen hours of sleep and still it wasn't enough to combat the bone-deep exhaustion.

By Monday, I mustered enough energy to leave my apartment. After I put in a load of laundry, I went to the grocery store and bought produce instead of frozen meals.

What did I do? I asked myself when I got home from the store, bracing on the kitchen counter. *Did I throw it all away?* All those years of hard work. My arms tingled and my heart rate quickened.

Deep breaths.

It's okay.

This is only a blip.
You just needed a break.
Your job is protected.
You'll get back on track.

I slumped to the tile floor, leaning against the lower kitchen cabinets, glad I didn't check the time before I did it, so I wouldn't know how long I sat there like that.

"I know you're a grown woman in your thirties and coming home to your parents' house in suburban New Hampshire is not very appealing, but I think you need a change of scenery. We can go for walks, and I'll cook healthy meals, and you can read and relax and get away from it all."

I lay on my back on my bed, phone pressed against my ear. The streetlights cast my room in a bluish glow.

My mother was right, of course. I'd never lived in NYC and been anything besides a Peters & Dowling associate. In the last week I'd started going to the gym in my building and cooking and sleeping more, but I didn't know what to do with myself here anymore. My desk, my couch, even my coffee machine reminded me of work.

"Okay," I replied.

"Okay?"

"You sound surprised."

"I am. I'm thrilled, but I'm surprised. You've never once taken me up on moving home and taking a break. Not since you left for college."

"I know." *Because it would have felt like admitting defeat.*

After we hung up, I placed my phone on the nightstand, stood, and spun in a circle, unsure where to start. I dropped to the floor next to my bed, slid a plastic bin out from under it, and popped the top off. It was filled with an array of summer clothing—a few sundresses and pairs of shorts, some open-toed shoes. I removed the contents and stuffed them into a duffel bag. It would be mid-July before I went back to work, so I'd need them.

Next I pulled out a smaller plastic bin. This one was coated in a thick layer of dust and it took me a moment to remember what it was.

My notebooks!

I ripped off the cover. My fingers ran across the notebooks, journals, papers, and folders of different colors before picking up a yellow spiral notebook with a worn, cracked cover. I opened it to the first page and discovered the story of two college students that fall in love while co-starring in a student play. They're friends, but they're both dating other people. Drama ensues. A smile spread on my face as I flipped the pages. It wasn't bad. After ten pages of notes, it ended. An idea that never got off the ground.

I picked up another journal and opened it. And then another. They were all the same: an idea for a novel or a movie, some bullets, and then nothing but empty pages waiting to be filled. I sat on my floor until I'd read through them all. The smile that widened on my face with each new idea felt foreign to my cheeks.

The notebooks spread around me on the floor reminded me that something I loved before work took over was books. The first love of my life was reading, and the second was coming up with stories in my head.

During college, I'd looked into creative writing courses almost every semester before dismissing them as impractical. After briefly entertaining the dream, I would always go back to Plan A: social studies degree with high honors, law school bound. Despite my interest, being a writer had little chance of resulting in the success I craved.

But now I let that pull to do something different than practicing corporate law—something I might love—take hold. Even if I could only do it for a few months, the idea stirred some long-latent excitement in my body. I removed all the notebooks and packed them in a bag to take with me to my parents' house, feeling like it was some sort of kismet that I opened this box before it ended up in storage.

I paid the hefty fee to terminate my lease, put my furniture in storage, and packed the rest of my belongings into bags and boxes that would fit into my dad's SUV.

Two days after my mom first suggested it, I waited for my dad in the lobby of my building, self-consciousness gnawing at me. I thought about how I would describe this scene in a screenplay: *A thirty-one-year-old woman waits in the sleek, marble lobby of a high-end apartment building surrounded by mismatched luggage and plastic bins. Other tenants scrutinize her on their way to and from the elevator bank. She looks like she'd like to disappear into the folds of her baggy sweatsuit.*

I didn't have a clue what the next scene would look like.

7

"How are you feeling?"

I zipped my dad's oversized windbreaker all the way up to my chin and lifted my gaze from the wet pavement to my mom. We crossed the street into the cul-de-sac neighborhood across from ours before I responded, "A lot better, honestly. I'm sorry that pretty much all I've done is sleep for two weeks."

It was the truth. Despite the fact that I was still grappling with my decision and had to self-soothe with breathing exercises almost every day, the four-mile walks with my mom, using the little home gym in the basement, eating healthy soups and high protein meals, and sleeping eight to ten hours a night had all had an irrefutably positive effect on my body. I didn't feel like I was constantly on the brink of tears either, which felt like a huge win somehow. Even the scale was a few pounds lighter this morning. It was small progress given I'd gained thirty since starting at Peters & Dowling, but I was happy about it, nonetheless. Mostly because I *felt* better.

"You know we don't mind. You haven't been able to sleep like that for six years, so you have a lot of catching up to do!"

I smiled at her as gratitude washed through me.

We spent the rest of the walk talking about the book she'd just finished for her book club. She always gave everything away, but I didn't mind. I'd probably read it anyway.

Drew drove home from Boston for dinner that night. At my mother's insistence, I suspected. Unfortunately, his wife couldn't join us—she was out of town for a medical conference.

It was the first time I'd seen Drew in person since my career imploded, and I was nervous to tell him. He didn't know how much his opinion of my success meant to me. Probably because I'd spent my entire life pretending I didn't care what he thought. But deep down, I did. Deep down, I still felt like the little girl who couldn't figure out the math problem at the kitchen table, waiting for her genius older brother to tell her she was smart, too.

Drew and I lingered in the dining room after eating, my parents busy in the kitchen assembling some kind of dessert. My hand ghosted over the smooth surface of the new table my parents bought a few years ago. They didn't have that kitchen table where Drew and I did our homework anymore. I couldn't decide if I missed it.

"Do you think you'll go back?" Drew asked me. "To your firm, I mean?"

A line formed between my eyebrows. "Of course I'm going back."

Ever since Mallory threw me the lifeline of taking a medical leave instead of quitting, I hadn't considered leaving my job altogether. I didn't need to anymore, now that I had this long break.

And then, defensiveness set in. Did he think I'd just quit?

I almost did, but he doesn't know that. I don't think.

I wasn't in the mood for his thinly veiled judgment. But when I looked at him, it wasn't judgment emanating from his facial expression—it was concern. Somehow that felt worse. Like I'd already tanked my career anyway, and he felt bad for me.

My eyes narrowed in on him. "Why wouldn't I go back?"

I waited for him to say something off-putting, like how I might be better off with a clean slate somewhere else, instead of going back and having to prove to them that I could handle the work-load without having another mental breakdown.

Before my brother could answer my question, my parents returned with a tray of Drew's favorite cookies. He grabbed four, said, "Thank you," shoved a full one into his mouth, and walked toward the front door. I rolled my eyes, and a smirk broke through my irritation. The thirty-four-year-old professor still ate like a thir-teen-year-old boy that just got home from track practice.

He squeezed my shoulder on his way past my chair. "You'll figure it out, Sis."

My parents walked him out. When I heard him zip up his coat I called, "Drive safe!" A moment later, the front door closed.

My parents had artfully avoided talking to me about work for the last two weeks. Now that blissful, avoidant bubble had burst. *Should I go back?*

What would it be like when I did?

I reached for the cookie tray but pulled my hand back. My stomach was chock full of dread now, thanks to the images of me walking back into Peters & Dowling's NYC offices in a few months flickering through my mind. I didn't have room for anything else.

Later that night, my mom and I lounged in the dining room with glasses of red wine. My dad was watching a college hockey game in the other room that wasn't quite close enough to draw me in there with him.

"I have an idea for you to think about," Mom said. "You know your father and I love having you here, and you can stay as long as you want. But I was thinking, maybe you should spend the rest of the spring and summer in one of your *other* favorite places." Mom raised her eyebrows at me.

"The Vineyard?" Enthusiasm crept into my voice.

"Yes."

"Hmm." I adored Martha's Vineyard. My grandmother had had

a house on the island off the coast of Cape Cod since before I was born, and Mom used to take me and Drew there every single summer growing up. I have so many fond memories of going to the beach, walking into town for ice creams and candy, riding our bikes everywhere.

"And not to pressure you, but it would be a huge help to me and your father to have someone there with Mimi. Since your grandfather died, I think the house has been a lot for her to manage on her own. As you know, your father and I have run ourselves into the ground every summer going back and forth to take care of her and the house."

"I don't hate the idea." The last few years, I'd only managed to squeeze in a quick weekend on Martha's Vineyard each summer because of work. I missed it.

"Think about it. You don't have to decide right now. We'll visit in July and periodically throughout the summer, like we always do."

I didn't need to think about it for long. I closed my eyes and transported myself to the top of the fisherman's pier in downtown Edgartown. I pictured the white and wooden boats moored in the harbor, little Opti sailboats crossing in between the Chappaquiddick ferries, the sun reflecting off the blue waves. When I imagined the steady wind that always blew through your hair up there, my decision was made. A summer on Martha's Vineyard, without a crushing amount of corporate legal work hanging over me like a black cloud, was *exactly* what I needed.

"Hey, Dad!" I called into the other room. "Wanna go buy a car with me tomorrow?"

I'd need one on the island.

8

The massive white and black ferry rocked in the spring waves as I drove the pre-owned, low-mileage sedan I bought three days ago up the car ramp. The inside of the car was still chilled from the gust of wind that burst through the window when I gave the attendant my passenger ticket: one-way to Martha's Vineyard.

It was the first time I'd seen the ferry terminal in Woods Hole, Massachusetts, with little to no car traffic, and even fewer walk-on passengers. It was also the first time I'd ever traveled to the island before Memorial Day.

After I parked the car, I made my way up to the little onboard galley, bought a beer, and settled into a seat by a window. I'd normally sit outside on the deck and let the cleansing ocean wind whip over my face. But today the cool temperature, gray sky, and choppy, dark waves kept me inside. I took my current romance novel out of my bag—my fifth since I started the medical leave—but I didn't open it. This journey typically inspired a sort of child-like excitement as I pictured trips to the beach and the boutiques in town, and anticipated the taste of handmade ice cream and lobster rolls on buttered, grilled buns. But this time, sipping my beer and looking out at the water, part of me felt just as listless as the crashing Atlantic waves.

Crushed shells and gravel crunched under my tires as I pulled into the driveway at Mimi's house. My tasks until Mimi arrived in mid-May were to open up the house, get it ready, and get settled in myself. A surge of nostalgia washed over me as I looked at the home. Weathered shingles covered the whole facade. Black trim surrounded the windows, and a black door stood in the center. It hadn't changed in thirty years.

I grabbed a bag and the key and headed inside. The door swung open, and a familiar smell filled my nostrils. But it was quieter than usual. I flicked on the lights. Like the outside, every-thing inside was the same: blue couches, nautical artwork, worn, dark wood cabinets in the kitchen. Collages of family photos filled gold standing frames on almost every surface. The oldest Drew or I were in any of them had to be about twelve. The bookshelf in the living room overflowed with my grandfather's well-loved paper-backs—all mysteries and thrillers. I'd have to read some of those this summer, too.

I followed the directions my dad wrote out on a note before I left, turning on the water and the heat and checking the basement for leaks.

Upstairs, I shook out the sheets I found in the linen closet and put them on the queen-sized bed in the larger of the two guest rooms, following my mother's lifelong advice to *always make the bed first because you'll be too tired later."*

I organized the handful of groceries I bought on the way here in the fridge, cracked another beer, and plopped on the couch.

Now what?

I drummed my manicured fingers on the dark wood coffee table until I finally gave in and opened that romance novel, ready to escape into another person's story for a few hours as a break from worrying about my own.

The next morning I woke up so early it was dark out when I opened my eyes. I'd had a nightmare that I had to explain to my law school professors why I wasn't working right now. I pushed the damp hair sticking to my forehead to the sides and sat up. My hand wrapped around my neck, feeling the pulse thrumming under the warm skin, faster than it should be. It was a familiar but (thankfully) increasingly infrequent occurrence in the mornings.

Still, the dream cracked open some of the mental floodgates I'd forced shut over the last few weeks. *Was I a quitter? I worked so hard in high school and college and law school, and then I just couldn't hack it? How come some people can? Are they just smarter than I am? More dedicated?*

At least the virtual counseling my primary care doctor recommended when she signed my medical leave paperwork was starting tomorrow. That should help. And Mimi would get here next weekend. Then I wouldn't be alone with my thoughts anymore.

I pushed the doubts down before I spiraled. Then I picked up the paperback from my nightstand instead.

Five chapters later, I stared through the kitchen window at Mimi's backyard with my second cup of coffee in my hand.

Sunlight reflected off the dewy, blooming flower bushes of her garden. They reminded me of the fresh flowers they always had at Morning Glory Farm, a small local farm a mile from Mimi's house. Grateful I didn't buy much produce at the grocery store yesterday, I skipped upstairs to change and smiled when a pair of jeans that hadn't been comfortable for a while zipped up easily.

This is what this break is for, isn't it? I thought as I drove. Sleeping, reading, cooking, enjoying my free time. If I focused on my physical health, then my mental health would follow, right? Hopefully my new therapist would know.

When I opened my car door in the Morning Glory parking lot, I caught an instant whiff of fresh flowers. The smell enveloped the entire property. The breeze rustling the leaves and the rhythmic whir of the windmill mingled with my crunching footsteps as I walked the flower-lined path to the door.

I picked up a wicker basket and a bunch of sunflowers from outside. Before I swung open the screen door the floral smell was overtaken by freshly baked muffins. This was dangerous, given the healthy eating kick I'd been on.

Vegetables first, then maybe some bakery items, I said to myself. *And I'm joining the gym tomorrow.*

The farm store was all light wood, like the inside of a barn, with wooden tables and crates filled to the brim with fruits, vegetables, and leafy greens. It was a kaleidoscope of colors, broken up by cheerful blackboard signs noting the name of each item.

I placed two fresh tomatoes from the table in front of the door in my basket. When I turned to look at the bakery section, there was a tall man with a deep tan skin tone standing there, reading the labels on the pie-shaped boxes in front of him.

He wore a black T-shirt, blue golf shorts, and a pair of boat shoes that looked like they'd traveled to the bottom of the ocean and back. His dark brown, almost black, hair was long, curling at the nape of his neck in the back, and sloping down from his hair-line to his eyebrows in the front. He pushed it back, and the pieces fell down to the exact same spot. As if he could feel me watching him, he turned and caught my eye. His eyes were a deep, warm brown. Inviting.

I realized too late that I was staring. My options were to pretend I wasn't and flee to another section of the store or say something to justify why I was looking at him.

"Hi," I blurted.

"Hi," he replied, amusement dancing across his face. One of his dark eyebrows rose slightly.

Why was I saying hi? Why would someone say hi to a stranger in a store?

"Um, so..." I nodded toward the stacks of pie boxes he was scrutinizing. "What do you usually buy here? I haven't been back in ages."

His face changed to a friendly smile, white teeth appearing within his neatly trimmed, dark beard. *Wow, he's handsome.* "The quiches are the best, and they change up the flavors regularly. Definitely grab one of those. And the zucchini bread. Plus, I mean, all the produce is great, too, because a lot of it is grown here." He gestured to the rest of the store with a muscular, tanned arm.

"Thank you. I'll definitely try a quiche then." I smiled at him. His gaze lingered on me for a moment, and I thought he might say something else. Instead, he added one of the boxes to the top of his basket, which was already full of green produce bags. He stepped aside so I could look at the display.

"Enjoy," he said over his shoulder as he walked toward the checkout area.

"Thanks!" I called back.

I wondered if he lived on the island full-time. It was mid-May, which was early if you only spent your summers here.

I wished I had thought of something else to say to him. I was out of practice at...well, everything that wasn't talking to partners, associates, and clients about purchase agreements.

Maybe I'd run into him again at some point. The island wasn't that big. I rolled my lips between my teeth and stole one more look at him in the checkout line.

I hadn't had the time or the desire to put myself out there in years. Maybe that was changing though, because one of the first things I noticed about him was that he wasn't wearing a wedding ring.

9

"So tell me what precipitated the medical leave."

I stared at the blonde, forty-something woman on my laptop screen. It was my first official counseling session with my new therapist, Wendy. Morning light streamed through the blinds above the little desk in Mimi's guest bedroom as I collected my thoughts.

After a deep breath I detailed the lifestyle of a deal lawyer for her—the hours, the client demands, the requirement to be available on short notice, even on the weekends. I told her about the panic attack I had, the fainting, the hand shaking and crying, followed by the feelings of hopelessness and apathy, all the while wringing my hands under the desk and attempting to maintain my composure.

When I finished, she looked at me for a moment—my glassy eyes and clenched jaw—and said, "I am *so* proud of you for taking this break and putting your health first."

I burst into tears.

Wendy waited patiently while I swiped at my cheeks, took deep breaths, and prayed it was normal for her clients to lose it during sessions.

"Sorry," I said once I caught my breath.

"Don't be," she smiled, like the tears were totally normal and didn't disturb her. That made me feel better.

With ten minutes left in our session she asked, "What do you like to do outside of work?"

"Um." I swallowed, my throat still thick. I hadn't maintained any hobbies since I started working sixty- to eighty-hour work weeks, unless you counted trying not to miss important events for my family and friends and attempting to get to the gym every once in a blue moon. Watching a few episodes of TV and drinking wine weren't hobbies. "I haven't had time for any hobbies in a long time."

"If you had more time, what would you spend it doing?"

I looked down at my legging-clad thighs. "I'm joining the gym today," I offered.

"That's great." She wrote something down in her notebook. "Before we meet next week, I want you to take some time to think about what makes you, *you*, outside of your career. Hobbies, interests, values... Ask yourself: What are your priorities that have nothing to do with your job?"

I looked at her blankly. I'd thrived for as long as I did at Peters & Dowling by wrapping myself, my time, my entire identity, in the job.

I wasn't sure who I was without it.

She ended our session at exactly fifty-five minutes past the hour.

Already in gym clothes, I pulled my thick, honey brown hair into a high ponytail and walked down the stairs. I topped off my water bottle and grabbed my headphones and car keys.

The smell of cleaning products, metal, and sweat filled my nose when I walked into the gym, but disappeared as I moved through my workout. It was quiet at the YMCA today, which I loved. I had the entire corner of the free weights section to myself. Upbeat dance music blasted through my headphones, keeping me motivated.

After I finished my circuit of weighted squats, walking lunges, dumbbell bench presses, and planks, I stretched on a yoga mat and thought about my therapy homework.

Reading novels counted as a hobby. I opened a note on my phone and wrote that down. I loved musical theater in high school, but that wasn't a hobby I had interest in pursuing as an adult, except as a spectator. My mind wandered to writing, the partially filled notebooks full of ideas I found under my bed and the flare of inspiration I'd felt when I read them. Why hadn't I started that yet?

I went through my final stretches as quickly as possible and jogged back to my car.

Sitting cross-legged on the carpeted floor, I scanned the open notebooks encircling me.

I'd reread all my old ideas since getting back from the gym, but, unfortunately, none of them stood out as one I'd want to pick up with again now. It had been a fun trip through my past, though. A reminder that I had other interests before I became a corporate lawyer. I chuckled when I read a story about some huskies that went on an adventure in Alaska. The penmanship left something to be desired, telling me I must've been about ten years old when I wrote it.

Some of the notebooks from my college years were romance ideas: small town romance, unforeseen circumstances causing forced proximity. I was so full of hope back then. I had a boyfriend I liked a lot for a couple of years at UPenn, but we broke up because he moved to California after graduation. I'd always wanted to write a romance novel because they're my favorite to read, but given my complete lack of a romantic life the last few years, and the toxic on-again, off-again relationship with Chris before that, I wasn't feeling romantically inspired.

I slid my laptop toward me and opened a search engine. Feeling foolish despite being alone in the house with no one to see, I typed 'how to become a writer' into the search bar. *Only Google's data records and I will know,* I assured myself as I pressed Enter.

One of the search results was an online writers' platform that ran short story competitions every month. They posted a number of prompts, and anyone could submit a story for consideration.

One of that month's prompts was about grief, another called for a ghost story. The third one caught my attention: Write a story about a lover's betrayal that isn't cheating.

I pressed my lips together and looked up toward the ceiling. What was something a lover could do that would cost you more than your heart? Murder, of course. But that seemed too obvious.

What if they did something that landed you in prison? My brain called up a memory from a lecture in Corporate Law. Our professor spent the entire first class warning us against insider trading. *"If you're on a first date and they tell you they're a day trader, run!"* I could hear my professor laughing at his own joke, and an idea came to life in my mind—a female public company mergers and acquisitions attorney whose boyfriend snoops in her home office and trades on the information. He gets caught, and they're both prosecuted for insider trading.

I'd read stories about things like that happening to people, and it always struck me what an enormous betrayal it was. When a person cheats, they break their partner's heart. When they do something like this, their partner loses their career and potentially goes to prison. All because they trusted their own boyfriend not to read their private documents. Plus, they say to write what you know. And the plight of a female corporate lawyer was something I considered myself an expert on.

I opened a blank Word document and started typing. First, bullets with the general idea, and then a potential first scene. They're at dinner, and he asks how her deal is going. He shows a bit too much interest, asks her too many questions, but she doesn't pick up on it.

By the time I looked up from my laptop, my stomach was growling and the sky had turned pink outside.

A few days later, I slid the latest hardcover Edward Phelps romance novel back onto the wooden shelf between its neighbors, and then pulled it back out again, balancing it on top of the three I already clutched in my arms. *Yep, I'm buying all four—Natalie said this one is great.* I turned and walked slowly to the front of the store, scanning the neatly packed shelves full of colorful book bindings as I passed.

My hair was still damp from the shower I took at the gym, but I'd finished the last paperback I brought with me to the island last night, so I'd parked my car in Mimi's driveway and headed straight to Edgartown Books. The bookstore had been my favorite since I was a child. My mind was full of memories set in this little, converted white house on Main Street: sitting cross-legged on the floor of the brightly colored children's section reading with my mom, and then when I got a bit older, wiling away hours perusing the back covers of young adult romance novels. The inventory changed every year, but my fondness remained the same.

Despite the books in my bag, I felt light as I navigated the brick sidewalk back to Mimi's. After a week on the island, I'd settled into a routine of my own making: gym or a walk or run in the mornings, writing in the afternoons, reading at night, with long phone calls with my mom or Natalie mixed in. I'd been off from the firm for a month now, and it felt strange and indulgent that *I* was the one who got to decide what I did each day.

I paused for a moment to admire the new dresses on the mannequins in the window display of one of my favorite boutiques. Martha's Vineyard had been quiet and calm without the summer surge, but that would come to an end soon. Memorial Day weekend was just over a week away, and the island was already coming alive. Each day more stores in Edgartown washed their windows and opened their doors, and the flower planters lining the sidewalks in town filled with petunias and coneflowers, as if by some sort of magic.

Later that night, after putting fresh sheets on Mimi's bed, vacuuming the whole house, and cleaning the kitchen, I sank into the couch and cracked open one of my new Edward Phelps romance novels, a fresh seltzer fizzing on the coffee table in front of me. It'd become my nightly ritual. It felt so luxurious, I almost felt guilty, but each day the urge to use that evening downtime for something more productive lessened.

I was enjoying reading again.

"Hey, Mimi!" I called out the window of Mimi's compact SUV at the petite woman with a white bob, a Burberry scarf, and the same red carry-on size suitcase she'd had for years. I woke up early and took the bus to the boat, and then another bus from Woods Hole to Logan Airport. I met Mimi's driver in central parking as planned, and pulled around to pick her up in the terminal. Normally it was my parents who helped transport Mimi back to the island every year. I didn't appreciate how time-consuming it was until today. But I didn't mind. For the first time in years, I had time to do something like this for her. It made me happy—being able to do things that helped my family.

"Hi, Val! Thank you so much for doing this." She kissed my cheek when I joined her on the curb. I picked up her suitcase and put it in the car.

As I drove us back toward Cape Cod, we caught up on her time in Florida and how my parents and my brother were doing. I told her about the books I'd been reading and the new shops that had opened in town. I briefly talked about my experience at work that led to my burnout and the need for a medical leave. I suspected she already knew most of it from my mom, but she listened attentively anyway.

When I finished, she said, "They worked you to death at that firm. I don't envy this generation with cellphones and laptops. I'm so happy you are taking a break and that you chose to spend it on the Vineyard with me. We're going to have the best summer!"

I smiled, and genuine excitement filled my veins.

A few days after Mimi arrived, I forgot to close my blinds before bed and woke up with the first rays of the sun. I wasn't used to how bright it was here in the mornings.

After a cup of coffee sipped in front of a lackluster pantry, I went back to Morning Glory Farm for provisions. Maybe the handsome, dark-haired stranger would be there again for another morning grocery run.

Unfortunately, he wasn't. But they did have some gorgeous pale-yellow sunflowers, a new quiche flavor (zucchini and parmesan), and heirloom tomatoes. I grabbed a bunch of fresh basil too, my mouth watering at the idea of Caprese salad for lunch. Knowing Mimi, a night owl, wouldn't be up for a few hours, I stopped in town for a second coffee.

Iced coffee in hand, I meandered to the fishing pier and climbed the steps to the upper deck observatory. I leaned over the railing, looking down at the waves that clapped against the edge of the pier.

Only a few fishermen remained down below, lines in the water. The rest would have packed up hours ago. The salty air was still cool, the heat of summer not yet upon us, especially up here where the wind roared through in a never-ending stream. The sun was only halfway up in the sky, its light reflecting off every wake in the water, making it shimmer and dance.

I tugged my sweater around me and sat down on a bench, watching the handful of boats passing by, breathing deeply. Easily. For once, I didn't feel like there was somewhere else I should be, something else I should be doing. There were no work deadlines or overwhelming projects hanging over me on this pier. Even the tick of checking my phone every few minutes had gone away. Another deep breath, and it got caught in my throat on its way out. I swallowed. My eyes filled as a sense of whole-body relief spread through me. The freedom of not being shackled to that phone, of not being beholden to deadlines that were always *"as soon as possible,"* and never soon enough.

I feel like I can breathe.

I shook my head, eyes brimming.

I don't know if I want to go back.

10

"How have things been going this week? Have you been able to work out, cook...read...and write?" Wendy tapped her pen on her notebook for each activity. Clearly, she took diligent notes during our session last week.

A smile spread on my lips, as if on its own. "Great, I'm still doing those things every day."

"When you go back to your firm, do you think you'd be able to set some boundaries so you could continue doing these things you enjoy?"

Of course not, my brain retorted. I took a moment before answering. "Honestly, not for long. Some weeks are a little slower, leaving me time to do those things. But more often than not, I'm working from 7:00 or 8:00 a.m. until after 10:00 p.m. every day, with limited breaks for meals and to commute."

She seemed stumped for a moment before she continued. "Well, stick with them for now while you're off, and then perhaps in our next few sessions we can brainstorm some ways that you could prioritize maintaining these activities—at least the ones that are most important to you—after you go back to work."

I nodded in agreement, but the churning in my gut told me no amount of brainstorming would help me maintain a workout and cooking routine for more than a week or two at a time once I got back, let alone reading or writing. It wasn't as if I hadn't tried in the past. Once my average hours of sleep per night dipped below six—and they would—it became too hard for me to justify spending my free time on anything else.

"What's your return-to-work date again?" Natalie asked, glancing up from her cutting board to her phone camera.

I sighed. She was cooking dinner, but I was already in my PJs, sitting cross-legged on my bed. "July 15th."

"Sorry to bring it up! You still have"—she paused to count—"eight weeks, though. That's a long time."

"I know." I forced a smile as my stomach roiled. I was just starting to feel whole, and I was just getting really into the writing. The last thing I wanted to think about was going back to Peters & Dowling. Eight weeks felt impossibly short.

"Do you even want to go back?" Natalie asked the question my therapist hadn't yet broached during our first three sessions.

I rolled my lips between my teeth as I considered telling my best friend the truth.

"No," I whispered.

Natalie stopped chopping. Her eyebrows rose, but a small smile emerged on her lips.

"I know I need to, but every time I think about it, I feel a sense of dread," I added. "But if I don't go back, then my paychecks will stop. I have savings, but not a ton because it took so long to pay off my law school loans."

"You could extend it a bit, right?"

"Yeah I probably could. But not much longer, I don't think. And it might not be paid."

Natalie tapped her pointer finger on her lips. "You could do something else, get a different job."

"You mean like go in-house?"

"Yeah, or something totally different. Work at a store or a restaurant or freelance. You won't make as much, but enough to defray your costs. Your expenses are low, aren't they?"

"For the most part. Mimi isn't charging me rent or anything. Car payment, groceries, other necessities. And eventually, health insurance."

Natalie nodded. "Couldn't you even find something on the Vineyard in the interim? There must be tons of summer jobs."

"I don't know why I didn't think of that."

"Could be fun, even."

I smiled. "That's a great idea. It would be really nice to feel like I have the freedom to *not* go back..." My shoulders relaxed. *Even though I probably will go back at the end of the day.*

I leaned against my pillows, content with this new idea and ready for a subject change. "Tell me about what's going on with you. Any interesting dates lately?"

"Oh, you will not believe what happened on my last one."

I made myself comfortable while Natalie told me all about the handsome but totally aloof grad student she went out with last weekend, how they got lost several times, and he'd made a reservation at the wrong restaurant. A smile stretched on my face as she gesticulated wildly, in full storytelling mode. Natalie found it all endearing, and said she'd go out with him again, but she would do the planning. He was a lucky man.

Over the next couple of days I meandered through town and looked online for job openings. My top choice would have been the bookstore, but they told me they already had their summer schedule covered.

I texted Natalie.

VAL

> Struggling to find a part-time retail job. And they're all pretty low-paying.

NATALIE

What else can you do? Did you have any other
jobs before law school?

VAL

Not really. Babysitting.

NATALIE

That's perfect! I bet tons of people on the island
need help with their kids over the summer. And
that would pay more than retail for sure.

VAL

You're brilliant, Nat.

11

On the Saturday morning of Memorial Day Weekend I walked into town before Mimi woke up with a stack of fliers I'd printed on my grandfather's old printer. Each sheet advertised my availability for summer babysitting or nannying, complete with my age and prior experience.

My first stop was the community bulletin board at the Edgartown Yacht Club, a boating club and restaurant that extended out into the water at the end of Main Street where my grandparents had been members for years. After securing the paper with a pushpin, I meandered to the front deck. Excited boaters heading out for the day streamed by in a parade of white and wooden motorboats, some with speakers blaring already. It was the first official weekend of New England summer, and those three beautiful, fleeting months stretched before everyone. A palpable sense of anticipation swirled through town, carried on the harbor wind.

I put a flier outside the youth sailing center and then headed back up Main Street to a popular coffee shop—aptly named *Behind the Bookstore* because of its location—got a cappuccino, hung my last flier above the syrups and creamers, and snagged a table in their garden. The sail-covered outdoor seating area had a patio of crushed white shells and smelled so strongly of espresso that I suspected the air itself might be caffeinated.

Headphones already in my ears, I sipped my cappuccino cautiously as my eyes scanned my notes: events in a bulleted list, roughly in the order I imagined them playing out for my main character. *This feels like a real story,* I thought with reserved optimism. The third bullet read *When she discovers his betrayal.* I transported myself to my character's office in my mind and my fingers danced across my keyboard, filling the page with details. Her deal has just been announced, and she has that exhausted but gratified feeling. She's asked to review the list of names of everyone that traded stock of the target company leading up to the announcement—a standard post-signing request she's completed a dozen times before, never recognizing any of the names. Except this time, when her boyfriend's name is on the list. *That can't be right,* my character thinks when she sees it, scrutinizing the spelling.

As I pondered what she would do next, my eyes lifted from the screen, and I gasped at the sight of a man standing right next to my table, not one foot away. How did I not see him? I took my headphone out of my ear. "Um... Hi?"

How long had he been there? Maybe he needed an extra chair?

"Sorry, didn't realize you were listening to something. I just asked what you were so focused on?" He gestured toward my laptop.

My lungs drew in another deep breath while I tried not to look too surprised that he, apparently, stopped by just to strike up a conversation with me. His blue eyes held eye contact with mine while he waited for me to respond. He was smartly dressed, holding a to-go coffee cup, looking unhurried. I'd bet good money he was in his early to mid-thirties—the smile lines, the posture.

"Um. Just a project. Of sorts." Lying wasn't in my nature, but I also didn't know him. I wasn't going to tell him I was writing a short story for fun because I'd recently decided not to deny my creative inclinations anymore. After answering his question in the vaguest way possible, giving him almost nothing to work with, I assumed he'd move on.

"Cool. So, are you visiting for the weekend or do you spend a lot of time here?" he asked, undeterred.

"Oh, I'm..." I hadn't had to explain my situation to a stranger before, and I was woefully unprepared for the question. What came out of my mouth was a version of the truth. "I usually only get over here once or twice a year, but this summer I'm taking a sabbatical from work, so I'll be here for a while."

"That's great. I'm spending most of the summer here, too. I go back to the city for important meetings here and there, but I'll work remotely from here for the most part."

"Boston?"

"New York."

My stomach churned. I nodded.

He shifted on his feet, seeming reluctant to leave, but not bold enough to sit down without an invitation. It was sort of...cute.

He was, too. His light brown hair was cropped on the sides, a bit fuller on the top. He had soft facial features and clear blue eyes. Clean-shaven. Quiet good looks.

"What do you do when you aren't on sabbatical?" he asked.

"I'm a lawyer."

His eyebrows went up. Was he impressed?

"Nice. I work with lawyers all the time. I'm in finance, wealth management." As soon as he said it, I realized I should've asked. When did I become so bad at making conversation with good-looking, age-appropriate men?

I took a breath and gave him a smile for the first time. "Do you want to sit down?"

"Yeah." He smiled back, brightening those blue eyes even more. I scanned his outfit as he sank into the chair next to mine at the little table—name-brand golf polo, shorts, and expensive-looking leather loafers.

I closed my laptop, giving him my full attention. "Do you have a place here?" I asked.

"My parents do. I've been coming here since I was a teenager. I stay in an apartment they have above the garage. What about you?"

"My grandmother does. No garage apartment, just the guest bedroom."

He smiled, and it again reached his eyes. "Guest bedroom works, too. What's your favorite thing to do on the island?"

I told him I love meandering through Edgartown and walking or reading at the beaches nearby, particularly Lighthouse Beach. When I asked him the same question, he said he liked boating. He didn't say whether they owned a boat, but I assumed the answer was yes.

The conversation was easy, pleasant. It became clear as he kept asking me questions that he was flirting with me. In a curious way —not overly aggressive or forward. It'd been so long since I went on a date or even flirted with anyone; I'd forgotten I was someone a person might *want* to flirt with. The flattery of it seeped into my pores, and a hum of something that resembled excitement built under the surface of my skin.

So I flirted back. I asked him about his job (wealth manager), where he lived in New York (Chelsea), where he went to school (Bucknell, and then Northwestern Kellogg for business school). He asked me all the same things, and I got a thrill out of how openly impressed he was when I said corporate attorney, Hudson Yards (formerly), and UPenn. I twirled my golden brown hair around my finger, pleased I'd thought to rim my green eyes with mascara that morning. I hadn't exactly dressed to impress today in my nylon tennis skort and V-neck T-shirt, but at least the outfit was consistent with what a lot of women wore on the island. And my legs were starting to look toned after all my trips to the gym.

"What's your name?" I asked, realizing he never mentioned it, and I hadn't either.

"Max." He extended his hand to shake mine. It felt a little formal after we'd just shared so many life facts with each other, but I took it anyway. Warm, firm.

"Val."

"So, Val," he held my gaze with a slight smirk on his mouth, drawing out my one-syllable name, "I have two questions."

I raised my eyebrows and let him go on.

"One, are you single? And, because I'm optimistic the answer is yes, my second question is, will you have dinner with me?"

My mouth quirked up as my cheeks heated. His assertiveness was so...flattering.

"Yes and..." I paused, holding his gaze the whole time, biting down the grin that threatened to spread across my mouth, "yes."

"Phew," he sighed, dramatically dragging the back of his hand across his brow. "In that case, I'll need your number." He leaned back, produced his cell phone from his pocket, and handed it to me. I typed in my name and number and passed it back.

"Val Leone," he said, reading the new contact on his screen as he stood up to leave. "I'm glad I met you. I'll let you get back to that project." He winked.

"I'm glad you, uh...stopped by." I gestured to the table.

"What can I say, nothing does it for me like a beautiful woman typing feverishly on a laptop."

A laugh rattled out of me.

A glint of pride sparked in his eyes at his joke landing.

I watched him walk away, noting the way the golf shorts hit just above his knees. He was muscular, but on the lankier side. No more than one minute after he disappeared around the corner, my phone buzzed.

617-555-0818

Hey, it's Max Phelps.

I smiled down at the little screen.

What just happened?

Just over twenty-four hours later, I took a seat at a small, white tablecloth-covered table on the second-floor balcony of Alchemy Bistro. It was a fancy (even by Edgartown's standards) restaurant on Main Street that I'd only been to once before with my brother, years ago.

Max had asked me if I was free tonight a few hours after he left the café yesterday. Mimi had invited me to have dinner with her and her friends tonight but was thrilled when I reneged to go on a date instead.

I peered over the railing after the waitress handed me the menu. "The people watching from up here is going to be amazing," I said to Max with a grin. *Wait, is that a weird thing to say?*

"Oh, for sure," he agreed. He'd swapped the golf outfit for salmon-colored chinos and a casual white button-down, rolled at the sleeves. Similar expensive-looking loafers. The ensemble was unabashedly preppy, but in keeping with how a lot of the men dressed here. Probably a nice break from whatever stuffy suits he wore to work.

"We should count how many people walking by are wearing Lilly Pulitzer dresses or some version of these pants." He gestured to his lap.

I laughed. At least he had a sense of humor about it.

When Max picked me up from Mimi's half an hour ago, I was wired with a sense of bubbly anticipation I'd been feeling since he asked me out over text the night before—a mix of first date nerves and excitement to be going on a date with someone I'd already met in person and hadn't weirded me out. It was an unfamiliar feeling after years of sporadic and disappointing dating app encounters. He'd looked me up and down from the bottom of her front steps. "I liked that tennis skirt yesterday, but I like this too," he said of my green sundress. It had thin straps, a straight neckline with a tiny cut-out that hinted at some cleavage, and a skirt that flowed to my knees. When the woman at the boutique I went to after I left the café yesterday told me the color made my eyes look even more green, I was sold.

"I didn't know you could be any more beautiful than when I first saw you," he added when we reached his car. I blushed at the compliment. I couldn't remember the last time a man called me beautiful, and he'd done it twice in under forty-eight hours.

I'd gone to the gym earlier, taken a long shower, and done my skincare routine meticulously. The slightly purple bags under my eyes that had become nearly permanent the last couple of years were gone now. I blow dried my hair and did my makeup, all while listening to music and puttering around in my bathrobe. Mimi had clucked her admiration at the dress and my hair. I felt good. Sure, I still had stress dreams where I was back at work sometimes, and I still wanted to get even stronger and leaner to undo some of the damage the stress of the last six years had done to both my mind and my body, but I already felt so much better than I had at any social event in recent memory. The result was that I was actually excited about this date.

By the time we ordered our drinks and some oysters, we'd counted two salmon-colored pants and three Lilly dresses.

"Tell me more about the sabbatical. What have you been up to? Have you traveled at all?"

I wrung my hands under the table, willing them not to start sweating. My normal-feeling first date nerves converted to a trickle of familiar cortisol-laced embarrassment, settling low in my belly. For some reason, I'd hoped I wouldn't have to explain why I was on a sabbatical on this date. It felt too soon to share how I'd actually had a big setback in my career, that it was a mental health break, not an earned extra-long vacation, and even calling it a sabbatical didn't totally feel right. I couldn't quite regret using that term, though. He looked so impressed when I told him I was a lawyer yesterday...

I met his gaze. His expression was casual, like he'd asked me a straightforward, easily answered question like have I been to Italy before. At least his phrasing allowed me to skirt around the *why* of it all. I schooled my face into a smile and said, "Not too much travel. I spent some time with my parents in New Hampshire, and

I've actually been on island since early May. I've been doing a lot of reading, long walks, gym. Clearing my head."

"That sounds great, honestly. I've traveled a bunch, but nowhere really beats here anyway."

"I agree! People come here from all over the world, and I'm just lucky my grandparents have a house here. When my parents suggested it, I knew it would be the perfect place to spend the time off." Relief to be moving on to easier topics settled my stomach. I crossed one leg over the other, ankle bobbing happily, ready for our drinks to arrive, ready for our conversation to continue.

He smiled. "It's a special place. I feel super fortunate my parents have the house here, too."

I wondered where their house was, what his parents did. Mimi had had her house since the early nineties, when homes on Martha's Vineyard were relatively affordable. Now it would be nearly impossible to buy a place on the island unless you had over a million dollars to spend.

The waitress returned with our drinks.

"To..." He paused. "A great summer on the Vineyard."

I clinked my wine glass against his near overflowing beer glass. "I'll drink to that." I held his gaze while I took a sip. One thing I should have done while I was puttering about getting ready earlier was remind myself how to flirt.

"So, what have you been reading?" he asked me.

I fought my smile while a blush surfaced on my cheeks.

"What?" he asked.

"Oh, um. Mostly romance novels right now. They're... comforting."

He barked out a laugh. "With that look on your face I thought you were about to say something horrifying. Don't most women read romance? I feel like that's totally normal, Val."

"I love them. What can I say?" I lifted both shoulders coyly.

His grin widened. "Plus, I wouldn't be here on Martha's Vineyard if it weren't for romance novels, so who would I be to judge."

"What do you mean?"

"My dad is a writer. Romance novels."

"Oh wow," I said, not thinking it through at first. And then I remembered the last name in his text yesterday. *Phelps.* "Wait. Noooo."

"Yup." Max took a big gulp of his beer.

"Your dad is Edward Phelps? One of the most successful romance novelists of all time. *The* most successful male romance novelist."

He blew out a breath. "The one and only." I couldn't read his expression.

"That's incredible! What was it like growing up with a novelist father? Was he locked in a study writing all the time? Did you realize when you were younger how famous he was?"

He chuckled at my rapid-fire questions. I wondered if he regretted bringing it up. "He definitely spent a lot of time locked in his home office. I remember that. And then when he was gone on book tours, it would just be me and my mom for chunks of time. Sometimes we'd meet him for a weekend in one city or another. Did I realize he was famous?" Max looked out at the white, colonial-style town hall building across the street and drummed his fingers on the table. "I think so, especially once I was eleven or twelve, and I started noticing the books with his name on them in every store."

"Crazy. But cool, too. Is he a romantic in real life?"

Max smirked. I was sure he'd rather not spend the whole date talking about his dad, so I vowed this was my last question.

"Yeah. He's always doing little romantic things for my mom, which I didn't notice until I was much older. And he used to give me speeches about what I should and shouldn't do before I went on dates in high school and stuff. So if I do or say anything right on this date, you'll know where I learned it from." He leaned back in his chair, a glint in his eyes as his gaze roamed from my eyes to my lips and back again. So unhurried, like he was indulging in something that fascinated him. Even his body language was a compliment.

Naturally charming, that was what Max was. Whether he learned it from his dad or not.

The conversation meandered to other pleasant topics: our favorite restaurants on the island, other places we wanted to travel someday. We both lost track of the outfit counting game.

The air was charged in his car on the way home. Did we both have a good time? Would he ask me out again? Would he try to kiss me?

Did I want him to?

I think so. I wanted him to want to, at least.

Max tapped his fingers on the center console, steering with just one hand, stealing little glances at me here and there.

Mimi's was so close to town we arrived in less than three minutes. Max bolted around the front of the car to open the door for me, and I grinned. He held his hand down for me to take, and when I stood up, he didn't let go. Instead, he used that hand to pull me toward him. *Smooth.* I steadied myself with my other hand on his chest, looking up at him. His blue eyes flashed to my mouth and then back to my eyes, and before I knew it, his lips were on mine. Soft and pleasant and warm. He held the kiss for a beat, then two, before pulling back.

"Phew," he said, his mouth tipping up in the corner.

"What?" A confused look spread on my face.

"I've been wondering if you'd let me kiss you all night. Now I don't have to worry about that so much next time." He squeezed my hand, still clasped in his.

I bit my lower lip and raised my eyebrows. "Next time, huh?"

His look of surprise made me proud of my teasing. "Well, I certainly hope there's a next time, Val," he said, adamant, staring me down with that ever-present glint in his eyes.

I stepped back onto the grass, holding his gaze as I slipped my hand out of his. "Me too." I offered him one more smile and turned to head up Mimi's front steps.

12

Optimism spurred me to sign up for a CPR certification course at the YMCA later that week. I figured it would help me get a nannying or babysitting job, if anyone ever reached out.

And because the universe works in mysterious ways, I got a text from an unknown number as I was walking to my car after the class.

617-555-6768

> Hi Val, my name is Luke and I'm looking for someone to help take care of my daughter after school for the next couple of weeks and over the summer between and after her tennis and sailing lessons. She's 8. Are you still looking for work?

I smiled at my phone in the parking lot, a sense of relief washing over me. I didn't know why I felt so concerned about having some supplemental income. I guess I just wanted the *possibility* of not going back to New York, to Peters & Dowling. If I had some money coming in, low expenses, maybe I could somehow justify pursuing my current flight of fancy: writing. At least for a while longer.

A voice in the back of my mind kept telling me it was silly, that

I'll probably go back at the end of the medical leave anyway. What else would I do? And why would I throw away years of education and hard work to struggle?

Still, I responded to the message, and we set an interview for Monday.

"You look stunning, as usual," Max said when I walked up to where he was waiting for me on the dock by the entrance to the yacht club. I was back at the café behind the bookstore earlier today, working on my insider trading short story when he'd asked how I'd feel about a sunset boat ride.

I glanced down at my outfit—white jeans, white sneakers, and a breezy blue and white striped button-down shirt, all from my favorite boutique in town. I shrugged and flashed him a smile. "You don't look bad yourself." *I can do this flirting thing.* He was sporting an expensive-looking pair of sunglasses that were shaped perfectly for his clean-shaven face.

He wrapped an arm around me and kissed my cheek. I wasn't used to it, didn't feel like I deserved it. The compliments. The affection. So unfamiliar it was almost jarring. *What's the catch?* I wanted to ask. Instead, I leaned into him.

We turned, pushed open the hip-height wooden gates, and walked out onto the dock. Max greeted the boat launch driver like an old friend, shaking his hand and clapping his back. Even though it was still bright out, most people were walking toward the dining room as opposed to the boat launch.

I liked our plan better.

We took seats at the back of the boat, and Max draped an arm around my shoulders. The wind whipped over us as we cruised out to the southern part of the harbor, the occasional splash of a wave misting water droplets into our faces. I closed my eyes and breathed in the salt.

The boat slowed and then idled alongside a pristine speedboat with three engines, plush seats, and dark wood sides, named *After Sunset*—the title of Edward Phelps's first novel. Max hopped from one boat to the other in a single, fluid motion and then turned back to offer me his hand. After we put down our things, Max produced a bottle of champagne out of a cooler he brought with him that was more expensive than I would have ever bought for myself, even with my senior associate salary.

"Spoiling me with fancy champagne?" I smirked in a way I hoped was flirtatious.

"Of course," he said with a wink before popping the cork into a towel effortlessly. He poured two glasses into flutes he'd retrieved from below deck and held his glass up to mine. "To the beautiful woman who keeps agreeing to go on dates with me."

I fought my grin and tapped my glass against his, unsure what to say to that.

"Shall we eat and sip these for a bit and then take her out for a spin before sundown?" he asked.

I glanced at the three engines attached to the back of the boat. "Sounds perfect. I'm kinda dying to know what three engines can do."

"Speed." A childlike excitement danced across his features.

We nibbled on a fancy charcuterie board full of cheese, meats, nuts, and dried fruits and chatted about the new client Max was excited he landed at work and the movie Mimi and I saw earlier that week. I gazed out at the passing boats full of sailors returning from an afternoon on the water, and the weathered-shingle mansions that lined Edgartown Harbor, as our conversation meandered from our weeks to our favorite spots in Manhattan. I had embarrassingly few favorite spots in that city, but I did a decent job faking it, I hoped. I didn't mention that I spent most of my free time writing this week. I wasn't sure why.

Just before sunset, he untied the boat from its mooring, navigated us out of the harbor, and then cranked up the speed. "Hang on!" he yelled, a devilish grin on his boyishly handsome face. I braced myself, holding on to a handle on the side of the boat as we took off. At moments, it felt like we were flying, barely skimming the surface of the water. I was grinning like a complete dork, water splashing onto my face, into my mouth, my hair, all over my clothes.

"Sorry!" Max called after a big splash crested over the side.

I shook my head emphatically. "It's awesome!" He cranked the engines even more, and I screamed, holding on for dear life.

A few minutes later the boat spun in a U-turn and started back toward the harbor at a slower pace. Eventually, he cut the engine so he could sit next to me to watch the last flashes of the sun. He pulled me under his arm, kissing my temple, and when I turned to look at him, my eyebrows slightly raised, he lowered his mouth to mine.

We both missed the sunset.

Back on dry land, when we got into Max's car, he asked if I wanted to go back to his apartment. The possibility should have occurred to me, but it hadn't. I declined in the flirtiest way I could think of on the spot: I turned in the passenger seat to face him and asked, "Next time?"

"I can live with that." He smiled at me, and to his credit, he didn't look overly disappointed.

For some reason, I never mentioned the babysitting interview.

13

On Monday afternoon I pulled up to a weathered-shingle, cape-style house about a mile farther from downtown Edgartown than Mimi's house. The hydrangea bushes lining the front rustled in the light wind and boasted blue flower bulbs so bright they almost didn't look real—like someone had dipped the flowers in dye, or painted them with a perfectly mixed blue oil paint. A white truck parked in the driveway said *Karas Construction* underneath a logo of a cape-style house, not unlike the one in front of me. I'd seen the same logo on lawn signs around town during my walks.

Luke—the dad interviewing me today—must work for a fairly big construction company here.

I walked up the stone front walkway, pulling down on the short-sleeve blouse I was wearing with a pair of jeans, hoping it was an appropriate outfit for a babysitting interview. The door opened before I could knock to reveal the tall, dark-haired man I'd awkwardly cornered into a conversation at Morning Glory Farm a few weeks ago.

Oh my god. I could already feel my face heating. Would he remember me, too? He was so handsome, I bet women try to talk to him at the grocery store all the time.

"Hey!" he said. "Morning Glory Girl." A genuine smile broke across his bearded face.

A matching smile stretched across my own, and my embarrassment faded as I drank in his eye-crinkling grin.

"That's me." I raised my arms.

"C'mon in." He held the black front door open wide.

Right inside the door was a bench with a number of shoes—comically different in size: tiny sneakers and huge boots—kicked off beneath it. To the left there was an open living room with two leather couches, an ornate mantle covered in mismatched photo frames, and a throw pillow on the floor.

"We can talk in the kitchen," Luke said, gesturing with his arm.

I followed him toward a rectangular wooden dining table on the far side of the room. But when we turned the corner, my eyes went wide. The kitchen took up almost the entirety of the back of the house: three windows over the sink looked out into the lush backyard, and a large, butcher-block kitchen island sported a bowl of fruit in the center. The cabinets were modern, the lower ones a dark gray and the uppers a lighter shade. A clean and somehow perfect white subway tile backsplash tied it all together. It was at least five times the size of my tiny galley kitchen in New York and twice as big as Mimi's.

"Wow, this kitchen is...incredible."

Luke's eyes met mine over his shoulder and held for a moment before he said, "Thanks! I built it."

"You built this? That's amazing!" I wasn't sure why I was geeking out over this man's kitchen. But it really was beautiful. I had a thing for kitchens, I supposed.

"I mean, I ordered the cabinets from a manufacturer, but I designed it and installed everything." The hint of pride in his expression was endearing.

I'd stopped by the table, and Luke pulled out a chair with both hands. Looking down at them before I dropped into the seat, my overly curious eyes again noted the lack of wedding ring. From afar the photos on the mantle looked like they were just of him and a young girl with long, dark brown hair. *Maybe he's a widower? Or divorcé with sole custody?*

He sat down across from me, and I waited for him to ask his first question. After a few seconds, he tucked his chin and chuckled to himself.

I scrunched my brows as the corner of my mouth lifted, confused.

"Sorry, I should have written down some questions or something. I've never interviewed a babysitter before. I've always had neighbors and their friends' teenaged kids to help out, word of mouth recommendations..." He ran a hand down his face and locked eyes with me again. "So, you have some experience with kids?"

I nodded, interview nerves dissipating by the second. Plus, I was ready for this question. Stories about babysitting in my hometown since I was a teenager, and the summer I was a nanny here on the island for a month during college flowed from my lips. "I mostly just made sure they got to and from camp and playdates on time, watched them when their parents wanted to go out to dinner," I added with a one-shoulder shrug, not wanting to oversell it. "Oh! And I just redid my CPR training at the Y."

He smiled at that last interjection, and I found myself mirroring it.

"Well, that's great because that's pretty much what I need, too. Get her to and from her activities, I mean. Hopefully no CPR, although that does put my mind at ease. Will you be on the island the whole summer?"

My smile disappeared. "Um, potentially? I'm off from work right now and my tentative return date is July 15th. I may be able to extend it, though. But there's a chance I have to go back to New York by mid-July. I totally understand if that won't work for you," I said, dread flaring in my belly.

He nodded, training his gaze over my shoulder for a second before asking, "Would you be comfortable helping a second grader with her homework for the next couple of weeks?"

"Of course. I always liked school."

Luke grinned at that answer. He asked where I went to school and I told him UPenn undergrad and Michigan for law school.

He let out a low whistle. "Damn. Safe to say second grade homework should be a cakewalk for you."

I bit down a smile. Admiration for my education was my kryptonite.

"You catch any football games while you were out in Michigan? I'm a fan."

"Me too! And yes—I dragged some of my classmates to a game or two at The Big House every year." I chuckled to myself.

"Were they bad games?" Luke asked.

"Oh no. They were good. I was thinking about how I became a college football fan in the first place. To my father's disappointment, my brother was more interested in philosophy than contact sports, so I'd watch games with my dad instead, because I felt bad for him. But then I wound up liking it, once I understood how it worked."

"You've given me hope I can turn my daughter into a football fan."

"If she's anything like me, she'll do it just to hang out with you. After that it's hard *not* to get sucked into the fandom."

"Perfect." Luke leaned back in his chair, clasping his hands and resting his head into them, revealing toned, larger-than-expected biceps and a glimpse of a tattoo on the outside of his shoulder where his sleeve hitched up. I couldn't tell what it was from this angle. "Okay, you seem perfectly well-qualified. Probably more qualified than Mrs. O'Neil across the street who I usually rely on. She's moved off-island for the time being to help her daughter with her first baby."

"Great for her! But I guess...not great for you."

"Exactly. Luna is pretty self-sufficient. She'd usually go over there after school for a couple hours and do her homework until I got home from work."

Luna. That was a pretty name. *Luke and Luna.*

"What made you decide to seek a nannying job?"

Maybe it was his casual posture, or the laid-back ease he exuded in his home, which was lovely but so cozy and lived-in, the type of place you weren't overly worried about spilling something. Or maybe it was that I hadn't felt nervous or self-conscious since the moment he smiled and called me the Morning Glory girl on his front steps, but I wanted to tell him the truth.

"The break I'm taking from my corporate legal career is actually a leave of absence. I..." I scanned his expression. Not a hint of judgment. "I burned out. Needed to reset and reevaluate. My parents suggested I come spend the summer on the island with my grandmother, both to help her out with the house and stuff, but also as an escape for me, I'm realizing. And..." I glanced up again. He was still looking at me with genuine interest, so I continued. "And I just want a little income to supplement, so I don't have to dip into savings for living expenses in case..." I swallowed. "In case I don't want to go back."

I held my breath and searched his face for any hint that he saw me differently now, but Luke simply nodded. "Makes sense to me. I have a lot of respect for people in those intense corporate jobs, but I don't think I could do it. Plus, I'm sure your parents are happy to have someone with your grandmother. I assume she's on her own?"

The tightness in my chest loosened with my exhale, and for the first time since I left New York, I wondered if needing this mental health break wasn't such a big failing, after all. "Yeah, my grandfather died a few years ago."

"Sorry to hear that." His deep brown eyes filled with empathy, like he knew a thing or two about loss.

"Thank you." I meant it. It didn't matter how long it'd been; every time I thought about hunting for quahogs or boating with my grandfather, it stole my breath. I probably would never have even been to Martha's Vineyard if it weren't for him. I tried to think of something to ask next, but Luke beat me to it.

"How's it been so far? Your island escape?" Our conversation had veered off so much that it didn't feel like an interview anymore. Hopefully that was a good thing.

"It's been amazing. I love it here. It's so different from New York." I shook my head slightly, picturing the view from the fish pier, and writing at the café, thinking about how my lungs felt bigger, capable of breathing twice as much air here. "I think my parents knew what I needed better than I did."

"I love it here, too. Moved here almost twelve years ago and never looked back."

"That's awesome. Can you tell me more about Luna?" In case this interview was going as well as it felt like it was, and my possible July expiration date and burnout hadn't disqualified me, I was curious what she was like.

He looked at the watch on his tanned, also muscular, forearm. "She should be getting back from school any minute now, so you can meet her."

That's a good sign!

"She's determined, spunky, lots of personality. She gives me a run for my money a lot of the time, but it's fun. She's competitive, but sensitive. Loves the summer because she's obsessed with her summer sports. I used to send her to camp, but last year she wore me down and got me to sign her up for tennis and sailing."

"A benefit of living on Martha's Vineyard!"

"Definitely. She's a little spoiled, but..." He paused. "She deserves it," he added softly, glancing over my shoulder. His expression was a mix of pride and something else I couldn't read.

"I can't wait to meet her." I smiled at Luke, and he returned it, the light reaching his eyes. It warmed my heart—this burly, dark-haired, bearded and, apparently, tattooed dad was obviously obsessed with his daughter. As it should be.

"I should mention, she's—" Before he could finish his statement, the front door opened.

"I'm home!" A girl's voice called into the house. Luke shot out of his seat and closed the distance to the front door in three long strides. I turned around in my chair as he helped her take off her backpack.

"Hey Luns, how was school?" He said it like *loons*. Paired with his doting expression, it was one of the most adorable things I'd ever witnessed. It was hard to decide who was cuter: her or her dad. *Both.*

"Okay. The same. Mrs. Coats still hasn't graded our spelling tests. How long can it take?"

I laughed, and Luna noticed me for the first time.

"Luna, this is Val. She's interested in hanging out with you this summer when I'm at work since Mrs. O'Neil is away."

I joined them by the door. "Hi Luna, it's nice to meet you!" I said in the cheeriest tone I could muster.

"Hi, Val." She was hesitant but warm.

"When did you take those spelling tests?" I asked. That one statement gave me my opening. She cared about her grades, even as a second grader. Girl after my own heart.

"Last Tuesday!"

"Wow, that is a long time, almost a week. Hopefully she finishes them soon. What were some of the words?"

Luke smirked at me over Luna's head as she launched into a list. If she remembered what the words were off the top of her head, I had no doubt she knew how to spell them. Luke put her backpack on a kitchen chair, and Luna walked over and sat down.

Luke asked, "You hungry?"

"Yes!" Luna said, a hint of incredulity in her tone.

"Alright, what will it be? Apple and peanut butter? Carrots and ranch?"

"Carrots and hummus? And some crackers too?" Luna asked, her big, brown eyes wide.

"You like hummus?" I asked her.

"Yeah, it's great. Do you like it?"

"Love it." I glanced at Luke, and he shrugged as if he knew what I was thinking. *What eight-year-olds eat hummus?*

"Do you want some too, Val?" Luke raised his eyebrows at me from the kitchen.

"Oh no, I'm good. Thank you."

Luke got Luna set up with her homework and her snack at the table. Clearly this was their daily ritual, at least on the days when he was home early. Once she was situated with a cracker in one hand and her pencil in another, Luke walked me to the door. "Thanks for coming to meet with us. I'll call you." He held the front door open for me. His tone didn't give me any indication as to whether he planned to hire me, but it was okay. He probably needed to think about it. Maybe he planned to interview more people. I tried to prevent any hint of disappointment from showing on my face.

"Okay!" I forced one more smile and turned to head to my car.

Seated in the driver's seat, I drummed my fingertips on the armrest and tried to think of things to do to distract myself while I waited to hear from him.

It's not the end of the world if he doesn't hire me, I thought, although my gut was unconvinced. He'd be better off with someone who could commit for the entire summer, anyway. I should mentally prepare myself for the letdown.

On my phone there were two missed text messages: one from Max and one from Natalie. As I slid the message from Natalie open, my phone vibrated with an incoming call from a Massachusetts number.

"This is Val."

"Hey," Luke's baritone voice said through the speaker. "You're hired if you'll still have us. Wanna come back inside and talk scheduling?"

I looked up. He was standing in the picture window of his living room looking out at my car, phone to his ear.

I didn't bother concealing my enthusiasm when I said, "Be right in!"

14

Later that night, I was reading in the living room while Mimi watched the news when my phone rang, jolting me. Sometimes I forgot that I wasn't at risk of incoming calls from partners or clients in the evenings anymore. At least, not for now. My pulse steadied when I saw Max's name on the screen.

"Hey, Val. How was your day?" I hadn't seen him since Friday —our boating date. He was just calling to check in?

That's sweet.

"It was good! I actually got a part-time job."

"Oh, really? Why?" His tone was hard with skepticism. It took me aback. Why would he ask *why* instead of asking what it was?

"Oh, um. I..." My stomach flipped over as I realized I never told Max that my sabbatical was actually an anxiety-induced medical leave, and while I probably would go back to my job, I wanted to have the option of *not* going back. "It's kinda complicated. With the leave from work, there's a chance I might want to...extend it, in which case I don't know if it would continue to be paid. And, you know, it's something to do."

"Oh, okay. I didn't realize you were looking for something, since you have your job at Peters & Dowling to go back to." His voice was so flat, so unlike the charming lilt he normally had in person. Neither of us said anything for a moment. The awkward-ness was palpable, even through the phone. Was he upset I hadn't explained more on our dates?

"I never fully explained. I'm sorry I didn't. Maybe we can talk about it more when you're back?" It was hard not to take his stunted responses personally, but I was partially to blame for not telling him the details of my situation.

"I got back a couple hours ago."

"Oh, great! How was your weekend? You said the client dinner went well?" I hoped a subject change would cut the tension.

Max seemed happy for the subject change, too, and spoke jovially about the dinner, the fancy food, the intricate drinks, the satisfaction that one of his biggest clients remained happy with their services. I listened and *ooh*-ed and *ahh*-ed appropriately, if apathetically.

We hung up after agreeing to go out for drinks on Wednesday.

Lying in bed that night, I replayed our conversation in my head. I didn't miss going to those fancy, budget-less client dinners like the one Max described so fondly, or the self-doubt they always inspired: Did I have one too many drinks? Did I say the right things? Did I come across as sociable and fun but still trustworthy and reliable?

Nope, I did not miss them one bit.

I waited on Luke's front steps for Luna to get off the school bus.

"Hi, Luna! How was school?" I asked once she got to the walkway.

She shrugged, her backpack lifting up an inch with her shoul-ders. "It was fine. We finally got our spelling tests back."

Her brown eyes were bright, so I asked, "And?"

"I got a one hundred." A smile crept across her tiny face. She had paler skin than Luke, but equally dark hair and eyes. Her brown hair was pulled up in a ponytail, with little wisps flying off in all directions from the humidity. She was adorable.

"That's amazing! Great job!" I held up my hand for a high five, and she stared at it for a moment, considering, before obliging me.

"Thanks." She shrugged like it was no big deal. Like she got one hundreds all the time. She probably did.

We went inside and she made her way to the kitchen table. I checked the fridge. "Do you want a snack? Hummus and veggies and crackers again?"

"Yeah!"

I brought her a little plate and a cup of water. She'd already spread open her books on the table. I made myself a small hummus and veggie plate and walked over to the couch. "I'll be right here reading if you need me."

Three chapters of my romantasy novel later, a dramatic sigh issued from the dining table. Luna squinted at the paper in front of her, hand poised over it with a pencil.

I tucked my bookmark in my book. "What's up?"

"I have a math test tomorrow, and I can't figure out one of the practice questions."

I walked over to the table and pulled out the chair next to hers. "Can I see?"

She pushed the paper toward me. The question was: *If seven students go to the park, and each student brings five tennis balls with them, how many tennis balls will there be to play with?*

I explained that the question was really just asking what seven times five was. Luna pondered this for a while and ended up solving it by adding up seven, five times. Oddly enough, I still remembered how hard it was to memorize multiplication tables at her age. And how innate it was for Drew.

"Nice work!" I said when she finished. "Let's do the next one."

For the next two hours, I didn't get up from the table except to refill our water glasses. We completed all the practice questions in her packet and practiced multiplication tables with flashcards. I felt bad that I didn't know any tricks to teach her, so I was more or less just providing moral support, working questions out alongside her and holding up the cards, telling her whether she got it right or not.

When she finally decided to take a break, she queued up *How to Train Your Dragon* on the TV. I smirked to myself because the book I was reading also had dragons.

I joined her on the couch. "You've seen this one?" I had no idea what was appropriate for an eight-year-old to watch. When Luke and I went over everything two days ago we discussed bus schedules and food allergies and homework, but not TV rules.

"Yeah! It's my favorite."

Perfect. "Throw it on!"

Half an hour later headlights flashed into the living room. In all honesty, I was thoroughly engrossed in this movie and somewhat disappointed Luke was home to relieve me.

"Hey!" Luke called as he opened the front door.

"Hi, Dad! We're watching *How to Train Your Dragon*."

"I can see that." His mouth curved as he spoke. He seemed amused to find us watching an animated movie.

I lifted my palms and smiled sheepishly.

Luna paused the movie and turned around.

"You finish your homework?" he asked. Luke leaned his elbows over the back of the couch, wearing a ball cap and a polo shirt with a *Karas Construction* logo embroidered on it.

"Yes, Val helped me study for my math test."

"Did she?" His mouth formed a *thank you* in my direction before tipping up into a grin.

This man had a nice smile.

Luna nodded before turning her attention back to the television and resuming her movie.

I joined Luke in the kitchen.

"Did it go okay?" he asked.

"I think she's still a little nervous about her math test tomorrow. But we did all the practice questions multiple times, and *lots* of flashcards. I think she has it down."

He stared at me with a slightly awed expression. I almost asked him *what?* but he said, "I'll go over it with her again after dinner, and give her a pep talk. I think it's awesome she's so motivated, but sometimes I wish she didn't put pressure on herself as a second grader. It feels too early. I didn't start taking my grades seriously until college, and even then, probably not seriously enough." He shrugged.

I chuckled at his admission. "I was more like her." I glanced over to where she sat on the couch. "I remember caring about my grades even in elementary school." *Probably too much, too.* "I agree going through it with her one more time will increase her confidence. And throw in that you're proud of her no matter what grades she gets. I used to like it when my parents would say things like that sometimes." As the unsolicited tip exited my lips, I had half a second to consider that Luke might not appreciate my parenting advice. I wasn't a parent, after all.

But I did remember what it felt like to be an oddly ambitious elementary schooler.

One look at his face told me my concern was unwarranted. His expression was open, and he was nodding. I was about to apologize anyway when he said, "Thank you. That's a great idea. I mean, I tell her I'm proud of her all the time, but I like how you put it."

I shrugged. "Just a thought from a former stressed-out student."

"Well keep 'em coming." He grinned. I stared at his perfect, straight white teeth and found myself wondering if he had dimples under that beard. "Do you want to stay for dinner? I'm grilling burgers, easy to make another."

"Oh, thank you, but..." I checked the time on my phone. "I actually have to get going."

"You have a date or something?" His eyes glittered, and I could tell he meant it in jest, but my own eyes flew open wide.

Before I could say anything, Luke said, "Oh! You actually do. Sorry. I mean, why wouldn't you? That...makes sense," he stammered. He seemed flustered all of a sudden.

"It's new." *Why am I telling him that?*

He swallowed. "Okay. Great. Good."

I raised my eyebrows and opened my mouth, but then I closed it again. I had no idea what to say next, so I figured it was time to go. "But thank you for the invite! I'd love to, another time." I held his gaze, willing him to see my sincerity.

A small part of me wished I didn't have somewhere to be tonight, so I could stay for dinner with them. *I hope this doesn't stop him from asking me ever again.*

"Sounds good." His expression returned to relaxed and warm. He walked me to the door and held it open. "See you tomorrow, Val."

My enthusiasm for this date with Max was somewhat diminished by the pit of anxiety that had lodged itself in my stomach. Our conversations had never been strained before that phone call on Monday. But, in his defense, I hadn't told him the real story, and calling my leave of absence a sabbatical probably didn't help. *It will be fine*, I told myself. I would tell him the full story this time. It'd only been a few dates, but he seemed like a great guy. *He'll understand.*

Or at least, I hoped he'd understand.

He insisted on picking me up again. When I stepped out the front door, he stared at me. "Hey, beautiful."

"Hi!" The bubbly feeling spurred by his compliment cut through my nerves.

Once we were seated in rocking chairs on the deck of the Harbor View Hotel, cocktails in our hands, a light breeze blowing through our hair, I decided to address the elephant in the room. Spinning my drink around on the armrest, looking at that instead of him, I said, "I'm sorry I didn't tell you I was looking for a part-time job. I also probably shouldn't have called it a sabbatical. It's a leave of absence." I glanced at him to gauge his reaction.

He nodded, contemplative. "Val, I get it. This is only what, our third date? You don't have to tell me everything. I was just surprised because you already have this great job to go back to, that's all. Sabbatical, leave of absence, whatever you call it, everyone deserves a break now and then. I think all companies should have them."

I nodded and forced the corner of my mouth up. "I agree." I wasn't sure what else to say. I was both surprised and relieved that he didn't ask what prompted the leave of absence in my specific case. At least he didn't seem to judge me for taking one.

"When is the leave up?"

"July 15th." I had the date memorized.

"Oh, that's so far away. You have plenty of time. You'll figure it out." He flicked his wrist.

"Right. Plenty of time." I swallowed and looked out at the view: Edgartown Lighthouse, its white facade and black door, window, and roof. It stood out against the deep blue background of the water beyond. Despite the serenity of my surroundings and the strength of the drink in my glass, I felt nervous.

It didn't feel like there was plenty of time between now and July 15th. Especially when I wasn't sure what I was going to do and hadn't spent enough time thinking about it. The freedom provided by having some money coming in now only contributed to my indecisiveness. I needed to talk to my therapist about it on Monday. Maybe she could tell me what I should do.

Max reached out, dragging his fingers lightly over my thigh, right above my knee. His hand was warm on my bare leg. It brought me back from my racing thoughts. "Still with me?" he asked, smile on his face, glint in his eye.

I nodded. "Yeah. I just..." *Feel super anxious and don't know what I'm doing,* I thought. But I didn't want to kill the vibe so instead I said, "I love this view. I used to go to this beach all the time when I was little."

"I've never actually walked down there."

"Really?"

Max chuckled. "Really. There's some beachfront at my parents' house so we didn't go to other beaches very often." I'd had a feeling the Phelps's house must be waterfront. "Let's walk down there after we eat."

"Sounds great."

Max left his hand on my leg until he got up to get us more drinks and order some food. I liked it. It was forward but somehow grounding. Before he stood, he said, "It's a gorgeous night, I'm in the company of a gorgeous woman, life is good. Let's get another drink and pretend tomorrow is far, far away, okay?"

That actually sounded...great. I turned to him, tilting my head and pressing my lips together to hold in my flattered smile. "Deal."

I watched him walk toward the doors into the restaurant. He was such a flirt. Handsome and confident. What was it about me that had drawn the attention of a man like him?

It'd been ages since I'd been showered with so many compliments. If anything, my time with Max was a fun distraction from my inner turmoil about what to do with my life. I didn't even want to drag down our conversations with all my fears and anxieties.

That was when I decided I'd be going home with him tonight.

15

My therapist refused to tell me what she thought I should do.

Over the last few weeks, we'd spent a lot of time talking about what I like to do outside of work, but not so much time talking about what I should do next.

"So my return-to-work date is July 15th," I said today. She nodded but said nothing, giving me time to go on. She did this often. "And...I don't know what to do."

"Do you want to go back?"

"I don't know. Do you think I should?" I'd told her all about what my life was like the last six years, and how by the end, I couldn't enjoy my time outside of work, either. I thought maybe she'd say something like: *Of course you shouldn't go back to a place that made you feel that way.*

But instead she said, "Do you miss it?"

Sometimes I wished she would opine more during these sessions. It seemed like her method was to ask me open-ended questions, let me fill the time talking, and then she would give me some things to think about at the end.

As I considered her question, images of my office, my computer, my phone, and my closet full of business casual attire flashed through my mind. Emotionally, I didn't miss it at all. But then I thought about the deal announcements, the accolades, my enviable salary, people's impressed reactions when I told them I was a Peters & Dowling attorney... Maybe I missed those parts?

"Not really. But I also know that this break, not working but still getting a paycheck, is temporary. It's not like I can do this forever. I don't want to deplete my savings. And I'm not the type to *not* work."

"Is there anything else you might like to do for work that isn't your old job?"

Write. The thought popped into my head reflexively. I squished it down. *I have a law degree and an expertise I worked really hard for; I have to use it.*

Don't I?

"I don't know," I said again.

"You mentioned you like writing. Is that something you've ever considered doing as more than a hobby?"

Honestly, it already felt like more than a hobby. Lately I'd been writing for at least a couple of hours per day. My first short story was complete. It ended up being longer than I expected, and I'd decided to turn it into at least a novella, maybe a novel. I read writers' blogs every day and looked for new prompts to spark new ideas. I had several partially written stories on my Google Drive now.

"Not seriously, no." Why was it so hard for me to be open with her on this topic? She gave me the perfect opportunity.

"Maybe you should think about it. Before next week I want you to imagine doing something else and consider whether it would bring more or less satisfaction than your old job."

On Wednesday it rained buckets, and I met Luna at the bus with an umbrella. She didn't have any homework since her school year was ending in two days, so we had over two hours to kill before

Luke got home. When we got inside, I took stock of the walk-in pantry and found a bag of chocolate chips, flour, sugar, and vanilla extract. Plus, they had butter and eggs in the fridge.

"Want to bake some chocolate chip cookies?" I called to Luna in the living room. I assumed she had flopped down on the couch and was about to turn on the TV, which was also fine with me, but I was endeavoring to not be the world's most boring babysitter.

"Yeah!" Before I turned around with all the ingredients cradled in my arms, she'd appeared in the pantry. "Do you know how to make those?"

I handed her the bag of chocolate chips. "Pro tip: there's a recipe on the back of the chocolate chip bag."

"Cool!"

Within the hour, Luna and I were insulated from the raw chill of the rainy afternoon by the rising temperature in the kitchen and the smell of sugar and butter and melting chocolate.

"Be careful, don't burn your mouth," I said as she took a small test bite of the hot cookie that threatened to fall apart in her hands. She gave me a thumbs up before taking an even bigger bite. I'd held her off for all of five minutes after the first batch came out of the oven. A little smile lifted her cheeks while she chewed. I stepped around her and grabbed one for myself.

Luna told me about her friends in her second-grade class between bites. I tried to keep track of all the names, but I could use a notebook. I was glad she was sharing things with me, even if I was the one to ask. She was becoming comfortable with me, I could tell. The cookies likely helped.

Luna was reaching for her second cookie when we heard the front door open. I raised my eyebrows at her and she took a huge bite of the gooey treat in her hand, her eyes wide. As Luke rounded the corner into the kitchen, she shoved the other half in her mouth, as if to hide the evidence.

"Hey! You're home." I said.

At the same time he said, "It smells like baked goods."

"Your nose is correct," I said.

"Oh my goodness." Luke laughed as he took in the disaster that used to be his kitchen—streaks of flour and dirty mixing bowls and measuring cups covering every surface. Then he smirked at Luna, who still couldn't speak because of the whole cookie she'd crammed into her mouth.

"We were about to start cleaning up. Last batch is in the oven," I said.

"How'd they come out?" He walked over to the stove and picked one up from the baking rack.

"Great!" Luna said, finally able to speak.

Luke took a bite and made eye contact with me, his brown eyes amused as he rubbed his pointer finger on the side of his nose.

"Flour?" I wiped my hands on both sides of my nose.

"Yup." He looked back at Luna. "So, whose idea was this, you or Val?"

"Val!"

I shrugged. "She didn't have any homework."

"Look, the recipe is on the back of the chocolate chip bag!" Luna showed Luke the bag like it was a grand revelation, and I felt an odd sense of pride. Something so simple sparked so much enthusiasm. We had fun making the dough, too, going through each instruction together. Luna was definitely ready to learn fractions.

"Nice. That's convenient."

"You must bake sometimes. You have all the ingredients," I said.

"Usually just when Nan is here. She makes banana bread," Luna said.

Luke lifted his palms, a diffident look on his handsome face. "I buy baked goods at Morning Glory."

The timer on the oven sounded. Luke grabbed the oven mitts off the counter and turned around to take the last tray of cookies out.

"They're really good. Nice job." He held his hand up for a high five, which Luna completed with a *clap*.

"Alright, Luna. Should we start cleaning up?" I asked.

She sighed. "I guess we have to."

I gathered the mixing bowls and measuring cups and walked over to the sink.

Luke placed his hand on my shoulder as I passed him, leaned into me, and said, "Thank you" in a low voice. I could tell he was referring to my baking with Luna, not just cleaning up.

I smiled over my shoulder at him.

Between the three of us, the cleanup took too little time.

Two days later I searched the pantry for a cookie to have while I read my book and waited for Luke and Luna to get home, but those little cookie monsters already ate most of them. Noticing there were only two left, I shut the pantry door and headed back to the couch empty-handed.

Since it was Luna's last day of school there was no bus service, and even though I offered to pick her up, she insisted it had to be Luke because *"everyone else was getting picked up by their parents."* So he agreed, even though he'd need to go back to work for a couple of hours afterward.

Four chapters of the most recent Edward Phelps romance novel later, they threw open the front door.

Before I could say *hi*, Luna ran upstairs with her backpack still on. The loud crack of a door slamming shut echoed down the stairs.

I glanced at Luke. His fists clenched and his jaw ticked. I could only imagine they'd had many a discussion about door slamming.

He sunk down onto the other side of the couch, dropping his elbows to his knees and his face into his hands and sighing loudly. "I was late. She's pissed."

"Ah." Everything made sense now.

"She was one of the last kids there. She said it was *so* embarrassing and then proceeded to not speak to me the whole way home." He groaned.

Man, he's really beating himself up for this minor transgression. I ignored my urge to scooch closer to him. "Luke, you're only twenty minutes later than I thought you'd be. It's not like you forgot about her."

He turned to face me, a smirk breaking on his frustrated face. "Do people really *forget* their kids places?"

"I don't know. Maybe not so much anymore, but my parents have all kinds of stories about being forgotten places when they were growing up."

Luke chuckled before leaning his head all the way back on the couch and closing his eyes. I'd probably find how distraught he was about this amusing if it wasn't so genuine. *It must be really hard being a single parent with a full-time job.*

"I got stuck in this new client meeting. If it was a client I knew better, I would've told them I had to leave. But it's a big project and I didn't want to be rude... I wish I just said something." I assumed most of his work was at the actual construction sites; he so often came home with dust on his boots, a hard hat tucked under his arm. *He must help with some of the back-office stuff, too.*

"I get it. No need to explain to me. Sometimes it's impossible to find an opportunity to extract yourself when you're in the middle of it."

He nodded but didn't seem to feel any better.

"I have an idea," I said.

Luke opened one eye and cocked his eyebrow.

"Why don't you take her for dinner or ice cream or something when you get home?"

"I like it." He stood, walked over to the stairs, and took them up two at a time.

After a knock Luke's voice said, "Hey Luns, wanna go to Edgartown Pizza for dinner when I get back?"

A door creaked open. "Can we get bacon pizza?"

"Yes, we can get bacon pizza."

A pause. "Okay." The door closed again, but the change in her tone was noticeable.

After Luke got back downstairs I said, "I think she's still a little too young to fully grasp the concept of bribery. Use that to your advantage." I grinned conspiratorially.

"You're brilliant."

He looked so relieved, I felt it in my own chest. A chuckle escaped my lips. "You'll be forgiven in no time."

"Thank you," he said, picking up his keys and heading for the door. He always said it so sincerely, like I was doing something much more remarkable than hanging out with his generally delightful eight-year-old and doling out arbitrary parenting ideas.

As soon as Luke's car pulled out of the driveway, I went upstairs, knocked on Luna's door, and convinced her to come down and watch a Disney movie with me until her dad got home.

Not long after our movie ended Luke came back in the front door and Luna popped off the couch. He didn't bother taking off his shoes or moving beyond the entryway. He knew they'd be turning right around to go get pizza, as promised.

"Is Val coming to pizza with us?" Luna asked her dad.

"She can if she wants." Luke looked at me, expression open. He hadn't asked me to stay for dinner since last week when I declined because I had a date.

When Luna turned around and said, "Please!" I was grateful I didn't have a date with Max tonight.

We slid into the worn, red leather booth at the casual pizza parlor. It was a cacophony of order-ready bell chimes and conversations. All the tables were full when we walked in, but a booth opened up just before our pizzas (one bacon, one veggie) were done.

I snagged two pieces of veggie. Luke leaned back in the booth, extending his legs. Several people nodded at him or said hello as they passed our table. Luna happily munched on her bacon pizza, all traces of her earlier attitude gone.

I took a bite of my pizza crust, then a bite of the slice, then one more bite of the crust, from the other side. It tasted like my childhood. They've been making the pies the exact same way since I was Luna's age. It was my grandfather's favorite pizza place on the island.

"Do you eat the crust first?" Luke asked me, one of his dark brown eyebrows raised.

I lifted one shoulder, unashamed. "It makes the topping and cheese to crust ratio better for the last few bites."

He scrunched up his face, said, "Let's test this theory," and took a comically large bite out of his own crust.

Luna and I made eye contact and chuckled as Luke struggled to keep his mouth closed while he chewed.

A few minutes later my phone vibrated loudly on the little wooden table, and then again thirty seconds later. Then again, three times, after that.

My hand shot out to grab it. "Sorry, group message."

Luke grimaced. "I wouldn't wish that many group texts on my worst enemy," he said, dead serious, a look of utter disgust on his face. Not even a hint of sarcasm.

I giggled. He clearly meant it to his core, and for some reason, I found it hilarious. His expression remained disgusted as my phone continued to vibrate in my hand. Uncontrollable laughter bubbled out of me.

"I honestly don't understand why you're laughing. I'm being completely serious." His expression matched his stony tone.

I clutched my stomach. "I know you're serious. That's why it's so funny." His face finally cracked. He turned to Luna, a glimmer of a smirk on his mouth. "I don't get her," he pointed his thumb at me. But Luna was also laughing. "Oh no, Luns not you, too."

"Look, see." I held up my phone, showing them both a picture of baby Mina trying to lift a Wiffle ball bat. "It's pictures of my friends' baby. And all the notifications are people liking the photos and saying how cute she is." I turned the screen back and smiled at my phone as I swiped through the photos.

When I looked back up Luke was staring at me. "What?"

"Nothing," he rasped. He shook his head, like he was trying to expel a thought.

Luke turned to Luna. "I remember when *you* were that little. I can't believe you're going to be in third grade next year, Luns. You're getting so old," he teased her.

"You're old!" she insisted.

"It's true. I am *so* old." He rolled his eyes and Luna giggled.

I shook my head, cheeks tugging my mouth into a smile, as they'd done frequently throughout this meal—pizza off of paper plates at the local pizzeria.

When we were done, Luke insisted I take some slices home for Mimi.

I laughed at myself on the car ride home for the little crush I'd had on Luke after I first met him at Morning Glory Farm. Little did I know he'd end up being my employer.

I couldn't help but wonder—again—what happened with Luna's mom. I'd never ask. He'd have to volunteer that information at some point, or it would remain a mystery. It occurred to me as I turned onto Mimi's road that I could do some sleuthing on social media, but I didn't want to.

I wanted him to tell me himself. If he ever chose to share that type of thing with me.

16

A s I drove up the cobblestone driveway to the Phelps compound, I felt almost proud that I had a date with an attractive, mature man on a summer Saturday. Theoretically, if things kept going well, Max and I could keep seeing each other back in New York. But that thought had me picturing returning to Peters & Dowling and brought my anxiety roaring back. *Nope, not thinking about that right now.* No need to get ahead of myself when we'd only been on three dates.

The sprawling seaside mansion came into view as I turned the last bend, along with Max, who leaned against the door that led up to his apartment over the three-car garage, sporting a more casual version of his usual uniform: long sleeve T-shirt, golf shorts, and boat shoes. When I stepped out of my car and closed the distance between us, I couldn't help but notice how much newer his docksider boat shoes looked than Luke's.

As we walked up to the main house, Max's arm slung around my shoulders, an older man and woman stepped out the front door. I was momentarily starstruck by the sight of one of my favorite authors. He looked exactly like the photo on all his book jackets, albeit a little grayer at the temples. They both smiled when they saw us.

"Hey, son," Edward called as the front door closed behind him. "Heading down to the beach?"

"Yes," Max replied. We closed the distance, intercepting them halfway up the front walkway.

"Mom, Dad, this is Val. Val, my parents, Brianna and Ed."

"Lovely to meet you, Val," Max's mom said with a sparkling smile, shaking my hand.

"You too, both of you." I extended my hand to Ed, and he took it with a firm shake.

"Hope our son is being a gentleman." Ed winked at Max, and a grin spread across my lips. *Guess the winking runs in the family.*

"Absolutely. Four dates and this is already our second picnic!"

They chuckled affectionately and continued toward the Bentley in the driveway that I had parked my sedan as far away from as possible moments ago. I didn't know much about cars, but I knew that one was extra expensive.

"Had you told them about me?" I asked as Max and I continued into the house.

"Of course," Max said, squinting his eyes at me, like it went without saying.

It made me feel giddy.

It was difficult not to gape at the gorgeous interior of the house. The kitchen had marble counters, an island the size of a vehicle, two fridges, two ovens, and counter-to-ceiling windows on the far side with an unobstructed view to the pool and pool house out back, a sprawling, manicured yard, and the ocean beyond it. It was stunning, if a little over the top. I didn't want to touch anything.

After we made our way down to the beach, we chatted about our favorite books and movies and television shows, sitting on a blanket in the sand. Apart from a brief discussion about the general inner workings of a New York City law firm after Max asked me whether I thought the show *Suits* was accurate, I avoided the topics of work and the future and New York, even though they were never far from my mind. He seemed content to stick with lighter subjects, too, and for that I was grateful.

We dined on expensive champagne and caviar and crab cakes Max had picked up from somewhere in town. I worried the real glass champagne flutes he brought down in a padded case would break and leave glass in the sand.

But the beach in front of Max's house was so serene and private, I found myself relaxing as the champagne seeped into my blood. Max held himself up on his palms and I leaned against him, soaking in the warmth of his body heat as the temperature dropped after the sun dipped below the horizon. *I think maybe I could get used to this.*

I looked up at him, the pink sky reflecting in his sunglasses. He took them off, and then mine, and pulled me into his lap. Taking my face in between both of his hands, he kissed me deeply. I let him. My fingers roamed through his hair, and he gripped me tighter around my waist. I hoped he wouldn't notice how soft I was in the middle. Maybe we'd remove each other's clothing right there on the private stretch of sand. But we weren't so far down from the house—someone could easily spot us from those kitchen windows.

As if reading my mind, Max pulled back, kissed my jaw, and whispered, "Let's go back to my apartment." Next he pressed his lips to my neck, and I closed my eyes. "Is that a yes?" I could hear the smirk in his voice.

"Yes."

He made quick work of packing up the blanket, the picnic basket, and the empty champagne bottle and then pulled me by the hand through the soft sand.

We barely made it to the top of the stairs before Max took off his shirt and mine and pressed me into the wall next to the door.

We'd taken it slower last time, after our cocktail date on the Harbor View Hotel deck, pretending we weren't only there to explore more physical intimacy. He'd made me a drink, we'd sat on the couch. Things slowly escalated from there and ended with us taking turns making each other come with our hands and tongues and mouths. It took me a while; I couldn't seem to get out of my head, worrying about what he thought of my body and whether he'd still be interested in seeing me after we'd hooked up. I almost gave up and asked him to stop, but he didn't seem to want to. I was smitten by his persistence, like my orgasm was a contest he was determined to win no matter how long it took. And I was happy to reciprocate. He made it a little easier for me, finishing within a few minutes after I started touching him.

As Max buried his face in my chest, pulling down my bra and brushing his lips over my nipples, I was glad we skipped the *do you want another drink* part this time.

"How do you turn me on so much?"

My stomach fluttered with butterflies.

"Mmm," I murmured in reply, pulling his face back up to kiss his lips. I parted mine and my tongue met his. Anticipation slowly built in my core. He grabbed my hand and led us to the bed, pulling me on top of him. I felt his erection pressed into my underwear under my skirt.

"Val. Let's have sex. Yeah?"

That's one way to ask.

"Yeah." I dipped down to kiss him again.

We shed the rest of our clothing, kissing and fumbling with buttons and clasps, and suddenly I felt more exposed than I wanted to be. I twisted to turn off the lamps as Max reached across me to one of the nightstands. *This will be fun*, I said to myself. *He's attracted to you, or else he wouldn't be doing this.* He wasted no time rolling on the condom he'd produced out of the bedside drawer, lining our hips up, and pressing himself into me. My breath sucked in from the pinch of it. I wasn't quite ready. I'd need more foreplay next time.

If there was a next time.

"So tight," he said after he pulled back and pressed into me again. *That's because it's been well over a year since I've done this*, I thought but didn't say.

After another minute of thrusts my body became used to his. I lifted my hips, trying for a better angle, trying to focus on the sensations and get out of my head. It was clear Max was enjoying it, at least. That made me happy. He rocked into me several more times and then finished with a groan, collapsing on top of me, kissing my neck. I hadn't finished this time, but that wasn't unusual for me. I wondered if he'd touch me, or offer anything else, but he didn't. *Maybe I'll start letting him go down on me before-hand?* He'd done a fine job with that last time.

"I'm glad I met you," he said, a sated glaze in his eyes as he kissed my palm.

I snuggled up under his arm, breathing in his subtle, expensive cologne. "I'm glad I met you, too."

I meant it. When I decided to move to Martha's Vineyard for the better part of this summer, dating was the furthest thing from my mind. I was clawing myself back from the brink of depression, and felt terrible about myself, both inside and out. Somehow after six weeks, I'd put a couple of my pieces back together. I'd discovered (or, more accurately, rediscovered) my passions for reading and writing. Having time to help Mimi and Luke and Luna made me feel useful and appreciated in a way I wasn't used to. My mentality felt stronger, like I was more capable of fighting off the anxiety, the tears, when they cropped up. I'd lost weight and gained muscle and felt so much better about myself, mentally and physically. Max's attention helped, even though during these last two hookups I'd still felt self-conscious. Nevertheless, it felt good to be desired by someone like him. And hopefully next time would be even better.

I enjoyed our dates, enjoyed him. Max was smart and fun and enthusiastic, never making me chase or pine for his attention. I couldn't predict what kind of a future we might have, but for now I decided this was a good thing we had going.

17

The sound of bouncing tennis balls greeted us when I dropped Luna off at her first tennis lesson. I watched her walk toward the weathered-shingle tennis center that stood between the parking lot and the courts in her matching pink outfit, twirling her racket bag. *Should I go in there and make sure she goes to the right place?*

I was about to unfasten my seat belt when a similarly clad little girl ran up to her. They hugged, racket bags clanking against each other, and a smile appeared on my face. When they reached the top of the porch steps, a teenager in an all-white outfit holding a clipboard guided them inside.

I exited the parking lot to head to the YMCA.

Shortly after Luke explained Luna's enviable summer schedule, I worked out my own. Every day after I dropped Luna off at tennis, I would go to the gym for an hour or so. Then I'd pick her up, we'd have lunch, and I'd drop her at the sailing center downtown on the harbor at 1:00 p.m. While she was sailing, I would write, either at a café, back at Mimi's, in the library, or at Luke's house. He told me I was welcome to hang out there whenever I wanted.

Max continued to text me consistently, and we usually saw each other every few days after I left Luke's house in the evening.

About a week into the new routine, Luke texted me in the middle of the afternoon when I was writing at his kitchen table.

LUKE

I'm picking up burgers to grill tonight. Want to stay for dinner?

A smile stretched on my face as I read the message again. I hadn't had dinner with them since we went for pizza after Luna's last day of school, but I felt the tug to stay more often than not after Luke relieved me each day. It was Wednesday, so Mimi had mahjong and dinner with her friends tonight. And I didn't have plans with Max, either.

VAL

Sure, that sounds great!

LUKE

What do you like to drink?

I got up and looked in his fridge. The only beverages were orange juice, milk, lemonade, and domestic beer. I could do a beer.

VAL

I'm easy! Whatever you're getting for yourself.

LUKE

Oh c'mon. Tell the truth.

I laughed. Was there a camera in here? How could he tell?

VAL

Okay, fine. I like rosé wine.

He liked my message.

My eyes landed back on the open spreadsheet on my laptop.

I'd decided to expand my insider trading story—the betrayed lawyer would form some kind of connection with the investigator after he offers her a deal that helps her avoid prison, and somehow her losing her job and having to reevaluate her entire life would end up being a good thing. I was still working out the finer points, but it was so *fun*—having the time to imagine the potential scenes like a movie in my head, getting hit with an idea at the gym or while out running errands and jotting it down in a note on my phone. Even the book on story structure I'd been working through sparked plot points and dialogue and character backstories, turning crackling embers of ideas into flames of inspiration that had me ripping open my laptop and typing for hours.

Envisioning writing instead of doing corporate deals was the easiest therapy homework Wendy had ever given me—I could absolutely picture myself doing this every day instead. I didn't know if I could ever make any money from it, but for now the first few babysitter checks were enough to quell my financial anxiety.

I still hadn't told anyone besides my therapist and my mom and Mimi about my newly discovered penchant for writing, but maybe I would at some point. I thought it was a little odd Max hadn't asked.

I wondered what he thought I did every day.

Luna ran inside, dropping her bag by the front door and rounding the corner into the kitchen like it was some kind of race. She must have noticed the classic rock playing through the speaker system —an irrefutable clue that her dad was home.

"Hi!" she yelled over the music, plopping down on a stool at the kitchen island, where Luke was chopping vegetables.

A wide smile transformed his handsome face into a beacon of light as he looked at her. "Hey, Luns! How was sailing?"

"Great. Clara and I won the practice race. We beat the boys."

"That's what I like to hear!" He held up his hand for a high five. She smacked it enthusiastically.

Standing a few feet from the island, I pressed my lips together to keep from smiling just watching them.

"Alright, first up, cheese and crackers." He placed a charcuterie plate in the center of the island and nodded me over to join them.

"Cheddar?" Luna clarified.

"Of course. That's the cubes. You could try the other one too," he suggested, pointing at a triangle of brie.

Luna stuck her tongue out. "No, gross."

Luke chuckled.

"Can I help with anything?" I asked Luke, gesturing toward the half-chopped tomatoes, zucchini, and summer squashes.

He shook his head. He held my gaze for a breath, some inscrutable expression replacing his smile, and then shook his head again, almost imperceptibly. It made me want to ask what he was thinking about when he looked at me like that. But before I could, he wiped his hands on a towel and held his pointer finger up, stepping toward the fridge. He pulled out a bottle of light pink rosé.

"This work? It's what the guy at the store recommended."

He handed it to me gingerly, our fingers brushing, but only for a second. I read the label. "Yes, perfect, thank you! Any French rosé with a recent year will be great." I moved toward the drawer that contained the wine opener.

"I got it," he said, taking the bottle back. Less than a minute later a half-full stemless wine glass appeared in front of me.

"Want some lemonade or something, Luna?"

"Yeah!"

Luke tapped something out on his phone, and grabbed the lemonade from the fridge, returning the bottle of rosé.

I spread some brie on a cracker and popped it in my mouth. Luna stared at me, agape. "You'll like it when you're older, promise. You already like hummus so it's only a matter of time."

Luke laughed.

"He's always saying stuff like that." Her little nose scrunched as she pointed at Luke.

Now I was laughing.

Luke clinked his beer glass against my wine glass and watched me take my first sip. I closed my eyes as the dry, tart, and slightly sweet wine splashed across my tongue. When I opened them, he was still watching me, looking satisfied.

"Like it?"

"Yeah, it's great. Thank you." It felt like special treatment that he went out of his way to buy something I liked.

He nodded and returned to chopping. I made another cracker, stealing a look at his muscled forearms as he chopped with a big chef's knife. It was hard not to stare.

"So, what's the occasion?" I asked. "Cheese board, wine, grilling up a storm. You have a good day?"

A smile unfolded on his face, like it wasn't on purpose. I bit my lip. *Damn.* I had no doubt that smile has gotten him lots of special treatment in his life. "Yeah, actually. We got a big contract with the town finalized today. We're building a whole neighborhood of bungalows and multi-unit condos about halfway between here and the airport. It's going to be managed by the company and will provide a bunch of affordable housing units for seasonal workers in the summer. We're adding a bus stop, too."

"That's awesome, Luke. Congratulations! So you'll be working on it?"

"Yeah, I mean, Karas Construction got the contract."

Realization hit me like a *thwack* to the back of the head. Luke's last name was Karas, as I learned from my first paycheck. Karas Construction was...his company. It all made sense now: how it seemed like he spent as much time at the office as at the construction sites, his coming and going at random times throughout the day.

His eyes narrowed. "You didn't realize it was my company, did you?"

I shook my head. "I feel stupid. I know your last name. Should have been obvious."

He shrugged one shoulder. "I never mentioned it."

"Still. Well, congrats!" I said again. "It sounds like something Edgartown really needs. Mimi's been complaining for years about restaurants and stores having to stay closed on certain days because there's not enough staff, and she always blames the lack of reasonable housing options for people who want to move here just to work for the summer." Mimi was particularly fond of the charismatic men that often came from Serbia for the summer to work at The Atlantic restaurant. "This will be so good for the island!"

The corner of Luke's mouth ticked up. "Thanks, Val. That's exactly why the town wanted this project." He clapped his hands. "Alright, I'm going to fire up the grill. Don't get into trouble while I'm gone." He looked pointedly at Luna.

She rolled her eyes.

Luke let me finish the salad while he grilled the burgers. I joined him outside when he went back out to flip them.

"How's it going? Is it a lot carting her from place to place?"

"Oh no, it's great. Her schedule keeps me honest. I go to the gym while she's at tennis, and then I write while she's at sailing. I like having lunch with her and hearing about her day. I think she's pretty comfortable with me now."

"Oh, definitely. I can tell. She talks about you after you leave, too."

My lips tipped into a smile. I didn't realize how much it would matter to me that Luna connected with me. That was the difference between babysitting here and there and seeing someone every day. "All good things?"

"Yeah, of course all good things." He said it like it was the most obvious fact he'd ever stated. "What do you write?" he asked after a moment.

My eyes widened. I'd been so nervous to tell people, and yet it had just slipped out here, on Luke's back deck. "Oh, um. Creative writing. Like, stories, maybe a novel. I've always had an interest in it, written down ideas over the years. And now I actually have time to pursue it, so I figured, why not?"

"That's really cool, Val. Impressive, too. Maybe one of your stories will take off."

I peered at him. His encouraging smile showed no signs of doubt. My cheeks tugged upward. "Thank you."

He dipped his chin and then pivoted to continue turning over the vegetables.

I leaned my elbows on the deck railing, looking out at the backyard. Flowers and a jungle of blue and purple hydrangeas lined the back fence. A weathered-shingle shed was tucked on the left side. Lush green grass covered the middle of the yard, leaving plenty of room for yard games. The faint din of birds chirping and bumble bees buzzing mixed with the sizzling sounds of the grill. A deep breath released from my chest.

"Whatcha thinking about?" Luke asked after closing the grill cover and joining me at the railing.

"Oh, nothing in particular. Admiring the yard. It's peaceful here. I didn't even have a balcony in New York, let alone a green space. It reminds me of New Hampshire a little. But the hydrangeas only take over like that here."

"It's gotta be the salt or something. My mom could never get the hydrangeas to thrive like this in Pennsylvania."

I turned to look at him. His expression was contemplative, looking at the same cluster of flowers that I was a few moments ago.

"She must admire them when she's here," I said, hoping it would prompt him to talk about his family.

I found myself wanting to know things about him.

"Oh yeah. She comments on it constantly. They're coming next week for July 4th. So I can give you some time back. They can help cart Luna around while they're here."

He meant it to be a relief, but my heart sank a little. I was starting to like my new routine with Luna. I didn't mind seeing him every day, either.

"Great," I lied.

He squinted his eyes slightly, like he could tell I wasn't being honest.

"Did you like it? New York? I know some people love it."

I took a long time to answer. "I liked New York in theory more than in practice. I love Broadway, and Central Park, and the fancy restaurants. But I honestly didn't do much besides work the last six years. Eighty plus hour weeks were the norm, and weekends were a time to catch up on everything I couldn't finish that week. Dinners out spent on my phone... I probably went to five total Broadway shows in six years because I never felt like I could be unreachable for three hours. And then when I took a vacation here and there, it was always to get *out* of the city."

When I finished speaking, Luke's eyes were so wide, you'd think he saw something shocking.

I shrugged and cast my gaze down to the deck, bracing myself for the usual comments questioning if it was really *that bad*. My standard response—that no, it wasn't *that bad*, I learned a lot and I was compensated well and I paid off my loans and when I did go out I could afford to order whatever I wanted—waited on the tip of my tongue.

I shouldn't have underestimated him.

"That sounds fucking terrible. No wonder you took a break."

Now it was my turn to be shocked. Giggles escaped my lips. "Thank you. That means a lot to me."

"Happy to help?" He scrunched his face, but he was smiling now, looking at me with equal parts concern and fascination.

"I feel like people don't usually believe me. Or they're not sympathetic because it was obviously my choice to take a job like that, which is fair."

"I believe you. And just because it was your choice doesn't mean you have to love every aspect of it."

I bit the inside of my lips, unsure what to say and wondering what I'd done to earn his confidence in such a short time.

And then his watch buzzed.

"That mean the burgers are ready?"

"Yeah."

Dinner at Luke's kitchen table felt normal and relaxed. He topped off my wine, cracked a fresh beer, talked to Luna about her activities. Luna and I decided to have lunch with Mimi at her house tomorrow, which Mimi would love. When we finished eating, Luna said she wanted to start biking to tennis in the morning.

"You're too young to bike two miles by yourself," Luke responded.

"But my friends do!"

"They might live closer or go with siblings or something. That's up to their parents. And I think you're too young to bike that far on your own." Luke's jaw ticked. His tone was calm but firm, like he was bracing for a debate.

Luna scowled with all her might, her expression so vehement I wanted to laugh, but that wouldn't go over well, so I pressed my lips together before saying, "Can I bike with you?" I glanced at Luke, and he nodded.

"Fine," she sighed dramatically, waving her arm.

I shook my head slightly, hoping only Luke noticed.

"I have an extra in the shed you can use," Luke said. "Let's go get it set up."

"Can I watch Disney?" Luna replaced her scowl with a pleading look.

"Yes, Luna, you can go watch Disney." He tried to maintain his serious tone, but the corner of his mouth tipped up as he shook his head.

"Yay!" She popped out of her chair in a flash and scampered into the living room.

I followed Luke out to the shed in the corner of the yard. He held the door open, and the scent of sawdust flooded my nostrils. The wooden work surface was lined with so many tools, I wouldn't be able to name them all. Deep shelves were outfitted with matching bins on one side and wooden boards and two-by-fours on the other.

When the door shut behind us, I suddenly became aware of our aloneness, the privacy of the enclosed space. He pulled a red bike down from an overhead rack, along with a hand pump. My eyes devoured the sight of his toned arms pumping the handle up and down as he added air to the tires. When he stopped and looked up at me, he pushed his dark brown hair out of his eyes. My hands were jealous of his, itching to know what his thick hair would feel like between my fingers.

Should I feel bad for admiring a man that was sort of my employer?

Probably.

"Let's check the height. C'mere." His hand gestured for me to come toward him and my legs obliged. He stepped to the side and guided me between him and the bike with a light nudge on my waist, just below my ribcage. "Seat should be level with your hip," he explained. His hands deftly moved the seat down, and he floated his palm across the top of the seat until it connected with my waist right at my hip bone.

"Good?" he asked, not moving his hand.

"Yeah." I hoped he didn't notice that my voice came out a bit hoarse. I didn't want him to move his hand. I wanted him to use it to grab that hip and pull me closer to him. What was wrong with me today? *I must be starved for male attention since Max has been out of town for several days.* That was all this was.

"Great." He swallowed. Was his voice a little throaty, too? *I must be projecting.*

His hand moved from my hip and shifted the bike so it leaned against his wooden work bench. He looked at me for a moment, lips pursed under his manicured beard. I was about to ask what he was thinking about when he held up his pointer finger and turned around. He plucked a blue helmet off a hook.

"Can I?"

"Yes," I said softly. He placed it on my head, carefully pushing a lock of my light brown hair behind my ear so he could secure the strap under my chin. The sensitive skin tingled.

He let go once it clicked but didn't step back, his face close enough to mine that I noticed some hints of golden brown in his chocolate eyes for the first time.

"How do I look?" I asked, biting my lip. It was a joke. Bicycle helmets were so not sexy.

It took him a moment to answer. He held my gaze, then the side of his mouth ticked up. "Like you're putting safety first."

A laugh sputtered out of me. "Thank you. That is *exactly* what I was going for." I flicked a lock of my hair over my shoulder with a flourish.

He chuckled before removing the helmet from my head and hanging it back on the hook. He turned back to me, not saying anything for a moment. That awareness of how alone we were descended again, making my breaths shallow and short.

"Should we go back in?" I asked finally.

"Yeah," he rasped. His Adam's apple bobbed as he swallowed.

I inhaled only when my feet hit the grass outside.

I said goodnight to Luna and Luke walked me to the door. "Thanks for dinner. That was fun."

"Anytime. Actually, do you like salmon? I was thinking of making it on Friday, and Luna won't eat it."

"Love it." I bit the inside of my cheek, not wanting the excitement filling me to be so obvious on my face.

I tried not to think about what it meant that I was happy Max wasn't getting back to the island until Saturday.

18

"Alright lady, time for sunscreen."

Luna's trademark dramatic sigh heaved from her little lips, but she ambled over to where I was waiting by the kitchen island, bottle of sunblock in hand. I held it out to her and said, "You do your legs and arms, and I'll do your back, shoulders, and face, deal?"

"Deal." Her tone was resigned.

"It prevents wrinkles, Luna. And skin cancer. Repeat after me, wrinkles and skin cancer."

Luke guffawed from where he was standing on the other side of the kitchen, packing his lunch.

I whirled on him. "It's true!"

"It is absolutely true." His brown eyes sparkled. "I just wouldn't have thought to incentivize an eight-year-old that way."

I shook my head, my lips pursed, amusement dancing on my face. I returned my attention to Luna. When I finished spreading the white lotion over her shoulders, back, and face, making the whole kitchen smell like coconut-flavored summer, she asked, "Do you have time to braid my hair today?"

I checked the time on my phone. "Sure do!"

Luna zipped past me and plopped down on the floor in front

125

of the couch. I climbed behind her and started finger-combing her hair. Fortunately, it wasn't too tangled today.

This ritual started last week when I picked her up from sailing with braids in my own hair. I was always playing with it and changing the style while I sat in front of my laptop. That day was more of a brainstorming day than a typing day, hence the braids. She asked if I did them myself, and if I could do them on her, too. I said, "Yes, of course." Her eyes widened with excitement. I'd done them for her almost every day since, except if we were running late and she had to do *"a boring ponytail"* instead. Luke was usually gone by the time we did the braids and sunscreen routine.

"One or two?" I asked.

"Two!" She was so enthusiastic about such a simple thing: getting her hair done in braids.

"You got it!"

Hanging with Luna the last few weeks, seeing things through her eyes, had helped me appreciate the little things too: like when you pick up enough speed on your bike that you don't have to pedal for a while, or an afternoon snack with a cold lemonade when you've been in the sun all day.

I briefly suspended my hand in front of my face before I began —not steady enough to perform surgery, but I could paint my nails without issue. Or braid hair. I separated her dark brown, almost black hair into two equal-sized clumps, making the part down the middle of her head as straight as possible. Her hair was as dark as Luke's. My fingers gathered three pieces and started folding them over each other.

My peripheral vision caught Luke moving to the edge of the kitchen that faced the living room a minute ago. "I can feel you watching," I sang. "You're gonna make me mess up."

"Sorry. I'm just fascinated." His voice rumbled from behind the couch, his breath caressing my bare shoulder and increasing my heart rate a click. He leaned closer, and I felt the back of the couch dip under his weight. "I don't get how it works. I've watched videos and still can't do it. Only Luna's grandmother can do it for her."

"He's hopeless," Luna added.

"Luna! That's not nice," I said, aghast, but also a little impressed with her vocabulary, as usual.

"No, it's true, I am hopeless," Luke admitted, not insulted at all. I laughed.

Luke pushed off the couch and I released my breath. He grabbed his lunch box from the kitchen and made his way to the door. "Have a good day, girls," he said from the threshold.

Girls.

Why did I like how that sounded coming out of his mouth so much?

"How about a snack?" I asked Luna when we got home two days later.

Luna folded her arms. We stood in the kitchen where she'd stopped after we got in the door like she didn't know where else to go. "I'm not hungry." Her tone was flat.

Odd.

Her French braid (a single today) was a wild mess, and her newly freckled skin was coated in sunscreen and salt, like it was every day when we got back. She was scowling, just like the entire car ride home. I left her alone in the car, letting her look out the window the whole time we normally talked about sailing and her friends, at least on the days that we drove instead of biked. I figured she was just hangry.

"What about a shower? It will probably feel good to wash off all the salt and sunscreen."

"I don't know," she sighed.

"Okay, Luna." I gripped her little shoulders. "What's going on? Did something happen today that upset you?"

"No," she said quietly, her voice a pitch higher than normal.

"You can tell me," I pleaded, starting to worry it was something serious that I wouldn't know how to handle.

She looked up from the floor then, her big, brown eyes glassy. "My tennis partner Rachel switched to a new partner for the tournament. She said she didn't think we would win because I'm too small, and I should be partners with Clara. I like Clara but she isn't as good as Rachel. And I really wanted to win!" Her fists were clenched now, anger emanating from her tiny frame.

I felt for her. I remembered what it was like to be young and invested in your activities. And even more than that, I remembered how hard it was to endure the cattiness of young girls. *This* I could handle. "I can't believe Rachel did that. That is so uncool to switch partners on you when you've already been practicing together for two weeks."

"I know! But I didn't say anything because I don't want her to hate me. So I agreed, but on the inside, I've been so mad. Do you think I should ask her to switch back?"

Hm. I didn't want Luna to put herself in that position because if Rachel said no, it would hurt even more.

"Clara is your friend, right? She's the one we got ice cream with earlier this week? I thought she was a pretty good tennis player, too."

"Yes, she's my friend we got ice cream with. And she *is* good; she just doesn't have a strong backhand like Rachel."

"It's hard because you don't want to hurt Clara's feelings, right? She would probably be hurt if you ask to switch back. I think you and Clara should practice hard and make it your goal to beat Rachel and...?"

"Zara."

"Zara, at the tournament."

"Okay." She blew her breath out through her lips and shrugged. "I don't know if we can do that."

"Not with that attitude. You're not that small, Luna. Plus, you're quick and smart. Tennis is a mental game as well as a physical one. I believe in you."

"Thanks." Her arms crossed in front of her. I was about to suggest a shower again when another idea occurred to me.

"Do you know what me and my roommates used to do when we had a big test the next day and we needed to pump ourselves up?"

"What?" Her tone was still flat, but her expression showed a hint of curiosity.

"We would play the song 'Defying Gravity' from the musical *Wicked*, dance around the room, and belt it at the top of our lungs. Have you heard of it?"

"No."

"Can we play it?" I asked her, already making my way to the living room.

"Um, sure."

"So the backstory is Elphaba is our underestimated and ridiculed heroine. She wants to learn magic and help animals, but she discovers that their leader is actually a bad guy. He tries to ensnare her in his wrongdoing, but she refuses and flies off to lead her life on her own terms. That's what the song is about— believing in yourself and defying everyone's expectations of you." By the time I finished the description, I had the video up on the TV.

"Ready?" My long-buried theater kid heart was actually pretty excited about this. "Defying Gravity" had never failed to improve my mood.

Luna shrugged and I said a little prayer that Idina's vocals could get this girl out of her funk.

"Oh, one more thing, we need microphones. I pulled up a version with the lyrics." I hopped over the couch and darted into the kitchen, pulling two kitchen spoons out of the holder by the stove. I handed one to Luna on the way back. She looked at me with thinly veiled skepticism.

I pressed play and Kristin Chenoweth's voice filled the house. "Give it a sec, it starts slow."

Luna had one hand on her hip, the other holding the spoon by her side.

I sang the opening lines, and by the time I got to the first time they say "defying gravity" I was fully belting into the black plastic spoon, gesticulating with my other hand, and moving around the living room. Luna was staring at me, eyes bugging out of her skull, with a closed lip smirk that revealed a hint of concern, like I just might be crazy. But that little smirk was stretching on her face, and the next time I looked, I caught her reading the lyrics on the screen.

"C'mon," I called over the music. "It's the defying gravity part again."

She timidly brought the spoon up to her lips and spoke—not sang—the first few words of the chorus. But it was progress.

I kept singing like I was back in my law school living room with Natalie. I walked over to Luna and sang the part about deserving a chance to fly just for her. *Damn, these lyrics are so motivational.* I smiled to myself before throwing all my vocal power into the final words.

Panting, I asked, "What do you think?"

She pursed her lips, but then a smile broke on her face. "I like it. You're a good singer, you know."

I laughed. "Oh, thank you, Luna. I did theater in high school." I never did *Wicked*, though. Even if the performance rights were available, which they weren't, it would have been too big a production for a small public high school theater program.

"It seems like it would be fun. I like singing sometimes, but only when I know the words."

"Want to play it again? So you can learn the words?"

"Yeah."

I tried not to smile too wide.

The second time through, Luna was a more enthusiastic participant. She scrutinized the lyrics on the screen and sang rather than spoke the choruses and some of the verses. By the end, we both screamed the final extended note.

Luna beamed. "One more time? I think I know the words now."

Got her.

By the fourth time through Luna—bless her—was really getting into it. I was out of breath. My vocal chords hadn't gotten a workout like this in a long time. I only sang in the car these days. But it was worth it.

Luna and I took turns singing certain parts and had climbed up on each of the couches. I'd turned the volume up the last time and wondered if the neighbors would hear us and question what the hell we were doing over here.

Luna belted one of the lines without looking at the screen, using the spoon microphone like a pro, and I beamed. For the last part, I jumped from my couch to hers, and we leaned our heads together, screaming into our respective spoons.

The music cut and the room filled with deafening silence mixed with our breaths.

Then, clapping.

I whipped around and found Luke in his dust-covered jeans and work T-shirt, leaning against the wall, gaping at us with an amused smile that made his eyes glitter.

"Oh my gosh, how long have you been home?! You're early!" Heat rushed to my cheeks. The music was so loud neither of us heard him come in. His arms crossed in front of his chest when he finished clapping, that amused grin still dancing across his face.

"Long enough to enjoy quite the Broadway show."

I shook my head, pulling my lip under my teeth. *He must think I'm such a geek. I bet he was a popular athlete in high school.*

But damn, he looked good leaning against that wall. I wondered if he knew crossing his arms like that, in a T-shirt, made his biceps so pronounced it was almost obscene.

Luna leapt from the couch and hugged her dad around the waist. She was still in her dirty tennis outfit, hair a wild mess framing her face. "Rachel made me switch tennis partners and now I'm playing with Clara but we're going to beat them in the tournament," she said with resolve. Pride filled my chest. I loved her fire.

"Is that so?" Luke ran his hand over her braid affectionately.

His palm was so much larger than her head it was comical. He stole a look in my direction.

I gave him a small nod. I'd tell him the full story later.

He crouched down so he was at her eye level. "Wanna take a shower while I get dinner going?"

She nodded, turned on her heel, and scampered upstairs.

"Sorry, she wasn't in the mood to shower when we got home."

"She was in the mood to sing instead?"

"Well...that was my idea." I walked in the kitchen and lowered my voice. "She was in a major funk about Rachel asking her to switch partners. So I suggested we do what I used to do when I needed a motivation boost." I popped my shoulder up.

"Seems like it worked!" His expression was something between mirth and disbelief.

"I think so!" A smile tugged on my cheeks.

"So Broadway music, that's the trick to pulling you out of a bad mood?" he asked, his head in the fridge, already taking out the bottle of rosé, a beer, a tray of chicken nuggets, and a white paper package I assumed contained the salmon he promised me.

"One of 'em." I pressed my lips together.

He turned, resting his hip on the counter, and raised an eyebrow at me. But I didn't go on, letting what other unnamed things could get me out of a bad mood remain a mystery.

Over dinner on the back deck, Luna asked me what theater shows I'd been in, had I ever done *Wicked*, had I ever *seen Wicked*, and can Luke take her to see it. Luke followed our banter back and forth between bites of salmon and rice, shaking his head occasionally. Our impromptu karaoke session might have opened a can of worms for him...

By the time we cleared the table, it was nearly Luna's bedtime.

We managed to carry everything back inside between the three of us. I was rinsing dishes and loading them into the dishwasher when Luna came up beside me and pressed her finger into my shoulder. The pressure made a white indentation before it turned back to an angry red. After the fuss I'd made earlier this week about covering Luna in sunscreen, I'd forgotten my own that day, a last-minute change from a T-shirt to a tank top leaving my poor shoulders defenseless.

"I know, I forgot to put sunscreen on my shoulders today," I said to Luna with a sigh.

She disappeared down the hall toward the first-floor bathroom and returned with a green bottle of aloe. She squeezed some onto her hands and started rubbing it into my shoulders. It was so sweet of her, my throat closed up. The slider screeched as Luke came inside from cleaning the grill.

"Thanks, Luna," I said to her softly.

"You're welcome!" She disappeared again to put the bottle back in the bathroom.

"That's a really sweet little girl you have there," I said to Luke, my voice hoarse.

"I know." He smiled proudly.

"I'm sorry," I whispered, embarrassed that I was having such an emotional reaction to the kind gesture.

"It's okay. You good?"

I swallowed the lump in my throat and told my tear ducts to calm down. "Yeah, I'm good."

"You sure? Because you have me tempted to ask who hurt you."

A laugh rippled out of me, cutting off the burgeoning tears, and soon I burst into full-blown giggling.

Luke started laughing, too. "Like, has no one ever given you aloe before?" he asked between breaths.

We were both cracking up when Luna reentered the kitchen. "What's so funny?"

"Oh nothing, Luns, your dad is just teasing me."

Luna turned a death glare on Luke, and I had to bite my fist to stop from laughing louder.

"You shouldn't do that," she said to her dad.

"It's all in good fun, Luns. C'mere." He lunged toward her, but she sensed he was about to tickle her and bolted into the living room. She squealed as his hand grazed her side before she spun out of his reach and jumped, giggling, over the back of the couch.

Luke's gaze snagged mine, a happy glimmer in his eyes. It was hard to look away.

Over her protests, Luke took Luna upstairs to bed a few minutes later. I put the rest of the leftovers in containers and placed them next to the fridge. Luke's footsteps sounded on the stairs as I washed the final dishes in the sink.

When I felt his large presence behind me, I looked over my shoulder. He stared at my back. "She didn't rub the aloe in all the way. Do you want me to, uh—" His low voice was tentative.

"Sure, thank you," I said quietly. Although I braced myself for the friction on my tender, burned skin, I still sucked in my breath when his fingertips landed on me.

"Sorry," he murmured. "Carpenter's hands."

I didn't correct him that it wasn't the feel of his hands that caused my reaction, but the fact that he was touching me in the first place. His touch was featherlight, barely enough pressure to massage the last of the gooey, cooling gel into my shoulders, like he was worried about hurting me. I glanced at our reflection in the window over the sink. Luke towered over me as I pressed my lips together and watched him. His head was lowered, a look of concentration on his face. The lock of dark hair that always fell down on his forehead somehow made his reflection even more handsome.

He massaged one last circle into my skin and removed his hands. "All good now," he rasped, meeting my eyes in our window reflection.

"Thank you." I smiled, letting out my breath.

He cleared his throat and leaned back on the kitchen island. After adding the last dish to the dishwasher, I turned to face him.

"So, you trying to turn Luna into a theater kid?" he asked, dark eyebrows raised.

"As a former theater kid, I'm not sure how I feel about your tone!"

He held up his hands, palms out. "No offense meant! I'd love if Luna found something like that that she adored. Her mom was a theater kid."

Her mom. Luke almost never mentioned her. *Was she Luke's ex? A former lover that didn't want to keep Luna?* That thought angered me.

Did she die? Empathy panged deep in my belly.

"Really?" I left my other questions unspoken, swirling only in my mind.

He rubbed a hand down his face, suddenly growing serious. "I can't believe I haven't mentioned this until now. Technically, Luna is my niece."

I gaped at him. In all the times I'd wondered about her mother, I'd never thought to question whether Luke was her biological father. They looked so much alike, she called him *Dad*...

Luke swallowed and looked over my shoulder, not making eye contact for the next part. "Her mom was my sister. She and her husband... They died in a car accident five years ago." It sounded like it took effort to force each word out of his throat.

I sucked in a breath. *Oh my gosh.*

When his eyes found mine again, I could tell he was trying to hold it together, that sharing this hadn't gotten easier for him over the years. My heart ached, and my body itched to comfort him.

"That's awful," I whispered.

He nodded before looking away again and clearing his throat. "They put in their will that if anything happened to them both, they wanted me to take her."

"Wow," I breathed. As if Luke couldn't be more admirable. He'd mentioned his parents in passing—Luna's grandparents. Maybe they were too old to take care of a child? It felt too invasive to ask.

After a moment he added, "It was my mom's suggestion that she call me Dad. Because she was so young, she probably won't remember them at all." He gave me a small shrug, like some part of him still questioned the decision. "She almost never asks, so I don't think she does. I'm glad she calls me that, though. Because that's how I feel." His voice turned to gravel by the end.

Was I allowed to comfort him? He just touched me, albeit under a totally different pretense.

Fuck it. I closed the gap between us and my hand reached out on its own to rub a comforting caress up and down his upper arm and then hold on just above his bicep.

He stared at my hand for a moment. When he lifted his gaze, it was all eye contact, his brown eyes glassy pools.

"You are her dad." I said softly. "It doesn't make your brother-in-law any less her dad. But you're who's raised her and loved her like a daughter. Not to mention sparing her spending her whole childhood explaining why she has no parents around." I couldn't look away as I spoke.

He nodded and lifted the corner of his mouth up, but his eyes were still sad. My eyes wanted to fill, too. Poor Luna, losing both of her parents so young, before she'd remember.

It was so quiet in this kitchen. What he shared was so personal. Under different circumstances, it might have felt uncomfortable, but instead I just felt honored that he shared it with me.

"Sorry. I don't know why it's always so hard to say it out loud," he added softly, voice hoarse.

"A loss like that will probably never get any easier to talk about."

He nodded.

I inhaled carefully, determined not to lose the battle with my tear ducts. "Luke, it's amazing you honored their wishes. You're doing such an incredible job with her." My fingers gripped his arm just a little tighter. I didn't know how, but I could tell he needed to hear that. I could tell he didn't always think so. I let go of his arm but didn't move back.

He swallowed hard, nodding almost imperceptibly. It didn't

seem like he believed me, and I vowed to myself that I'd keep saying it, as long as I was here.

I kept it together for the handful of minutes it took to finish putting away the leftover food. We parted on a slightly somber note, but Luke still walked me to the door and told me to get home safe, even though Mimi's was only a mile away.

He did that every time.

As soon as my car door closed, a sob ripped out of me. I couldn't believe what he went through. What Luna went through. What got me the most was that she would've been too young to have memories.

She has no memories of her biological parents.

And Luke. He was probably only twenty-eight or twenty-nine years old when he lost his sister and became a guardian to an orphaned three-year-old. I shook my head, swiping at my cheeks. He might notice if I didn't pull out of the driveway soon, so I put my car in reverse and drove carefully toward Mimi's house.

What a beautiful thing Luke had done, fulfilling his sister's wishes, giving Luna every bit of love she deserved after she lost so much. I thought of Drew. Would he do the same for me? Would I do the same for him? Despite our differences, I knew the answer to both of those questions was *yes*. It made me want to talk to him.

"Hey, Val. Everything alright?" Drew's voice came through my car speakers.

"Yeah, I'm good. Just saying hi." My voice was still a little strained from the crying, but I hoped he couldn't tell.

"Are you sure nothing is up? You're not one to call to check in."

"People can change, Drew," I teased.

He chuckled. "You bored on that medical leave?"

"Actually, not at all. I love it."

Drew told me about the classes he was teaching next semester and the medical paper his wife published recently. I told him how Mimi was doing and how great it's been to spend more time on Martha's Vineyard like we did when we were younger.

"I'm jealous. I'm going to try and get over there when Mom and Dad visit next month."

"That would be great."

"Yeah?" The lack of certainty in his tone zapped me like a bee sting. Did he really question whether I wanted him to come? I'd snapped at him the last few times we talked, and I felt bad about it. He'd actually been a lot more sensitive lately, hadn't said anything patronizing that made me feel inferior in a while.

"Yeah, Drew. I'd love to see you," I assured him. "Mimi would, too."

"Cool, I'll make it work."

I smiled to myself after we hung up, already looking forward to it. Until I remembered that the week my parents were coming to the Vineyard was after July 15th.

19

The well-manicured lawn of the glitzy restaurant buzzed with Saturday evening excitement. Max and I were sitting at a little table on the lawn at Atria, another upscale Edgartown restaurant on Main Street. The weather was perfect—only a smattering of clouds to break up the sun, a light breeze, low humidity. It was the type of summer day New Englanders waited all year for. Condensation glistened on my wine glass as I wondered what Luke and Luna were up to today.

"Peters & Dowling must be missing you," Max said as he took a sip of his gin cocktail. He was just making conversation. It wasn't Max's fault a rock made of granite formed in my gut every time someone mentioned that firm's name. I lifted my wineglass to my lips but placed it back down on the beechwood café table without taking a sip.

"Maybe!" I shrugged, wracking my brain for a subject change. I'd rather talk about anything else. *Like my novel.* I wished he would ask me what I did during the day, while Luna was at tennis and sailing. Then I'd tell him about my writing. For some reason, I was having a hard time bringing it up without an invitation.

"I was so impressed when you told me you were a lawyer that

day at the coffee shop. I thought, wow, she must be as smart as she is beautiful."

A grin spread on my face. Max's flattery was like water to a parched flower.

I considered telling him how I really felt—that the more time that passed, the more writing I did, the more conversations I had with my therapist, the less I wanted to go back to the firm. That the real reason I took the job with Luke was to make sure I had at least some income in case I decided not to go back at all. But I didn't want to disappoint him, tarnish this positive impression he had of me. The initial excitement at the compliment settled like bile in my stomach. *Would he think I'm not smart or ambitious if I told him the truth?*

I decided I didn't need to tell him yet, because I hadn't decided for sure what I would do. I still had two weeks.

Why disappoint him when I might go back after all?

Later that night, tangled in his sheets, I rested my head on Max's chest after a short but fun hookup. It really was getting a little better each time—ever since I plucked up the courage to tell him I needed more foreplay, he'd taken the time to make sure I was ready before sex. Tonight I'd even gotten close to finishing a few times, until I thought about it too hard. But that was clearly a me problem. Moonlight streamed in the window above his bed, casting us in a glow as Max traced little circles on my bare shoulder. "Can I call you my girlfriend?" he asked.

My eyes widened, but my head was on his chest, so he couldn't see. *Already?*

"I've been meaning to ask," he added. "Introducing you as anything else just wouldn't feel right."

Would it feel right to introduce Max as my boyfriend? I twisted to look at him. Sandy brown hair mussed, blue eyes sincere. It was a bit of a leap, if I was being honest. But if I said no, or that I wasn't ready to call each other that yet, then I'd be rejecting him, and that would probably be it for us. That wasn't what I wanted.

"Yeah," I said, jumping in. "You can call me that." I kissed his cheek.

When his breathing evened out, I scooched to my side of the bed. My eyes closed but my mind wouldn't find sleep.

All I could think about was how much I didn't want to tell Luke about my new relationship status. *It's just new,* I told myself. *And my last official boyfriend was an asshole.*

And for some reason you have this hot dad fixation on Luke that you need to shake off.

Besides, I had more in common with someone like Max, didn't I? And Max was an attractive, smart, fun, well-adjusted man who treated me well and made me feel good about myself.

I should be thrilled he wants to be my boyfriend.

It had to be 3:00 a.m. by the time I fell asleep.

The next morning we cooked breakfast in the big kitchen at Max's parents' house. They were out of town for the weekend, so we had the place to ourselves.

"What was your favorite sport growing up?" I asked him. "I feel like you must have played something."

"Sailing, if that counts. I went to this boarding school in Massachusetts that had a well-established sailing program. And then I did it competitively in college, too. I've been saving to buy a sailboat to have here."

"That would be nice! Especially if you keep spending so much of your summers here. I'm sure you miss it."

"Oh, yeah. As you know, not a ton of time for leisure activities in New York. But I kinda love the grind, so I don't mind."

I nodded, not sure what to say next. I emphatically did *not* love the grind. Not anymore.

"My brother went to a boarding school, too." The detail left my lips without forethought.

"Oh yeah? Which one?"

"Franconia."

Max laughed. "That one is a *lot* better than the school I went to."

"It's a good one." I hoped my tone didn't reveal the hint of bitterness I still felt about it. The rejection letter I got from Franconia seventeen years ago flashed through my brain like an intrusive thought. I didn't think about it as often these days as I did during school, but for years that letter was what drove me—to get the best grades, go to the best law school I could, and then work at the most prestigious firm.

"I'm sure he's a great guy. I'd love to meet him."

"He's going to try to visit this summer. But he's a professor, so I'm not sure. You'd think they get the summers off, but he says the summers are when he gets all his research and writing done."

"Makes sense. So, a lawyer and a professor, your parents must be thrilled."

"I think so. But I think they've always been proud of us, honestly." Spending time with Luke and Luna had me thinking about parenting a lot more than I ever had before. It was hard to articulate the subtle difference between the pressure some parents put on their children and the inspiration and encouragement my parents instilled in us. I wanted to succeed and make them proud, but it came from a place of desire, not fear.

Max nodded and took a sip of his coffee.

I followed suit, taking my first sip of the morning. It was the richest, smoothest black coffee I'd ever tasted. "Mmm," I hummed. "This coffee is so good. I'm surprised we even met that day at Behind the Bookstore. Why would you get a coffee there when you have this at home?" I swirled my cup.

He popped one shoulder up. "Something to do, get out of the house. Good thing I did." He reached for my hand on the table, rubbing circles on my palm with his thumb. "When I saw you at that café I thought—that's the prettiest girl I've ever seen. I almost walked past you but then I said to myself, you'll regret not at least finding out if she's single."

"Hmm." I was skeptical those were the *exact* words that floated through his mind. "I don't know about that."

"Learn to take a compliment, Val. There's more where that came from."

His smug grin had me smiling too.

"Oh, you think you're so charming, don't you?" I teased.

He shrugged one shoulder, smug grin maintained. "Well, kinda, yeah."

I shook my head and leaned over and kissed him. He rested his hand on my bare thigh under the table and took another lazy sip of his coffee.

I thought about that day, and it dawned on me—I was writing my short story when he walked up to me. This was my chance to tell him.

"You know what I was doing that day when you approached me?" I asked, leading.

"You said you were working on a project?"

"Yes. But I was already on the leave of absence, so it wasn't a work project. I was writing." *Why is my heart rate climbing?*

"Oh yeah? What were you writing, an article?"

"No, actually. A short story, which is now more of a novel. I found this prompt online that resonated with me. I've always loved books and reading, had always thought about writing my own stories. And now I have the time to do it, so I figured, why not?"

I searched his face for his reaction, hoping his confidence in my legal skills extended to my potential as a writer. Maybe he'd even offer for me to talk to his dad about it.

"That's cool. Writing is a fun hobby."

The word *hobby* landed like a blow.

What if I didn't want it to just be a hobby?

"It's your dad's career," I argued without thinking.

"I know, but that's him." His blue eyes shone with mirth.

Mine felt like they might fill with tears.

"You're not considering a career change, are you, Val?" He chuckled, like it would be silly to change my career now.

It would be silly to change your career now, a voice in the back of my head agreed.

"Ha, no," I lied, hiding my face in my coffee mug. "How would my private equity clients survive without me?" I added drily.

Max leaned back in his chair and crossed his ankle over the opposite knee. "Not well, I'm sure. Us finance people need our lawyers." He winked.

I nodded and schooled my expression to conceal the disappointment roiling in my stomach. When I stood to go top off my coffee from the dedicated coffee bar in the kitchen, I wished I had something stronger to drown in.

"Want to take the boat out later?" he called from the breakfast nook.

I closed my eyes and took a deep breath. "I so would but I made plans with Mimi. I haven't spent much time with her lately and I feel bad." Between staying until Luna's bedtime on Friday and going to the gym first thing Saturday, I'd only seen Mimi for a little while on Saturday afternoon before I left to meet Max.

"Oh, okay." The disappointment in his voice had me considering changing my mind, but he added, "How about on the Fourth? We can take the boat out for the afternoon with my parents, then have dinner and do the fireworks at their club?"

I joined him at the table again, steaming mug clutched between both hands, the sweet aroma filling my nostrils. "That sounds like fun."

20

On Monday, Luke asked if I could stay a few extra hours because he needed to work late.

Luna and I had macaroni and cheese for dinner (her request), and I convinced her we should read a book together before bed. It was the first time I'd gone into her bedroom. Her bed was a custom, wooden work of art, built to look like a sailboat. It had nooks and crannies for books and other things, and even a cup holder for her water cup. Luke obviously made it himself. Admiration flooded my bones as I took in all the beautiful details. *What a good dad.*

As I descended the stairs, I was already mentally cracking my book open on the couch before I noticed Luke sitting in the living room. Still in his dusty jeans and work boots, he was leaning over, elbows on his knees, rubbing his temples.

"Hey," I said softly.

He lifted his head with a start. His eyes were red, beard longer than usual, hair disheveled, dark circles under his eyes. "Hi." He forced the corner of his mouth up, but the smile didn't reach his eyes. "Is she asleep? I just got in."

"Yeah, totally passed out."

Luke sighed. "I hate it when I only see her in the morning."

"It happens," I reassured him. "Work's been crazy, huh?"

"More so than usual, yes. That renovation has been a lot. I wish I didn't promise it would be done by the Fourth. Today I had to make them rip up the tile in the bathroom because it wasn't aligned perfectly. I don't know that the client would notice, but *I* noticed, and I couldn't leave it like that. Now I'm going to do it all over again tomorrow, after I check on all my other sites and have a meeting with the town about the new development. So it's going to be another long day." He pushed both of his hands through his hair.

"I can stay late again tomorrow. I don't have any commitments."

"Thank you. I'm really sorry. I wasn't planning on you having to do this so often. Things will slow down after this reno is done and my people get back from their holiday vacations." His employees were taking time off around the Fourth, so he'd been picking up more of the heavy lifting.

"It's no problem, seriously. I want to find out what happens in this Magic Tree House book. I don't know why I didn't read more of them as a kid. They're gripping."

Luke smiled, eyes crinkling. *That's a real one.* My stomach fluttered.

"Thanks, Val."

I sat down on the edge of the couch, not ready to leave yet. Luke hadn't made any move to get up either. His eyes scanned the living room, kitchen table, and the bench by the front door. He sighed again, his mouth forming an O like he was trying to calm his breathing. I could feel the anxiety wafting off of him from across the room.

"Is it just work that has you stressed?"

"That obvious, huh?"

I nodded.

He blew out a breath. "My parents get here late tomorrow night." He let that statement hang in the air for a beat.

Is that a bad thing? I waited for him to continue.

146

His eyes found mine. "I need to clean the house and get their room ready. I need groceries. I don't know when I'll be able to get to it, probably late tomorrow before they get in. It will just have to be good enough."

I scanned the open living area. Some of Luna's things—books, shoes, toys, tennis equipment—had piled up. There was a growing stack of mail, several water bottles, and a few tubes of sunscreen on the counter. Some dust and dirt had accumulated in the corners from the constant coming and going of all three of us. But it wasn't bad by any means. Nothing a quick tidy and vacuum couldn't fix.

"I can help tidy tomorrow. It's not in bad shape, and I'll be around anyway."

"No, absolutely not. Your only job is taking care of Luna. You're not a cleaner."

"I know, but I can still help."

"Seriously, you don't have to. You have Mimi, and your books to read, your writing, and your return-to-work stuff, plus all the extra hours I've needed you to stay with Luna. It's not necessary."

I tried not to read too much into him mentioning my writing like it was important. I'd only told him about it that one time. Now he asked me how the writing was coming or if I got many words in almost every day.

"Okay." I sensed I should drop it for now.

He ran his hand down his face. "I love it when they come to visit. We have a solid relationship, and they adore Luna. She's so excited to see them. But I always feel like..." He paused, searching for the right words. "I feel like they're judging me, if I'm doing a good enough job, and our whole life is under a microscope. They always end up saying something about taking her, like she's some kind of burden to me, or like she'd be better off with them than just with me." Anger laced his tone.

I'd be angry, too.

He shook his head. "I thought they would have stopped by now." He glanced around the room again, and I could tell he was mentally cataloging everything that needed to be cleaned up so there'd be nothing for his parents to critique. "They're not happy that Monica chose me, that I didn't decline becoming her guardian, and that I didn't move back to Pennsylvania with them. But I had just bought this house and started my business here and I wanted to stay."

"That makes perfect sense, Luke. You were building a life, and you brought Luna into it."

He nodded and swallowed, but he didn't look convinced.

"They could move here," I suggested. I assumed given his parents' age, they might have some flexibility.

"Ha. It does not go well when I mention ideas like that." Luke shook his head. "My dad's business is in Pennsylvania, and I'm pretty sure he will keep working until the day he drops dead."

My eyes flew wide.

"Sorry. That was in jest. Somewhat. He's just...intense. Super reliable, and I know he loves us, he's just...*intense* is really the only word for it."

"I get it." I opened my mouth to ask a question that popped into my head but thought better of it.

"What?"

"Oh, it's nothing. I'm sure everything will be fine." I smiled.

"C'mon, I like knowing what's going on in there." He tapped his temple.

I chewed the inside of my lip, contemplating whether to ask my question.

He raised his brows, egging me on.

"Why do you think your sister and brother-in-law chose you and not your parents?"

I wasn't sure how he'd react to such a personal question, but the smile he gave me certainly wasn't what I was expecting.

"It took me a while to figure it out. I actually do know why. But I've never told my parents, so it's a secret." He gestured for me to come closer, like he didn't want to say it at full volume. I got up from the couch I was sitting on and joined him on the other one.

148

He shifted so his body was angled toward me. We weren't touching, but we were only separated by a few inches now.

"Everyone was surprised they picked a twenty-eight-year-old bachelor as their preferred guardian over my parents, or Gardner's parents. My parents offered to take her, but I declined. If that was what Monica wanted before she died, then I wouldn't let her down. It's because she didn't get along with Dad. Nothing too bad, they just didn't see eye to eye on a lot of things, especially parenting."

He paused but I didn't say anything. I wanted him to go on.

"We were raised in a tough-love household. Dad thought, 'the world will be hard on you, so I'm going to be hard on you so you're prepared.' Monica hated it. He's not a bad person, and not even a bad dad; he's just not warm. And in hindsight, he may have taken the tough love thing a little too far sometimes. It didn't bother me that much growing up—his criticisms about sports or school or some mistake I'd made. But it bothered her. She'd always pull me aside, tell me she was proud of me, that I was doing my best, that I was human, that she loved me no matter what."

He shook his head and swallowed hard. "I adored her." He sucked in a breath before continuing. "My mom is the same way, ya know? Soft and kind and loving. That's where Monica got it from. But my mom never really stood up to Dad. After Luna was born, Monica was always saying how she wanted to raise her kids in a haven—a place that protected them from all the hard stuff out in the real world. I want to prove her right for choosing me, so that's what I'm trying to do for Luna. Give her a home that's soft and safe. When I'm not sure how, I ask myself, what would Monica say right now? And that helps."

When he looked up at me, his dark eyes shone with reverence. "It's amazing, sometimes I know exactly what she would say to Luna when she has a hard day, like I can hear Monica say it in my head. Is that strange?"

My body moved a millimeter closer to him, all on its own. "No.

You knew her and loved her. Her personality lives on in your mind."

"I like that." His voice was soft. I could tell how hard he was trying not to get choked up. I wished he wouldn't. "She'd have loved that you used Broadway music to pull her out of a funk."

I smiled at that, and feelings I refused to name flooded my chest. This smart, handsome, strong, successful man who exuded strength and confidence from every pore was putting so much pressure on himself to be a perfect dad. No wonder he was stressed out today.

I wished I could tell him I was sure he was proving his sister right, that I was positive she'd be so happy to see how he was with her daughter. But I didn't know her, so it felt strange to put words in her mouth. Instead, I said the closest thing I could think of. "You're doing it, Luke. Luna is so well-adjusted, and she's the sweetest kid but also so full of personality. This home *is* a haven." It'd been a haven to me, too, somehow.

He raised his glassy, brown eyes to mine. "You think so?"

I grabbed his forearm and squeezed lightly. "Yes. You are doing an *incredible* job." I said it again because apparently not even his parents told him this as often as he deserved. I'd said the same thing on Friday, but that was an eternity ago, before I understood the depth of the responsibility he felt.

He nodded and swallowed. When his eyes met mine again, they were full of an emotion I couldn't quite place. He shook his head slightly. "Thanks, Val. That means..." His low voice cut off, like he was struggling to come up with the words.

"I know." I rubbed my thumb over his forearm and let go. It felt wrong to let go when all I wanted to do was hug him, wrap my body around his and absorb some of the emotional weight he was carrying. But that wasn't the kind of relationship we had, so I just sat there and let him collect himself before he walked me out, as always.

"Okay," I said aloud to myself when I stepped into Luke's house the next day. "I have four hours to get the guest room ready, clean two bathrooms, tidy, vacuum, dust the entire downstairs, and scrub every inch of this kitchen until it gleams." I blew out my breath in a huff. "I can do this."

Instead of going to the gym, I'd biked back to the house. The deep cerulean blue bulbs of the hydrangea bushes that greeted me when I pulled up were photo-worthy perfection, and the lawn looked freshly mowed, so I was focusing on the inside.

I took the steps two at a time, headed for the laundry closet. I was sure Luke's parents were good people, but right now, I had an ax to grind with them. By the time I was done today, they would not find one damn thing to critique about this beautiful home. He told me not to, and it wasn't part of my job description, and I would likely be sacrificing a day of writing to do this, but none of that would stop me. I wanted to do this for him, and I refused to question my motivations beyond that.

The dryer was full and so was the washing machine. *Luke must have put these in this morning.* I grabbed an empty basket from the bathroom and pulled the clean, dry clothing out of the dryer: men's T-shirts, socks, golf shorts, and...soft, black boxer briefs. *Dammit, these are all Luke's.* I reached deeper into the dryer's barrel and started pulling the clothes out even faster, in big armfuls.

Do not go through his laundry, and whatever you do, do not picture him in those black boxer briefs, you weirdo.

Pulling my lip in between my teeth, I spun around in the hall-way, itching to put this basket away somewhere. I made for Luke's room at the end of the hall, vowing to toss the basket in there and close the door.

Except I'd never gone in his room before, and I couldn't help but take inventory when I crossed the carpeted threshold. A king-sized, black wooden-framed bed held court in the center of the room, flanked by matching nightstands. The only decorations were some framed photos on the dressers and nightstands. Two stacks of parenting books—edges turned up, bindings creased—

stood in piles on the floor next to the bed. As I bent to place the basket by the bigger dresser, the picture on top caught my eye. A couple stared lovingly at the brown-haired baby they're holding between them. It had to be his sister Monica and her husband with a baby Luna. Monica was as beautiful as Luke is handsome.

I pivoted and closed the gap between me and the hallway in an instant, swallowing the lump in my throat before closing the door.

I found the vacuum in the front-facing office downstairs, which contained more boxes than furniture and appeared to be used primarily as storage right now. By the time I left to get Luna for lunch, I'd finished vacuuming upstairs and was nearly done cleaning the upstairs bathroom. We had grilled cheese sandwiches at a place in town, and I dropped her at the sailing center with her instructors a little early.

When I returned and went back upstairs to put the dry, clean sheets on the guest bed, I walked into a small bedroom Luke clearly used as his actual home office by accident. A large desk with two big monitors and a few file cabinets lined the wall, leaving just enough room for a rolling chair. Above the desk hung two diplomas: a bachelor's degree from Franklin & Marshall and an MBA from Southern New Hampshire University. A little surge of pride filled me before I closed the door and located the real guest bedroom.

My arms tingled with fatigue as I wiped down the kitchen island. My phone buzzed in my back pocket.

MAX

Finished work early today. Want to hang out?

What he meant was: did I want to come over for an afternoon hookup before I picked up Luna? We'd done it once before. *But I still need to vacuum the whole downstairs.* I had no interest in leaving this task unfinished, but how could I explain that I couldn't come over because, despite being told not to, I had to help Luke clean his house before his parents arrived, so he wouldn't crumble under the weight of the pressure he puts on himself? I slid my phone back into my pocket and didn't respond until an hour later, when it would be too late to go over anyway.

VAL

Sorry I can't today, raincheck? ;)

Five minutes before I had to go get Luna, I collapsed on the couch. The house had the faint scent of lemon cleaning spray and Pine-Sol, and there were no dust bunnies or dirt in sight. A sigh released from my chest as I sank further into the worn leather cushions, not daring to close my eyes. Cleaning a whole house is a lot more work than going to the gym, and I was a disheveled mess, but the house was above reproach. Mission accomplished.

I bribed Luna to go to the grocery store with me after sailing by telling her she could pick out three things she wanted. We filled a cart with burgers, hot dogs, chicken, salmon, cheese, buns, salad, berries and other fruits, vegetables, hummus, chips, and breakfast items—everything they could possibly need to host his parents for a few days. Luna's selection was not one, not two, but *three* boxes of sugary cereal. I laughed when she dropped them in the cart.

"You said three!" she insisted, eyes narrowed.

"I know. That's why I didn't say anything." I patted her head. This girl was good at finding a loophole.

Just after 9:00 p.m.—Luna long asleep after three chapters of *Magic Tree House*—I was curled up on the couch with a glass of that rosé Luke had been keeping on hand for me when the front door opened.

"Hey," Luke said. His eyes crinkled when he took in my glass of wine and the romance novel in my hands.

"Hi, how'd it go?"

"It's done." He ran his hand down his face and started to kick off his boots. He looked at the clean bench—which had previously been covered with junk mail and a number of Luna's socks, shoes, and tennis accessories—and paused what he was doing.

"Val," he said in an admonishing tone.

"If there's anything you can't find, check the downstairs office. Or if it's Luna's, it's in her room."

He narrowed his eyes at me, finished taking off his boots, and walked into the kitchen. I got up to follow him and found him gaping, holding himself up with both hands on the counter. There was a bowl full of apples and bananas on the island, but otherwise it was spotless and gleaming, showing off the many attributes of the stunning custom kitchen.

"I told you you didn't have to."

"Well...I didn't listen."

His head shook before he looked up at me, his shoulders releasing down from his ears.

"The guest bedroom is all set," I went on. "I dried and put the sheets on the bed, and washed all the towels I could find so there's lots of clean towels in the bathroom now. I cleaned the bathrooms, too. Well, not yours. The only rooms I didn't touch are your bedroom and your office."

His head nodded slowly. Then he noticed the full bowl of fruit for the first time, and he pivoted and opened the fridge.

He closed it and turned to face me again, his expression full of meaning, his eyes shining. "Thank you. No one ever..." He swallowed. "Thank you."

I felt his relief in my own chest. And the realization hit me like a blow—I'd do just about anything to make him happy, to make things easier for him, to make him cry tears of joy again.

This wasn't a shallow fixation at all.

I needed to lighten some of the emotions building in my bones, so I lifted the corner of my mouth and said, "Don't thank me too much, I charged everything to your credit card. I took a load of your laundry out of the dryer, but I didn't fold it. I just put it in a basket and left it in your room, so it's probably all wrinkled. Also, I did Luna's laundry, but she is missing *several* socks. Like, there are almost no matches. It's just all singles. She must hide them somewhere? Or the dryer eats them? I scoured her room and the rest of the house, all of her bags. Nothing."

He'd started shaking his head halfway through my diatribe, a smirk tugging at his lips, and he was fully laughing by the end. It was music to my heart.

"I have to buy her a new pack of socks like every other month," he choked out between laughs, gripping the counter. "It's a scientific phenomenon."

I beamed at him. "I'm glad it's not just me."

He watched me from across the kitchen, not saying anything for a moment, the relief mixed with disbelief still shining clear in his deep brown eyes. "Now that you picked out all of this awesome food, it's only fair if you get to eat some of it. What are you doing on the Fourth?"

21

Fourth of July. New England's favorite summer holiday. Fireworks and cookouts, parades and parties. Everyone clad in red, white, and blue. It had been years since I fully enjoyed one. It was so often an arbitrary deadline by which clients wanted their deals to sign or close. So, I usually spent the days leading up to the Fourth working around the clock.

This year was different. I had plans I was looking forward to. I'd gotten full nights of sleep the last few days. I snuck over to the gym before Mimi woke up. I showered, dried my hair, lathered a base layer of sunscreen on my unusually sun-kissed skin, and put on a blue and white patterned dress that hit me at mid-thigh (but was designed to avoid wardrobe malfunctions with built-in shorts underneath). I spent some extra time on my makeup and added white sneakers and pearl jewelry.

"Don't you look beautiful," Mimi said when I walked in the kitchen.

I twirled. "Thanks!" I felt good, too. "Alright, Mimi, chop chop, gotta get ready for Luke's."

She took a big gulp of her coffee and popped out of her kitchen chair, surprisingly spry for an eighty-three-year-old. "I wish I could still wear dresses like that," she grumbled as she climbed the stairs.

"You'll look fabulous anyway, Mims!"

The plan for today had worked out better than expected. Luke was having a few friends over to join him, Luna, and his parents for a lunch barbecue before the parade at 4:00 p.m. and had invited Mimi and me. Max and his parents were planning to take the boat out before the parade to avoid the chaos of downtown. Which meant I could go to both. I'd bring Mimi to her friend's house near the parade route before joining Max.

"Val!" Luna jogged over and hugged me around the waist when we arrived in their backyard. Then she ran back to where she was playing a game with Clara, her new tennis partner. The sun beat down, but gratefully, the trees provided some shade to the yard and a retractable gray awning covered the deck. I wondered if Luna had sunscreen on.

I scanned the yard for Luke but didn't see him. An older couple stood on the side of the yard, watching the girls play and chatting with Clara's mom. *Luke's parents.* An attractive, younger couple pulled canned drinks out of a cooler on the deck. Mimi took a seat in the shade, and I told her I'd grab her a drink before slipping in through the slider.

When Luke saw me, a smile filled his whole face.

My stomach somersaulted. He'd trimmed the beard, so I could just make out his one dimple. He was wearing red shorts, those impossibly weathered boat shoes, and a white golf shirt with blue and red stars on it. A half-drunk Corona bottle sat on the counter next to the tray of hummus, carrots, and pita chips he was creating. Relaxation wafted off of him.

"Hey, you made it!"

"We did. Thanks for inviting us."

"Of course. Do you want something to drink? I grabbed another bottle of that rosé."

I bit down on the smile tugging at my cheeks.

"What?" he asked.

"It's just nice that you keep getting it for me."

He shrugged. "Or there's lemonades and iced teas and stuff in the coolers outside if you aren't trying to get after it yet."

I leaned my hip against the counter. "It's the biggest day-drinking day of the year, so who am I to resist?"

He grinned and pulled the bottle out of the fridge. I poured two glasses: one for me, one for Mimi. I took a sip and said without thinking, "Does, um—Nevermind."

"Tell me." Luke looked up from the tray where he'd added some cucumber spears.

I pursed my lips. *Will he be insulted if I ask?*

He stared at me expectantly.

"Does Luna have sunscreen on?"

His mouth quirked up in the corner. "Yes, covered head to toe."

"I figured. I'm sorry."

"Don't be. The times I've forgotten and she's gotten burned, I felt so bad. She's fairer than I am, so I have to be super aware of it."

He had a way of doing that: never making me feel bad for saying what I was thinking, even when I thought it might not come out right or land well.

He returned the wine bottle to the fridge. Then he held up his finger, opened it again, and removed a plastic bag with half a banana in it, still in the peel, hopelessly browned. My cheeks flamed.

"Why do I always find half bananas in the fridge in plastic bags? Does Luna not want the other half or something?"

"Oh, um, that's me. I don't think I can eat a whole banana," I said as shame continued to rise to the surface of my skin. It was ridiculous that I regularly tried to save the other half. This one was from several days ago.

"You can't eat a whole banana?" Luke asked, dark eyebrows raised, a smirk spreading over his face.

"Yeah, I don't know. I always think I want one, but then I get sick of it before I can finish it. Maybe I just don't really like bananas?" I raised both my palms up, like I still wasn't sure.

He laughed, full-bellied, supporting himself on the counter. When he stopped he shook his head, smiling at me with a glimmer in his eyes.

I shrugged sheepishly.

"Sorry, that's...hilarious. What a quirk. And I live with an eight-year-old. I think you don't like bananas, Val. Do we need to expose you to some other fruits?"

Now it was my turn to laugh. "You're probably right."

"There's apples, grapes, all sorts of berries..."

He thinks he's so funny.

I let him tease me, shaking my head and fighting my smile. Then I threw a carrot at him. He caught it in one hand and popped it into his mouth, and my smile broke free.

When I walked back out to the deck, Luke was right behind me, still smirking.

"Mimi, Luke. Luke, Mimi," I said as I set down her glass.

"Great to meet you." Luke took her hand gently. "Thank you for getting Val over to the island and for hanging out with my kid the past few weeks. Luna has told me your flower garden is much better than mine and we should try and make ours look like yours."

Mimi laughed, clutching her chest. "Oh, of course. Luna is just a delight. And I am very proud of those flowers, so that means a lot to me."

Luke turned to me. "Want to meet my parents?"

I looked at Mimi, and she waved me off, content to relax on the deck. Knowing her, she'd have some new friends by the time I returned.

Luke led me out to the yard to make introductions to his parents, Alex and Elena. His father's handshake was firm; his mother's smile was welcoming.

"I'm so happy to meet you, Val," his mother said. "Luna has said some wonderful things. She seems to be really enjoying spending time with you this summer."

"It's been great for me, too. I feel like I'm living the best summer ever vicariously through her."

"The two of them rave about the summers here," his dad chimed in. "I find it to be a tad crowded, but I can see the appeal."

Luke shook his head slightly when he could tell his parents weren't looking, his subtle grin all but hidden under his beard.

"Summers on the Vineyard are the best," I said.

I joined Mimi on the deck a few minutes later, unsurprised to find her chatting away with the couple I noticed by the coolers earlier.

"Val!" Mimi's smile reached the green eyes I inherited from her. It was always the same, whether she saw me a few minutes ago, or if it had been months: like my presence made her whole day. "My new friends Jeremiah and Francesca were just about to tell me all about their wedding at the Martha's Vineyard Museum."

Jeremiah was Luke's close friend from college and second in command at Karas Construction. Luke had mentioned him several times, but this was my first time meeting him in person.

"The one on the hill in Vineyard Haven?" I asked them as I took a seat.

Francesca nodded.

"Wow, that must have been spectacular. I'm Val, by the way." I reached my hand across the table.

"Great to meet you. Luke and Luna have told us all about you. All good things." Jeremiah smirked and draped his arm around the back of Francesca's chair.

My stomach flipped over. *What did they say?*

"Did you do a tent on the lawn?" Mimi asked.

"Oh, yes. The white tent on the lawn, live band, views of the harbor below, blue and white flowers everywhere." Francesca turned and grinned coyly at her husband.

"She knows how I feel about the flower budget. Highway robbery." He lifted his dark brows at Mimi and me and shook his head.

"They make the whole event, though," I said.

Mimi nodded emphatically.

"Exactly, Val! That's what I keep telling him." When Francesca looked at her husband again her eyes shone with victory.

He shook his head again, smiling affectionately. He was outnumbered, but he didn't seem to mind it.

"I loved planning it so much, I quit my high-stress start-up job and started my own event planning business," Francesca added.

Wow, good for her. Pangs of both envy and admiration rattled inside me as she explained how the start-up grind was not for her, but she loved being her own boss, putting together beautiful events on the island after she moved here to be with Jeremiah.

While we chatted, Luke turned on the grill, refusing our offers to help until everything was almost done. Luna's friend Clara and her mother left before we ate, but we still had to push two patio tables together for the rest of us.

Luna, Mimi, and I made our plates of burgers and chips and salad first.

"Why do we celebrate July Fourth?" Luna asked after we sat with our food.

Mimi nodded in my direction, lobbing the question to me.

"Originally another country, Great Britain, controlled the United States, but we decided we wanted to be our own country and be independent, so our representatives sent this letter to the king of Great Britain telling him that the United States would no longer follow their laws or pay their taxes. The letter is called The Declaration of Independence, and it was published on July 4, 1776." *Thank you,* Hamilton *(the musical) for inspiring me to refresh my memory on U.S. history.*

How exactly did people parent before the internet?

"Cool," Luna said before taking a huge bite of her burger, clearly satisfied with my answer.

I can't wait for the day she's old enough to watch Hamilton, I thought, watching her chew and kick her feet happily under the table. But a zap of reality forced my gaze down to my plate and wiped my smile off my face.

I won't be here when that time comes.

When Luke, his parents, Jeremiah, and Francesca finally joined us, I suppressed my anticipatory disappointment and asked Luke and Jeremiah to tell us more about their business.

They launched into it like a well-practiced duo. It was Jeremiah's family that had a home on Martha's Vineyard, and they started coming here together in the summers during college. They loved it and came up with the idea of opening a business here. Luke had known he wanted to do some sort of building since he made his first birdhouse in woodshop class in high school. He did carpentry throughout school, and by junior year of college, they both got summer jobs over here with a different construction company. That company still existed, and that was where they'd worked for a few years before they broke off on their own. Luke looked at his dad when he finished speaking.

"Was your boss upset?" Mimi asked.

"He wasn't thrilled," Luke responded. "But he understood. And there was so much work, he was turning down jobs left and right. So we're a bit competitive with each other, but we don't let it get ugly because we also end up referring each other for jobs the other can't take."

"And it seems like business is booming for you guys," I complimented.

"Oh, yeah. This guy has been working hard. And he got that huge contract from the town," Jeremiah announced, a proud smile on his face.

"*We*," Luke corrected his friend. He didn't respond to the other compliments. *So humble.*

"If work is getting too busy for you, son, and it gets to be too much, there's great schools in Radnor," his dad said, taking a bite of his food and looking straight at his son, like what he said was totally casual.

I nearly dropped my fork. Luke chewed and swallowed,

lowering his hands to squeeze his own thighs. He looked pissed. He glanced at Luna, who was engrossed in a side conversation with Francesca about tennis. Before I could think better of it, I reached for his hand under the table and gave it a squeeze.

"I know, Dad. I went to them. The schools here are great, too." His tone was cold as ice, his brown eyes suddenly black. Damn, Alex struck a nerve.

I squeezed his hand again, and he squeezed back, almost a little too hard. *He's wrong,* I tried to say with the pressure of my fingers. *Luna belongs here.*

"Of course they are," his dad said. Sensing he'd opened an old wound, he backed off. "Didn't mean anything by it." He looked at his granddaughter with adoration. "She loves it here, obviously."

It was the first time I detected a hint of hurt in Alex's tone, and his eyes. My indignation immediately lessened.

Luke let out a breath and released his iron grip on my fingers. His father's obvious pain seemed to take the wind out of his sails of anger, too.

Luna probably looked just like Monica to them. Even though I was certain Monica and Gardner made the right choice choosing Luke, if I looked at it from his parents' point of view, I could see how much that must have hurt, especially if they wanted her.

An awkward silence descended on the group. Jeremiah popped out of his chair. "Anyone want an ice cream sandwich?"

Luna's hand shot in the air, along with Mimi's. *Phew.*

When he returned, he also had a paper grocery bag tucked under his arm. He handed out navy blue ball caps that said *Karas Construction* with a little American flag underneath. "You're all expected to wear these to the parade," Jeremiah commanded.

I laughed and put it on my head.

Not that I was going to the parade, I thought with a pang.

Luke's mother insisted on clearing our plates when we were done. Francesca and Mimi said something about needing to sit in the air conditioning for a while, and Luke, Jeremiah, Alex, and Luna started up a game of cornhole in the yard.

I grabbed a seltzer from one of the coolers, content to watch them play while I tried not to think about how right it felt to reach for Luke's hand earlier. I probably shouldn't be holding my boss's hand under the table at a barbecue, probably shouldn't even *want* to do that, given I was seeing someone. *But it was harmless,* I convinced myself. *We're friends.* Friends could support each other with little gestures like hand squeezes in tense moments.

That's totally normal.

After a few minutes, Luke's mother joined me, leaning against the porch railing.

"So, Luke told us you're taking some time away from work?"

I turned to her and nodded. Her brown eyes were a slightly lighter shade than Luke's, but just as warm.

"I think it's so great, and brave, that you made a change," she added before I had a chance to respond.

"Thank you. I—thank you." I was so used to justifying it, even to myself, I didn't know what to say to someone who automatically thought my leave of absence was a good thing.

"You never know what is going to happen in life." She stared at Luna, who was concentrating so hard on her next toss, she'd pulled her lip between her teeth. There was a sadness in Elena's eyes. She must be thinking about her daughter, the car accident. "You need to live it every day, enjoy it, because you just don't know."

I felt myself getting choked up, not only because of their loss and the deep sympathy I felt for them, but because for the first time since March, I stopped doubting my decision to leave Peters & Dowling, whether temporarily or permanently, no matter what happened next. The doubt just vanished. I could almost feel it leaving my body, like saltwater evaporating off my skin in the sun.

It wasn't worth it. The sacrifices. Living to work instead of working to live.

There was so much more to life.

When it was time to leave to drop off Mimi and meet Max, I felt like a child getting picked up from a playdate she didn't want to end.

But I was going boating in Edgartown Harbor on the Fourth of July with my attractive boyfriend who spoiled me with fancy champagne and compliments every time I saw him. I should be excited.

I *was* excited.

"Max told us you're on sabbatical from your law firm this summer?" Max's mother asked after we settled at the front of the boat, glasses of champagne in our hands.

"Yes, I...needed a break. It's been great," I said, hoping to avoid a deeper dive.

She popped a grape into her mouth. "I wish he would take a break," she nodded toward her husband, who was standing in front of the controls, navigating us out of the harbor.

Maybe he just loves it, I thought, relating deeply. I didn't see myself getting sick of writing any time soon.

Edward Phelps handed the controls over to his son, picked up his glass of champagne, and sat down next to his wife.

"I just finished reading your latest, *Something In The Water*. It was great!" I said to Ed.

"Oh, did you now? I'm glad you enjoyed it. That one was fun to write."

I felt the urge to tell him I'd started writing, but I chickened out, hoping Max would bring it up for me and maybe Ed would share his advice. "I bet." I trained my face into a grin. "I'm going to check on Max."

I swallowed the rest of my champagne in one gulp before I joined Max at the controls and leaned against his side.

"Hi." He beamed down at me. I could see my reflection in his sunglasses, my honey-colored hair whipping in the ocean breeze. He tucked a strand behind my ear. "Having fun?"

"Yeah, you?"

"Absolutely."

I refilled my wine and took another sip, the bubbles popping on the roof of my mouth, and gazed out at the water. A boat passed us, going twice as fast as we were, with an inflated tube dragging behind. The two children, a boy and a girl, called, "Faster!" from the tube, their voices barely audible over the engine and the wind. I chuckled. *I bet Luna would love tubing.*

Max followed my gaze. "If they go much faster, they're gonna get tossed."

"I think that's exactly what they're hoping for."

"Probably," he agreed.

I turned and looked at the back of Max's boat. Perfectly polished dark wood and plush padded benches stared back at me. "Can we hook up a tube to this boat?" I asked, my inner child jealous of those kids.

"No. No hookup on this beauty, unfortunately."

"Bummer."

"But I can take us out farther and crank up the speed, if you want."

"About time!" his dad hollered from the bow.

Max gave me a knowing grin and steered us out of the harbor, accelerating once we rounded the lighthouse. I sat back down in the chair next to his, tied back my hair, and stared out at the waves, smiling every time ocean spray collided with my face. I was determined to be in the moment and tried my best not to spend the whole time wondering if Luke and Luna were having fun at the parade.

When we got back to the Phelps compound, Max's mom went up to bed and Max and his dad went to the living room and cracked open an expensive bottle of bourbon. I was exhausted. A few hours ago, my day drinking had turned the corner from a buzz to the beginnings of a hangover. Maybe I should've kept drinking like Max had. He and his dad both looked a little flushed. It was definitely the most drunk I'd ever seen Max. But he seemed happy, at ease.

I was jealous. I hadn't felt at ease all night.

At dinner at the yacht club, Max's mom, already a little drunk from the champagne on the boat, mentioned that they weren't surprised Max found a new girlfriend on the island. I wasn't sure what she meant by that, and Max shot daggers from his eyes when she said it, so she didn't elaborate.

Sensing the need for a subject change, I asked his parents, "Do you get here for dinner often? The food is excellent."

"Oh, yeah. This is one of the only places we can have dinner during peak season. Everyone here is too interested in themselves, or too proud, to stop me and ask for a photo. If we go anywhere else, the interruptions from fans are constant." Ed chuckled, and Brianna and Max joined in.

I forced a smile. Wouldn't it be nice to be so beloved by your readers they want pictures with you? I'd almost asked, but I refrained.

Ed brought up his writing career a few more times throughout the night, and my heart hoped Max might mention I'd started writing, but he didn't.

After dinner we'd gone to *another* private club that Max's parents were members of. There must've been about a hundred people there, enjoying an open bar and a clear view of the fireworks from the back dock. Max introduced me to everyone as his girlfriend. Almost everyone's first question was: What did I do for work? Each time Max proudly said I was a Peters & Dowling attorney, it made me feel weird. Despite the relaxed and celebratory vibe, it felt like we were networking.

Some people asked how we met first. Those conversations were more fun. Max told them how he saw a stunning woman working at the coffee shop behind the bookstore and he somehow came up with enough confidence to talk to me.

"By the end of the conversation, I realized he was flirting with me," I would add at that point. "He asked me out, and the rest is history, I suppose."

When Ed put the bourbon glasses on the round, white coffee table in the center of the Phelps' palatial living room, I excused myself to go to bed, saying I wasn't a bourbon drinker. Max followed me into the hall, lifted my chin, and stole a kiss.

"Want me to come up with you?"

"No, it's okay. Enjoy the time with your dad!"

"You sure?"

"Yes," I said, rising on my tiptoes to kiss him again.

I slipped out the front door and crossed the driveway to his apartment, oddly content with being alone for the first time in hours.

When Max got back to his room an hour later, I still hadn't fallen asleep, but I kept my eyes closed and lay there motionless. Pretending.

Like I had been since the moment I left Luke's.

22

I spent the Saturday after the holiday at the beach with Max. It was hazy, a bit cooler on this side of the island with the wind careening around the sandy, burnt orange cliffs. We spread out a blanket, and he knelt behind me to rub sunscreen onto my back, taking his time, and leaning over me to kiss my cheek when he finished. We read our books for a while—a romance novel for me, a business-y nonfiction book for him. Then Max asked if I wanted to go for a walk along the shore.

I was unintentionally quiet at first, lost in an idea that the book I was reading had sparked. The two main characters begin at odds with each other—it was a rivals-to-lovers romance—until one day the male main character reveals something personal about himself that makes the female main character soften toward him. I needed a moment like that for the characters in my story. I looked down at the sand, watching the frothy water slip over the tops of our feet before being sucked back out into the ocean, considering what personal detail my main character could reveal to make the SEC investigator see her in a new light.

"I think this is my favorite summer yet." While I was looking at the sand, Max was looking at me.

I smiled. "Oh, yeah?"

"Yeah." He squeezed my hand. "My life was just going along, linear, boring, and then all of a sudden, there you were. Like a shooting star landed right in front of me."

A giddy, bubbly feeling filled me, and I tilted my head to grin at him. He was so sweet. I didn't feel like I deserved it.

How'd you know? I wanted to ask. *You didn't know anything about me yet...* But I left those questions unspoken. Instead, I pulled his face down to mine and kissed his lips. He'd shaved that morning, and it always made his lips feel super soft.

"I'm having a great summer, too," I whispered.

On our way back to the Edgartown side of the island from the beach, I knew the moment I got service back because my phone vibrated several times in my bag. I took it out to check.

LUKE

> Hey Val, I'm sorry to ask, but any chance you're free this evening? My parents are leaving in a few hours and Jeremiah and I got a last-minute opportunity for a dinner meeting with a potential new client. No worries if not, I know it's a Saturday and I'm sure you have plans.

I rolled my lips through my teeth. Two of Max's friends from business school were on the island this weekend, and he'd invited me to join them for dinner tonight. I felt torn. What would Luke do if he couldn't find someone to watch Luna? Luke had mentioned that Jeremiah's wife Francesca watched Luna sometimes, but she was probably working an event tonight. He'd likely just have Jeremiah take the meeting. Jeremiah would do a great job, I had no doubt, but I had enough experience with client interactions to know it would be infinitely better if they were both there.

Hopefully Max wouldn't mind if his dinner with his friends was just a guys' night.

VAL

What time should I come over?

Luke responded immediately.

LUKE

6:30? Reservation is at 7. Thank you so much.
You're a lifesaver.

VAL

I just hope Luna didn't get too far ahead of me in
Magic Tree House. I wanna know what happens.

He replied with a bunch of laughing emojis. My stomach filled with excitement. Luna and I could eat dinner on the deck, watch a show, do some reading, and then I'd probably have an hour to write before Luke got home.

When we got back to Max's apartment, I said, "I actually can't make it to dinner tonight. Luke needs someone to watch Luna last minute."

Irritation flashed across his face. "Seriously?"

"Yeah, he has a client dinner."

Max's lips pressed into a thin line.

I felt the need to justify it further. "He usually pays me time and a half when I work off-hours. I thought you wouldn't mind because now tonight can just be a guys' thing with your friends?"

Max blew a breath out through his teeth. "Okay," he said, resigned. "I still don't understand why you took that job this summer. Aren't you still getting a check from the firm?"

For now.

"I am, but I guess I didn't want to be dependent on it. I wanted to have the option to extend the leave, even if it was unpaid, or..." My body urged me to hold back.

"Or what?"

I took a deep breath, steeling myself. "Or...if I quit altogether, I'll need money for health insurance and living costs. I don't want to plow through my savings."

Max nodded, brow furrowed somewhere between surprise and concern. "I didn't know you were considering quitting altogether."

"I know. I'm still not sure what I want to do." Even as I said it, it felt like a lie. "I just wanted to have options, if that makes sense."

"It does." His lip quirked up and his eyes softened. "I just wish it didn't mean I got to spend less time with you. I'm greedy when it comes to you." As he said it, he reached for me.

I closed the gap between us and let him wrap his arms around my waist. *Does this mean he'd be cool with it if I quit?* I decided not to ask.

Nine more days until July 15th. I sighed into Max's shoulder. The truth was, I knew what I wanted to do. I just wasn't sure if I had the courage to go through with it.

Luna filled me in on the rest of her time with her grandparents, how much candy they got at the parade, and their trip to the Flying Horses Carousel, over macaroni and cheese on the deck.

After dinner we watched a Disney show and got through two chapters of *Magic Tree House* before she fell asleep.

I tiptoed downstairs, got my laptop and a glass of wine, lit a sea salt-scented candle, and set up at Luke's kitchen table. For some unknown reason, I always got the most writing done here—on his deck or at this table.

The more layers of my characters I pulled back, the more convinced I was that they'd be good together, romantically. I was starting to love the idea that their meet-cute happened because he was investigating her. After a scene break, I dove into the conversation where she tells him how hard she worked to put herself through school and he begins to soften toward her. I'd been writing more than usual the last few days, bringing my laptop with me into Mimi's living room when she watched the news at night. I felt like I was running out of time, and I hated it.

After I got up to refill my water and wine glasses, unwelcome thoughts about my return-to-work date seeped in, distracting me from my characters' story. Dread formed a rock in my stomach.

I didn't want to go back. I could ask my therapist to sign a note recommending an extension, but even that thought provided no relief. I didn't want a date looming.

I wanted to be done.

But how would I explain it? To my friends, my family, my old coworkers. Max.

The conversation played out in my mind: *I'm quitting this career I've been dedicated to for almost ten years, if you include school, to try my hand at writing. In the meantime, I'm a babysitter.*

I slumped into the back of the chair. I could feel their judgment already.

"What's on your mind?"

I gasped, my hand slamming into my chest. Luke's large frame cast a shadow on the table.

"Oh, um. I don't know," I said softly once I caught my breath.

His eyebrow rose skeptically. "C'mon Val, you were so absorbed in your thoughts, staring into space, you didn't even hear me come in. Unless there's a ghost in that corner of the room you can see that I can't? Are you a medium?"

His joke cut through my melancholy and a laugh released from my throat. "Okay, *fine*." I sucked in air, holding it in my chest for a moment before spilling my thoughts in a stream. "I'm upset because...I only have nine days to decide if I'm going back to work. And..." I took a breath and looked at him.

His open expression urged me to continue.

"When I took this babysitting job I was just hedging, I wanted the concept of flexibility, but I still assumed I'd return to the firm, if not in mid-July then after a brief extension. But now I'm thinking thank god I did hedge because I actually don't want to go back. At all. I don't want to make those sacrifices anymore. I want to have time for other things. I didn't like the person that job made me into. I'm just starting to feel like myself again..."

When I looked at him this time, he was biting the inside of his cheek, fighting a smile that'd already reached his eyes.

I blew out my breath as all the needling insecurities rushed in, just like they always did when I thought I'd made up my mind. "But I know everyone is going to ask me what I'm going to do instead, and I don't know how to answer. Max called my writing a hobby." My voice cracked slightly on the word 'hobby.' Why did that word bother me so much? I gave Luke a small, one-shoulder shrug.

He opened his mouth but closed it again without speaking, as if he could tell that wasn't it.

So I continued. "I know that's how everyone will think about it. And I'm embarrassed to be pursuing this pipe dream that I have no relevant experience to do. People from my prior life will think it's dumb. A waste of my education and work experience. A silly flight of fancy that will never work out. I just..." I swallowed, lowering my voice to a whisper. "I don't even want to tell anyone else."

Luke nodded, his arms crossed in front of his chest, biceps straining the fabric of his button-down shirt. "You don't know until you try, right? And knowing you, you'll need to try your absolute best, make the writing the best it can be. And that's going to take time and a lot of believing in yourself. I say go for it."

I gaped at him. "Really?"

"Yeah, why not? All careers and businesses start out with risk. You gotta do it anyway. You're smart and passionate; I have no doubt you could write something great. You probably already have." His palm gestured toward my laptop.

A lump formed in my throat. "Thanks, Luke."

"Let's talk about the practical plan. Don't go anywhere." His pointer finger wagged at me, an order to stay put. He strode to the fridge, took out a beer, and placed it on the table next to my wine glass. Then he bounded up the stairs. He returned moments later with a legal pad and a pen.

He dropped into the chair beside mine, took a big swig of his beer, and wrote, *Author Business Plan* at the top of the page. His hand pushed the notepad to his right, positioning it between us.

"I mean, I don't know if I have a plan per se, it's more at the dream stage right now."

"That's why we're making one. This is what they taught us in business school. You gotta take the vision and turn it into a plan."

What had I done to earn this level of confidence from him? Maybe he was just an encouraging person. Either way, a smile spread across my face and happy tears brimmed in my eyes. *He's taking me seriously.*

"Okay." I swallowed.

"The first thing is a summary." He gripped the pen in his fingers and scrawled: *Lawyer and reading addict to write her own novels about:* "We'll leave that blank for now and come back to it. Next is goals."

I chewed on my lip.

"These can be objective and start small." He turned in his seat to face me, his thigh colliding with mine under the table. His face was so close, I felt his breath on my cheek when he released it. He didn't pull his leg back, leaving it there, flush with mine, making my breaths shorter, my neck warmer. Should I scooch back?

I didn't want to.

Hyperawareness of how alone we were—sitting in this quiet kitchen, the world dark outside the windows—set in. I lost my train of thought. What did he just ask me?

Oh right, goals.

He took a sip of his beer, watching my face intently, a ghost of a grin on his full pink lips, like he knew he'd distracted me.

"Goals," I repeated. "I want to write at least four times per week, either for three hours or 1500 words." He jotted those down in bullets. "I want to read books about writing, learn more about the craft, self-educate, you know?"

"Great." His pen raced across the page.

"I want to turn the story I'm writing into a full novel and look into publishing it." It was the first time I'd said it, even to myself.

"What are you calling it?"

"I don't have a title yet but let's say...*Insider Trading Meet-Cute*."

A laugh rumbled from deep in his chest. "I need to hear more about this." Black ink appeared on the page next to a new bullet: *Turn Insider Trading Meet-Cute into full novel, then publish.*

Ten words, now in writing, in the universe.

"Alright now let's start with money. Like any new business, you'll be operating at a loss for a while, but you still need to support yourself in the meantime."

He jotted down categories: monthly expenses, monthly income, business investments. He turned and looked at me, nodding to the page.

"My expenses are pretty low, living with Mimi." I estimated what my health insurance would cost if I quit, gas, groceries, and car payment. "And I'd insist on paying Mimi to cover taxes and utilities after she goes back to Florida."

His eyes whipped from the notepad to my face. "You're considering staying on the island full-time?"

I met his gaze. Wide-eyed, sincere curiosity stared back at me. I almost took it back, told him I had no idea if I'd stay on the island, but the look on his face stopped me. I nodded.

Did he want me to stay?

The corner of his mouth ticked up, my only clue the answer might be *yes.*

Luke cleared his throat and looked back down at the page. "What was that estimate again?"

I repeated what I'd want to contribute to Mimi's taxes and utilities, and he jotted it down.

In the income category, he wrote down what he pays me. "Do you have enough time to write now? With all of Luna's commitments?"

"Yes. Her schedule is actually good for me. It keeps me disciplined."

"Good. And every six months you should negotiate a pay

increase. Because of inflation. And increasing job challenge as Luna continues to hone her spunky attitude."

"Luke, you don't need to pay me more."

"I'm just giving you objective advice I would give any business mentee."

I shook my head but didn't bother objecting aloud for a second time. Under no circumstances would I be asking him to increase my pay.

He stretched his long legs under the table and leaned back in his chair. My knee silently protested the loss of contact. My fingers skated along the spot where our legs had been pressed together for the last several minutes. He looked like a man that was so comfortable—in his house, sitting at his kitchen table—there was no place he'd rather be.

"So, tell me about this Insider Trading book," he beckoned.

"No shit, this dude goes into his girlfriend's home office, goes through her private work documents, and then invests $100K into a company he *knows* is about to be bought."

"It actually happens more often than you'd think."

"Fuck, I feel bad for her. It's not her fault she trusted the wrong person."

"I do too! That's exactly my point. But the investigator—he doesn't feel bad for her at first. He thinks it was reckless she left the documents lying around. Until he gets to know her better and realizes what she's lost far outweighs the magnitude of her error."

Luke watched me intently as I spoke. "I think it sounds great. I want a signed copy."

I shoved his shoulder. His body didn't move at all.

"What?" he asked, eyes flaring with mock indignation.

"You're humoring me."

"I am not! I listened to the whole pitch, and it sounds good. I'll watch the movie, too. I love that white collar crime shit."

I didn't fight my smile for once.

He'd opened another beer and refilled my wine glass while I rambled about my story and how I started writing it. We hadn't moved from the table, but we'd turned our chairs so we were facing each other. I sat cross-legged, my sundress draped over my knees. He'd undone the top two buttons of his shirt, unfortunately only revealing the neck of a white undershirt.

Eventually, I looked back down. He watched me fidget with the skirt of my dress for a moment before saying, "I'm sorry your boyfriend called it a hobby. He probably didn't mean it to be hurtful, but I know it sucks to hear stuff like that when you're dreaming about making it a bigger part of your life."

I looked at him. "It sounds like you're speaking from experience?"

"Yeah. I had more stable options back in Pennsylvania. Established construction companies where I could have gotten a desk job after college. People told me moving to a new place and opening my own business was risky and likely to fail. But I didn't listen to them. I wanted something that was mine; I wanted to create jobs, provide a more affordable option for people. Our old boss always only wanted to take the big jobs, the most expensive renovations and new builds. Anyone who called that just wanted a new bathroom, or a new deck, we'd turn down. So I made that part of my mission: we'd do big *and* small jobs. Starting out, it was a lot of the smaller jobs, but eventually those created relationships and leads, and now I get just as many big jobs, too."

"That's a pretty awesome origin story for Karas Construction."

He shrugged, humble.

This man.

"I mean it, it's impressive." I grabbed his forearm for emphasis, but quickly removed my hand. His gaze moved to the spot where I'd touched him.

"Thanks, Val," he murmured.

"It's inspiring, too," I added. His eyes widened, like it meant something to him that I found him inspiring, like he was surprised I said that.

I finished my glass of wine and angled my head up to the ceiling, a soft sigh escaping my lips as my mind reverted to my own next steps.

Sensing the train of my thoughts, Luke said, "Honestly, Val, and I mean this in a nice way, but who cares if they don't get it? You get it. You know why you're doing it. So who cares what your old coworkers or anyone else thinks?"

Luke was right, of course. My therapist had been asking similar questions lately, too, especially after I finally revealed to her how much I loved writing, how I would be excited to wake up every day if that were my real job.

"I know you're right. I'm…" I pursed my lips to the side. Luke's gaze flashed to my mouth. "I'm working on it."

Then my eyes caught the time on the stove: 11:00 p.m.

"It's late," I said. "I should probably head home."

Luke nodded but didn't move.

My legs found the floor and as I pushed myself up, the room tilted. *Crap.* Half a box of kids' macaroni and cheese was no match for three generous glasses of wine.

"Actually, I don't think I can drive," I admitted, embarrassed. He glanced at the wine glass and then at my face. "I know it's a short drive but…the wine went to my head." I felt the need to explain and apologize. "I'll just walk and come back in the morning to grab my car."

"Absolutely not."

"Luke, it's only a mile—a twenty-minute walk, tops."

"It's dark, there aren't many streetlights in this neighborhood, no sidewalks, and there'll be a bunch of drunks driving home from dinner right now. *No.*" His voice was a command. "You're sleeping here. Text Mimi, I'm sure she's still up."

He was standing now too, towering over me. I tipped my head up and opened my mouth to protest again, but it was plain from his expression that he would have none of it: lips a thin line, dark eyes serious as sin. It was hot as hell. The untamable part of my mind was already wondering how I could get him to boss me around again.

"Okay," I whispered. "I'll sleep on the couch."

"Nope. I'm going to go change the sheets in the guest room."

"Luke," I whined, dragging out the monosyllabic name. "You don't need to do that." *I'm his babysitter, I'm supposed to be helping him, not burdening him.*

In a few big strides, he was at the base of the stairs. "Help if you want, but I'm doing it anyway."

I groaned quietly, grabbed my things, and followed him up the stairs.

"Thanks again for all the cleaning you did. My parents didn't make any comments about the house other than to say it looked great," Luke said as he tossed a corner of the fitted sheet in my direction.

"I'm glad." I tucked the sheet around the edge of the mattress before moving to the foot of the bed. "Did you have a good time with them overall? Luna told me she did."

"Yeah, it went well. They didn't say anything else that implied Luna would be better off in Pennsylvania for the rest of the week, and Luna always has a great time with them. I'm happy when she's happy." He shrugged, and warmth filled my veins. "My dad actually mentioned the idea of retiring. I don't think I've ever heard him say the word before. My mom said they'd love to spend more time here after he retires. And I do kinda miss them, honestly."

"I'm sure they miss you, too. That's awesome he's considering retiring and they'd spend more time here when he does. They'd have to get their own place, of course."

"Of course." He grinned.

He fluffed the last pillow after putting on the fresh case. "Need anything else?"

"If I do, I know where to find it."

"True."

He walked slowly toward the door. I followed, so I could shut it behind him. As soon as he crossed the threshold, he turned. I stopped short. He lifted his arm, leaning his elbow on the door frame. It was the perfect position, his head leaning just low enough that I could lift my mouth to his if I wanted to. His eyes roamed to my lips, and my heartbeat thundered in my ears. *Was he doing this on purpose?*

"Night, Val." A smirk played on his lips as his gaze lifted back to my eyes. Slow. Covetous.

He didn't move until I said, "Goodnight, Luke."

I closed the door and leaned back against it. My fingers found my lips, my pulse still roaring. *Maybe my little crush on my boss isn't one-sided, after all.*

I think he wanted to kiss me just now.

And I wanted to let him.

An image of Max's goofy smile and wind-blown, light brown hair at the beach earlier today flashed through my mind like a tocsin. *I have a boyfriend,* I reminded myself. I wasn't allowed to want Luke to kiss me.

Guilt crashed over me like a bucket of ice water, dousing the flames I'd just felt down to nothing.

23

O ver FaceTime, I filled Natalie in on the last few weeks with Luna—baking cookies, getting her to work through her disappointment by singing "Defying Gravity" with me, reading *Magic Tree House* on the nights I stayed until bedtime.

"You are so in love with that little girl. It is so cute. Who knew you had this nurturing, maternal side," Natalie cooed, sipping her wine.

"I'm maternal! I've always said I wanted to have kids someday."

"I know, but that was conceptual; this is real practice."

"Well, I do love her. She's the best. And I'm totally turning her into a theater kid." I said it with pride.

Natalie shook her head lovingly. "Her poor dad."

"He's on board...I think." My cheeks tugged up reflexively thinking about Luke.

"I think you're in love with her dad, too," Natalie commented.

"I am not! I'm seeing Max, remember?"

"Yeah, yeah. Finance bro. You don't light up when you talk about him the way you do when you talk about Luke."

I scoffed. I loved that my best friend read me so well, but sometimes it was very inconvenient.

"Hasn't there been tension? Deep conversations? A little flirting?" she asked.

"Yes. I mean, I think so. But he hasn't given me any reason to think he'd ever act on it." By now I'd convinced myself his pause in the doorway to the guest room couldn't have been as loaded as I thought. "He knows I'm seeing someone. And he's...my employer. Wouldn't that be inappropriate?"

"Eh, I don't think so. I'm sure he wouldn't take it lightly, given the situation, but if there are real feelings there—"

"There aren't. We're just friends. And you're right, he wouldn't want to jeopardize the good relationship I've built with Luna and the working relationship I have with him. And I have a boyfriend, so, yeah, no 'real feelings' are happening." I added air quotes for emphasis.

"It sounds like you're trying to convince yourself as much as me." Natalie lifted her perfectly shaped brown eyebrows at me on the screen.

"That's not true!"

"You doth protest too much, babe."

"I *like* Max, and you'll like him, too. You guys can meet when you visit in a week and a half. He is so romantic. I've never been showered in praise and compliments like this before. It's so nice for a change. The other day on the beach he said, 'My life was just going along, linear, boring, and then suddenly, you were there, like a shooting star landed right in front of me.' He, like, inherited his dad's way with words. Isn't that so sweet?"

She poured another splash of white wine into her tall, stemmed glass and walked over to her dark blue, velvet couch while I spoke.

"It is..." she drawled, like she hadn't made up her mind yet. She took a sip of her wine and then stared at something off-screen.

"You hesitated," I accused.

"It just sounds familiar, like it's out of a movie or something." Her eyes squinted.

"That's my whole point! It's romantic."

"I'm happy if you're happy." She shot me a smile. "In other news, your return-to-work date is around the corner, right? Have you decided what you're going to do?"

I inhaled, inflating my chest, and then blew the breath back out. "Yes. I'm going to quit. For real."

"That's great! Why don't you sound more excited about it?"

"I know I don't want to go back, and that I want to keep writing. I guess I still feel like a failure. I'm *so* nervous to tell the partners and my other coworkers. And it makes me feel like the last ten years of hard work were a waste."

Natalie nodded, chewing on her lip. "If you end up regretting the decision, you could go back to another firm later. Or an in-house job. A resume gap is not a big deal these days. Look at Tyler—he already has an in-house job lined up for the fall, despite taking ten months off."

"That's true." I mulled it over. This decision wasn't as permanent as it felt. I could quit for now and take some more time to make sure it was what I really wanted. I was free to change my mind later, and my background and experience would still get me a job practicing corporate law somewhere else.

The vise on my chest loosened; relief expanded my lungs.

"Okay. I'm doing it," I said finally, a lilt in my tone.

Natalie's expression gleamed with pride, like somehow she knew I was doing the right thing.

Curling iron in hand, I was twisting a strand around the hot metal when my phone buzzed on the vanity in my room at Mimi's house. Max was due to pick me up in thirty minutes for dinner at some place he wouldn't share with me because he wanted it to be a surprise. I carefully placed the curling iron down and answered.

"I'm sorry, I can't make it to dinner anymore," Max said. "They moved my meetings from the afternoon to the morning tomorrow, so I have to fly back tonight."

"Oh, okay. That's fine. I understand. The client's schedule takes precedence." I'd been in his shoes before, so I didn't blame him, even though I was a little disappointed to miss out on this secret restaurant he'd been teasing.

"That's what I love about dating a lawyer—I know you get it. You'll be canceling on me in no time once you're back to crushing those private equity deals."

My stomach knotted. *I'm quitting on Monday.* Ever since my conversation with Luke and then with Natalie I felt like I was lying to Max. I needed to find a way to bring it up.

"Would you want to come to the city this weekend? I'd love to take you to this dinner we're doing tomorrow night. It includes significant others. It'd be fun to introduce my new girlfriend." He said it with pride, which only made me feel worse about my immediate reaction: dread.

"Oh, um."

"I know it's not that desirable compared to the Vineyard, but we could hit a rooftop bar, spend some time in my apartment..."

The desirability of spending a Saturday tangled in Max's expensive sheets wasn't enough to combat the unease I felt about going to a fancy networking dinner with his colleagues and clients. Part of me wished I'd met Max five or six years ago, when I still lived for the job and needed a boyfriend to support me but also not mind when I had to cancel plans or work all weekend long. We'd have been a great fit back then, but I was starting to realize that...maybe I wasn't the same person anymore.

"I don't think I can this weekend. I told Mimi we'd do something together. But thank you for the invite!" It wasn't a lie. Mimi and I had talked about going to buy some new plants before the rain came on Sunday, and I was looking forward to it.

A little alarm bell sounded from the recesses of my brain. *Are Max and I compatible?* it said. I pushed the thought down, assuring myself that I could enjoy those fancy client dinners again someday, once I'd recovered more, especially if it was Max's clients and not mine. *I'll say yes next time, if he invites me again.*

"Okay, no problem." He sounded disappointed. I almost changed my mind to please him, but he went on to say, "We could do something Sunday night, when I'm back?"

"Yes, that would be great."

"It's a date then. Wear that green dress I love. I didn't get to take it off you last time."

I grinned and shook my head even though he couldn't see it. "So bold."

"I can't see your face right now, but I think you're smiling."

"I might be," I sang.

"Good. Sweet dreams, Val. I hope they're about me."

I giggled at him this time, not holding it in. "I'll let you know. Night, Max."

I texted Luke the next morning.

VAL

> Can you recommend someone that could fix Mimi's front porch stairs? I think a few boards need to be replaced.

LUKE

> I'll come take a look this afternoon. What size are the boards?

VAL

> We can hire someone! And it's not urgent.

LUKE

> Board size please.

VAL

> 2 x 5.5

LUKE

> See you around 1:30.

I shook my head. Of course he would volunteer to do it

himself. I should have thought of that. I texted Mimi to let her know and got out of the car to go into the gym.

The gravel in the driveway crunched under Luke's truck tires at 1:20. He wore his usual uniform: jeans, boots, a ball cap, and a Karas Construction T-shirt. At least on days he didn't have client meetings. On those days, it was golf pants, a collared shirt, and a cleaner pair of boots. I liked knowing what he wore every day. I felt like I had some inside scoop that other people didn't have.

Instead of knocking on the door, he stopped in front of the steps. He examined them with a flashlight and tested each one by lifting them forcibly with his hand and then walking up and down them with heavy steps. I watched from the front window before opening the door.

"Luna's right," he said in greeting, "Mimi's flowers are better than mine."

"You should see the back," I teased.

"I don't know if I want to!"

"Do you need any help? I can...hold tools, or something."

"Nah, I'm good, but thank you." He walked over to his truck, dropped the tailgate, and pulled out his massive toolbox, arm muscles flexing. I stood in the threshold, watching.

When he turned and saw me standing there, his mouth quirked up. "Seriously, I got it. Go write, you."

I smiled. I loved it when he said things like that. "Okay. Come inside if you need anything."

He gave me a little salute before crouching down and opening his toolbox at the foot of the stairs. It was blazing hot, not a cloud in the sky, the sun beating down like it had a vendetta. I shut the front door and retreated to the safety of the air-conditioned living room.

Four hundred words flowed from my brain to my keyboard with an ease that resembled breathing. I was writing from the SEC investigator's point of view—a man I'd begun to picture with thick dark hair, brown eyes deep enough to get lost in, and a chiseled jawline that spoke of authority. In this chapter he finally admits to himself that he can't stop thinking about my main character after the case closes. It made me wonder if Luke ever thought about me when we were apart. Not that I should be pondering things like that. I double-checked that my document was saved, and next thing I knew, I was standing in front of the window.

Several boards were now missing from the stairs and a saw was set up on the tailgate. Sweat dripped down Luke's temples and pooled around the collar of his light blue T-shirt. He tossed the pencil he'd held between his teeth into his toolbox and lifted the hem of his shirt up to wipe the sweat from his face, revealing a tan, toned stomach. Dark hair dusted his chest before narrowing and traveling downward to his belt buckle.

"That's the best view I've seen out these windows in a while."

I jumped.

Mimi stood over my left shoulder, watching Luke, too.

"How long have you been standing there?"

She shrugged one shoulder and smirked unabashedly. "About as long as you have."

I huffed and shook my head. "Think he knows we're watching?"

As the words left my mouth, Luke took off the ball cap, removed the T-shirt entirely, and put the cap back on, backward. *Damn.*

"Yep," Mimi replied. "I think he likes you."

"He's just a good guy, Mimi. He'd do this for any neighbor or friend. And look at him." I gestured toward the window. "He could probably have any woman he wants." I often wondered why he wasn't dating anyone already. There had to be a number of single women on the island that would love to date him...

Mimi turned to face me, lifting my chin with her hand. "Look at *you*, my dear. You are astonishingly beautiful. Always have been." She smiled and gazed off, like her mind was traveling else-where for a moment. "Even when you were in middle school, you didn't have an awkward phase. You looked so darn cute in braces."

I laughed. I definitely had an awkward phase. "Thanks, Mimi."

"And the best part about you is your beauty isn't just on the outside." Warmth bubbled through me. Mimi had known me my whole life, so I should believe her, right? At a loss for words, I pulled her in for a hug.

After a moment of embracing her fragile frame, I said, "I had beautiful role models."

She pulled back and smiled at me. Then she tossed my hair, twirled it over my shoulder, and pinched both of my cheeks. "Now, go bring that man a glass of ice water."

I guffawed. Mimi, always with her eye on the prize.

"I have a boyfriend, Mimi."

"It's just a glass of water, Val," she sang as she walked into the living room.

I shook my head and entered the kitchen.

Water in hand, I stood at the top of the steps and watched him cutting the boards at the back of his truck. Sweat glistened on his bare, sculpted back, and his abs flexed each time he brought down the saw.

When he turned the saw off, he caught me staring.

"Enjoying the view?" He removed his safety glasses, and a smug smirk took over his face.

Shoot.

I shrugged, feigning nonchalance, and trained my gaze to Mimi's neighbor's house across the street. "Eh, it's just the same street and houses as it's been for thirty years. I like it, though."

He shook his head, seeing right through me, but he let me get away with it.

"I came out to bring you some water."

"Thank you." He set down the boards in the grass and leaned over the treacherous stairs to take it. His rough fingers brushed mine as he closed his hand around the glass. The spot on my fingers where he'd touched me tingled after I drew my hand away. It took all of my self-control not to watch him drink it.

I left through the side door when it was time to go get Luna from sailing. Wallet in my hand, I was pulling out a couple fifty-dollar bills when Luke said, "Don't even think about it."

I didn't realize he'd even seen me, let alone my wallet. "But I feel bad, it took your whole afternoon. You could have been doing something else."

"I didn't have anything pressing today, and besides, I like getting out from behind the desk sometimes."

I opened my mouth to object, to insist that I at least pay for the materials, when he added, "Seriously, Val. Do *not* try to pay me." His tone was low and final. I pushed the bills back into my wallet and shivered despite the heat.

"Fine. Thank you."

"You're welcome." A small, victorious smile appeared under his dark beard.

"See you at home?" I asked as I walked toward my bike. "I mean, your house," I corrected myself quickly.

He nodded, staring at me, face unreadable. "Yeah." He swallowed. "I'll be back shortly. Just finishing this and checking on one more site."

I waved and swung my leg over my bike, letting out my breath when I sat down.

That was quite the slip.

24

Sunday night, July 14. The night before my scheduled return-to-work date.

Max and I were at dinner at the Edgartown Yacht Club, this time just the two of us. The dining room had windows on all three sides, usually offering endless water views and a sea breeze, but today it was gray and stormy outside. Wood floors and paneling, blue and white wicker chairs, vintage ships' wheels hanging on the few walls that weren't comprised of windows—it was incredibly well-kept, but the old-fashioned, nautical vibe of this club hadn't changed since my earliest memories. That was probably why the long-time summer islanders loved it. Subtle, old-money elegance. And apparently, the only place a famous author could go to dinner.

Max had just returned from New York, and I'd barely seen him since the holiday weekend. It felt like more than just time had separated us over the last ten days, and I knew closing the gap would involve telling him I'd made up my mind that I wouldn't be going back to work tomorrow. But first, I needed a drink.

"I'm sorry I missed dinner with your friends when they were here over the Fourth," I said.

"It's okay." Max reached for my hand on the white-clothed

table. His blue eyes were soft, like he really didn't mind. I was about to let out my breath when he added, "We can see them whenever in the city."

I gulped a sip of my Cosmo, my stomach turning over. The martini glass landed half on, half off the coaster when I placed it back down, and I had to fist the entire stem with my free hand to stop it from tipping over. I'd told him I hadn't made up my mind about going back, hadn't I?

The scraping of cutlery against plates at the tables surrounding ours sounded like nails on a chalkboard as Max's eyes narrowed on me, like he understood something I hadn't said.

"I've been thinking about what you said, about the leave, and not being sure what you want to do. Why don't you just extend it through Labor Day, if you can?" he asked. "Even if it's unpaid, it's not that long. Then you can really enjoy the rest of the summer here. We'll go back to New York in September and start crushing it again at work. We can support each other, you know? I'll go to your events, you can come to mine." His eyes were bright as he rubbed his thumb over my hand affectionately.

Why didn't it sound good to me? I forced a smile before taking another big sip of my cocktail. The vodka burned slightly as it slid down my throat. They made the cocktails strong at the yacht club, I'd give them that.

Max watched me keenly, assessing my reaction. I glanced down at our intertwined fingers on the table. Would it make him happy if I agreed that what he described for me—for us— sounded perfect? But I couldn't say that. And I didn't know how to tell him I didn't want that without it sounding like I didn't want *him*. Why did he have to make it so much harder to tell him?

Before I could respond he added, "And then you can quit the nannying gig, really enjoy the last eight weeks of summer."

My brow furrowed in confusion. Why would I quit my job helping Luke with Luna?

I loved it.

And I couldn't quit on them. He could probably find someone

else, and the neighbor that usually helped him was getting back soon, but still.

"I wouldn't want to leave them in a lurch, especially if I'm staying on the island anyway."

"You could help him find a replacement. There must be tons of babysitters on the island. College kids staying with their parents," Max suggested. He dropped my hand and leaned back in his chair, sipping his gin and tonic. He nodded at someone passing by our table. The person stopped and shook Max's hand. He introduced me as his girlfriend with his trademark charming smile. He made small talk with this man who looked to be the age of Max's father, but I didn't hear the words.

The idea of someone else spending time with Luke and Luna —braiding Luna's hair, taking her to tennis, being in Luke's kitchen when he got home from work—made me nauseous.

I glanced back at Max, this handsome, charismatic man who'd plucked me from a crowd and pursued me, who'd made me feel beautiful and alluring at a time when I was still so down on myself in every way. But he didn't seem to get me at all. Not the version of me I was becoming.

We're at a crossroads, I thought as I swirled the light pink liquid in my martini glass and looked out the rain-splattered window at the roiling waves.

And I need to decide which way to turn.

I steeled myself, and as soon as the acquaintance moved on from our table, I said, "I'm going to quit."

His brows knit so hard it was condescending. "Are you sure you want to do that?"

I couldn't help the surge of defensiveness that rose within me like a tidal wave when he looked at me like that. Like I didn't know what I was doing.

"Yes. I've thought about it a lot. I don't want to go back. And I don't want to have a set return-to-work date hanging over me either."

He nodded, brow still furrowed.

I clenched my hands in my lap.

"I guess you don't care what I think about it."

I bristled. "That's not true. C'mon, Max. You have no idea how hard it was for me to make this decision, but it's the right one. I want a break, I want to write, I want to wake up every day and look forward to what I am doing that day, not *dread* it." I searched his face for some sign of understanding.

His blue eyes finally softened, but his words still weren't what I was hoping. "Alright, Val. It's your life. If this is what you need to do, then it's what you need to do. I just thought—" He stopped himself.

"You thought what?"

A deep breath left his throat. "That we were on the same page. We'd have fun here for the summer and go back to New York and our careers and keep seeing each other. It was sort of perfect really. I'm just disappointed."

Does he not want to keep seeing each other if I'm not a New York City lawyer anymore? I could still move back there and be a writer. But we weren't serious enough to be talking about moving for each other, so I didn't blame him for not bringing that up.

"I'm sorry," I said, although I wasn't sure what I was sorry for. He'd come up with this whole idea on his own based on things he assumed about me but never actually inquired about. "It's not that I don't want to see you; I just don't want to work for Peters & Dowling anymore."

"I know," he said, his expression inscrutable.

The awkwardness in the air was as palpable as the thick humidity that had settled over the island before the storm broke this afternoon. It didn't improve for the rest of the night as we fumbled through safer topics—the food, the weather, how his client meetings went and what Mimi and I did this weekend. Max usually seemed so pleased with me whenever we were together, and I couldn't tell if he was anymore.

By the end, I asked if he could just drop me at Mimi's, since I was stressed about tomorrow. I'd hoped he might say something encouraging when we parted, but he just kissed my cheek from across the console in his car and told me he'd text me.

I couldn't tell if he meant it, and I wondered how I'd feel if he never texted me again.

Relieved, maybe.

Laptop open on my lap in bed, the cursor hovered over an unsent email to Mallory requesting a meeting for tomorrow morning while guilt gnawed at me. She'd given me so many opportunities to work with our most established clients on high profile deals. My lungs took in a breath and held it as my trembling finger pressed Send. She'd been supportive about the medical leave, hopefully she'd be understanding about my departure, too.

And I can't make big life decisions based on guilt, I reminded myself.

"You shouldn't worry more about disappointing others than you do about disappointing yourself," my therapist said when I told her how guilty I would feel if I decided to quit. That advice resonated with me, like a long-awaited and hard-fought revelation. I'd repeated it to myself daily when the doubt slipped back in.

I tossed and turned in bed as fat raindrops pinged on the metal air conditioning unit in my bedroom window before giving up and turning on the light. I picked up my book, but after I'd read the same paragraph four times, absorbing nothing, I put it back down on the nightstand that Mimi and I had painted white ten years ago, during a summer while I was in college. I ran my fingers over the worn, chipped edge.

What would college-age Val think of me quitting my job tomorrow?

As I replayed my conversation with Max in my head, twisting and untwisting the sheets around my legs, my phone buzzed. I picked it up, expecting a text from Max, but instead Luke's name appeared on the screen, and my heart trilled. *I'm sure it's just something logistical for tomorrow*, I cautioned myself.

But it wasn't.

LUKE

> I know tomorrow's the big decision and you're probably freaking out. I wanted you to know that whatever you decide, Luna and I will be fine. You have a job with me as long as you want it, but we will figure it out if you don't. I think you should do what feels right. It will all work out.

I read the text three times, my eyes welling. He probably had no idea how much I needed to hear that.

Or maybe he did know, somehow.

I puzzled over how to respond. How could I tell him how much his encouragement meant to me without revealing too much?

I went with:

VAL

> Thank you so much for saying that. It's exactly what I needed to hear tonight.

LUKE

> Good. Try and get some sleep?

The question mark said it all.

VAL

> I'll try!

I fell asleep eventually but woke up at 3:00 a.m. feeling wired. *May as well start getting this over with.* I padded downstairs as quietly as I could, made a cup of coffee, and opened my work laptop for the first time in over three months.

I can do this, I told myself as my hands started sweating.

By 8:00 a.m. I had gone through hundreds of emails and set meetings with the partners I needed to tell about my departure. Palms damp, laptop burning a hole in my bag, I left for Luke's to get Luna.

When I got there, Luna was already ready, and they were both gathering their things by the door. "Hey, I meant to text you, I can take Luna to tennis this morning."

"Oh, okay." I was in a bit of a daze, exhaustion and anticipation battling for dominance in my veins. I made to turn back for my car.

"You have your work stuff on you?" He nodded at my bag.

"Yeah."

"Stay here. It's quiet and private, plenty of coffee."

I wrote at Luke's house a few afternoons a week anyway, so it wasn't as if I hadn't been alone here before, but for some reason this felt different. It was preferable, though. Mimi's walls were thin, and she usually slept until after 10:00 a.m.

"Okay." I offered him a half smile. He squeezed my shoulder with his large palm as he passed me on their way out the door.

"Good luck," he said, "it's going to all be fine."

"Thank you." I watched them depart. He ruffled Luna's ponytail lovingly as they walked toward the car and I smiled. I could hear Luna's voice in my head calling it a "boring ponytail." I made a silent promise to get here early enough tomorrow to put it in braids for her, if she wanted.

"Oh." Mallory's shock was clear from her widened eyes, her short intake of breath, and the pause she took before she said anything else after I told her I'd decided to put in my notice. "I'm saddened to hear that, Val. Of course you need to do what's right for you, but we'll miss you in the practice group."

Her surprise stung, but I resisted the urge to overexplain my reasoning. The call was short. There wasn't much else to add after I told her that I didn't have a new job lined up, that I was taking some time to figure things out. I appreciated that she ended things on a positive note, saying, "Give me a call if you change your mind, we rehire people all the time."

"Thanks, Mallory. I really appreciate your support and mentorship over the years."

Mallory was one of the people I'd miss. She'd been my role model for so long—the youngest female partner in the male-dominated practice group, balancing work and a family somehow. But she still only saw her kids for an hour or two each day, and only on the days she didn't have client dinners or evening conference calls. They had a full-time nanny.

I used to think that was what I wanted if I found a husband and started a family. But this summer, spending time with Luna made me realize that an hour or two on the less busy days wouldn't be enough for me. I respected that it worked for her, but it just wasn't something I could picture for myself anymore.

After I spoke to Mallory, Luke texted and said Clara's mom was taking the girls to lunch, and they were going to her house after sailing for a playdate.

He probably initiated those plans so I wouldn't have interruptions today. My throat tightened with gratitude. He was so busy, and yet he took the time to make this stressful day easier for me.

In between each call, my heart pounded so hard it felt like it might fall out of my chest and onto Luke's kitchen table. My breaths came in shallow, deliberate puffs, the air only reaching the top half of my lungs.

By midafternoon, I'd survived all but one of the necessary meetings. My resignation wasn't official until I told John, and of course he wasn't available until 4:00 p.m., so I puttered around the first floor of the house like an anxious, poorly programmed Roomba vacuum for over an hour until the clock struck 4:00.

"Val, are you in today? Feel free to come by my office if you are." I clenched my jaw. He could tell from my background that I wasn't, so it felt like a jab at me for failing to go into the office on my first day back.

"I'm not, actually. I've been having my meetings virtually today."

He nodded for me to continue.

I dove into the speech I'd rehearsed and repeated several times already. "I've decided to leave Peters & Dowling. I really appreciate the opportunities I've had while working here. I can't imagine starting my legal career anywhere else, but I'm planning to pursue other passions now."

"Did you get an in-house job somewhere?"

I took a deep breath. He wasn't the first partner to ask this. "No, I'm planning to take some time away from work to figure out my next steps."

"Oh." His eyes were wide with surprise. "It's a shame that the leave wasn't enough of a break. You've developed a valuable skill set, Val. The other partners and I had high hopes for your future here. But I understand that this work is just *too grueling* for some people." He paused for a moment, letting my stress-addled brain catch up to his words. *Oh, he means me.*

He spared me having to respond by adding, "If you do decide to seek an in-house job with one of our clients, let me know, and I'll see what I can do."

I fisted my hands under the table, steeled my expression, and forced the words "Thank you" out of my mouth. I should've known he'd say something that implied I was quitting because I wasn't good enough to keep ascending at his firm. I took a breath in through my nose. *Just keep your composure until you're off this call.*

"So, in terms of notice," I went on. "I know the typical time-frame is two weeks, but I'm not on any active deals right now, so I could do shorter."

"Think you can file all your emails and everything by Friday?"

"Yes."

I clicked the end call button after he told me "good luck" in a tone that left me wondering exactly what he meant by it. A deflated sigh heaved out from my chest. I hoped to never speak to him again.

My body was still vibrating, my breaths stilted.

It's done, I thought.
I'm done.
What now?

25

I stared at my screen until it turned to the screen saver and then turned black. My legs carried me to the fridge. My hands poured a glass of wine. My bare feet took me out to the deck. Wrung out like a washcloth that'd been twisted too many times, that was how I felt.

All the certainty I had drummed up leading into today had depleted with each confused look and pitying comment.

"The work is just too grueling for some people." John's condescending comment rattled through my brain on a loop. I spent my entire life trying to prove how smart and hardworking I was. But in the end, he was right. I couldn't do it. I was *"some people."*

I fixated on the half glass of pink wine on the wooden table, now glistening with condensation. The first few sips didn't provide the relief I was hoping for, and I'd forgotten about it while I ruminated.

The sliding door squealed open. I turned as Luke stepped out. "Hey," came the deep timbre of his voice, "I was hoping you'd still be here. How'd it go?"

I shrugged, a single, stubborn tear burning a stream down my cheek.

He sat down across from me, elbows resting on the table, leaning toward me, giving me his full attention.

A deep breath escaped my lips. "I quit."

His eyes brightened. "That's great, right?"

"I don't know. Yes. I mean, I made up my mind, and I'm glad I'm not going back but I also..." I shrugged again. "I feel like a failure," I whispered, like it was a secret I didn't want anyone but him to know.

"Val, you are not a failure. You changed your mind about what you want."

I nodded, pulling my lips between my teeth.

His head tilted back to the sky and then he stood abruptly, his large frame towering over me. "C'mon. Let's get out of here. I have an idea."

"What's your idea?" I asked even though I was already pushing my chair back to follow him inside.

"Do you trust me?" He pulled a cooler out of the pantry and added some ice packs, beers, and the nearly full bottle of my rosé from the fridge.

"Of course," I said, though my tone was skeptical.

He tipped his head toward the table. "Close that laptop and leave it behind."

Windows down and Rolling Stones on the radio, Luke drove his truck along the beach road that ran from Edgartown to the neighboring town of Oak Bluffs. I waited for him to pull into each open spot that appeared along the beach, but he kept driving, tapping his hand on the steering wheel, peering over at me every few minutes.

For the first time all day, my body relaxed, sinking deep into his passenger seat. It was hard not to let the salt in the air, the warm wind whipping in through the windows, and the views of the happy beachgoers and the Atlantic beyond lift my spirits.

At least I get to enjoy a full summer here.

The next time Luke turned to look at me, I smiled at him.

His cheeks tugged up too, his brown eyes glittering like he was keeping a secret. *So freaking handsome, this man.*

When we eventually passed a sign for Aquinnah and Menemsha—named for the island's Native Wampanoag roots—I figured out where we were headed.

"Are we going to Menemsha?" I couldn't conceal the excitement in my voice. I glanced at the clock on the dash: 6:30. The sunsets at the beach in Menemsha—a tiny fishing village on the western side of the island—were unparalleled. Mimi and I drove out there in May to try and catch a sunset, bringing sweatshirts and blankets, but it was so cloudy that we couldn't see anything. I leaned my head out the window. Clear blue sky stared back at me.

Reading my mind, Luke said, "We can stay for the sunset. Luna is all set at Clara's."

I wondered how long he'd planned this, or if he got the idea when we were sitting on the deck.

We rolled past the rock walls that lined the road. The farms and little houses zipping past us were so much more spread out on this side of the island. I envisioned the beach and the jetty and the little inlets of Menemsha. Drew and I used to hunt for crabs and other critters in the shallow, rocky inlet for hours when we were young. When things were simple.

"Did you ever bring Luna to that little inlet where kids always look for crabs?" I asked Luke, raising my voice enough that he could hear me over the wind and the radio.

"Oh, yeah. She loved it. Never wanted to leave. Pruned up like a raisin by the time I dragged her out."

I smiled, picturing it.

We parked at the end of the lot, where the sand spilled over the low wood retaining wall right onto the pavement. Some people were packing up after a day at the beach, and others, like us, were just arriving for the sunset. We backtracked to the fish market that sold only fresh, raw fish and plastic-wrapped, pre-made lobster rolls.

Luke bought us two rolls and guided me back out the door with a soft nudge of his fingers on my lower back that sent shivers up my spine.

We set up beach chairs near the rocky jetty, right above the line of seaweed left behind from high tide. Luke poured me a glass of wine into a red Solo cup. "Sorry, no fancy beach-worthy wine glasses."

"It's perfect."

He took out a can of beer for himself, cracking it open with a *snap.*

Warm wind blew in off the waves. A few children still swam in the water, their parents watching from the sand. A sailboat and a motorboat were anchored a hundred yards out from the frothy shore. It was much quieter here than in Edgartown Harbor, which boasted hundreds of boats on moorings and stakes, shuttles constantly traveling out and back, and fifty-foot yachts regularly docked near the yacht club. Despite the quaint beach's popularity with locals and tourists alike, Menemsha had maintained its fishing village vibes—like nothing had changed since the filming of *Jaws.* At the end of the jetty, the silhouettes of a few evening fishermen held their lines in the water.

I sipped the wine, the slight citrus notes bursting on my tongue, the tartness cleansing the back of my throat. It was impossible not to let the peacefulness of this place sink into my chest. My next breath came out as a shudder. Water filled my eyes.

I cried because I was relieved, and sad, and because I didn't have a concrete goal for the first time in my life and the uncertainty of it overwhelmed me. As much as I tried to talk myself out of it, I felt like I'd failed.

Luke squeezed my knee briefly but didn't look at me, somehow giving me both comfort and privacy while I had this moment. *Please leave it there,* I wanted to say when his fingers released. My body craved the warmth and the weight and the tethering effect of his hand on my skin. A minute later he silently handed me a napkin.

"Thank you." I laughed through the tears.

He peered over at me. "Wanna talk about it? We don't have to, if you want to just process. I'm content with silence."

He meant it. Our conversations were always easy, but he never spoke just to fill the air.

I watched the calm waves ebb and flow. "Part of me feels like there's something wrong with me, and that's why I couldn't do it anymore. I wasn't smart enough or hardworking enough to hack it. Other people could, but I couldn't, so they must be smarter or better or tougher than I am. That's what one of the partners said: 'The work is just too grueling for some people.'" I lifted my fingers to make air quotes. "I feel like it's a waste that I spent ten years of my life—more if you count college and high school—learning this skill and attaining this earning potential and now I might not use it."

I turned to face him when I finished speaking, and Luke's gaze pierced through me. His jaw flexed. "I don't think that's true at all," he said, adamant. "I have no doubt that if you decided your purpose and joy in life was to make partner at that firm, then you would have done it. I don't think it's that you can't, or that people who can are somehow better than you are. You just decided you want to do something different, something you seem to love more."

I closed my eyes and pictured it: making partner, the announcement, the fancy celebration dinner, the congratulations from colleagues. How would I feel? Proud of myself, sure. But would I be happy? Would it feel worth it to have spent a decade of my early adulthood crunched behind a computer screen, running on little sleep, barely being present for important events with family and friends?

No, I wouldn't all of a sudden be happy.

And no, it wouldn't feel worth it.

Maybe it was okay to want something different.

"You're right," I said. This time I felt like I believed it.

"And in terms of feeling like you're wasting those hard-won skills... Have you heard of the sunk cost fallacy?"

I chewed the inside of my cheek and shook my head.

"It's this economic psychological principle. Almost all people feel that if they've sunk a lot of resources into an endeavor, then the right thing to do next is to continue sinking resources into it, even if that's not rational and leads to a worse outcome."

I nodded. That was exactly how I felt.

"So that little devil on your shoulder telling you that you have to keep doing it because you already put so much time and effort and money into it might be totally wrong," he added.

His eyes searched my face.

My mouth curved up as the tightness in my chest loosened. "You're so right," I said again, the image of a little red animated devil on my shoulder making me smile.

My gaze swung back to the horizon. The sun was still high in the sky, reflecting off the gentle waves. I tipped my cup, swallowing a gulp of wine. I believed him, but that same uneasiness I'd been feeling all day slipped back in. Even if I wasn't a failure, even if it wasn't a waste, I'd still never felt this much uncertainty about who I was and what I was working toward.

"What else is on your mind?"

I turned my head to find Luke still looking at me, reading my face. *How can he always tell?*

"I feel like...like I don't know who I am without the job. It was such a big part of my identity—my whole identity, really—for so long. Now I have to redefine myself." I shrugged.

His brown eyes narrowed, dark eyelashes almost touching. "You haven't been a law firm associate the entire time I've known you, Val. So you may think that job was who you are, but I don't. Other than being impressed with your education, intellect, and drive, I've never thought about the fact that you're a fancy lawyer from some fancy law firm. No offense." He glanced at me.

I fought my smile.

"When I think of you, I think about how thoughtful and funny you are, how great you are with Luna, how perceptive you are with me. The way your face lights up when you talk about Mimi, or Broadway shows, or lobster rolls, the story you're writing, or anything else that you love." His own face lit up as he was talking about me, and I felt like my chest might crack open.

He was making me want to cry for an entirely different reason. *Is that really how he sees me?*

"Luke," I said softly.

But he kept going. "And you should see yourself with Luna. She reveres you. It's always Val this and Val that. Sometimes I'm like, what about me, Luna?" He laughed humbly. "And I'll tell you one thing I know for a fact: kids do not give a shit about careers and accomplishments. They care if you're kind and fun and attentive, if you make time for them and care about their interests. You're all of those things, too."

He shook his head, looking at me like I was something remarkable. "Caring for and about others seems to come so naturally for you. You're intuitive and creative and empathetic. Brilliant of course, but that doesn't mean you're obligated to apply that intelligence to winning the corporate race. You can apply it to whatever you want." He reached for my knee again, and I wanted to hold his hand there forever. "You're still ambitious, Val, you just want to do something else now, something you love, something that's on your own terms and lets you have a life in the meantime. The best decisions I ever made in my life were when I ignored everyone else and listened to myself instead."

I swallowed the lump in my throat. "Thank you."

He shrugged one shoulder, like it was no big deal, even though to me, it was the biggest deal in the world. "Just being honest."

"Still." I looked into his eyes, willing him to see how much his words meant to me. "Speaking of," I said after a moment, smiling. "I'm ready for my lobster roll now." I extended my hands.

A laugh bubbled out from deep in his chest. He took it out of the cooler and handed it to me, taking out his, too.

We ate in silence, both looking out. I savored the sweet, tender lobster pieces, lightly coated in mayo. How did something so simple taste so good?

I peered over at Luke when we were done. The beach chair was too low for his long legs. His arms wrapped around his bent knees, holding the beer can between them. Wind tousled his dark, wavy hair as he stared out at the water, giving me a perfect view of his chiseled profile. The question he asked me at Mimi's last week rang in my ears: *"Enjoying the view?"*

Yes, I thought now. *More than I should.*

As the sun plummeted, the wind gave the air a chill, raising tiny goose bumps on my skin. I rubbed my hands up and down my upper arms. Luke's eyes tracked the motion. Without a word he popped out of his chair and jogged across the sand back to the parking lot, calves flexing. His agile body made it look like jogging across sand was easy. Did he forget something in the car? He seemed to have thought of everything, as if this were a real date he'd been planning for a while.

I wish it was a real date.

He approached my chair silently. My notification he'd returned came in the form of a forest green hoodie dangling in front of me. I grabbed it.

"Thank you!" I squealed, relieved. My black cotton dress wasn't cutting it anymore.

"You looked cold."

He sat back down in his chair, stretching his tanned legs in front of him. He pulled a navy crew neck sweatshirt with the same logo over his head and then used both of his hands to push his dark hair out of his face. I slipped my head and arms into the hoodie. It smelled like pine and sawdust. *Like Luke.* The urge to pull it up over my face and breathe it in was instant. I schemed about how I could keep it for a while. Forever.

"Sorry, I'm a walking advertisement," he said.

I looked down at the *Karas Construction* logo on the top corner of the sweatshirt, a mirror to the one on his.

"I love it," I said, and his eyes crinkled in the corners in response. "Besides, you never know when you might meet a potential customer," I added.

"That's what I was thinking."

He refilled my Solo cup and cracked another beer. I soaked it in: the salty breeze, the unreal neon colors filling more and more of the sky as the orange sun continued its descent, the hum of relaxed conversations by relaxed people sitting around us, all enjoying the same spectacle that was a western-facing sunset with colors so fluorescent, it seemed impossible they came from nature.

My bare feet made little valleys in the pebbled sand in front of my chair while we talked about Luna's tennis and Natalie's upcoming visit and his housing project. He told me the town wasn't providing as much funding for the project as he'd applied for, so most of the construction costs would have to come out of pocket for Karas Construction, and they'd have to recoup the investment once rental income started coming in.

"I'm sorry, that's frustrating you're not getting the funding you originally planned on."

"It'll be fine," he said, unfussed. "We crunched the numbers, and it will just take us an extra year to get in the black."

A whole year? That sounded like a long time to me.

When the last strip of orange disappeared beyond the water line, I realized I hadn't thought about Peters & Dowling, or felt that stomach-plummeting self-doubt, since I took the first bite of my lobster roll, after Luke helped me see myself and my decision in a new light.

I turned to face him after the sun took its exit, expecting to see the neon lights splashed across his face. But he wasn't looking at the horizon—he was watching me.

"What?" I gushed.

"Just watching you watch the sunset. It was like you were watching an intricate scene in a movie and you didn't want to miss anything."

I bit my lip. "I just love them, I guess."

He looked at me with something like endearment. "Wanna get going?"

"Sure." I pushed myself up from the arms of the chair. "Luke?"

He turned his attention from the cooler back to me.

"Thank you. For this, for what you said. I—" I sucked in a fortifying breath, and then released it. "I feel like I can talk to you about things I don't usually feel comfortable discussing with anyone else."

"Me too." His gaze held onto mine for a heartbeat after he said it, and warmth filled my veins despite the chill in the air.

Something shifted between us tonight. I spent the whole car ride back wishing I could reach for his hand. Before I got cell service back and got Max's text—which said he was sorry and asked if we could hang out this week—I'd already made up my mind. I needed to break up with him.

I had real feelings for someone else.

I just hoped everything Luke said tonight meant he had them, too.

26

I climbed into bed that night playing and replaying what Luke said in my head, excited butterflies dancing low in my stomach. I wanted to write it down. All summer, he had made me feel so comfortable. I never felt like I had to put on appearances for him. I cared that he felt I was being responsible with Luna, but beyond that, I'd been completely present with him. Completely myself. When I was with him, with both of them, I wasn't in my head. I was just *there.*

The rattling of my phone on the wooden surface of the nightstand assaulted my senses. I snatched it up, my naive heart hoping the name on the screen would be Luke. It wasn't, but a smile still found itself on my face when I saw it said Natalie.

I rubbed my eyes and answered the FaceTime call. "Hi!"

"You know how I told you that thing Max said to you about the shooting star sounded familiar?"

"Yesss." I scooched up to lean against the headboard.

"It's because it's word-for-word pulled from *Never Forget Me!*" She flashed the paperback copy of one of our favorite Edward Phelps novels in front of her camera.

"You're kidding."

"Wish I was, babe."

"I'm sure it's only a coincidence? I mean, I didn't remember that part of the book."

"Tell me some of the other romantic things he's said to you."

"Hmm." I wracked my brain for examples. Max's courting style was flattery. *The quickest way into my insecure little heart,* I thought darkly.

"There was the shooting star thing. The other night he said, 'Sweet dreams, I hope they're about me.'" I combed through our conversations in my head, trying to remember the times he'd made me blush. "When he talks about the day we met, he says he thought I was the prettiest girl he'd ever seen, and he'd regret not at least finding out if I was single. But that's kinda standard flattery, right?"

"True. Anything else?"

I told her about the time he said to learn to take a compliment because there was more where that came from, that time he said he was in the company of a gorgeous woman on a gorgeous night, and let's pretend tomorrow is far, far away. My embarrassment climbed with each example I shared.

Natalie jotted the keywords down on her phone.

"Which Ed Phelps books do you have there?"

I climbed out of bed with a groan and padded over to the bookcase in the corner of the bedroom. "I have *The Impossible Dream, The Rest of Our Summers, Something In The Water,* and *Hope Against Hope.*"

"Okay, you take those. I think I have the rest."

I pouted. "I don't know how I feel about this."

"Your text a few hours ago said you're going to break up with him anyway, so what's the harm? I think it's kinda funny, in a slightly dark way..."

I pouted harder.

"I'm sorry, Val. If you don't want us to look, we don't have to."

"No, I'm curious now. And yes, I have already decided to break up with him. I just feel like...a sucker. Like I got faked out. I feel like next thing you know we'll find out it was some sort of bet."

"I doubt it. I think he just stole his game from his dad's books."

I grabbed *Hope Against Hope* from the shelf after we hung up and started rereading it. *I'd better not discover any familiar lines in here.*

I found one before I fell asleep.

The next night, Natalie and I were up until midnight on FaceTime, pouring over all our Edward Phelps paperbacks.

Sitting cross-legged on the floor of my bedroom, I read the words the male love interest said to the main character after their third date in *The Impossible Dream*.

"Shoot."

"Did you find another one?" Natalie asked, reluctantly lifting her head up from the paperback in her own hands.

I underlined the quote in pencil—*Introducing you as anything else just wouldn't feel right*—and read it aloud to Natalie. "That's what he said when he asked me to be his girlfriend."

"Damn," she said. I bookmarked this page with a tiny pink sticky note, closed it, and tossed it into the growing pile of similarly bookmarked paperbacks in the middle of the carpeted floor.

"I can't believe a real-life man said all these things to a woman he was pursuing, and it worked?"

"Yeah... It kinda worked," I admitted.

Natalie broke into a fit of giggles and then noticed the look on my face—a mix of embarrassment and awe. "I'm sorry, I shouldn't laugh. I honestly don't blame you. If a handsome, mature man said these things to me, I'd *swoon*."

"Ugh," I groaned, lying back on the floor and looking up at the ceiling.

"Don't you want to keep reading? See if there are others?"

Natalie asked, her voice emanating from my phone where it leaned against the stack of books.

"I think it's safe to assume the answer is yes at this point."

"Probably true... Hey, on the plus side, at least he likes romance novels? Not that it matters, since you're breaking up with him. But I'm sure he'll make some other romance novel-loving woman happy someday." She chuckled, obviously trying to lighten my mood.

"He likes them too much, Natalie, *far* too much. This is so ludicrous."

"Agreed. You literally cannot make this shit up."

"Unless you're Edward Phelps."

"Unless you're Edward freaking Phelps," Natalie agreed. She picked up another book from the unchecked stack on her coffee table and opened it.

Ever the charmer, but he couldn't even use his own words. And I fell for it, for a time. Shame washed through me, settling in my stomach like a stone.

For the rest of the week, I spent my writing time sorting and filing emails to the Peters & Dowling server—a permanent legal record of everything I'd worked on over six years. It was cathartic to go through it all, reminding me that while I'd chosen to leave this career behind, at least for now, I had done a lot in my time there. I'd worked on investments in companies that had gone on to change the status quo in their industry and negotiated mergers that led to new medical devices being distributed all around the world. I decided I was allowed to be proud of what I'd accomplished, even though I didn't want to do it anymore.

Telling the handful of associates I'd made friends with over the years was less nerve-wracking than telling the partners, but harder in some ways because I felt like I was abandoning them, especially the junior associates. But they were all supportive. Some even said they were jealous and wished they had the courage to quit, too.

I slipped my work phone back into my bag when Luna hopped into the backseat of the car Thursday afternoon, braids long since lost to the harbor winds.

"How's tennis going?" I asked as I turned right to get back onto Main Street and drive toward their house.

"Great! I still don't know if we can win, but we're getting better. I think we're a good team. And now Clara's my best friend at tennis *and* sailing." She shrugged, like it wasn't a big deal she had a best friend.

A dopey grin spread on my face. "You still working on her backhand?"

She nodded. "She's gotten a lot better. I have, too. But I think Rachel is still better than us at that." Luna scowled.

"You can keep working on it. When is the tournament?"

"August."

"You have plenty of time." I met her eyes in the rearview mirror for a second. "I think all the hard work is going to pay off."

When we got back, Luke pulled into the driveway next to us moments later.

Luna jumped out of the car the moment I put it in park. "Dad!"

"Hey, Luns." A smile took over his face as she launched herself into his arms, caring nothing for the bag in his hand.

He embraced her and kissed her temple. "How was your day?" He ran a hand over the back of her shirt. "I see you didn't capsize. Or you already changed."

Luke made eye contact with me over Luna's head and inclined his head toward the door—an invitation to follow them inside.

"Nope, didn't capsize. Pretty much everyone else did though."

He laughed as he put her back down in the walkway.

When we crossed the threshold he guided Luna by her shoulders to the staircase. "Go take your shower and you can watch Disney before dinner." Luna jogged up the stairs.

"That's some good negotiating. I often have to bribe her with a pre-shower snack," I said.

He chuckled. "I take that as high praise. It doesn't always work, but it's usually worth a try."

"I'll add it to my arsenal." We stood by the door, facing each other, no more than a foot apart. Neither of us moved farther into the house. The room fell silent, the air suddenly charged. I watched Luke's chest rise and fall. Were his breaths shorter than usual?

Did that evening at the beach change everything for him, too?

I tilted my chin up, lifting my gaze back to his face. His brown eyes were waiting for me, and time stood still while we just... looked at each other, words eluding us equally, until the squeak of the shower being turned on upstairs broke our trance.

Luke cleared his throat. "Do you have plans tonight? I bought a bunch of steak tips to grill. Mimi can join us, too."

"She has book club tonight. But I can stay."

He smiled like that was the best news he'd heard all week, and my heart stumbled. "Great," he said. "I need to respond to like three emails, then I'll be down. Don't go anywhere?"

I nodded, wondering if he knew how special he made me feel with that smile.

"Help yourself to whatever. You know where everything is," he called over his shoulder as he bounded up the stairs.

I hadn't seen Max since Sunday, and we hadn't spoken much either. We had plans tomorrow night, and that was when I planned to break things off. He already felt like a stranger. I also had this odd grudge against him for using lines from books to woo me. I wasn't sure why it bothered me so much, but it did. Even though it wasn't malicious, it ruined something for me. I felt commoditized.

When Luke got back down, he poured himself a glass of water and joined me on the couch.

"Do you play tennis?" I asked.

"No, I didn't have the forethought to stick Luna only in sports I actually know how to play. Jeremiah is a great tennis player, though."

"That's perfect! Ask him if he can make time for a few extra sessions with Luna and Clara? Luna says they need to improve their backhand skills to beat Rachel and her partner in the tournament at the end of the summer."

His brown eyes glittered, and I knew he was about to tease me. "Feeling a little competitive about girls' eight-year-old tennis, Val?"

"One"—I held up my pointer finger—"the word 'girls' in that sentence is completely irrelevant—"

He raised his hands in surrender. "You're right. Absolutely irrelevant. I need to get better at that, being a girl dad and all."

I fought the smile that had my cheeks tugging upward, both because of his lack of defensiveness and because him referring to himself as a 'girl dad' did something to my insides.

"And two"—I let my smile free—"I just want her to win, okay? Does that make me a bad person?"

"One," he mimicked me, a smile appearing on his mouth at his own cleverness. "There's almost nothing you could say that would make me think you're a bad person, and two"—he held up another finger, pausing for added effect—"in this specific instance, also no. I want her to win, too. I'll text Jeremiah tonight."

The urge to kiss that smirk off his gorgeous mouth hit me like a sudden gust, unprompted. Undeniable.

"I was thinking about what you said the other day, how the town isn't providing as much funding as you hoped, and it will take you that much longer to break even on your investment. What if you did a fundraiser?" I scanned Luke's face for his reaction as he chewed.

"A fundraiser." His expression revealed nothing.

I continued, undeterred. "Yeah, you know, sell tickets that cost more than the food, cash bar, an auction. Mimi calls them 'parties for a good cause.' She goes to one for the Martha's Vineyard Preservation Trust every summer." This idea came to me when Mimi mentioned that specific fundraiser over dinner last night.

"I'm open to it, but I don't know much about fundraiser planning. What do you think, Luna?"

Luna shrugged. She hadn't spoken for a while. Her hands were tucked under her legs and her plate was clear. It was obvious she was waiting to be excused from the table to go continue watching the movie she started before dinner.

"Go ahead," Luke said, gesturing toward the sliders.

"Thank you!" She popped out of her chair and took a step toward the door before pivoting quickly to grab her plate to bring inside.

"I wouldn't know where to start," Luke went on. "I've only ever gotten funding from business loans and investors."

"We do know an event planner..."

"True. We could see if she thinks it's something we could pull off and actually make money. I also don't love asking people for money..."

"I understand. But Luke, no one is obligated to come or to donate anything, so if people choose to, then it's because they want to. I think solving the seasonal worker housing issue is probably a pretty popular cause."

Luke pursed his lips to the side, considering. After a moment he said, "Okay, let's at least ask Francesca if she thinks we can pull something like that off. I'll see if she's free for lunch tomorrow."

"Can I come? I mean, if that's okay? I've been wanting to hang out with Francesca again and helping brainstorm ideas for an event sounds kinda fun. My last day at Peters & Dowling is tomorrow." In fact, I planned to go to the post office and mail my firm laptop and phone back to Peters & Dowling LLP by noon.

"Of course. This is perfect, actually. She keeps asking me to give you her number, and I keep forgetting. She says she wants to be friends with you."

"Really?!" I squealed. I liked Francesca, and I loved the idea of having a friend that lived on Martha's Vineyard full-time.

"Yes, really." Luke laughed, eyes crinkling in the corners. The orange hue of the sunset reflected off the angular planes of his face as he shook his head slightly.

My enthusiasm rang clear in my voice when I said, "I like this plan."

27

The high of the positive response Luke and I got from Francesca about the fundraiser over lunch came to a swift end when I pulled into Max's driveway later that evening. Resolute in my decision to end things, I nevertheless hated the idea of disappointing him. "You can do this," I whispered to myself as I opened the car door. *And don't delay with pointless small talk.*

When we got up to his apartment, I blurted, "I don't think we should keep seeing each other."

His eyes widened like he'd been slapped, and then he gave me that condescending brow furrow again. "What do you mean you don't want to keep seeing each other?"

"I just don't think we have very much in common," I rushed to explain. "And you haven't been all that supportive about what I've been going through with my career. It's made me feel like we aren't a great fit, after all." I wanted to be honest, and hopefully part on okay terms. I wasn't planning to bring up the recycled Edward Phelps lines he used on me, even though that bothered me enough to make me more than certain breaking up was the right thing to do.

He ran a frustrated hand down his face, and his voice was

laced with incredulity when he said, "Really? I take you on all these nice dates, text you constantly, invite you to the city... And now *you're* dumping *me*?"

The condescension in his tone snapped my nervousness in half, and anger flooded in to replace it. Where did he get off being so surprised? Obviously, his last question was meant to be rhetorical and insulting, and I took it as such, which was probably why I threw up my hands and said, "You used your dad's romantic lines to make me like you! They were all copied from his books! Were any of the compliments real?"

"Isn't that what all women want to hear, Val? So sue me for trying to be romantic. Jesus!" He paced in front of me.

I stayed within a few feet of the door.

All women.

Tears filled my eyes when I realized all at once it wasn't really me that he liked, but a set of assumptions he made about me. An attractive lawyer, someone he thought he could bring to parties and client events, make her fall in love with him by showering her in compliments that *all women* want to hear. *Am I really that insecure?* I wrapped my arms around my torso—putting up a barrier, making myself smaller.

Misinterpreting the tears, he said softly, "Hey, why don't we work through this? I know you're going through a rough patch, but I'm sure it's temporary. We can stick it out."

I shook my head and swallowed, taking a step backward toward the door. "I'm sorry, Max. I don't want to."

His eyes flared with anger. "Really?" He laughed darkly. "This is unbelievable, Val. Whatever. Good luck finding someone better when your life is such a mess."

His words stung, and my eyes widened with hurt.

"Fuck, Val. I'm sorry." He reached out, and I recoiled.

"We aren't good together, Max. We just aren't. I don't regret anything; I had a great time with you this summer, but you'll have to find what you're looking for with someone else."

I fled before he could try to talk me out of it again. Tears threatened as I jogged to my car. I willed them down until I was safely back at Mimi's house.

Thank goodness Natalie's flight was arriving in two hours.

Natalie's black curls bounced into my face as I embraced her at the airport. Had it really been months since I'd seen her?

"I'm so happy to be here and get out of the baking concrete that is New York right now. I seriously need a summer home somewhere. And a new, fully remote job," she jabbered as we drove to Mimi's house.

"No kidding."

"Sooo, how do you feel? You're a free woman!" she said.

"Do you mean free from BigLaw or single?"

"Oh my god, right! You just broke up with him. Tell me everything."

I relayed the whole conversation to her. She nodded and gasped, "He did not!" at one point, but otherwise listened silently until I was done.

"Your life is not a mess, Val," she said, honing right in on the words that hurt the most. We'd parked a few minutes ago to pick up lobster rolls and a few bottles of wine to have with Mimi when we got back.

"Thanks." I smiled at her. But I didn't fully believe it.

I didn't regret my decision—to leave Peters & Dowling or to break up with Max. But his words had played on a loop in my head for the last few hours and I couldn't help but feel there was a kernel of truth to them. I had no real job. I was living with my grandmother, pretending to be a writer when I had no relevant experience or schooling for it. At thirty-one with a doctorate level of education, my main source of income was babysitting.

Maybe he was right.

My life is a mess.

I buried the thoughts down as deep as I could, looked back

over at Natalie, and forced a smile. I refused to let him ruin my weekend with my friend.

"Did Val tell you Luke came over and fixed my front steps the other day?" Mimi told Natalie, her eyes glittering with mischief. I knew exactly what she was trying to start.

Sure enough, Natalie's light brown eyes whipped to my face. "No, she did not!"

I lifted my palms, fighting a sheepish grin. The sweet, buttery lobster rolls, fizzy prosecco, and self-perpetuating conversation with two of my favorite people had broken through my sour mood, and by the time we retreated from the dining room to Mimi's sunroom I was feeling relieved more than anything.

"That was nice of him. How'd that come about?" Natalie asked.

"I asked him to recommend a contractor or one of his guys who could do it, and he insisted on doing it himself."

"He's a contractor too, right? Works in construction?"

"He owns the business actually, and he has an MBA."

Her eyes widened with glee. She tucked her legs underneath her on the couch, settling in. "Ugh, I love a white collar, blue collar man," Natalie said. "Mmm," she hummed like she'd taken her first bite of a delectable dessert.

I laughed at her.

"What? I am so sick of the men in New York. Maybe I'll move here, too."

"What does a 'white collar, blue collar man' even mean?" I asked, smirking. I missed her so much.

"You know exactly what I mean. Right, Mimi?"

"Mmhmm," Mimi sang, nodding for emphasis, enabling her.

I shook my head.

"He knows his way around a spreadsheet *and* a toolbox. Like yes, please talk dirty to me about contracts and supply and demand while you fix my shower head." My smile widened with every image. This was getting oddly specific, but she was on a roll, so I didn't dare interrupt. "His muscles come from manual labor and not just the gym, and his hands are always a little *rough*." She waggled her eyebrows suggestively as she said 'rough.'

"You're ridiculous, you know that?" I shook my head again and attempted to tame my smile as I wondered if his hands were, in fact, always a little rough. The time he tentatively rubbed aloe into my shoulders or put his hand on my knee at the beach hadn't been enough contact to form an opinion on the subject. I needed more data points.

"Oh, give me a break, like you haven't thought the *exact* same thing since you met him." She waved her hand in my direction dismissively.

I bit my lip but didn't protest. She could always tell when I was lying, anyway.

Mimi the traitor said, "Val watched him from the window for most of the time."

"You did, too!" I defended.

Mimi shrugged, completely unashamed.

Natalie erupted into giggles and tipped over on her side on the couch. I laughed too, infected by their energy—these two women I loved so much—not caring one bit that their entertainment was at the expense of my crush.

We all stayed up talking until midnight.

"I need a drink," Natalie said.

After a day of shopping downtown, we'd come back to Mimi's and settled in on her back deck. She'd just finished telling me about the hospital merger she closed recently. While she hadn't had to put in as many hours as her outside counsel, she still needed to be available around the clock to get it done. "I did not miss those types of deals, and I hope I don't have to work on another one for a long, long time," she'd said.

Her story brought back dozens of unhappy memories and a surge of relief that I wouldn't be working on anything like that for the time being.

"Welp, when life gives you lemons..." I held her gaze.

"Make Paper Planes!"

A wave of nostalgia and a deep craving for the boozy cocktail hit me at once. Tyler was always trying to get Natalie and me into whiskey in law school, and we didn't like it. His solution? Paper Planes. Bourbon mixed with Amaro Nonino, Aperol, and fresh lemon juice. It was slightly sweet and bright and shockingly refreshing.

We raided Mimi's well-stocked bar cart in the dining room, finding almost everything we needed. "Mimi, do you have Aperol?" Natalie called into the living room.

"Check the hutch," she answered. An unopened orange bottle greeted us when we opened the wooden door. "I'll have one too!"

We drank two rounds of cocktails with Mimi before she all but shooed us out the door. "You're too young to stay in with me all night. Go out. The Wharf will be packed with young people tonight," she'd said.

Natalie and I split one more Paper Plane to bring upstairs and sip while we got dressed. She helped herself to my closet, tossing each dress she deemed a worthy contender onto the bed.

"Oh, this. This is gorgeous." She pulled out the green dress I wore on my first date with Max. "And the green with your eyes." She kissed her fingertips. "But maybe a little too classy for tonight." It returned to the closet.

I ended up in a dark purple dress with a cowl neck and two slits, one on each side of my legs. Natalie wound up in one of my go-to little black dresses that highlighted her curves perfectly. I should just give it to her.

"I can't believe we lived in New York City for six years and almost never went out to the clubs," I said as we walked down Main Street. At 9:30 most people were on their way home from dinner, but a line had started outside The Wharf—a seafood restaurant by day, dive bar/club by night.

They'd cleared the tables in the back of the restaurant and a DJ was set up in the corner. A long bar spanned the length of the room in the back. We navigated in that direction.

My heart caught in my throat when I saw the most handsome brown-haired man I'd ever seen in my life leaning against the dark wood bar. The sight of him made every nerve ending on the surface of my skin prickle with awareness. And for once, I didn't feel guilty about it. *God bless Natalie for making me wear the hottest dress in my closet tonight.*

Not once had it occurred to me that I'd run into him out on a Saturday night. But we didn't talk much on the weekends, so I didn't know what he usually did. Maybe he went out all the time.

Who was watching Luna?

By the time my mind ran through its stream of questions he caught me looking at him. First, a hint of surprise. Then, a smile that spread across his face like a reflex.

I smiled back just as broadly and stopped walking for a moment. His grin was infectious, and I had this feeling I could look at that stunning face—his dark eyes alight, that wide, easy smile—forever.

He waved us over and I grabbed Natalie's hand to weave through the growing crowd on the dance floor. "That's Luke," I said. Natalie's head swiveled and she found him right away, gaping. He was wearing a black T-shirt, shorts, and those boat shoes. I could see the tattoo on his shoulder peeking out from under his sleeve. His dark brown hair was tousled, but his beard was trimmed and tidy. He was the tallest one in the group of guys he was standing with. I didn't blame Natalie for staring. *He looks hot.*

"That's him?" Natalie asked, shocked.

"Yep."

"Wow," she said as we closed the gap between us, waiting,

probably deliberately, until we were in earshot to add, "you told me he was handsome, not that he's a Greek *god*."

Luke's lip ticked up. *He must have heard her.* We were two and a half strong cocktails deep at this point, so we weren't being particularly quiet, even with the music blaring.

"Hi!" I shouted. "This is my friend Natalie. Natalie, this is Luke."

"Hey, nice to meet you." She took his hand. "Thanks for keeping my friend here gainfully employed."

"She's very employable," he said, licking his lips and flicking a glance in my direction.

I tried—and failed—to bite back my smile. *What does that even mean?*

Luke introduced us to his friends—Jeremiah and one of their other friends from college who was visiting and apparently the instigator of this night out. Natalie and I ordered vodka sodas and lingered by the bar with them.

"Good thing Auntie Francesca was willing to babysit," his friend—his name was Clark—clapped Luke on the back.

I pouted.

"What's that face about?" Luke asked.

"I'm jealous. Do you think she likes Francesca more than me?" I whined. I had no idea where this stream of consciousness admission was coming from.

"Are you an *in-your-feelings* drunk? Because it's kind of adorable." His smile seemed like it was just for me. "Also, it's not a contest. My kid can have more than one female role model."

"You think I'm a role model?" I squeaked. That was such a nice thing for him to say. *I don't know if I'd consider myself a role model. I did fail at my job, after all.*

"Of course," he said, furrowing his eyebrows like it was a silly thing to ask.

I beamed at him. He was so nice. And nice to look at. And strong. And sensitive. *Damn, I'm drunk. I should get out of here before I embarrass myself.*

The music changed to one of our favorite songs from law school and Natalie grabbed my hand. "The dance floor beckons!" she said.

"You coming?" I called over my shoulder.

Luke shook his head. "Yeah, no," he drawled. "I don't do"—his hand gestured in the direction of the dance floor—"*that.*"

I popped my shoulder up as if to say, *suit yourself*, and followed Natalie into the crowd, hips swaying.

I looked over after a song and made eye contact with him from across the room. He was leaning an elbow on the bar, a beer in his hand, not even pretending he wasn't watching me dance. My stomach somersaulted.

Clark and Jeremiah joined us on the dance floor for a few songs, and then I made my way back to the bar to get us more drinks, pulled like a magnet to Luke.

"I didn't expect to see you here tonight," I said.

"Not my usual scene, but my friends drag me out a couple of times a summer."

I nodded, watching his face for longer than I'd dared to in the daylight.

"Where's your boyfriend tonight?" he asked. The slight flush on his cheeks told me he might be a little drunk, too. His eyes moved slowly from my face to the rest of me, raking down my body and back up again. Unrestrained. I could melt under the heat of his gaze.

Butterflies filled my stomach. *This is my chance to tell him.* With the way he was looking at me, I wanted nothing more than to confirm I was single now.

But I didn't get the chance. My best friend's familiar arms wrapped around my shoulders, one hand taking a full drink from the bar in front of me and the other pulling me back into the crowd.

I woke up the next morning with a pounding headache and a smile on my face.

I'm pretty sure Luke said I'm adorable last night.

28

S itting at Luke's kitchen table two days later, my throat tightened as my fingers flew across my keyboard.

I wanted to believe everything Luke had said to me when we went to the beach the day I quit—the myth of sunk costs, that it was valid to choose to exit the corporate race and pursue different passions—so badly, but Max's words still struck a nerve. I told my therapist about Max calling my life a mess, and as my therapy homework, Wendy recommended I write about some of my experiences at Peters & Dowling as a way to process my departure.

It was more difficult to find the words to describe my fainting incident in John's office than I imagined it would be, and as I wrote each painstaking word, my shame came roaring back, but also my indignation. Articulating it in detail helped me see what happened through a more objective lens. I didn't deserve the dressing-down he gave me. I'd been working so hard, and I hadn't made any mistakes or missed any deadlines.

By the time I got to the part where I'd turned to flee but couldn't make it to another office fast enough to stop myself from fainting, it was hard to swallow, and my eyes were full. Writing it felt like reliving it—the panic, the embarrassment. My pulse thundered in my ears, just like it did that day.

"Val?" Luke's voice called from the front hall, making me nearly jump out of my chair, my psyche yanked suddenly from the fiftieth floor of Peters & Dowling's New York office back to Luke's house in Edgartown. He rounded the corner toward the kitchen and said, "You know, I'm starting to get—" I tore my eyes from the screen. He stopped when he saw my face. "Hey, what happened?" His brow furrowed, voice laced with concern. "Did you get bad news?"

I shook my head. "No." My voice was hoarse. "Sorry." I cleared my throat. "I was just writing something that made me kind of emotional." But Luke's presence was already having a calming effect on my nervous system, causing my pulse to quiet. *How does he do that?*

He closed the distance between us. "Wanna talk about it?"

"It's okay." My forced smile was weak and unconvincing.

"Well, I want to talk about it, if you think it would help. But I understand if you don't want to tell me." Worry was written all over his handsome face.

Suddenly, I did want to tell him.

"My therapist told me to write about some of the events leading up to my burnout. She said she thought it would help me process them and make peace with the decision to leave. In addition to being a good writing exercise, since she knows I've been writing."

Luke nodded, clearly following along with every word.

"I was writing about something that happened at work the week before I left, and it brought back some...feelings."

"What happened?"

I wasn't sure how to explain it. But of course, I just had. "Want to read it?"

"If you want me to."

I nodded and turned the laptop toward him. He sat down and pulled it closer. I watched as his pupils moved side to side, his face almost immediately turning cold. His brow furrowed deeper, his lips a thin line. I knew when he was done because he stood up from the dining chair violently. It fell over with a slap.

"This really happened?" His tone was menacing. I could tell he wasn't asking whether what I wrote was the truth, but expressing disbelief that it happened at all.

"Yes."

"What the fuck? I can't believe he said all those things to you, made you so upset you fainted." He started pacing, fists clenched at his sides. "What a sexist piece of shit." His hand reached up and gripped the back of his neck. "I'm sorry. I feel like I'm supposed to be supportive right now, but *that*"—he pointed at the computer—"pisses me off. No wonder you left. Fucking assholes."

I bit my trembling lip, my eyes welling. It was so validating—his reaction, his wrath. Just like when Drew said John was a sexist asshole, implying the ridicule wasn't my fault. I didn't believe him at the time, but I was starting to.

I was about to say thank you when Luke took in my expression. In an instant he picked up the chair and dropped back into it. "Oh no, she's crying again. Um, fuck." He pushed both hands into his brown locks. "I don't know how to say the right thing."

"No, no. It's not that, your reaction"—I shook my head and wiped away the tears, replacing them with a reassuring smile—"it's validating. It makes me feel like...like it wasn't my fault. I was so embarrassed, I didn't want anyone to know. I thought it made me weak, proved I wasn't cut out for the job after all."

He rubbed his thumb over the back of my hand, and a feeling of safety—the opposite of panic—emanated through my body from the spot where our skin touched. "You're not weak, Val. That's called a hostile work environment."

I nodded, willing myself to believe him.

His soft eyes searched my face.

"It was the perfect thing to say. All of it."

"Ha," he breathed. "Good." He leaned back in his chair but didn't let go of my hand.

The afternoon light streaming in the kitchen window reflected off the countertop behind Luke like a mirror.

After a moment he added, "That's some damn good writing, Val. Who knew two pages of text could infuriate me so much I nearly broke one of my own dining chairs."

I bit the insides of my lips, a smile begging to break free. "Thanks, Luke." Relief coursed through me, my heart rate long steadied.

He left his hand on mine, like he had nowhere he'd rather be. I stared at the tanned fingers, noted the roughness of his callouses. *My anchor in this confusing storm of mine.*

"What were you going to say when you got home, before you saw I was upset?" I asked softly, voice still a little hoarse. I lifted my gaze to his face, wondering if he'd remember.

His chocolate eyes bore into mine. His jaw flexed, like he was questioning whether to tell me. "I was going to say...I'm becoming addicted to seeing you at my table when I get home every day."

My breath caught, and those brown eyes begged me to admit that I was addicted, too. I opened my mouth. And then my alarm sounded, my phone vibrating violently on the wooden surface of the table. I exhaled. "We need to go get Luna."

29

It'd been two days since Luke told me he was getting addicted to seeing me when he gets home, and for some reason unknown even to me, I haven't told him I'd broken up with Max. I played Luke's comment over and over in my head, exhilaration swirling through my insides each time. I stirred the vegetables I was sautéing on Mimi's stove, psychoanalyzing myself. *Why am I reluctant to tell him I'm single now?*

No longer emboldened by alcohol and wandering eyes, I was afraid to find out if the flirtation between us was the crackling surface of something real, or just for fun. I didn't know if he dated or was interested in dating. He'd never talked about it. And even if he did feel something, I worried he wouldn't want to risk it, given how well things were going with me babysitting Luna for him.

Mimi was due home any minute from running errands with her friend Cathy. Cathy had been one of Mimi's closest friends on the island for as long as I could remember. She often reminded me that she's known me since I was a child digging for crabs and other critters at the beach.

My phone buzzed on the table. I turned the burner down and grabbed it. It was Cathy.

"Val, everything is okay now." My stomach dropped. "But we're at Vineyard Hospital."

The room froze as my panic spiked. "What happened?"

"We were at the store, and your grandmother started to feel faint. Before we could find her somewhere to sit, she collapsed."

"Did she hurt herself?"

"No, just a bruise on her arm. She didn't hit her head or anything."

"I'll be right there."

I turned off the stove, threw on flip flops, and ran out the door.

An hour later I sat in a chair next to Mimi's bed while she rested. The doctor said she was only dehydrated, and there was nothing to indicate the fainting spell was caused by her heart. She'd had an arrhythmia in the past, so of course that was immediately where my mind went as I drove five miles an hour over the speed limit on the way here. I called my mom on the way. My family was visiting us starting that weekend, and my mom changed her plans so she'd arrive tomorrow instead.

They planned to give her fluids, run a few tests, and monitor her for the next twenty-four hours, but expected she would be released by tomorrow morning. Mimi herself was fine—personality fully intact, embarrassed that people were making a big deal out of it.

Sitting here, looking at the monitors, leg bouncing, I was beyond uncomfortable, and it had nothing to do with the hard plastic chair beneath me. Mimi's personality was so youthful, I sometimes forgot she was in her eighties. She'd long felt more like a friend than my grandparent, always showing interest in my life, my friends, and my boyfriends, and sharing stories of her own. She stayed strong through grieving my grandfather, but that had to have taken a toll on her. Aging was so cruel. I usually made it to Martha's Vineyard at least once per summer, but I often spent most of the time upstairs in the spare bedroom, hunched over my laptop, stressing about whether the internet would hold. I shook my head at the memory. With Mimi's age, who knew how many more summers we'd have together. *I can't believe I missed some.*

I chewed the inside of my cheek until it hurt, willing the moisture in my eyes to evaporate before it escaped. My legs carried me out of the room to the hallway. I closed the door to give her a shred of privacy. Hospitals were so revealing.

I dropped into a chair a few paces beyond the door to her room and stared at my phone in my lap. Calling my mom again wouldn't be productive. She was already upset, and I didn't have any updates to share. Still, I opened my contacts. Acting on natural impulse more than conscious thought, my finger tapped Luke's name.

He answered on the second ring. "Hey, Val."

I heard a second "Hi, Val" in the background from Luna and a smile cracked through my somberness.

"What's up?" he asked. I took a deep breath before answering, and he added, "You okay?"

I blew out my breath and steeled myself. "Yes, I'm fine, but Mimi had an episode, felt like she couldn't breathe while she was at the store, fainted. She's okay now, the doctors said she was probably just dehydrated. I'm waiting outside her room while she rests before they run a few more tests. I—I don't know why I called, actually."

"Because you're upset, and you need a friend right now. Pretty normal thing to do, Val. I'm glad you called."

For some reason his kind words made my eyes well up. My throat constricted. "Thanks, Luke," I choked out, hoping he couldn't hear the tears in my voice.

"Have you eaten?"

"No. I was cooking us dinner when Cathy called me. I'm too emotional to eat anyway."

"How about this, Luna and I will come by and check on you

and Mimi, and I'm bringing you both dinner, in case your appetite comes back. Okay? The hospital food sucks."

I opened my mouth to object, but something told me Luke wouldn't take no for an answer even if I did. He phrased his suggestion like a question, but there wasn't any uncertainty in his deep tone.

I sniffled. "Okay. If Mimi wakes up while you're here, I'm sure she'd love to see Luna."

"It's settled then. See you soon."

The book I attempted to read on my phone while I waited didn't hold my attention for long. I poked my head into Mimi's room a couple of times and found her sleeping.

The pitter-patter of a child's footsteps down the linoleum-tiled hallway announced Luke and Luna's arrival. Luna threw her arms around my neck, my shoulders at the right height for her arms while I was seated—saying nothing. I started to choke up again but banished the feeling quickly.

"Hi, Luns," I cooed. "Thank you."

"Is Mimi okay?"

"Yes, she's okay. Let me go see if she's awake, and you can go see her."

"Okay! I brought my book." She held up a *Magic Tree House* paperback like it was a trophy.

I smiled. "That was a great idea."

When I looked into the room again, Mimi was up, changing the channel on the TV. "Are you up for a petite visitor?"

"Of course."

I told Luna to come in. She plopped right down in the chair next to the bed and asked Mimi if she wanted to read *Magic Tree House* with her.

"Oh, yes," Mimi said, her smile encouraging.

I stepped out of the room again, closing it only halfway. Luke had set down the soft-sided cooler he brought with him on the chair. I didn't know what to say. *Thank you for coming when I called?*

I missed you in the three hours that have passed since I last saw you?

"Hey," Luke said softly. It was less of a greeting and more of an invitation as he opened his broad arms and tipped his head in a way that said, *come here.* Pulled by an invisible thread, I stepped into him, and he wrapped his arms around me without hesitation, holding me flush against his body. I rested my cheek on his chest, letting out a full breath for the first time since I flew out Mimi's front door. The next breath in was Luke: pine and a hint of sawdust and warmth. The sound of his heartbeat filled the ear I had pressed against his shirt. His arms tightened around my back.

It was not a friendly hug. This embrace spoke its own language —sturdy and true and full of care. I kept a tight lid on the pressing emotions crackling beneath the surface of my chest—my panic about Mimi's wellbeing earlier, my somber thoughts about her age, my mom's fear when I told her, all mixed with the relief and comfort and safety I felt when I let myself lean on the man before me.

I refused to let the emotions bubble out while he held me. Although, I suspected he wouldn't mind if I did.

He ran his palm over my hair, from the crown of my head to the spot between my shoulder blades, before stepping back. He looked at my forehead and bit the inside of his cheek. If that meant he wanted to kiss it, I wished he would.

"Thank you," I whispered.

"Don't mention it. Least we could do. Is your appetite back at all?"

I looked down at my stomach, waiting for it to tell me. The sound of Luna reading her book out loud to Mimi floated out the open door. "Maybe?"

He nodded to the row of chairs and sat down, then handed me a fork and a Tupperware container filled with rice, beans, peppers, and grilled chicken he'd sliced and placed on top. The scent of cumin and chili powder wafted up to my nose, and my stomach grumbled.

"This smells really good."

He did a mock bow, twirling his hand and dropping his head.

I took a bite, consciously chewing. "Max and I broke up," I blurted.

Cool, Val. Way to ease into it.

I checked his face for his reaction. He pressed his lips together like he was fighting a smile, but the little crinkles around his eyes gave him away. I didn't know what I expected, but my stomach somersaulted nonetheless. Then he schooled his expression to neutrality and cleared his throat.

"Are you...upset?"

So diplomatic.

"No, I'm relieved. It was enjoyable for a while, and I kept waiting for it to grow, but it never did. We didn't really click, you know?"

Not like I do with you.

He nodded and didn't say anything for a moment. His eyes followed a nurse that strode by in front of us in a blur of lavender scrubs.

"That makes sense," he said finally. His brown eyes met mine, but I couldn't tell what he was thinking.

I wanted to say more, but it wasn't the right time or the right setting. He seemed to tacitly agree. "Want to bring this in to Mimi? See if she's hungry?" He gestured to the other Tupperware he had in the cooler.

"Yes. Thank you so much for doing that."

He squeezed my knee for a millisecond before I stood. "Of course. We wanted to."

I believed him.

By noon the following day, Mimi was at home, released with a clean bill of health and a daily water intake requirement. By 2:00 p.m., I'd picked my mom up from the boat. Luke had insisted I take the day off, saying he had a light day and could take care of Luna's drop-offs and lunch hour.

After Mom's arrival, the three of us went to the beach in the early evening with our books and beach chairs, letting the wind and salt and indirect evening sunlight seep into our souls.

The following morning, I had my session with Wendy. Even though my mom was here and my dad and brother were arriving that evening, I decided not to reschedule.

"How do you feel about the decision to leave, now that it has been a little while? Did writing about it help?" Wendy asked.

"Relieved, I think. And yes, writing about it helped me feel confident that quitting was the right decision. But for some reason, I still feel unsteady. I spent so long focused on being super successful... Making peace with giving up is hard."

"I wouldn't call it giving up."

I raised my eyebrows.

"What does success mean to you, personally?" she asked.

I looked out the window above my laptop screen, rolling my lips in between my teeth. I'd grown pretty fond of Wendy the last few months, but sometimes it drove me crazy that most of what she said during these sessions were questions back to me. This one in particular gave me pause.

Wasn't success just an objective goal? That was how I'd always thought about it. But Wendy's leading question suggested she thought otherwise.

"I don't know." It was an honest answer.

Her mouth quirked into a small smile.

"Is that my homework for next time?" I asked.

"Sure is!"

I huffed out a breath.

"I often encourage my clients to think about their life goals not just in terms of *what* they want to do, but who they want to be. Think about that, too, while you craft your personal definition of success."

I thought about what Luke said to me on the beach in

Menemsha, all the qualities he'd listed off, how it made me feel. Maybe I'd been thinking about everything the wrong way this whole time.

"Anything else on your mind before we wrap up?"

I nodded slowly as my stomach turned over. "I'm nervous about telling my parents I quit. And my brother."

The only words I'd spoken after I greeted my dad, mom, brother, and Mimi at the restaurant were the ones conveying my drink order. Even though my dad initially told me to quit, when I took the medical leave instead, I got the sense that he was relieved. At the time, I was too. But now that I'd done this about-face, I didn't totally know what to expect from the man who had always taught me to strive for big things. I wrung my hands under the table while we waited for our drinks to arrive. That spot behind my sternum where my throat met my lungs pinched, making it that much harder for air to get through. A deep breath in through my nose, and then another, and it bent to my will and released. *I'm getting better at that.*

As soon as my grapefruit Paloma appeared in front of me, I said, "I quit my job."

My dad raised his eyebrows. Drew's blue eyes focused on me like a camera lens. My mom patted my leg under the table. Mimi sipped her drink nonchalantly—it wasn't news to her.

Before they could ask any questions, I launched into my defense. "I realized this summer that, while I wanted to be a BigLaw partner someday, it wasn't worth everything I felt like I was giving up for it. I've felt so much better not being tied to my phone, beholden to so many demands. Sounds crazy, but I feel like I can breathe more easily than I have in years. I feel healthier. And I want to have time to pursue other passions and enjoy my time with my friends and family more." I caught my dad's eye and forced a smile.

"I'm working as a babysitter and have enough to get by for now. I'll have to figure out something for income eventually, but I feel like I will." *Maybe someday I'll even be able to sell my novel.* "Worst case scenario, I regret it in six months and get a job at a different law firm or private equity firm."

I let out my breath and shrugged.

"Okay," my dad said.

"Okay?"

"Yeah, honey. It sounds like you thought it through. And I know how miserable you were at that job. You already seem happier?" He raised his eyebrows again, this time with a smile.

I smiled back, genuinely this time. "I am."

My mom patted my leg again.

"Good for you, Val," Drew said.

I didn't know what to make of his tone, but I was too relieved by my dad's reaction to dwell on it.

"Do you need money to bridge the gap? I know we didn't have a ton to spare when you kids were growing up"—he glanced at me and then at Drew—"but we're doing pretty well now."

I couldn't take money from my dad. "No. But thanks, Dad."

Mimi lifted her cocktail glass. "To new beginnings."

We all brought our glasses together over the top of the table.

Throughout dinner, I caught my dad and my brother looking at me with a hint of concern in their eyes, but they didn't say anything else about my career decisions. Maybe they were disappointed, despite what they said.

Or maybe they were just worried about how I was going to support myself going forward.

I was a little worried about it, too.

30

The week with my family flew by. My mom and I shopped in town, Dad and Drew fished, and we wound up at the beach or out to dinner downtown most evenings. One night, all five of us went out for an evening sail on the big catamaran that went out of Edgartown Harbor. I didn't get as much writing done as usual, but I didn't mind. Luke handled as many of Luna's sailing pickups as he could so I could spend time with my family. But I missed my favorite father-daughter pair, which was why I invited them to dinner at Mimi's tonight.

I set out hummus, pita chips, and veggies because Luna liked them. Before dinner, we broke out a dusty cornhole set from Mimi's basement and played several rounds. Luna was a little ringer now.

"Have you guys been practicing?" I asked Luke after she sunk one right through the hole in the board—her third of the night.

"Yes." Luke laughed, dragging a hand down his face. "Sometimes if it's still light out after dinner, we play a few games."

"You're doing that *and* your extra tennis sessions with Jeremiah? Your energy levels astonish me, Luna," I called to her across the yard where she stood next to Drew by the opposite board.

"Me too," Luke said for only me to hear. He took a swig of his beer and shook his head.

"She'll keep you young."

He laughed, full-bellied, at that comment. I felt like I won a prize at the fair.

The sound of a bag slamming on top of the board broke our semi-private exchange. "Okay, eleven to seven," Drew pronounced, calculating the score in his head in a fraction of a second.

Luke tossed my bags toward me for the next round, catching my gaze, a competitive glint in his eyes. He crushed me the last round, but I was having too much fun to mind.

Sitting at the dinner table in Mimi's dining room half an hour later, plates cleared, conversation long from over, I surveyed the table. My mom had asked Luke about how he started his business, and Luke was telling us about his first visits to the island with Jeremiah. I knew the story already, but I listened anyway. It was like catching a scene of a favorite movie when it was on TV.

I feel present. The thought came to me with a rush of clarity. I was totally in the moment with my parents and Mimi, Luke and Luna, and my brother, in this house that felt like a childhood home full of fond memories, on this island I'd loved my whole life. My mind wasn't half here, half somewhere else, worried about a deadline or a draft I didn't make enough progress on or a client I might hear from with an urgent request at any moment. I was just *here*, mind and body.

Nowhere else to be.

Nowhere I'd rather be.

My parents and Mimi turned in shortly after Luke and Luna left, but Drew and I stayed up in the sunroom. We sat in silence with fresh glasses of wine, letting the sound of the crickets and the soft nighttime breeze sneaking in through the screened windows fill the room. It was the first time we'd been alone together all week.

Even though I knew I might not like the answer, I asked, "Do you think I'm doing the right thing? I mean, I'm sure you aren't surprised I quit. I know you probably think I already tanked my career there anyway."

He squinted at me. "When did I say that?"

"You didn't have to." My eyes were glued to my wine glass as I recalled the concerned glances he shot my way at dinner the night I told my family I quit and the pity in his eyes when we talked at our parents' house at the beginning of my medical leave.

"I didn't think that. Although, I wouldn't be surprised if they held it against you, which would be wrong of them, but not unbelievable. What I was actually worried about was *you*, my little sister, and how unhappy you seemed."

He paused, and I lifted my gaze to him. "It seemed like you felt bad for me that I blew my chance at making partner."

"That wasn't it at all," he defended. "Why would I care if you ever become a big law firm partner? I don't care what you do." His tone bordered on incredulous.

My eyes widened with hurt.

"Sorry. That's not what I mean. I do care, I just..." he trailed off, and his consternation seemed genuine.

I held my tongue and let him collect his thoughts.

"If that's what you wanted, then I'd support you. And I'd be impressed as hell when you got it. And pissed on your behalf if they passed you over. But either way, I'm already impressed with you—the job title wouldn't change that."

My throat tightened and I gaped at him. I knew my brother cared about me as a person, but I could never really tell if he was proud of me, and I definitely couldn't remember him saying anything like that to me before. I couldn't form words for a moment.

"I don't say that enough, huh?"

I shrugged. "You've always said my deal announcements were impressive."

"Yeah, but that's different." After a pause he added, "I'm sorry."

I wasn't sure if he was apologizing for not saying he was impressed with me enough, or if it went deeper than that, to all the times he made me feel less than in my life. All I knew was my entire body forgave him instantly, and I felt lighter.

I caught his eye and my mouth ticked up. "Thanks, Drew."

"As for whether you're doing the right thing—I totally respect your decision to make a change. You're only thirty-one, Val. You have your whole life to keep changing it up—quitting shitty jobs, finding better ones..." he said.

I nodded. "That's true."

"Subject change?"

I cleared the last of the emotion in my throat. "Please."

"So, you're in love with the dad, huh?" His earlier sincerity was replaced with a teasing lilt in his tone.

I glared at my older brother. "I see subtlety is still lost on you."

"What?" His tone was indignant. "You're my sister, I can't tell you what I think?"

I sighed. "I don't know if I'm in love with him."

Liar, a voice in my head said. I ignored it.

Drew popped his shoulder up, like this was the most casual topic in the world. We didn't talk about our love lives that much. Once or twice he asked my advice when he was still single, but he'd been married for years now.

"Well, whatever it is, seems mutual to me," he said.

My hopeful little heart latched on to that. I absconded any sense of mystery to ask him, "How can you tell?"

His mouth curved upward annoyingly, satisfaction rising to the surface of his blue eyes.

"Because he looks at you the way I'm sure I looked at O all those years. Like he kinda can't believe you exist."

Oh, god. The hope that filled my chest was overwhelming. *Does Luke really look at me like that?*

Drew thought he did, and Drew was the bluntest person I'd

ever met. Despite our tender moment earlier, and no matter how much my brother loved me, he'd never say something he didn't believe to be true.

I buried my face in my wine glass, a pitiful attempt at hiding my smile.

"See? That's what I mean."

"Do you ever tire of the elation you feel when you're right?" I teased.

"You wound me." He clutched his chest dramatically. "But yeah, no, it doesn't get old."

I threw a pillow at him, and we both laughed.

"You seem happy here, Val. Are you going to stay?" Drew asked, light brown eyebrows raised.

"Hmm." After mulling my decision to quit endlessly, I'd spent precious little time thinking about what I'd do once the summer ended. Mimi would go back to Florida. Did I want to stay here without her? I assumed I could keep helping Luke with Luna; he'd implied as much, but we hadn't talked about it since I officially quit my job. He'd only need me for a couple of hours a day when Luna went back to school, so I'd be making less money than I am now.

But I'd have even more time to write. That thought drummed up some excitement in my veins.

"I don't actually know," I said to my brother finally. "I haven't thought much past the summer."

He shrugged again. "You'll figure it out." He stated it as an irrefutable fact.

"Thanks, Drew," I said, meaning it. I looked at him—sitting in this house where we used to play in the yard in wet bathing suits and watch movies on rainy days before the more serious aspects of life took over—and questioned why I'd always felt like I needed to compete with him. Who signed me up for this race, with society, with my brother? We're really different people, Drew and me. We always had been. *And that's okay.*

"You looking forward to heading back to Boston tomorrow?" I asked.

"Oh, yeah. I love you guys and all, but I miss my wife."

The corner of my mouth turned up. Maybe I should be taking Drew's relationship advice after all.

31

L uke and I watched Luna until she disappeared inside the tennis center before pulling out of the crushed shell parking lot. He'd invited me to check out his housing project site with him today.

Within two days of mentioning it to her last month, Francesca had secured the Daniel Fisher House—one of the Vineyard Preservation Trust's most beautiful properties—for the fundraiser on a Friday night the third week of August. She even convinced them to cut the reservation fee as a contribution to the cause. Ticket sales were off to a great start. Francesca was handling almost everything, but she kept me in the loop. I'd gone with her the other day to seek donations and ticket purchases from some local business owners. Not everyone was an affordable housing enthusiast per se, but most people agreed they'd prefer their favorite restaurants and businesses on the island be open seven days a week and recognized the need for more housing options to achieve that.

I was holding my breath now that we were alone in his truck. It made me think of the night he took me to Menemsha in pieces and brought me back feeling more whole.

I glanced at his profile. The angular nose, full lips, long lashes.

He'd always been incredibly handsome, but now that I knew him —how beautiful he was on the inside—he was devastating.

"Whatcha thinking about?" he asked, his deep voice carrying easily over the tones of the classic rock song on the radio.

How good-looking you are.

Some women would say it. But I wasn't a confident flirt like that, despite the numerous indications he'd given me that he was interested. Despite what my brother said about the way he looked at me.

It'd been almost two weeks since Luke visited me in the hospital and I told him Max and I were over. He hadn't done anything. I wasn't surprised. He didn't seem like the type to move in on someone who'd only been single for a couple of weeks. I tried not to let it make me think there weren't feelings on his side. It wasn't like he had many opportunities while I was spending so much time with my family over the past week. But in quieter moments, I'd begun to question whether he reciprocated my crush after all. *Maybe he's just a good friend. Maybe he isn't looking for anything right now.* I couldn't let my mind linger on those thoughts for long, though. The disappointment was too overwhelming.

He stole a quick look at me in the passenger seat, reminding me he'd asked me a question. "I'm excited to see the site!" I said finally.

He chuckled. "I appreciate the enthusiasm. The model home is just a slab foundation and the frame right now, but I can walk you through what it will look like." A lock of hair fell into the middle of his forehead, and he pushed it back reflexively.

Within five minutes, we pulled up to the construction site. It was tucked in a neighborhood off the main road, perfectly situated just outside of town and along the bus route. We climbed out of the car—Luke tucking his hard hat under his arm—and walked over to the only structure on the site. Three men in yellow hard hats, jeans, and T-shirts boasting the *Karas Construction* logo lugged two-by-fours and power tools to different spots in the structure.

Luke grabbed an extra hard hat from a folding table set up outside the framed-out door opening. He motioned me to him with his hand, and my body obeyed. He lifted both arms to place the hat on my head, and the motion brought me back to that night alone in his shed for a second. I tucked my light brown hair behind my ears and looked up at him from under the little brim. He was already looking at me, and our eyes locked.

He shook his head almost imperceptibly as the corner of his mouth lifted, revealing his dimple under his freshly trimmed beard.

What? I almost asked him, but he was already turning to enter the site.

When I looked up, all three of the workers were watching us. "Hey, boss," one of them called.

"If I hear one whistle, you're all fired," Luke said.

My cheeks flamed as I looked down at my outfit: a V-neck T-shirt, a tennis skort, and sneakers.

"Alright, boss," the same worker said, winking at me.

"I don't even know how to whistle," another one called from the far corner.

"Shut up, Tony!" Luke and the third worker said in unison. Luke was shaking his head, but a smirk tugged on one of his cheeks.

I smirked, too. They clearly had a good rapport.

"Alright, so, this is the front, obviously. We'll hang a bunch of hooks here and build a closet here." He gestured to each side of the entry. "The first bedroom is right off the entry to the left. If you walk straight back, there will be a kitchen and living room that spans most of the back of the house, full bathroom in the far corner where Tony's working, and two more bedrooms off this hall with a Jack 'n' Jill bathroom in between. Oh, and a deck off the back of the kitchen. And that's it." He spread his arms wide in what will be the kitchen area. His words were humble, but his excitement was as clear as day.

This is what it looks like when you love what you do.

"I like the layout. It's going to be so nice. You have me wishing I was twenty again with a job here for the summer. I'm jealous of these future renters."

"Me too, honestly. You should have seen the place Jeremiah and I rented. It was...not nice."

I giggled at his tone.

"Wanna see the rest of the property? Most of the other lots are cleared."

"Of course."

Luke turned to his employees. "Keep up the good work, guys. Let me know what you need. I'll swing by later to help out."

"See ya!" they called. A chorus of nail guns and country music on a radio sang us farewell.

I followed Luke down the makeshift dirt road created by tire treads from heavy vehicles. Luke explained that there will be four bungalows at the beginning of the property. Then on each side of the road, there would be some multi-level townhomes. When it was done, there would be fifteen bungalows and fifteen town-homes, for a total of ninety bedrooms.

At the end of the road, he motioned to a large, cleared area. "The last thing we'll build is a pool, small indoor gym, and basket-ball court."

"This is so cool, Luke. No wonder you got the contract from the town. It's going to be incredible." I spun in a circle, visualizing what the idyllic little rental neighborhood would look like when it was finished. "And I can't believe how much progress you've already made. I'm so impressed. Plus, this is going to preserve some of the culture of the island—the seasonal workers traveling from around the world to live and work here for the summer. You must be so proud."

He looked at me from under his eyelashes. "Thanks, Val." He said it quietly, like he wasn't sure he agreed.

"What?"

He swallowed, looking around. It was just gaps in between green trees, but with a dream's worth of potential. "I am proud."

He said it like he was trying to convince himself. "I built something."

"You did." I couldn't help my smile when I added, "Literally and figuratively." His eyes flashed to mine and his own smile broke on his lips. "Why does it sound like you don't fully believe it?"

He inclined his head in the direction we came from, and I fell into step next to him. The sky was gray, humidity making my T-shirt stick to my skin. The foretellings of a summer storm.

Luke finally answered my question. "My dad was one of the people that wasn't super impressed with my career plan. He didn't think construction was sophisticated enough work for his son. He considered it...I don't know. He never said it like this, but I could tell he considered it a low-education, blue collar, last-resort job you did if you couldn't get something else."

"You have an MBA!" I all but shouted.

His mouth curved. "Yeah, but it's an online one from Southern New Hampshire University. They let everyone in. It's not exactly Wharton."

I stopped walking, wanting to look at him. "I know, but that doesn't make it inferior. You learn the exact same things at Wharton. And most people who graduate from there are too confident for their own good. Successful businesses don't spring up naturally from a Wharton diploma frame like a weed. It's hard work. You found something you loved, learned a skill, started your own business, decided to further your education to enhance your business, you're working your ass off, and you're thriving. That's *so* impressive. And even if you didn't have that MBA, I still can't see how your dad would be anything but proud of you." I was pacing in front of him, gesticulating wildly, not even trying to temper the flare of indignation I felt on Luke's behalf. He probably thought I was a crazy person. I looked up, expecting to see a look of bewilderment at my outburst.

But instead he was staring at me with something that resembled admiration.

"Sorry," I said, sheepish.

"Don't be." He stepped forward, pulled me into him, and wrapped his arms around my back. It was as if he couldn't express what he wanted to say with words, so he said it with his body instead. He kissed the top of my hair, and I swore my heart stopped. He stepped back but didn't break our contact.

We walked to his truck with his arm around my shoulders. Like we did that all the time. Like it was the most natural thing in the world.

The little touches continued after that—knocking his knee against mine under the table on the nights I stayed for dinner, a hand on my back when he walked me to the door. Some days he would lean his elbow on the doorframe mid-conversation as I exited the front door, like he did that night when I slept in his guest room. When I'd turn around, the urge to raise myself up on my tiptoes and kiss him goodbye would be so powerful it nearly overcame my reluctance to make the first move. But I hadn't.

On the Wednesday before the fundraiser, I met Francesca for a late lunch at Among the Flowers Café. It was right up the road from the sailing center where I'd just left Luna. It was so sunny today, the rays beating down and warming any exposed skin in an instant. I'd reapplied Luna's sunscreen with a heavy hand during her lunch break.

"How are you feeling about Friday?" I asked after the teenaged waiter placed our salads on the little white-painted iron café table we'd selected in the shady part of the patio. "Is there anything I can help with?"

"I think we're in good shape." She scrunched her petite nose like she was running through a mental checklist. I took a bite of my spinach salad and let her think.

"Yeah, I can't think of anything. We have fifty gift cards and twenty bigger excursions to auction off, including private charters on the Mad Max catamaran and the Tigress sailboat, fishing tours, windsurfing lessons. I think those will all go for a lot. Plus there's the raffle and the online donation page. I'm cautiously optimistic we'll hit the fundraising goal."

"Everyone I've spoken to is really looking forward to it."

Francesca sucked in a breath and expelled it through pursed, pink lips. "I'm a little nervous. This is one of the biggest events I've planned."

"It's going to go great," I said. "And we'll get lots of pictures you can use for your website, show future clients you can handle a 300-person event."

She nodded, a glimmer of excitement in her bright, brown eyes.

After a few more bites of our salads, I asked, "So, tell me the full story about you and Jeremiah. How'd he convince you to move here?"

She smirked, wiped her hands on the napkin on her lap, rested her elbows on the edge of our little table, and leaned in conspiratorially. "It is the most random story," she warned.

"I can't wait."

"We met out at a bar in Boston. He was in town for a wedding. I was out with my single girlfriends. He walked in around midnight—suspenders, loosened bowtie, jacket over his arm. There's just something about a man in a white dress shirt and suspenders, you know? I think he saw me too, because he wedged himself between my barstool and my friend's to order his drink. He turned to me and said, 'Hi,' with a little nod.

"We flirted for the rest of the night, and he came back to my apartment with me. We had drunken, sloppy sex, and then we had coffee together in the morning and talked and talked, I think sharing more of ourselves because we both assumed we'd never see each other again. I told him about my disenchantment with my job. He told me about the Vineyard, his dreams for his and Luke's company. When he left he said, 'If you ever want a tour of Martha's Vineyard, call me.' And that was it for months."

"And then...?" I'd stopped eating my salad.

"I had a rough week at work. Finally realized start-up life might not be for me. We ended a really tense investor call on a Friday afternoon and I just *fled*. Before I knew it, I had a suitcase packed and was walking to South Station, checking the bus schedule on my phone. When I got on the bus to Woods Hole for the Martha's Vineyard ferry connection, I texted Jeremiah asking if his offer of a tour still stood. I figured I wouldn't hear back from him."

"But you did of course." I looked at Francesca, her deep tan complexion, brown eyes, and dark brown hair that fell almost to her waist. She was memorably beautiful. I noticed people noticing her every time we went somewhere together. I bet Jeremiah couldn't believe his luck when she reached out.

She smiled, looking at the flower box hanging from the railing beside us. "Yes. He saved me the embarrassment of admitting I was already on the way because he asked if I was already on the island. Then he called me!"

"On the phone? Like it's the nineties and we don't have texting?"

"Yes! He convinced me to stay with him for the weekend. It was, hands down, the best weekend of my life. We just clicked, you know?"

I swallowed. I knew exactly how that felt now. Probably for the first time in my life. "Absolutely."

"From there it was easy. We saw each other almost every weekend. I'd come here, he'd come to Boston. When I quit my job and came here to stay with him for a while, I just kinda...never left." She shrugged one shoulder, beaming.

"I love that story."

"Me too." She smiled to herself and took a sip of her iced coffee. "That's why I'm so proud of you for quitting your job. It was the best thing I ever did—taking a step back, thinking about what I wanted for the next chapter of my life."

I choked up a little. Francesca and I had only hung out half a dozen times since we met, but she was quickly starting to feel like a real friend, someone I could be my true self with without fear of judgment. Besides, I'd never judged her for leaving a high intensity job that she fell out of love with, for making a career change to something totally different in her thirties. I admired her.

I drank in my flourishing surroundings and the flourishing woman across from me as I sipped my iced tea. *I think I'm proud of myself, too.*

"How'd Jeremiah convince you to do winters here? Is it as long and cold and boring as everyone says?"

"Honestly, I kind of like the winters here. Everything slows down by October, and the fall is beautiful. The air gets crisp, the leaves change color, the rhythms of the island slow. I hole up and read books and work on my website and marketing materials, do some self-education, long phone calls with friends and family. And then when it gets really cold, work slows down for Jeremiah, too. We watch movies every night, that kind of thing. We go off-island for the holidays, and then again in January or February for a vacation somewhere warm, and before you know it, it's summer again."

"That sounds really nice actually." I pictured myself holed up with a book reading, or my laptop writing.

She pursed her lips as a knowing look spread on her face. "I think you'd like it."

I had a feeling she was right.

32

I watched myself in the mirror as my fingers twirled the pieces of hair that framed my face this way and that, making sure the soft curls I put in would hold for a while. I'd finally found a dress this week at my favorite boutique downtown—the one I stopped in so often after dropping Luna off at sailing that they recognized me now. It was a deep emerald dress in a rayon material that hung like silk down to just below my knees, with a modest slit on one side and a cowl neckline. It hugged the curves of my hips and my butt just enough that I was proud of them, not insecure about them.

I told myself I didn't buy it specifically because I hoped Luke would like it, but that was a lie.

I was more nervous about this fundraiser than I had a right to be. It wasn't my project, my company, or even my event. But I'd been so involved with certain aspects of the planning with Francesca, I wanted everything to go well for her. I also hoped Karas Construction would hit its fundraising goal. Tickets were sold out, but they'd need some generous bids on the bigger ticket auction items, a ton of 50/50 raffle sales, and many direct donations to get there. Maybe nervous wasn't the right word. More like invested and excited and dying to see Luke.

After adding gold dangling earrings and scrutinizing my makeup for a little too long, my phone buzzed on the hard surface of the vanity. Incoming call: Luke.

A butterfly fluttered in my belly like it always did when his name popped up on that screen.

"Hi!"

"Hi, Val. So, we have a tiny crisis happening over here, a braid emergency, if you will."

"Dad!" I heard Luna call from the background, her tone accusatory.

I chuckled. "Luna wants braids in her hair for her playdate, and you can't do it."

"Precisely." I heard a door click in the background before he said in a lower tone, "I know we need to leave for the event in half an hour. Maybe we can pick you up?"

"I can drive over and leave my car, get it tomorrow. Cathy and her husband were going to pick up Mimi and me anyway. I'll just go with you and meet them there."

"Are you sure you don't mind? Do you need more time to get ready?"

I met my eyes in the mirror. "Nope, I'm pretty much ready. I'll be there shortly."

"I owe you."

I grabbed my strappy gold heels and headed for the door.

When I parked in Luke's driveway a few minutes later, I touched up my lipstick in the car mirror. The front door opened before I got up the steps.

"Val! Thank goodness," Luna sighed.

"Hi, Luna." I smiled. Luke appeared behind her but didn't say anything for a moment. He watched me walk up the stairs, dark brown eyes flitting from my head to my shoes before returning to my face.

"You look really pretty," he said in a low voice as I squeezed past him into the door.

I pressed my lips together, a fruitless attempt to hide that I was beaming.

My eyes took him in, too, traveling down and back up. Dark navy suit that hugged in all the right places, white shirt, no tie. He didn't have his shoes on yet, which gave his formal look a dash of fitting humility.

When I turned to face the living room, Luna was already sitting cross-legged on the floor in front of the couch, brush in her hands.

Luke puttered listlessly around the kitchen while I wove Luna's hair into two matching French braids. We chatted about her plans with Clara and their other friend tonight. Apparently they were making their own pizzas and watching movies. Clara's mom was an innovator on how to entertain little girls.

"Maybe next time we can do it here," Luna said.

"I'm sure you can talk to your dad about that." I caught Luke's eye over my shoulder.

He looked mildly terrified at the concept of entertaining three eight-year-old girls, but he said, "Yes, we can do that. We'll do make your own...snack mix?"

"Yeah!" Luna agreed.

I giggled. It was a great idea. And a lot easier than pizzas.

When I was about done with Luna's second braid, she said, "Next time, can you teach my dad how to do the braids? So he can do them after you leave?"

The words hit me like a blow, stealing my breath. My throat constricted. *What does she mean, after I leave?*

Who told her I'm leaving? I hadn't talked about leaving since I quit my job a month ago.

"Yes, of course I can show him." I forced the words out softly.

My hands trembled, threatening to unravel the taut hairstyle. I had to focus ten times harder than usual to finish the braid and tie it off with her little black hair tie.

"All set." I tapped both her shoulders, hoping she couldn't hear the emotion in my voice.

I dashed from the couch to the little office off the entryway, closing the door behind me. My heartbeat roared in my ears.

Two raps on the door. "Val?" Luke's voice floated into the room.

"Yeah," I choked out. He slipped inside and closed the door behind him, assessing me from head to toe. When he saw the look on my face, he closed the gap between us in an instant.

"Hey, hey." Luke reached for my face, wiping at the tears I didn't realize had pooled under my eyes with his thumbs. I tried to steady my breaths, forming an O with my lips.

He pulled me into his strong arms, wrapping me up, his hands stroking my hair gingerly. "Tell me what happened."

"She said she wants you to learn to braid her hair. For when, when," my voice quivered, "I *leave.*"

Luke continued to hold me, rubbing soothing circles into my bare shoulder blades. After over a month of pondering and weighing my options, what I wanted was suddenly clear. "I don't want to," I added after a moment.

Luke took a half step back and gripped my shoulders. He bent slightly to look at me through the curtain of my hair before he tucked it behind my ears. The empathy, and the longing, in his eyes were plain as day.

"I don't want to go back," I whispered. Not to corporate law. Not to New York or any other city. Not to anywhere that wasn't here.

He nodded, swallowing. "So don't."

"But what will I—"

"Stay."

I gaped at him.

"Stay, Val. Just stay. You're happy here."

My panic converted to curiosity; my tears stopped in their tracks. I opened my mouth to inquire further. *What do you mean by stay? In what capacity? As your nanny, or...something more?*

Before I could voice my thoughts, Luna knocked on the door.

"What are you guys doing in there? Don't we have to go? I don't want to be late." She opened the door, and Luke and I broke apart. Caught.

"Yeah, Luns. Let's get going." He gave me a meaningful look before we left the room.

I nodded, letting him know I was ready to go.

I took a deep breath, straightened my dress, and followed them out. He held the door open for me. His hand reached for mine, giving it a squeeze. A gesture of reassurance. An underscore to his words.

A silent promise.

The event was breathtaking. Live music, a clear tent strung with spheres of light, bright floral centerpieces on white-clothed tables set up across the lawn. Smartly dressed adults mingled, enjoying a dinner of heavy appetizers and serving stations.

The first couple Luke and I talked to asked what I did for work after introductions and appropriate accolades to Luke for winning the project and organizing the fundraiser. My pulse thrummed and words eluded me. I didn't know how to answer this question anymore.

Luke noticed my hesitation and brushed his knuckles against mine before saying, "She's a lawyer-turned-writer."

I stole a glance at his face. His eyes gleamed with enthusiasm and my chest ached with a feeling I'd definitely never felt before.

Luke and I stayed close for a while after that, but I knew he needed to work the room and thank everyone for their generosity, so I tried not to be a barnacle.

I sat with Mimi, Cathy, her husband, and another woman Mimi was friends with a bit later to eat. Then I found Francesca and Jeremiah on the lawn at the edge of the tent. I told Francesca how amazing the event was.

"It's tough because I want to mingle with Jeremiah but I'm also working," she said.

"I'm good, babe," he said, pulling her toward him by her waist and kissing her temple, a look of pride on his face. "Do what you need to do."

I recalled the story Francesa told me at lunch about how she and Jeremiah met. He really did clean up well in a suit. Just like his business partner.

"Ok!" She squeezed his arm. "I need to go check that we're on schedule for the speech." In a flash of red, she was gone.

I scanned the crowd under the tent for Luke. Jeremiah planned to go up there with him, but Luke would do the talking. I knew he was nervous about it.

"I went into construction for a reason," Luke had said earlier that week when he practiced his speech for me. "No public speaking."

"Just think of it as a client dinner where a client has asked you about this project," I'd suggested. His speech was great; he just needed to get up there and get it done.

My eyes found him near the entrance. His back was to me, but his full dark hair, large frame, and blue suit were unmistakable. Moments later Francesca tapped him on the shoulder. Then she turned and nodded in our direction. Jeremiah said, "That's my cue," and made his way to the side of the tent where the band was playing. The music paused, and I gingerly maneuvered through the crowd to a better vantage point.

I looked to my left and my right as conversation quieted and people turned their attention to the man with the microphone. A head of sandy brown hair snagged my attention. Max.

Shoot. I hadn't seen him since our breakup, somehow. Why was he here? But then I noticed his parents standing next to him. Of course, they're exactly the type of people we hoped would come to this event. People with deep pockets, a deep attachment to the island, and an annual charitable giving goal set by their financial advisors.

As if he could feel me watching, Max turned in my direction and caught my eye before I could look away. The floor was nearly silent now, Luke would be speaking any second. I nodded, acknowledging him, hoping my facial expression didn't reveal the tension I felt in my gut. He nodded back, eyes widening before he turned away.

I shifted my stance so Max and his parents were no longer in my periphery and focused all my attention on Luke.

"Thank you all for being here. Jeremiah and I and all of us at Karas Construction are truly humbled by the community's support for this housing project. When the town started discussing housing solutions that could help with the seasonal workforce shortage, we were immediately in favor. We're honored we won the bid, and so grateful that the community here tonight has generously contributed to the cause, which will directly support our ability to keep rent low and manage the neighborhood once it's built. We hope you all enjoy the rest of the event and thank you again."

Short, sweet, perfect.

He handed the mic to the band lead, and the din of conversation under the clear tent resumed. He scanned the crowd. His eyes found mine immediately, and a smile spread on his face.

I beamed back at him.

He strode toward me as the crowd continued to disperse, headed for the bars, the food stations, or the tables on the lawn.

"How'd I do?" he asked, standing in front of me looking handsome and relieved.

"Perfect."

His mouth ticked up. "I need a real drink now. Come with me?"

He nodded in the direction of the bar in the far corner of the tent, extending his hand. I took it, and we navigated through the clusters of people like that, hand-in-hand.

Once we got to the front of the line he said, "I'll have an old fashioned and she'll have..." He turned to me, eyebrows raised.

"Rosé, please." Francesca, bless her, had ensured the bar stocked a good rosé.

Luke smirked knowingly and I shrugged. His hand found my

lower back while we waited. I was becoming dangerously accustomed to his little touches.

Once we had our drinks he guided me along the edge of the dance floor under the tent, toward a less populated part of the lawn. Pink streaks lingered in the sky, the last traces of the sun's departure a few minutes ago. A pleasant, tingling warmth emanated through me from the place where Luke's hand rested on my back as we walked. At an event among hundreds of people, it felt like a secret just between us.

When we turned the corner around the end of the tent, we nearly collided with another attendee.

"Sorry," I said reflexively. My stomach dropped when I saw who it was.

Max's sky blue eyes were a storm as he looked between me and Luke. His gaze stopped where Luke's hand met my back.

"The nanny sleeping with the single dad, very original you two," Max said with venom. He looked directly at me. "I thought you were better than that, Val."

Luke removed his hand and clenched his fist at his side. "Don't disrespect her, Max," he said slowly, firmly. Of course he knew exactly who he was.

"Or what?" He must be drunk, antagonizing a man he'd never met like this.

"Or you'll be heading back to the city with a broken jaw."

"Like you'd risk an assault and battery charge," Max sneered.

"Wanna test that theory?" Luke's tone was steady, almost blasé, but his eyes were damning.

"Whatever, asshole." Max gave me one more disgusted look before passing by, bumping Luke's shoulder deliberately. Luke clenched his fist at his side again but didn't turn around.

"Were you really going to hit him?"

"Probably not. Especially here. But he's lucky he was smart enough to walk away. I can't believe he fucking said that to you."

"It's okay. I mean, it's not, but I'm okay. I think he's just bitter... maybe." My pulse was still racing.

My eyes drank in Luke's face. His jaw was tense, but his eyes were clear. We walked farther away from the tent. It was hot, Luke defending me. I realized he never tried to say Max was wrong in his assumption that we were sleeping together.

"Why didn't you correct him?" I searched his eyes. *Please put me out of my misery and say something direct about wanting me—about wanting what Max had inferred to be true.*

The look of hurt that flashed across his face stung me like a wasp.

"I'm sorry." His brows furrowed and his face went from open to closed in an instant. He finished his drink in one gulp.

"I'm going to go grab another one." He tapped the side of his glass. "I'll find you later." He turned and strode back to the tent, leaving me standing on the lawn alone. Stunned.

When my body unfroze, I turned around. Relieved to spot Mimi's white bob at one of the tables on the other side of the lawn, I beelined in that direction. The conversation between Mimi and her friends was nothing more than background noise as I stared into my wine glass, puzzled and distracted. After a while, I excused myself and walked toward the bar near the dance floor.

My head was on a swivel, looking for Luke, trying to figure out what it meant that he'd looked hurt. I questioned whether it was hurt after all. Maybe I made him uncomfortable? Was I too direct?

Our flirtation was a spinning top— it had to fall down eventually. I'd assumed for a while that when it did, we'd fall into place, *together.*

Not fall apart.

Francesca found me wandering. "I think I saw him slip out the other side of the house, to the garden. He probably needed a break from all the schmoozing."

I nodded. *I should give him a minute to himself,* my brain said. But my feet didn't listen.

I made out his figure in the shadows as I descended the steps. The lush garden was dark, the only light coming from the street-lights a hundred yards away. The flower bushes that swayed in the light evening breeze cast long shadows on the ground. I walked toward him on the narrow brick path carefully. The only sounds were the dampened notes of the band on the other side of the building, the crickets chirping, the trickle of the fountain in the center of the garden, and the clinking of glasses and plates and metal serving trays just far enough away that we felt alone.

"Hi," I said.

He turned. "Hey." His expression was inscrutable.

"Francesca said I might find you out here."

"Just needed a minute. We can head back." He started in the direction of the house.

"Hey." I grabbed his arm, forcing him to look at me. I let go once he stopped and faced me. "What's going on?"

"I'm sorry about earlier, Val. Not correcting your ex. I should've known you'd be embarrassed if someone like him thought you were dating a townie construction worker." By the end, he was looking over my shoulder.

My brows knit together. *That's why he's upset?*

That's what he thinks?

"I was not embarrassed." His eyes found mine, irises oscillating as he scanned my expression. I grabbed his forearm again, needing to have some part of me touching some part of him. "*Never* say that. I would never be embarrassed to be with someone like you. You're smart and driven and sensitive, you're the best dad, the best friend. You're, well, you look like that"—I gestured to him with my other hand—"and you—you *see* me. Not what you want to see, but the real me."

I held his gaze, sure that my eyes were shiny by now. "If I was with you, I would be so proud." My voice broke.

"You would?" He brought his thumb to my lip.

"Yes," I whispered. I wanted him to kiss me so badly I could scream. "Do you...have feelings for me, too?" The question my heart had been chanting for weeks came out so softly he wouldn't have heard me if he wasn't standing so close.

He looked at me like I was insane.

"Of course I do." His face was adamant, incredulous. "Isn't it obvious? I can't help myself when I'm around you. I want to be near you all the time, talk to you all the time. *Touch* you all the time." My skin exploded with tingles with the way he said *touch*.

So touch me, my body answered, stepping closer. He stood so close to me now, I could feel his heat, tempering the post-sunset chill in the air.

"But, Val. You just broke up with someone. I didn't want to swoop in too fast. And with everything you've been working through this summer. It's a lot." His hand cupped my chin, giving me nowhere to look except his face, his lips, while his thumb continued to stroke my lower lip. "I—*we* are a lot to sign up for."

We.

Him and Luna.

"It doesn't scare m—"

He replied with his lips instead of his voice, lifting my chin and bringing his mouth down on mine. Firm. Wet. Uncompromising. I dropped my bag to the ground and pushed my fingers into his hair, pulling his face harder into mine. His tongue pressed at the seam between my lips, and I parted them for him. His tongue swirled. Took. Claimed.

I claimed his mouth too, exploring and savoring as relief and pure excitement coursed through my veins.

He tasted like whiskey and my favorite fantasies.

His strong hands moved from my back to my hips, clutching them tight and pulling me into him where I could feel he was hard for me. I whimpered into his mouth. Tension spooled low in my abdomen.

He dragged his lips along my jaw, pressed them to the spot just below my ear.

"Luke." The noise that left my lips was something between a whimper and a whine. I wanted—needed—more.

But we were in public. Any passersby that looked hard enough might see us in the shadows. Any partygoer might find us if they noticed we weren't back.

That restlessness building below my belly button told me I shouldn't even care.

"You keep saying my name like that, and I'm going to lose my damn mind," he drawled.

I pulled his lips back up to mine, my tongue finding his immediately. He gripped my hips so hard through the thin layer of my dress, part of me hoped I'd wake up with little bruises where his fingertips dug into me, evidence that the insatiable longing I felt for him was reciprocated.

Laughter from pedestrians walking up the sidewalk just outside the garden's fence sliced a hole in our lustful bubble.

Luke pulled back, looking at me. His eyelids were heavy, eyes darker than I'd ever seen them. "We should stop. Someone is going to come out here," he rasped.

I bit the inside of my lips, resisting the urge to reach up and touch them, to make sure they remembered what Luke's felt like. I nodded. "But not because we're embarrassed if anyone thinks we're together," I clarified, my voice a murmur.

His flushed cheeks tugged upward. "No. Not because of that." His hand brushed my hair off my shoulder. He leaned down to whisper what he said next into my ear, his breath hot on my neck. "Because if we keep going, what I want to do next is definitely illegal if done in public."

I shivered involuntarily, clenching my legs together, silently cursing the universe that our first kiss had to be here instead of somewhere private.

But I wouldn't change it. Not one second.

Kissing Luke...I wasn't just in the moment, I was completely lost to it.

33

W e walked back into the tent holding hands. The crowd had thinned considerably, but a dozen people were still on the dance floor, swaying to the final songs by the band.

Luke was almost immediately pulled into a conversation with an older couple. He introduced me, but I didn't have much to contribute to their conversation about whether Luke's company built docks, too. I scanned the crowd for Mimi, but I didn't see her. I checked my phone.

MIMI

Heading back, see you at home! Enjoy :)

Francesca approached moments later and gave me a knowing look, glancing pointedly at the space between my hand and Luke's, where they'd been clasped together moments ago. I was sure I was flushed, too. *I should have checked my appearance before walking back in here.* I stole a look at Luke's profile as he spoke. He didn't look disheveled at all.

I lifted both shoulders, unable to stop the smile that played on my just-kissed lips.

She beamed and whispered, "Finally," before grabbing my hand and pulling me toward the bar.

"You were gone for a while," she said after we got our last-call drinks.

"Is it that obvious?"

"Yes, but only to me. I'm very observant." Her eyes twinkled.

I laughed. "Phew."

"We won't know for sure until tomorrow, but I think we hit the fundraising goal."

"What!? That's amazing! Francesca, this event was incredible. I'm in awe."

Her warm smile took over her whole face. She looked out at the lingerers in the tent, the band, the handful of people still clustered at the tables on the lawn—surveying her work. "I'm happy with how it all came out. I got a few referrals, too."

"As you should! You deserve it."

Luke and Jeremiah found us. Luke brushed his knuckles against mine before slipping my hand into his again. "I need to go get Luna. You good?"

"Yep!" I swirled the last few sips in my wine glass. "I'll walk back after I finish this."

All I wanted since the moment Luke pulled back and his hands left my waist was to sneak away together, alone. But it would have to wait.

Luke kissed my cheek firmly before he left, leaving me blushing and fighting a smile in front of his friends.

When I got into bed that night, I replayed my time with Luke in the garden in my head.

"I can't help myself when I'm around you." His low timbre filled my mind, making my stomach somersault. My fingertips brushed over my lips.

When my phone buzzed on the nightstand, my hand shot out so quickly that I knocked it to the ground with a thud. I scrambled out of bed to grab it.

LUKE

Can I take you to dinner tomorrow night?

And, two seconds later:

I already got a sitter.

"So, you hit the fundraising goal?" I drummed my fingers on the console, pulled at the hem of my floral sundress, looked everywhere but at Luke.

"We did. Can't thank you enough for the idea." He stole a sheepish look at me in the passenger seat before training his gaze back on the road, left leg bouncing uncharacteristically.

"Francesca deserves all the credit."

Luke swallowed, saying nothing as he pulled into the parking lot behind his office near the top of Main Street.

We navigated through the other pedestrians as we headed toward the harbor, hands brushing but not grasping, continuing to talk about the event but studiously avoiding my favorite part: our kiss in the dark garden. I couldn't stop thinking about it—the whiskey taste of his tongue, the firm press of his erection through the thin fabric of my dress. My stomach flipped over every time I called the memory back into my mind, including right now.

The whole way down Main Street, it was tentative glances, small talk, silence. For all the time we'd spent together this summer, everything we'd shared, the kiss last night confirming the attraction was mutual, this felt different. Formal.

I was nervous. He seemed nervous, too. *I like you so much,* I wanted to say. *You have nothing to be nervous about.*

Luke held the door open for me when we got to the restaurant attached to one of the hotels downtown. I'd been here before, but not yet this year.

There were two restaurants in this hotel. One was a swanky patio and pool bar right off the main road near the harbor. The other—the one we just entered—was around the corner, its entrance just below street level. It was more casual, off the bustling main stretch. Quieter, smaller. More private. Cozy, even with the A/C blasting to combat the August heat. Almost everything—the tables, chairs, bar, floor, and walls—was dark wood, making it feel like we were inside an old wooden ship. That was the intent, if I had to guess, given the multitude of paintings of such ships hanging on the wood-paneled walls.

"Is this okay? I know it's more casual. But I wanted to go somewhere we might actually be able to hear each other." He peered at me earnestly, brown eyes wide with trepidation.

"It's perfect."

He nodded, but his face told me he was still questioning his restaurant choice. *"I should have known you'd be embarrassed if someone like him thought you were dating a townie construction worker."*

I thought I did a great job allaying his insecurities last night, but the tension in his shoulders told me they might still be there, swirling under the surface. *How on Earth could someone like me make this gorgeous, accomplished, incredible man nervous?*

"I really like you, Luke. I'm happy we're here."

He smiled genuinely, shoulders dropping. "I really like you, too. Do I seem nervous?" The corner of his mouth ticked up, like he knew he was tense.

I fought the smile that pulled on my lips as soon as he said he liked me too. "A little, yes."

He barked out a laugh. "I'm sorry. I... It's been a while."

"What happened to the man that asked if I was enjoying the view of his abs while he worked the saw?"

His laugh was even louder this time. It was exhilarating, making him laugh like that. His shoulders relaxed further. He ran a hand down his face, then pushed both hands through his hair. "You make a great point."

I shook my head. A gorgeous anomaly, that was what he was. Confident, but not all the time.

The waiter showed up at that moment to take our drink order —beer for him, wine for me.

The drinks loosened us up almost immediately. We'd gone on dates before, in a way. We just didn't call them that. Why was it any different now?

Because you've kissed, because you like each other and you both know it, because it's real now and not just a flirtation.

"Why has it been a while?"

His eyes narrowed a bit, like he was considering how to answer. "Long version or short version?"

"Long version, obviously."

He smirked and took a swig of his beer. "I haven't gone on a date in almost two years. Jeremiah gives me endless shit about it, but the summer flings with people visiting the island just...lost their appeal. I dated a teacher that lived here year-round for a while. We got set up. She was nice, attractive. I thought being a teacher would be a good thing because I figured that means you love kids, right?" He moved his beer bottle in a small circle on the table. "And she did, but I felt like she didn't connect with Luna, didn't know what to make of me being a single dad. She was a little younger than me, and it was a few years ago, so I think she was like, twenty-six. So I get it.

"In an attempt to open up, I told her about the whole thing with my parents, how they wanted Luna to move to Pennsylvania and live with them in the beginning. One time she asked me if I ever seriously considered taking them up on it—"

"What the hell?" I interjected. I couldn't see my own facial expression, but I knew it was murderous. "How could she even ask that?"

Luke's chocolate brown eyes found mine, the look full of meaning. "That's how I felt. I know she didn't mean anything by it. It didn't mean she didn't like that I had Luna but...I just couldn't get past it. I realized it wasn't just Luna she didn't fully connect with, but me, too."

I nodded and sipped my wine, holding his gaze, hoping he'd go on.

"After that I just didn't see the point of dating for sport, you know? I've been content to hold out for something that was really worth it, even if that meant holding out forever."

My eyebrows rose. *Is that how he still felt? Like he was holding out?*

He read my mind. "I'm glad I didn't have to wait forever." He said it casually, like it was an obvious fact and not something that set my heart on fire.

I smiled into my wine glass, a poor attempt to conceal that I was beaming, and probably blushing, too.

"That"—he nodded at me—"that smile, is the definition of worth it." His hand squeezed my bare leg under the table.

I giggled and stopped trying to hide it. Momentarily rendered speechless, I stared at him. I couldn't believe he existed, and that I got to exist with him. "I can't believe she said that about Luna," I said.

He shrugged like it didn't bother him, but a flicker of some emotion broke through his facade. "It's a lot. I get it."

He kept saying that.

"We are a lot to sign up for."

"It's a lot."

I disagreed.

Our meals appeared on the table. I hadn't even noticed the waiter approaching us.

"Well, I can't say I'm sad it didn't work out with her." I bit my lip.

His mouth took on a devilish grin. "I can't say I'm sad it didn't work out for you and Max."

"On my god," I groaned. "I'm so embarrassed. I can't believe he was so rude. I can't believe I dated him in the first place."

"Eh, I'm sure he was nicer when he was trying to date you, and now he's just jealous." I loved the confidence in Luke's tone, such a contrast to last night when he thought I was embarrassed of him.

I leaned across the table conspiratorially, motioning him to lean in, too. He obliged, ducking his head, that rebellious brown lock falling in between his eyebrows.

"I'm not gonna lie, it was pretty hot when you put him in his place last night," I whispered.

His hand found my leg again, tracing soft circles on the inside of my knee, leaving a trail of tingles. My thighs clenched.

"My threat of bodily harm to your ex do a little something for you, Val?"

"It's doing a lot of somethings for me."

He rolled his lips together as his gaze bore into me.

After a moment he leaned back. My knee felt exposed without his touch. He took a lazy bite of his food, letting the silence linger, leaving me squirming from a hand on my knee and a hushed conversation. I looked at my plate, but food was the last thing on my mind.

I lifted my eyes back to his. Confidence back, the smirk on his full lips was his smug one. It looked good on him.

When we left the restaurant Luke draped his arm over my shoulder, leaned down, and pressed his lips to my temple. He already felt more like my boyfriend than Max ever had. I couldn't remember the last time I felt this drawn to someone. The attraction buzzing beneath the surface of my skin, everywhere.

I thought—hoped—it was the same for him. For the rest of dinner and one more drink after he kept finding ways to touch me: rubbing his thumb over my kneecap under the table or playing with my hand on top of it, guiding me to the door with his hand on my lower back.

As the sidewalk narrowed, he switched to holding my hand. When we neared the parking area behind his building I said, "I don't want to go home yet." I craned my neck to look up at him.

"Let's go up to my office," he said quickly, like that was already what he was planning.

My stomach fluttered. "Okay," I whispered.

He locked the door behind him as soon as it swung shut. Hands grasping mine, he walked backward, sat down on a couch and pulled me on top of him. I didn't have time to take in any details of his office.

I straddled his muscular thighs and kissed him feverishly, pulling him by his neck toward me. His tongue dipped into my open mouth, dancing with mine. I gave in almost immediately to the urge to roll my hips against him. His erection provided the exact pressure I needed to start soothing the ache between my legs that'd been building since dinner. A sigh escaped my lips.

"Fuck, Val."

His hands squeezed both of my hips, pressing me down even harder on top of him. "Mmm," he groaned into my mouth.

We were a storm of lips, tongues, and teeth. Kissing, nipping, playing. Intentionality gave way to chaos. I grinded shamelessly on top of him; the only things separating us were the thin fabric of my underwear and his shorts. I wasn't thinking about what I looked like, what he was thinking, if he was enjoying it. The sounds breaking from his throat and the grip of his rough hands on my hips told me enough. It felt so good; I never wanted it to end.

I pulled back and started kissing his neck, licking it, and then breathing on the same spot, over and over. Another groan, like a prize. His hand reached into my hair, grabbed hold of it, and angled my head back, exposing my neck to his hungry lips. He pulled the sensitive skin into his wet mouth, kissing at first, then sucking.

I squealed with delight but said, "You're going to leave a hickey."

He released my skin from his lips. "Sorry," he whispered to the tender spot on my neck.

"It feels so good, it might be worth it."

"No, no. I'll be gentle." He kissed the same spot again, lightly this time, licked it, and continued peppering both sides of my neck with featherlight, torturous grazes of his lips and soft swipes of his tongue. I was unraveling, grinding my hips into him, his hands holding me in place, the forcefulness of the union between my wet core and his erection a sharp juxtaposition to the gentle torture he was enacting on my neck.

"Luke," I whimpered, the tension building in my lower abdomen. He hadn't even touched me where the nerve endings between my thighs were humming, and I was already building toward release. My whimpering his name tipped him off. He knew I was close.

"Yes," he said, to what I didn't know, and crashed his lips back onto my mouth. My lips parted, taking as much of his tongue as possible. I'd have half a mind to be embarrassed by how needily I was rubbing myself against him, but I didn't have half a mind right now. It's all skin and breath and tension and passion and this overwhelming sense of *rightness*. Like we were finally doing the natural, obvious thing, acting on what has felt right for a long time. I no longer felt like I was being torn in two, denying the feeling in my gut.

Right here. Right now. With him. This was exactly where I was supposed to be.

He pulled down the straps of my sundress, exposing both of my breasts. He stared at them for a moment, as if in awe, and then covered them with both his palms. The friction of his calloused hands on my sensitive skin accelerated *everything* that was happening inside my body. My forehead dropped to his shoulder as an involuntary moan flowed from my lips. He released one hand to lift my chin, pressing his lips to mine. His back arched, his hips bucking into me. I wasn't sure if he did it to increase the friction for my benefit or his, but it worked. I resumed moving on top of him, the pressure in my abdomen heightening.

"Luke, I'm so close," I whined.

"Keep going baby, I've got you." He captured my mouth with his, one hand pressing down on my hip, guiding my movements, the other finding my breast again. When he started working my nipple between the pads of his fingers I let go, my orgasm crashing over me in multiple bursts. He clutched me to him, catching my moans in his mouth.

"Mmm," he hummed, like he could taste the sounds I was making, and they were his favorite flavor.

I kissed him deeply, and then moved my mouth to his jaw, then his neck. I pulled the hem of his shirt up, and he lifted it off over his head in one fluid motion. I ogled him, rubbing my lips together. My hands moved over his chiseled pecs and then down over the taut plane of his stomach. The tan skin, the dusting of dark hair. It was as fun to touch as it was to look at. He watched me observing and feeling him, both of our chests rising and falling with heaving breaths.

His hands moved up my waist to my exposed breasts. He cupped them, staring openly. The look almost wasn't sexual, but like he was studying them.

I reached for his belt buckle, undoing it. I slid down further to remove his shorts, my feet finding the floor. I licked his abs before inserting my hands into his black boxer briefs. The same ones I saw in his laundry that time and vowed not to picture him in.

My imagination wouldn't have done him justice.

"You don't have to," he said.

"Are you crazy? I've wanted to be...like this, with you, for so long."

"I've wanted this for so long, too. Basically since the moment I met you. And it's only gotten stronger as I've gotten to know you. I —" He shook his head, swallowing, looking at me with untempered awe.

"Me too," I said, not needing him to finish his statement to know I felt the same way. Whatever this was, it was mutual.

I was kneeling now. "Can I?"

He nodded, pupils wide like he couldn't believe his luck. He helped me pull his briefs off, releasing him. It was as perfect as the rest of him. I ran my tongue from the base to the tip.

"Oh fuck, Val. I'm not going to last."

"So don't," I murmured, looking at him one more time before

taking him in my mouth. I'd never wanted to do this for someone as much as I did right then. His hips bucked in a gentle rhythm with the bobbing of my mouth. I caught my breath for a moment, swirling my tongue over his head.

"Val. Now. If you—" I felt him grow harder between my lips. I knew what he was trying to say—if I wanted him to finish anywhere other than inside my mouth, then I needed to move now. But I didn't want him to, so I didn't.

I crawled back into his lap after swallowing. "Oh my god baby, you're incredible," Luke said into my hair, wrapping his arms around me like a vise, still coming down from his release.

A moment later, he pushed me down on the couch next to him. His hands yanked the skirt of my dress, pulling it down further. "Does this have a zipper?"

I shook my head *no*, and he pulled harder, sliding it down my hips and off my body before discarding it on the floor.

"Luke," I giggled.

"Only fair."

He climbed on top of me, holding himself just above my body, biceps straining. I ran my fingers over his arms. His arm muscles were so big, it was such a turn-on. It made me picture how easy it would be for him to toss me around if we had more space. He lowered his lips to mine. The kisses were soft at first, and then more frantic.

I wrapped my hands around his neck, through his hair, sucking his tongue into my mouth. A groan rattled up his throat. His lips pulled away from mine and he kissed my cheek, then my jaw, my neck. He lowered himself on his knees between my legs and bent to take my breast into his mouth, sucking and licking attentively before moving to the other one. My hips shifted involuntarily, muscles coiling just from the sensation of his mouth on my nipples. *It's never felt this good before.*

Sensing my neediness, he continued moving down, planting kisses and swipes of his tongue on my stomach while his hands pulled my underwear down and off.

When his face reached the apex of my thighs, his breath caressed my core. He touched me first, then kissed my sensitive clit.

"Oh my god," I whined.

"Tell me what feels good," Luke instructed before licking me from entrance to clit.

"That."

He did it again and my hips writhed in response. Then his lips sucked my clit into his mouth. "Less sucking and more of—" He licked again, this time in a circle. "Oh my god more of *that*," I gasped, digging my nails into his shoulders. I'd never been this vocal about my preferences, but it was like I couldn't deny his request to tell him what felt good.

His tongue kept working me in mind-blowing swirls. Tension spooled low in my stomach, building steadily toward a release. I was already excited for it, knew it was going to be more intense than the first one. Luke looked up at me from between my legs.

"It's so good, Luke, I'm already cl—" I unraveled at the next press of his tongue. The release was deep and long—not a quick snap, but a lingering, drawn out, multi-wave explosion. He kept lapping until my hips stopped wiggling.

I reached down and pulled him up adamantly. I wanted, needed, his weight on top of me while I came down.

His bare body pressed against mine, head to toe, skin to skin, I threaded my fingers in his hair and pulled his mouth to mine. His kissed mine back insistently. When we broke the kiss, he shifted to the side, pulling me half on top of him, our chests heaving.

Lying on the couch, propping my head on my palm, one leg over him, we looked at each other in sated silence.

"Thank you," he said.

I couldn't help but giggle. *I suppose that's the polite thing to say after an exchange of sexual favors.*

I was about to say *thank you*, too, when recognition flashed across his face. He laughed. "No, I mean. Thank you for telling me what you like. I'm not always sure what to do. I always want you to tell me what feels good."

I was aghast. He saw it on my face.

"What?" he asked.

"Luke, you're like, the best-looking man I have ever seen. I find it so hard to believe that you feel you're inexperienced. You just told me about your last relationship..."

"Well, it's not really because I've sought it and failed, but more that I haven't sought it that often, and I'm out of practice. That relationship was short; we didn't experiment that much. I was shy in high school and most of college. I only cared about sports. And then I became a single dad at twenty-eight, so my window wasn't very long, and mostly just alcohol-fueled summer flings. So..."

I could feel my heart expanding in my chest. As if he couldn't be any more endearing.

I cut him off with a kiss. "You do realize you just made me come twice in the span of twenty minutes."

A smile broke through his sheepish expression. His eyes shone with a glint of pride. Even his dimple made an appearance. "I guess that's true."

I rolled my eyes playfully, smiling too. "So proud of yourself," I teased.

He looked at me and popped his right shoulder up, the self-satisfied grin still plastered on his face, and I giggled.

I love this.

Going from intense intimacy one minute to joking friends the next.

I love him.

The realization got caught in my throat, and something must have changed on my face because he asked, "What is it?"

I shook my head, closing my eyes briefly. "Nothing, I just like this."

He leaned down, pushed his fingers into my hair to hold it back from my face, and kissed me deeply. "I like this, too," he said into my lips, our foreheads touching. He pulled back, only a few inches, and looked at me like I was something remarkable. "Who'd have thought I'd have the Morning Glory girl all to myself on my office couch."

My cheeks tugged my face into a wide, disbelieving smile. "Did you really call me that?"

"In my head, yeah. I regretted not learning your name or really anything about you that day."

"I went back." The confession bubbled out of me, unprompted. "Once, around the same time, wondering if I'd see you there again."

"Really?" His eyes squinted in confusion, like he didn't believe it.

This man.

I shook my head incredulously. *Did he already forget what I just told him?* "Well, I don't know if you know this, Luke, but you're, like, ridiculously handsome."

He chuckled, his white teeth and dimple showing, as if to prove my point.

He twisted a strand of my honey brown hair with his fingers. "I don't know if you know this, Valerie, but *you* are ridiculously beautiful." I could melt from hearing my full name come out of his mouth.

I beamed, wrapped my arms around his neck, and buried my face in his broad chest. In that moment I didn't care if anyone else in the world told me I was beautiful ever again. Only him.

34

My fingers were clasped so tightly together I'd lost circulation. Sweat pooled in my bra and under the band of my ball cap as the sun beat down relentlessly. I couldn't imagine how hot these little athletes in front of us must be.

My eyes followed the little green ball as it bounced and flew from one side of the court to the other. It was the final match of the seven- and eight-year-old girls final tennis tournament, and Luna and Clara were playing her old tennis partner, Rachel, and the girl who Rachel asked to play doubles with over Luna, whose name I could never remember.

It was the final set, and if Rachel and her teammate won the next point, then they would win the match. Rachel served. The ball sailed over the net, bounced, and Clara returned it. Rachel's partner hit it back after a bounce, sending it in Clara's direction, to her nondominant side. I nearly covered my eyes with my hands. I said a silent prayer that those extra sessions with Jeremiah paid off. Clara cracked a perfect backhand, and I heard Jeremiah hiss, "Yes," under his breath from beside me. I smirked briefly before the prickling anticipation resumed in my fingertips.

I'd been so impressed all game, all day. These girls were eight years old and already so skilled—fast, accurate, agile. The instructors, some barely teenagers themselves, should be so proud.

Please let them miss it. But no, Rachel returned it again, lobbing it in Luna's direction.

Oh no! It was high; it was going to go right over her head. And Clara was on the other side of the court. I sucked in a breath as Luna's arm shot up. She spiked it down, hard and fast, right over the net. *Yes!* I started to lift out of my seat. *No way they can return that, it's too fast!* Rachel and her partner and everyone in the bleachers watched the ball with rapt attention as it zoomed toward the back corner of the court.

And landed just outside the baseline.

No! My stomach dropped.

My gaze whipped to Luna. Racket hanging by her side, head drooped, her little lip trembled.

Shit. I couldn't cry at a children's tennis match, but boy did I want to. Luna worked so hard. She must be so disappointed. I looked at Luke. He was looking at his daughter, lips a thin line, expression inscrutable.

I turned my attention back to Luna as she lifted her head and walked to the net, shaking both Rachel's and her partner's hand, then embracing Clara.

"Alright, let's go get her," Luke sighed. He gave my thigh a quick squeeze before he stood up.

Luke, Jeremiah, Francesca, Clara's mom, and I all approached the girls and helped them gather their things. Jeremiah told them how impressed he was and that he'd be honored to play more tennis with them next summer.

"You did amazing, Luna," Luke said, clapping her on the shoulder.

"Thanks," she said, sounding utterly defeated. She hugged Clara goodbye. The areas surrounding the court started to clear out and the three of us walked toward Luke's car.

"Luke!" A man a little older than us jogged over from one of the other courts where a boys' match was still underway.

"Hey, Jack. How's it going?"

"Oh, good. Just watching Charlie's final match. You up for a round of golf tomorrow? Tee time is at eleven. I have an extra spot."

"Let me shoot you a text in an hour? I'll check my schedule."

"Sounds good." Jack noticed me standing next to Luke and Luna. She was bouncing on her toes.

"Jack, you know my daughter, Luna. And this is Val, she's... been helping me with Luna this summer."

That introduction sliced through me like a paper cut. I schooled the hurt off my face and reached out to shake Jack's hand. "Nice to meet you," I said. *Thank goodness for sunglasses.*

"You too. Hey, I better catch the end of this match. I'll look out for your text." He turned and jogged away.

We continued toward the main building that stood between the courts and the parking lot.

"I'm sorry," Luke said as soon as Luna was a few paces in front of us. He brushed the back of his fingers against mine.

"It's fine. It's true." I forced a smile.

The truth was, I was hurt but I wasn't actually mad at Luke. I didn't know how I would have answered that question. He'd been amazing since our date—texting me good morning and good night every day, sneaking kisses and hand squeezes and other affectionate gestures whenever we had a moment alone.

We hadn't told Luna yet, and it was clear to me he didn't want her to see anything that confused her before we did. We just hadn't talked about it. Maybe we needed to. I had no doubt we had feelings for each other. But what were we?

Luna climbed into the backseat of her dad's truck. Luke and I both turned to look at her once we got in, A/C blasting through the vents. Luna looked out the window, eyes wide and shining. I felt her disappointment in my own body, like I was the one who lost something I'd been working toward.

"You did so great, Luns," Luke said.

"Thanks. Can we just go home please?" she said quietly.

Luke pulled out of the parking lot.

"Want to get an ice cream from Dairy Queen?" I asked Luna, looking for her in the rearview mirror. Luke caught my eye and nodded.

"No, that's okay." Her tone was so morose. *Maybe we need to let her mope...*

But she was eight. And it was so hot. There was no way a sugary frozen treat wouldn't help, at least a little.

"Do you mind if we make a quick stop there on the way anyway? I really want one."

"Sure," she huffed.

Luke's mouth quirked up. He knew my ploy.

When we pulled into the parking lot, I turned around in the front seat. "Sure you don't want a small chocolate peanut butter cup Blizzard? Since we're already here?"

She looked out the window at the little white house-turned-ice cream shop. Reconsideration glimmered in her big brown eyes. *Got her.*

"Okay," she said. Luke told me what he wanted (a medium strawberry shortcake Blizzard), and I headed inside. They were talking when I got back with the ice creams.

"Luna, I'm so proud of you. You worked so hard and played so well. I know you wanted to win, and it's so disappointing you didn't, but I'm proud of you anyway."

She nodded noncommittally.

"Whether you win or not," he went on, "I'm proud of you and I love you. Nothing will ever change that. I don't care if you lose every other tennis game or sailing competition, I love you and I'm proud of you. No matter what."

Oh my gosh. His speech was so sweet. He was going to make me cry. The words were familiar. *"She'd always pull me aside, tell me she was proud of me, that I was doing my best, that I was human, that she loved me no matter what."*

"I know," she said softly between bites of chocolate ice cream.

I'd stopped eating mine. It was too hard to swallow over the lump in my throat.

"Can you say it for me?"

"You love me and you're proud of me," she mimicked.

"No matter what."

"No matter what."

I had to look away, out my own window, emotion seizing me. This wasn't the first time they'd had this talk. It wouldn't be the last time, either.

I took a deep breath and turned to face them again. I looked at Luke, tacitly asking if I could say something, too. She wasn't my kid, so it wasn't necessarily my place. He nodded his encouragement.

I turned around in my seat. "You two looked amazing out there, Luna. I was so impressed. You worked hard all summer, did your best, and had fun doing something you love—that's what really matters. And you were so poised. It's not easy to shake the hand of your opponent after you just lost, but you did it. I'm so proud of you."

Luke smiled at me privately, reassuring me. *Is this what it would be like? The two of us working together to build Luna up?*

"Thanks, Val," she murmured before asking, "What's 'poised'?"

A chuckle escaped me. "It means being kind and treating others with respect even when we're upset."

She nodded.

"How is it?" I asked, gesturing to her ice cream cup. "They put in enough peanut butter cups?"

"Yeah, lots this time." A little grin appeared on her lips.

I didn't miss the smirk and slight shake of Luke's head. Luna and I had snuck to Dairy Queen for a pre-dinner ice cream here and there this summer, never mentioning it to Luke. Guess our jig was up. Luna didn't seem to realize she'd revealed our secret as she scooped big bites into her mouth. We ordered the same thing every time, including today. I'd given her the one that looked like it had more candy pieces in it.

When we got back to Luke's house, Luna dragged herself up the stairs for a shower. It was still early—sailing was canceled today because so many of the sailors had their tennis competitions. I followed Luke into the kitchen and discarded the ice cream cups. We washed our hands in silence, dancing around each other.

As soon as we heard the shower turn on upstairs, Luke said, "I'm sorry, Val."

I finished drying my hands and turned to face him. "It's okay, I promise. I wouldn't have known what to say either."

"I know, and I believe you. But you were hurt and I'm sorry anyway. I *never* want to hurt you."

"How could you tell I was hurt?"

"I don't know." His brown eyes were so soft and emphatic as he scrutinized me from across the kitchen island. "I can just tell."

I nodded. I supposed it wasn't a bad thing that he could read me so well.

"Can you come here?" he pleaded.

I rounded the counter and stepped into his arms. He wrapped me up, kissing the top of my head. I let myself sink into him, breathe in his piney scent mixed with a hint of sweat and sunscreen after today. It unlocked something in my chest, and I shuddered.

"We haven't told Luna," I said into his shirt, voicing my unfiltered thoughts.

"I know." He pulled back to look at my face. "What's going on in the beautiful brain of yours that's got you emotional?" His thumb traced a soothing stroke on my cheek.

I chewed the inside of my lip and glanced out the window above the kitchen sink. Hot sun poured in through the glass. How could I articulate the feelings swirling through me right now?

I think I love you.

I think I want this. Tennis matches and coming back to this house every day. Helping Luna through all her tough times— together.

It scared me, wanting something that looked so different from what I'd pictured for myself for my whole life. Was I getting carried away?

When I met his eyes again those deep brown pools said I could tell him anything. So I shared a shorter version of the truth. "I'm feeling really attached. But it's new and we've only gone on one official date, and I understand if you're not ready to tell Luna and—"

I stopped myself when Luke opened his mouth to speak.

He cupped my chin in his calloused hand. The intensity of his gaze burned. His thumb moved to press gently on my lower lip, and I sucked in a breath. "I can guarantee you," he said slowly, "there is no way you're any more attached than I already am."

I nodded as my heart galloped.

"I'm ready to tell her," he said. "But I don't tell her about things that are casual or temporary. Is this casual for you? Temporary?"

I shook my head *no*. I couldn't speak with his thumb pressing into my lip, begging me to lick it, or pull into my mouth.

"Good. It isn't for me, either." His eyes seared me, like me admitting I was emotionally attached had unlocked some new level of lust in him.

I gave in to the urge to swipe my tongue across the pad of his thumb. He groaned before pulling my face into his.

The kiss was wet and urgent. We'd barely had a moment to ourselves since Saturday night. I'd thought about it over and over. I wondered if he did, too. His body was telling me *yes* right now. I dug my fingers into his back, through his shirt, pressing our bodies together as tight as I could, desperate to line up my hips with his.

When I did, his hands gripped my waist.

And then turned me around.

He walked us up to the opposite counter, in front of the window. I had to grip the edge to stand upright. His whole body pressed into my back. I could feel his erection, and I rolled myself back into it. His hands moved greedily from my hips to my chest, gripping my breasts through my dress, before dropping lower, lifting my skirt up, and flattening his entire palm between my legs.

I nearly cried out, forgetting our surroundings. He bent his neck down from behind me, capturing my mouth with his, our tongues swirling from this new angle.

I'd pictured a bed for our first time, but in that moment, if he lifted the back of my skirt and asked for permission, I'd let him take me just like this.

But he didn't.

Instead, his fingers slipped into the front of my underwear, down to my wet, swollen clit. His fingertips worked small circles exactly where I needed them, just like he'd done with his tongue on Saturday. *Fast learner*, I thought, already dangerously close to finishing.

When he moved his mouth to my neck, the combination of his soft lips and coarse beard on the sensitive skin near my throat sent sparks through my entire body. "I don't think you're going to need much more instruction," I whispered.

He chuckled. The sound was deep and guttural, with a slightly sinister edge to it. I shivered.

"Maybe not," he murmured before pulling my earlobe gently between his lips.

His arm banded across my chest, his hand cupping my breast, while the other remained pressed firmly between my legs, working magic. My knees started to tremble with the impending release. He held me tighter.

"Shhhh," he whispered as I bit back the cry that wanted to expel from my lips when my muscles contracted and released with sweet agony.

I turned around and pushed my fingers into his hair, burying my face in his neck as I came down. A few breaths, then I reached for his belt, eager to reciprocate, eager to touch the erection that'd been pressed adamantly into my backside while he'd focused on my pleasure. As soon as I undid the buckle and moved my unsteady hands to the top button of his shorts, the sound of rushing water through pipes upstairs abruptly stopped.

Luke grabbed my wrists and pushed my hands back to my sides. "We can't."

"I know."

He looped his belt back through the buckle and paced, adjusting himself. He turned to look at me, shook his head, and chuckled darkly. "Grown adults, sneaking around like a couple of teenagers."

I giggled. "I know!"

He came back and stood in front of me. "We'll tell her when she gets back from my parents', alright?"

"I think that makes sense."

On Sunday, Luna would go to Pennsylvania to spend a week with Luke's parents before she went back to school. From the way she talked about it, they'd done the same thing for years.

"You sure?" he asked.

My brow furrowed in confusion. "Sure that I want to tell Luna?"

He nodded.

"Of course," I said.

"Okay." He held my gaze for a moment before continuing. "And then, I mean, we can't ever get caught doing...*that*"—he gestured to the space between us—"I think that would be mildly traumatizing."

I huffed a laugh and nodded in agreement, feeling my cheeks heat.

"But I feel like you could stay over after that. I don't think it'd be a big deal if she saw you, knew you were there, in my room?"

"Yeah. I mean, if she knows we're together, I think that would all be perfectly fine and normal." *Like parents*, my brain filled in. But I didn't want to say anything like that yet. That seemed a bridge too far—for Luke, for me.

He smiled, liking my answer. "It's a plan." His hand reached out and squeezed mine, then footsteps sounded on the stairs.

Luna sat in one of the stools in the kitchen, looking at us expectantly.

"What do you want to do for the rest of the day?" Luke asked her.

"I don't know," she huffed.

"Want to go up island to the fair? Ride some rides?" he asked.

Her eyes widened with excitement. "Yeah!" She turned that enthusiasm in my direction. "Are you coming, too, Val?"

How does he ever say no to her?

"Yes. I love that fair. I used to go to it when I was your age." I smiled at her. She popped off her chair and scurried back upstairs. To get ready to go, I assumed. I turned to Luke. "Let me call Mimi and see if she wants to come, too."

35

The next afternoon I had a session with my therapist. I didn't have to keep doing the therapy sessions as a condition of my medical leave, but I felt like they were helping, despite all the questions she answered with questions. I'd reduced it to twice a month but planned to stick with it at least until the end of the year.

"I got an email from a legal recruiter the other day." I wasn't sure why I wanted to tell her, honestly. Maybe because I was proud of myself for declining the opportunity the recruiter presented without agonizing over it.

"How did that go?"

"The opportunity was with a firm that just opened their Boston office. They're looking to build out their private equity practice group, so it's a good fit for my background, but I don't think I want to go back to a firm." *Maybe not ever.* "So I responded right away that I wasn't interested at this time."

"How did you feel after you sent that message?"

"Good. Relieved. I haven't second guessed it. I'm not ready and I think I might not ever be..."

Wendy nodded. "Have you thought about your personal definition of success lately?"

"Yes. I thought about what you said, about *who* I want to be. This summer...I've felt like I'm getting to know myself again. Who I was and what I wanted before my career became everything, and who I want to be now."

She raised her eyebrows, indicating I should go on.

"I want to be an optimistic person, someone that lifts up the people around me and makes them feel important. I want to show up and feel present with loved ones. For myself, I want to learn to appreciate simpler things again, keep prioritizing my physical and mental health, and learn to not be so focused on accolades and money as representations of my worth. And I do want to give writing a go. I'm finding that I love it. I wake up every day excited for my day." I shook my head. "It's such a strange feeling."

She gave me the widest smile I'd ever seen from her. "That's great, Val."

I felt a surge of schoolgirl pride, like I'd made some progress after all.

She looked down at the notebook on her desk. "Who are the people you want to lift up? Natalie and your other friends, your grandmother, your parents?"

"Yes, all of them. And Luke, my, uh...boyfriend. And his daughter, Luna. The little girl I've been watching this summer that I told you about?"

"The one who lost her parents?" Wendy clarified.

I nodded. I'd asked her a few weeks ago about Luna and how losing her parents so young would impact her. Luna seemed well-adjusted now, so loved by Luke and her grandparents, but I worried that someday that wouldn't be enough to fill the void left from losing both biological parents.

I'd asked Wendy if she thought, in her professional opinion, that this would be the case. She essentially agreed—that at some point Luna would ask more questions about where she came from, and she would feel the grief like it was the first time, once her more mature brain comprehended the loss anew.

"It's going to be hard on her," Wendy had said. "It's going to be hard on her uncle, too." *I'll help them through it, however I can,* I vowed in my head. Nothing had happened between me and Luke yet by that time, but that hope was already there—that I'd stay in their lives.

"You feel good about this new relationship?" she asked now, a hint of skepticism in her tone.

My mind raced through scenes of this summer: sharing confidences, sharing meals, the trip to Menemsha where he told me how he saw me after I said I didn't know who I was without my job. "Yes," I said, absolutely certain. "He's been really good for me. Luna, too. She reminds me what matters in life, you know? It's been fun hanging out with her, seeing the world through their eyes. Rooting for them, feeling needed."

Her pen raced over her notepad. "It sounds like it's been very positive, then," she said finally. I could almost hear the *but* that threatened at the end of her statement.

"You have qualms?"

Her eyes flashed to mine through the screen. "I think qualms is too strong a term. I just want you to look out for yourself, stay in touch with yourself, you know? You've been through a lot, but it seems to me you're a lot happier, and more comfortable in your own skin, now. Keep in mind that taking on a family, especially one that has been through what they've been through, is a big undertaking."

I nodded. I knew it was. Irritation at the constant reminders of what a big undertaking Luke and Luna were mixed with my own trepidation over the degree to which my life had changed in the last five months. Nevertheless, it just felt *right*.

"I know. I won't lose myself. I actually feel like he's helped me rediscover parts of myself that I like, parts that got buried under my work and ambition."

"Well, that is a *really* good thing." Her eyes twinkled with encouragement.

And then our time was up.

I went downstairs to fill my water bottle and found Mimi sitting at the kitchen table, a crossword spread in front of her.

"How was your session this week?" she asked. I'd kept Mimi in the loop about the therapy sessions, usually just that I was having them and not necessarily the details of what we talked about. But today I broke tradition.

"Everyone keeps saying—Luke, my therapist—that embarking on a relationship with Luke and becoming a part of Luna's life is a lot to take on." I searched Mimi's face for her reaction, but her expression revealed nothing of what she was thinking. "It bothers me." I pushed a breath out in an exasperated huff and dropped into a kitchen chair. "I mean, I get it. It's not exactly what I pictured. I pictured meeting someone a similar age to me that wanted a family but didn't have one yet and starting that family together. I didn't picture having an eight-year-old stepdaughter at thirty-one years old. It *is* a lot. But...I don't know. I just can't imagine anything else now. If that makes sense."

"It does," Mimi said.

"Am I missing something? Should I feel more nervous about it than I do? Because the idea of *not* being there, with both of them, is so much scarier to me than the responsibility I'd be taking on trying to learn how to be a mom." I thought about the conversation we had with Luna in the car after she lost her tennis match, how Luke encouraged me. He didn't want me on the sidelines, that much was clear. We'd be a team. In a way, we already were. "The idea of not being there as she grows up feels like a knife in the stomach," I added.

"Then I think you have your answer," Mimi said, sincerity shining clear in her eyes.

I nodded, brows furrowing. *Why do I always let what other people say make me question myself?*

As if she could sense my need for more reassurance, she went on, "Life is never what we picture. It gets complicated whether it starts out that way or not." The wisdom of her words struck me. "Now that they're in your life, what do *you* want?"

"I want to be with Luke. I want to be the best mother, or mother figure, I can to Luna. I want to write, and keep figuring out what makes me truly happy, because it wasn't climbing the corporate ladder." I paused. "But I also want to get married and have some of our own children someday, too."

Mimi's smile reached her eyes. "I don't see any reason you couldn't have all those things."

"But Luna deserves a real mother, someone who loves her unconditionally. And if I still want to have my own children, will she feel left out?" I asked, voicing a fear I'd barely formed or articulated, even to myself.

"You wouldn't let that happen." Mimi reached for my hand on the kitchen table, her hand soft and delicate, resting on mine. "Val, I have known you your entire life, and your heart is so big. Your capacity to love is infinite. You already love that little girl, I can tell."

My chest constricted and my eyes filled. "I do," I choked out. Mimi stood up and pulled her chair next to mine so she could wrap an arm around my shoulders.

"You'll be an amazing mother figure, an amazing female role model for her after she hasn't had one for a long time. You'll give her the chance to be a mother's daughter and, hopefully, a big sister someday." Mimi gave my shoulder a squeeze and dipped her head to look at me. "What a beautiful thing after all that she lost. All that Luke lost, too."

I nodded, not able to form words over the lump in my throat. After a few watery blinks and deep breaths, I said, "I already love her so much, I couldn't love her any more." I wanted to be there for every one of Luna's first days of school, all her graduations, her wedding, and all of her triumphs and losses. *When did I get so invested?* It snuck up on me, and it couldn't be undone.

"I know," Mimi said. I could tell she believed me.

"But this is so complicated. What if I get attached to her, and to Luke, and then I'm the one that gets hurt?" *I'm already in too deep.* I couldn't imagine leaving them, but what if he left me?

"Do you think that's going to happen? What do you feel in your gut?" Her tone was leading, like she already knew what she thought, but she wanted me to get there on my own.

I hadn't asked myself that question before. I swiped under my eyes, considering. I had always trained myself to assume my relationships might not last, because none of my prior relationships had. But with Luke, it felt so different.

"Caring for and about others seems to come so naturally for you. You're intuitive and creative and empathetic."

"Stay."

"Isn't it obvious?"

"I want to be near you all the time, talk to you all the time. Touch you all the time."

"I can guarantee you, there is no way you're any more attached than I already am."

"No," I said to Mimi, my tears quelled for the moment. "I don't think that's going to happen. My gut is telling me he's just as invested as I am."

36

I picked Luna up from her final sailing practice later that day. Their regatta was tomorrow, and that marked the end of the summer season. Clara's mom and I took the girls to get ice cream. They bounced back quickly from yesterday's loss, already talking excitedly about the regatta and their back-to-school plans.

Melting cups of ice cream in hand—mint chip for me, cookie dough for Luna—the four of us sat on a bench facing the harbor, watching the boats dock and leave, and the group of ducks floating in the water right near the edge, hoping for scraps of bread and potato chips from passing children. Sunlight reflected off the choppy waves in a way that made the surface look like it was covered in sparkling diamonds. The slight breeze made the August heat more bearable.

It made me nostalgic for my own childhood, sitting on these same benches, eating ice cream with Drew and my parents or grandparents—whoever we'd convinced to take us into town for a frozen dessert. Sometimes we were in regular clothes, coming down from Mimi's house before or after dinner, and other times we were still in our damp bathing suits, sand sticking to our feet and legs, coming directly from the beach.

I watched Luna from the corner of my eye, happily licking her cone, swinging her little legs back and forth, chatting with her friend, her dark hair a wild mess only half contained by her ponytail. Freckles that weren't there when I met her in May dotted her cheeks. She had Luke's same deep brown eyes and enviable eyelashes. Her smiles were like sunshine in spring, and looking at her, seeing her happy, filled me up.

I wonder if this is how Luke feels all the time.

When we got home, Luna didn't protest heading right upstairs for a shower. Then we settled into the air-conditioned living room, me with my book, Luna with an animated movie she liked. I heard the rumble of a truck pulling into the driveway, but after a few minutes the telltale sound of a car door closing hadn't come. Maybe it was just a car going by. I read a few more lines, but my curiosity and uncontained excitement for Luke to be home had my feet carrying me to the window.

His truck was in the driveway, but he stayed in the front seat, arm draped over the steering wheel, head resting on his forearm.

My stomach plunged with fear. Did something bad happen?

"Luna, I'll be right back." I didn't bother to put on shoes before I bolted down the walkway.

I tapped on the window and his head popped up with a start. The car locks clicked. I climbed up into the passenger seat and reached for his forearm.

"What happened?" I asked softly, trying to stop my mind from jumping to horrible conclusions.

He took a deep breath and blew it out. His eyes were glassy and contemplative. My chest ached before he even said a word. "I ran into one of Monica's friends from high school. Totally random, first time she and her family went on vacation here. She was with her husband and—and little kid." His voice broke, along with my heart. "Fuck." His hand ran roughly down his face.

He looked at me, his face broken. "That should be her, you know? Vacationing with her husband and kid." He turned back and stared out the windshield. "It fucking sucks that she's gone."

I climbed over the center console and wedged myself into his lap between his chest and the steering wheel. I wrapped my arms around his neck, and he dropped his head on my shoulder, holding me tight in his arms. He shuddered into me. It may as well have come from my own body. *Let me take some of it,* I begged the universe.

But that wasn't how life worked. So I held him, running my fingers through the ends of his hair and over his shoulders in a way I hoped was soothing until his breaths steadied. Fingers still locked behind his head, I pulled back enough to look at his face. "It's not fair," I said. "It should be her. You and your sister, her husband, Luna, your parents—you were all robbed."

After a minute of holding each other, breathing into each other, I asked, "Wanna go in? I could hug you forever, but I think you need one from the little girl inside right now."

He swallowed. "I think you're right."

Luna was right where I left her. Luke circled the couch and said, "Hey, Luns."

"Hey, Dad," she said, not looking away from the screen, where dragons flew through clouds to an inspirational song. Luke sat down next to her, pulled her into his lap and hugged her, kissing the top of her head. "Dad!" she squealed at the distraction. When he didn't let go, she looked at him for the first time since he walked in the door. Then she squeezed him back, no longer squirming to break away and focus on her movie. *That beautiful, intuitive little human.* Another quick squeeze and he plopped her back on the couch.

"How about pizza for dinner?" he asked her.

"Yay!" was her only response. A smile broke through on Luke's face. I chuckled internally. Ice cream and pizza, what a day for an eight-year-old.

He needed her today. And she was going to need him on lots of days, for the rest of her life, not least of all once the magnitude of what she lost when she was young sinks in. Maybe someday, when she was older, they'd be able to talk about it more.

But today it seemed like having each other was enough.

All day Sunday I bounced around Mimi's house and yard, cleaning, gardening, cooking, checking the clock. When would Luke get home from dropping Luna off with his parents at their agreed meeting point in Connecticut? I wished I'd asked.

I'd offered to go with them, but he insisted I stay back to get some writing done and spend some time with Mimi before he got home. When he said it, he gave me a knowing look that sent heat through my body.

I could call him to ask, but I didn't want to seem *so* eager to spend an entire week alone with him. Even though I absolutely was.

When my cell rang just after 6:00 p.m., I lunged for it like a nineties teenager lunging for the landline. After telling me the drive went well, he asked, "Is it weird if I ask you to be there when I get home?"

"No." I laughed.

"Why is that funny?"

"Because I've been thinking about how badly I want to see you when you get back, but I was worried you might be too tired."

"I've never had more energy," he deadpanned. I smiled giddily at my phone.

My skin buzzed with anticipation as I all but ran down the hall to shower.

I drove to Luke's house an hour later, and when his headlights flashed into his living room through the front-facing picture window, I abandoned my wine and book on the coffee table to meet him at the door.

I opened it when he reached the bottom step.

"Hi!" I said, heart thundering.

He looked at me as his feet carried him up the front steps two at a time, eyes blazing. He didn't say a thing. His hands grabbed my face and brought my lips to his in an urgent kiss, greeting me with his mouth instead of his words. It might have been the hottest thing I'd ever experienced. My body lit up with a rush of excitement.

The kiss deepened and got sloppier as I backed us into the house, closing the front door behind him. His lips pressed into my neck, leaving goose bumps. His hands turned me around by my waist and nudged me up the stairs, no detour to the living room. He kicked off his shoes aggressively and followed me, a hasty, calloused hand pushing me up each step. I giggled, looking over my shoulder. The heat in his gaze only got more intense.

We barreled into his room in a tangle of limbs. He walked me back until I was sitting on the end of his bed. He kissed me firmly, but then stepped back, held up his pointer finger, and strode to the *en suite* bathroom.

The faucet turned on and I walked over, my bare feet soundless on the plush bedroom carpet. I watched as he scrubbed his hands with soap in the sink. Leaning on the doorframe, I smiled at him. He looked up at me, smirking as that piece of unruly dark hair fell in front of his forehead. *So freaking adorable.* I couldn't explain why I loved it so much when that happened.

He dried his hands and walked toward me. "Hi, baby," he said finally, voice a mix of lust and levity.

"Hi." I beamed. One hand found my waist, the other wrapped behind my neck, and we picked up where we left off.

Shirts were removed and discarded on the floor, then my bra. He dropped his head immediately to pull my nipple into his mouth, licking and sucking gently.

"Luke, oh my god," I moaned. My underwear would be soaked through by the time we removed any more clothing.

Our bodies moved toward his bed once more, unclear if it was me pulling him or him pushing me. Both.

My knees bent, my half naked body sitting down, legs parted, waiting for him to fill them. Luke stood in front of me in nothing but shorts. I pulled my lip under my teeth as my eyes roamed. His did the same. My hands reached for his belt. I wanted as little as possible between us when he finally pressed me back down on his bed.

His bed.

I'd spent almost no time here—in his room. When I came up here to do laundry that time, I felt like an interloper, peering into a private part of his life. We barely knew each other, but I already felt at ease in his presence. I wanted to share things with him, do things for him, even then.

He looked down at me, his hooded eyes a mix of hunger and adoration and disbelief, like he'd pictured this before and wanted to pause for a second to take it in. And then he stepped out of his shorts and crouched to his knees, pulling my athletic skirt off and adding it to the trail of strewn clothing on his floor. He stood again, looking like an underwear model in his black boxer briefs. Well, apart from the sizable erection pressing through the material, the sight of which sent a flutter of electricity right to my core.

"Scooch back, against the pillows."

I did as he said, moving until my light brown hair was spread across his gray pillows. He climbed on top of me slowly, eyes as dark as night, drinking in my body greedily. I never once thought about how I looked when we were intimate, as comfortable with him in this context as I was talking to him at his kitchen table. My mind only focused on the sensations in my body, how badly I wanted to make him feel good too, and my urgency to feel *closer* to this man I'd fallen for, in every possible way.

In the moment.

I smirked. He caught me. "What are you thinking?" he asked.

"I'm thinking it's fun having more space than the couch."

"Mmmm." He kissed my neck, dragging his tongue over the sensitive skin, lining his body up with mine. I grinded myself against his erection needily.

I reached down between us. I wanted to feel how hard he was for me right now. He did the same, slipping his fingers in between the apex of my thighs, pushing the lace thong I was wearing to the side.

"I'm so wet for you," I whispered.

The groan that left him then came from somewhere deeper. Instinctual, not based on thought. I wrapped my own fingers around the smooth skin of his shaft, which was hard as marble. His hip bucked at the contact. I loved seeing him like this—uninhibited.

"Val," he breathed. "Do you— Can we—"

"Yes." My actions matched my words as I pushed the black cotton of his boxers down over his muscled thighs. He dipped to his side, pushing them off before pulling my thong over my legs, too. He removed a condom from the drawer in the nightstand and knelt between my legs, dark eyes watching me. I adjusted myself, lifting my hips, opening my legs further. He circled his thumb over my clit, then slid two fingers inside of me. With his other hand, he gave himself a tug. *Oh god, I'll never get this image out of my head.*

When he removed his fingers and ripped open the condom package, needing both hands to slide it on, my core was on fire from the absence of him, so much so that when he finally lined himself up and I felt his head right where I needed it, I begged, "Now, please."

He pushed into me, filling me, letting his weight fall on top of my body. I kissed him with everything I had as he rocked his hips in between my legs, as my body stretched and relaxed to accommodate him, letting him in deeper. Our tongues swirled, our breaths tangled, our bodies rolled in a newfound rhythm.

I clenched around him, lifting my hips to meet each of his thrusts. I relished the closeness—our sweat-slicked skin touching, lips pressed together, tongues devouring, him inside of me. As close as we could possibly be physically, somehow not close enough. Maybe if we do this another thousand times...

"I'm close, baby," he rasped in my ear. "Can I go faster?"

"Yes," I nearly cried. "Oh my god, yes."

"How can I make you come too, with me?"

I was close, too, riding that edge for a little while now, especially when his pelvic bone provided some friction near my clit.

His huge body caged me with both arms pressing his chest up. I licked a path from his chest to his neck and met the dark, lust-filled pools of his eyes again. "If you touch me, but only just before."

He nodded and his mouth crashed back into mine, tongue delving deep. He pulled almost all the way out of me before slamming back in with more force than before. A cry of pleasure left my throat, captured by his mouth. He did it again and then kept rocking into me almost twice as fast as he had before, taking what he needed to come, and boy did I want to give it to him. One, two, three, four thrusts later he reached down, pressing his hand between our joined bodies until his middle finger found my clit. I exploded almost immediately, crying his name. One last slam inside me as I clenched and writhed around him, and he let go, too. He came with a guttural groan before dropping the rest of his weight on top of me, head turned to the side, panting. I clung to him as we both came down, pressing my hands into his bare back, massaging his taut muscles.

"Oh my god," he said finally.

"I know."

He rolled onto his side, pulling out of me, a sated sigh leaving his lips. When I turned to look at him, his eyes were on me. Not my body, but my face. He reached out and twirled a piece of my hair in his hand before gently pushing it behind my ear. It was so tender, a lump formed in my throat. I ran my fingers up and down his arm, pausing on the tattoo on his shoulder. Three rows of numbers, with slashes in between. *Dates.*

"Can I ask what they are?"

He nodded, eyes locked on mine.

"April 10, 1987?"

"Monica's birthday."

"September 15, 1990?"

"My birthday."

I knew the next one. "And Luna's," I whispered. "I love it." I pushed myself up and kissed his shoulder, right over the ink, before lying back down and returning my gaze to those chocolate eyes.

"Mom and Monica had a thing about birthdays. Always made a big deal about them. So, I don't know, this is symbolic of my commitment to keep up that tradition."

"You celebrate your sister's, too?"

"Yeah, I take Luna on a fancy dad-daughter date. Francesca's idea. We don't talk about why, but I want to when she's older."

"I think that's a great tradition." I smiled, and he brushed his thumb over my raised cheek.

We lay there, exchanging gentle caresses, heads resting on his pillows, facing each other on our sides, until our breaths were soft and easy.

He opened his mouth to say something but closed it a breath later.

"Tell me," I whispered.

"I'm falling in love with you."

My heart trilled. "I love you, too." No hesitation, no doubt in my mind.

His brown eyes lit up. "Yeah?" He inched closer to me, touching our noses together.

"Yeah," I affirmed before his lips found mine. It was soft and exploratory, full of care. Cherishing.

A kiss that said *I love you.*

I never wanted to be kissed by anyone else.

Luke and I spent the next two days tangled in his sheets from the moment he got home from work until we drifted off after midnight. Talking, touching, experimenting. Only short trips to the kitchen for food and water.

As I expected, he didn't need any more instructions on what did it for me—he was already a pro.

And he knew it.

On Wednesday, we decided we should leave the house, at least for a few hours. We drove to the beach when he got home from work.

We settled on top of the still warm sand, sitting on a blanket, me between his legs, using his knees as armrests while we watched the waves.

"I want to ask you something but I'm nervous it's too soon," I said. Ever since my conversation with Mimi I'd been wondering if Luke wanted more kids, or if Luna was it for him. I looked at him over my shoulder, my green eyes wide with trepidation.

"Please tell me."

I chewed my lip, pulse thrumming.

"Valerie, I love you, you can tell me," he urged.

I love you. He said it so freely and easily now that we'd admitted our feelings. Every day, multiple times a day. My heart swelled. We'd only been together, romantically, for under two weeks, but with all the time we'd spent together both before the fundraiser and this week, it felt like much longer than that. My mind told me it was too soon to bring something like this up, but my heart disagreed, so I took a breath and asked, "Do you want to have more kids? More than Luna, I mean?"

He wrapped his arms around me and squeezed before spinning me to face him. I sat cross-legged in front of him, his eyes locked on mine from under the brim of his ball cap.

"Do you?" He scanned my face, trying to read me.

"But I asked you first."

"Fair enough." He ran his hand over his face, and a tinge of anxiety hummed under my skin. "Yes. I always thought I'd want a family with multiple kids someday. And then Luna being born, and then me becoming her guardian, confirmed it."

I squeezed his forearm.

"I wouldn't do it alone, though..." he added, leading me.

"I want them, too," I was quick to confirm. "I think Luna would be a great big sister."

An uninhibited smile broke across his handsome face, white teeth on full display in the early evening light.

I beamed back at him, and relief that bordered on elation filled my heart.

"So, how soon we talking? Should we ditch the condom tonight?" He raised his thick, dark brows.

"Luke!" I shoved him playfully.

"What?" he asked, brown eyes dancing with mischief, mock indignation in his tone. "I'm not...not serious."

My eyes flew wide, but my smile stretched even bigger on my face. Even though I was starting to feel really good about my decisions—to quit the law firm grind and write, to stay on the island with Luke and Luna—it would be a lot to add another child to the mix right away.

From his grin and his tone, I could tell he was teasing me, at least partially. Saying something crazier than what I said presumably so I stopped feeling self-conscious for asking. I had no idea if he did it on purpose or if it was just natural for him—his uncanny ability to say what I needed him to say. Every time.

I stood, removed my cover-up, and dragged him into the crashing waves with me, reminding him August was the only time the water was passably warm in New England. He picked me up once we were out past our waists, but a swell crashed over our heads, toppling us. We came up sputtering and laughing.

"I forgot how strong the waves are here!" he called over the surf, whipping his dark hair out of his eyes. I treaded a few feet away and watched him, water droplets glistening on his tanned, toned shoulders, before dropping my head back to look at the deep blue sky. Floating on my back, the Atlantic waves lulled me. I turned and saw Luke doing the same, not two feet away. *I don't think it gets any better than this.*

It almost felt too good to be true.

37

Guilt gnawed at me for leaving Mimi on her own all week. So when she asked me if I wanted to join her and her friend Cathy and her husband for dinner at the yacht club on Thursday, I said yes.

"It's okay, Val. Go have fun with Mimi," Luke said when I told him about the dinner this afternoon like I was breaking bad news.

"I could come over after?" I asked. That still felt like ditching her, but I didn't want to miss a private night with Luke.

We'd discussed that I could stay over after Luna comes home and we tell her about us, but it wouldn't be every night starting out. We both wanted to let her adjust gradually. And we'd have to be a little bit...quieter, once we no longer had the whole house to ourselves.

"It's okay, hang with her after dinner, too. I genuinely need to get some stuff done before Luna gets back, and I won't do it if you're here distracting me." His flirtatious tone told me he didn't mind my distractions.

I sighed.

His voice dropped lower. "We'll make up for it tomorrow, I promise."

My thighs clenched.

"Okay, *fine*," I whined.

He laughed at me. "Text me when you get home. Love you."

"Love you, too."

We arrived early for our reservation and went to the bar in the corner of the dining room for a drink. The windows were all open, water views on three sides, wind flowing through the room in a pleasant cross-breeze.

Mimi and I ordered Cosmos, and Cathy and her husband ordered glasses of wine. We took seats at a high top, watching boats arriving and departing the harbor outside the row of windows behind the dark wooden bar. I scanned the room: tables with three generations of families—grandparents, adult parents, and children in little dresses and collared shirts. My eyes snagged on an older couple at the end of the bar and my stomach dropped. *The Phelpses.* I stared long enough to confirm it was just Brianna and Ed. No sign of Max, *thank god.*

I returned my attention to the conversation with Mimi and her friends. They were discussing their plans to head back to their winter residences in the fall.

"What are you doing in the fall?" Cathy asked me.

I considered telling her the truth, even though it would be news even to Mimi—that I was planning to stay on the island, I wanted to write instead of going back to corporate law, and I wanted to keep living near Luke and Luna. Instead, for some reason, I said, "I haven't fully decided yet."

"That's okay, dear," she said. "No need to wish the rest of the summer away."

But the summer was nearly over, and while I wanted to stay here, I didn't have a plan for how to support myself. My only source of income was Luke's babysitting checks, and I needed to tell him I wouldn't accept those anymore. We were together now, and it would feel wrong to let him pay me to spend time with Luna.

I'll just need to dip into savings for a while, I thought with a gulp of stress.

The hostess came over to tell us our table was ready. I went to the bar to close our tab, telling my dinner companions I'd meet them at the table.

I checked the corner of the bar where the Phelpses had been sitting as I walked over, hoping they'd left, and accidentally caught Edward's eye instead. *Crap.* He gave me a nod of recognition, so I compelled myself to go say hello.

"Hey, Ed."

"Val, right? My son isn't very happy with you."

"Oh yeah, that... I'm sorry." Why didn't I just wave instead of coming over here?

He batted his hand into the air. "He's a grown man. He'll recover."

I smirked. So much for sympathy from the romance-novelist father. But something told me Max had had many girlfriends, so maybe his parents didn't think much of his breakups. Ed didn't seem the least bit concerned.

"I hope so." His wife was thoroughly engaged in conversation with the person to her left. I waited to get the bartender's attention, facing the bar instead of Edward Phelps.

"So, you're heading back to New York at the end of the summer?" he asked.

I took a deep breath. I'd told his parents I was only taking a sabbatical from work because I was too embarrassed to tell them the truth—that I was on an anxiety-induced medical leave and may or may not quit by the end of it. Which, of course, I had.

"No, I—I actually left my job, for good."

A flash of surprise crossed his face. He looked so much like Max, with the sandy brown hair and blue eyes. I smiled, trying to display confidence on the outside even though, on the inside, I was feeling the opposite. But when will I get another chance to talk to a famous author? Luke kept trying to get me comfortable with calling myself a writer, so what the hell. "I've actually been writing. I've always wanted to. I've been working on something this summer."

"Novels?" His brows went up further.

"Yes." I held my breath, hoping for some golden kernel of advice from one of the most successful novelists of all time.

"What a shame to waste the skill set you already have. You'll have a hard time making half as much money as a struggling novelist. I wish you luck, though." He raised his glass in my direction. The din of conversation and glasses clinking and cutlery scraping against plates sounded far away, all of a sudden. All the air left my lungs. *Did he really just say that?*

Confusion overtook my features. I said, "Thanks" meekly, grabbed my drink, and bolted for Mimi's table in the corner of the crowded dining room. The bartender would have to find us with the bill.

I found it hard to focus on the conversation for the rest of dinner.

That night, I lay in bed, staring at the ceiling, unable to fall asleep. A few sleepovers and already it felt strange to be alone at night. I missed Luke. Maybe I should have gone over there anyway.

Edward Phelps's voice echoed in my head. *"A shame to waste the skill set."* His words tangled with his son's. *"Your life is such a mess."*

I spent all this time learning this valuable skill, how could I throw it away? I had no formal writing education; I would be crazy to think I could just start doing that as a career. And what other opportunities would I have on the island? I could work in a small law office...but my skill set was specialized: private equity transactions. In order to do that, I'd need to work at a law firm in a city, or in-house at a private equity firm, *in a city.*

I picked up my phone and dug out that recruiter email I received a few days ago. I stared at it, reading it again and again. Maybe this firm would have a better culture. Maybe I'd like Boston more than New York. And I could easily get from Boston to Martha's Vineyard every weekend.

My fear outweighing any doubts in my mind, I typed out a new reply.

On second thought, I am interested in interviewing with the Boston firm. Can you please set it up? Thank you!
– Val Leone

38

On Friday, Luke cut out of work a little early. We held hands in the grocery store before heading home to have wine on the deck. We cooked a real dinner for the first time that week: grilled salmon and salad and orzo dressed simply in olive oil and spices.

"You must be excited for Luna to get home tomorrow," I said to him. Empty plates sat in front of us on the outside dining table. We nursed the last of our drinks, watching the sky turn pink.

"Yeah." He looked from the sky back at me. "Don't get me wrong"—he reached for my knee under the table—"I've been having an amazing time with you this week. But it's kinda weird not having her here."

"I agree." I was excited for her to come home, too. The house felt a little empty. Not enough Broadway sing-alongs or *How to Train Your Dragon* on TV. I missed reading with her. "I hope she and your mom didn't get too far ahead of me in the *Magic Tree House* books."

Luke laughed like I'd told an intentional joke. His laugh was infectious, so I giggled too, even though I was being serious to begin with.

We did the dishes together before he took my hand and led me upstairs. We were up even later than usual that night, taking our time, trying new positions, laughing when they didn't work, repeating them when they did.

I completely forgot about my conversation with Max's dad last night, and the email I sent after I got home.

My memory loss was short-lived, however.

I woke up to bright sunlight streaming into Luke's bedroom through the cracks in the blinds. I loved how bright the morning light was here, like even the sun was excited for the day to begin.

To my right, Luke was sleeping soundly, his chiseled, tanned back rising and falling with each breath. His head was turned on its side, one hand under his pillow, the other extended toward me. I studied the long black eyelashes resting on his cheeks. *So gorgeous, this man.*

I didn't want to wake him yet; he had a long day of driving ahead of him. So I rolled over as quietly as I could and distracted myself on my phone, scrolling social media before opening my email. Tucked in between advertisements and my credit card statement was a response from the recruiter.

Val, So glad you reconsidered. They can meet with you in Boston at 1 p.m. on Tuesday. They want to move fast and said the signing bonus will be generous. Let me know if that works for you, and I'll send over the details.

Oh my god. My stomach plummeted, and not with excitement. As if he sensed the trepidation radiating off me, Luke stirred.

He opened one eye first, saw I was awake, and propped himself up on the pillows. "Hey," he muttered sleepily.

"Hey." I slid down a bit and ran my fingers through his hair.

"Mmm, I love it when you do that."

A laugh escaped my throat. "I know."

I looked back at my phone, chewing my lip as I reread the email. Did I want to meet with them on Tuesday? I supposed one interview couldn't hurt. I didn't need to take the job, even if I got it. I sighed more loudly than I intended.

"Whatcha looking at?" His eyes were open now, assessing me.

"Oh, um. Just an email from a recruiter. There's this firm that's opening an office in Boston and they need lawyers with my background. I, uh, got an interview."

Luke sat up, brows furrowed, not saying anything for long enough that it made me nervous.

Compelled to fill the silence, I said, "The summer is ending, and I don't feel right having you pay me to spend time with Luna now that we're...doing this." I gestured between us. "I have enough savings to last a while but..." I shrugged.

"Val, I don't want you to go back to a job you didn't like because you don't want me to keep paying you to watch Luna. I'll keep doing it; I can afford it."

"No, Luke. It's weird. It feels wrong. Please."

"Okay, well, let me pay for other expenses you have. So you can take your time and keep writing. That's a totally normal thing for a boyfriend to do... I'm your boyfriend, right?" The question was earnest.

I smiled. We'd said I love you but had skipped the boyfriend/girlfriend conversation. "Yes. I mean, that's what I want. That's how I feel."

"Okay, good. So that's established." His dark brows were still furrowed.

"But I don't want you to pay for my expenses. I have all this education and work experience. I can't just...*not* contribute."

He looked at me for a long time, like he didn't know what to say. He sat all the way up, turned to face me, and took my hand, a tortured look on his face. *He's upset.* It hit me like a blow to the chest. I didn't think a simple interview would spiral like this.

"But Val. I've watched you work through this the entire summer. I've seen the change in you. You're happy. I can tell. Why would you go back to something that made you miserable?"

I swallowed, emotion caught in my throat. Hurt because he

was upset. Worry that he was right—that even entertaining returning to a law firm was a mistake. And perhaps most powerfully, the deafening self-doubt and insecurity I felt deep down, drowning everything else out. I closed my eyes and told him the truth. "Because I worked my entire life for this. And when people look at me—the education and experience I have—and find out I'm an unemployed, aspiring author, they look down on me."

"Who? What people?" Indignation laced his tone with acid.

"I don't know, everyone!"

Me.

I flung the sheet off my lap and got out of bed, needing to pace. I loved how he saw me to my core, understood me in a way that was sort of remarkable given how long we'd known each other, sometimes even better than I understood myself. But right now, as his concerned gaze bore into me, I was overcome with the feeling that he saw too much.

"They don't matter," he said. "They don't know you. And they don't know the key to life either, despite what they might think. No one does."

I stopped and looked at Luke. His chest was heaving, his legs tangled in the sheets, barely awake but fuming. "It's just an interview," I said quietly. To him, to myself. He climbed out of bed and stood in front of me—him in his boxers, me in my silky PJ set. He pushed my hair behind my ears and lifted my chin to look at him.

The look of hurt on his face cracked my heart wide open. I lowered my gaze.

"Is it too much? Are we moving too fast?" he asked.

"No! This has nothing to do with us. This is about me. I promise." I gripped the wrist of the hand that was still holding my cheek and turned my face to kiss his palm. "I just... I don't know how to let go of my entire career. It was my whole world before this summer."

"Can I ask you something?"

I nodded cautiously.

"What would you want Luna to do? Twenty-plus years from now, if she was in the exact same position?"

I'd tell her to stay here and be happy. The answer came from my gut. My soul.

"You're not fighting fair," I whispered, eyes filling.

"When it comes to you two, my girls, I will *never* fight fair."

I choked on a sob, and he pulled me into his strong, warm arms. He kissed my hair. "Hey, no crying. You're right. It's just an interview. See how it goes, see how you feel, and we'll talk about it, okay?" His fingers stroked my hair, holding me tight until I got my emotions under control.

"When is it?" he asked when I lifted my head off his chest.

"Tuesday."

He nodded, somber. His eyes were glassy. My strong man. I hated myself for making him cry. At the same time, I didn't fully understand it. It was just an interview. I probably wouldn't even take the job. But I felt compelled to add, "Boston isn't that far. It's easy to get back and forth."

"That's true," he said, but his smile didn't reach his eyes. His lips pressed to my forehead. "I'm going to take a shower."

I nodded, words eluding me.

He didn't fully close the bathroom door, and the intimacy of it struck me.

I sat on the corner of his bed, head in my hands. *It's just an interview*, I repeated to myself. *Why did it feel like more than that all of a sudden?*

I got dressed slowly, listening to the sound of running water from the bathroom. He stayed in there long enough that mist wafted through the crack in the door. I watched the spirals of steam rise, tranced.

Where did that confidence I found to live on my own terms this summer go?

Luke and Luna got home late that night. Since we hadn't told Luna we were together yet, I didn't go over to the house. It hurt to not be with them when they were only a mile away. *Tomorrow*, I said to myself. Surely we'd tell her tomorrow and then start figuring out what our new normal would be.

The next day, Luke told me they were running errands in the morning, buying back-to-school supplies. I went over to hang out with them in the afternoon.

"Hey, Luna!"

She ran over and hugged me.

"You don't usually come on Sundays," Luna said. Nothing got past her.

"I know." I glanced up at Luke. *Should we tell her now?* But he didn't say anything, so I said, "I missed you and wanted to come hang out, if that's okay with you?"

"Obviously," she waved her hand in front of her and returned to the living room.

"What do you want to do today? Do you have any summer bucket list things you didn't get to do yet?" I asked her.

"What's a bucket list?"

"It's a list of things you want to do before a certain time, in this case, before school starts."

"Hmmm." Luna pursed her lips, concentrating hard.

"We were thinking the beach, but it's not that nice out," Luke added. He felt far away, sitting on the opposite couch. Every other time I'd been here in the last week, some part of our bodies was touching, or at least within reach.

Pulled by a magnet, I crossed the room and sat down next to him. I checked the weather radar on my phone. It was a little misty and chilly, but no rain was expected.

"What about a bike ride? We could take the bike path along the beach to Oak Bluffs. Maybe get a ride in on the Flying Horses Carousel?"

Luna's face lit up. She turned to her dad for his agreement. He nodded and said, "Go up and put on some leggings so you don't get too cold, Luns."

After she scampered up the stairs, Luke leaned over and kissed my cheek. "Have I told you how smart you are?"

I smiled. "Not today."

A laugh rattled out of his chest.

He stood from the couch. "I'm going to change, too." He scanned my outfit, lingering on the bare legs extending from my short denim shorts. I wanted him to touch them, but I sensed his hesitation. We both knew Luna would be bounding back into the room at any moment.

"I'll grab you a sweatshirt," he said before jogging up the stairs.

The slight chill in the air made the bike ride refreshing. Luna rode ahead of me, Luke behind both of us. A few undaunted beach-goers set up at the beach, wrapping themselves in towels and sweatshirts. Several kids and preteens splashed in the waves, unconcerned with the air temperature.

When we got to Oak Bluffs, the town was full of day-trippers, kids and families, and couples young and old, shopping and dining. The whole downtown buzzed with end-of-season energy, everyone squeezing in some quintessential summer experiences before school and work and reality crashed back down on them all.

With that interview coming up, I felt that same urgency to soak it all in while I still could. I pushed it down, trying to be in the moment with Luke and Luna.

On the third turn around the carousel, Luna got the sole brass ring from the dispenser that extended over the wooden horses. This earned her one more free ride, a fist of victory into the air, and a big smile splashed across her adorable little face that made me feel like a kid again, like her dopamine flowed right into my own system. Luke looked similarly elated, leaning on the half wall next to me, beaming at Luna and giving her a whistle of praise.

We wandered through town as a trio, eventually stopping at one of the casual seafood restaurants along the water for an early dinner.

Luna told us all about her week with her grandparents, what they did each day, the new clothes she bought for school with her grandmother. Luke brushed his hand over my leg under the table once or twice. I wanted to reach down and hold his palm there, resting on my bare thigh, but I resisted. He'd been hesitant about touching me all day. *It's because we haven't told Luna yet, and he doesn't want her to be confused,* I reminded myself.

What were we waiting for?

We biked home after eating and put the bikes away in the shed. The day's cloudiness made it feel later than it was.

"Alright, two hours to your bedtime. Wanna watch a movie?" Luke asked as we walked around to the front of the house.

"Yeah. *How to—*"

"Luna, I love the little dragons as much as the next guy, but can we *please* watch something else?"

I bit my fist to keep from laughing. There was true anguish on his handsome face. Luke caught my eye over Luna's head. *How many times?* I mouthed to him.

"Hundreds," he muttered under his breath as he unlocked the front door.

"Fine," she droned, recalcitrant. "I guess we could watch something new."

"Thank goodness, I'll pick it out." Luke launched himself over the back of the couch and lunged for the remote.

"Dad!" Luna squealed, running around to the front of the couch, throwing herself across his lap, and reaching for the remote too.

"Nope, it's my turn." He held the little black device up over her head where she couldn't reach. "But you have veto power, deal?"

She sighed dramatically. "Deal."

My heart expanded in my chest just watching them.

"C'mon, Val." Luke tapped the couch cushion on his other side.

They picked a cute Disney movie about a little Italian sea monster. The darker it got, the more I leaned into Luke, feeling starved for his touch after playing platonic friends all day. Eventually, his arm wrapped around my back and his thumb rubbed soothing circles on my shoulder.

When the movie ended, Luke turned to Luna and said, "Alright, go brush your teeth and put on PJs. I'll be up in a few minutes."

"Night, Luna." I smiled at her.

"Night, Val!"

When the upstairs bathroom door closed, I turned to face Luke on the couch.

"I guess I shouldn't stay over, since she doesn't know yet?"

My eyes searched his for an explanation. It was dark in the room now, the only light coming from the muted credits running down the screen. The low lights flickered across his chiseled features.

"Yeah, uh." He ran a hand down his face. "I think that's for the best." He leaned over to kiss my lips, soft and tender, like he was trying to reassure me.

"Okay," I said softly. "Why—why didn't we tell her today?" We'd agreed to tell her when she got back.

She was back.

He considered how to respond for a long moment, face unreadable. My heart thundered like a bass drum in my chest, accelerating with each second of silence. "There's a lot going on right now. She's going back to school in a couple of days, we need to work out a new schedule—hers, mine...yours."

Oh, right. He had no idea what I was doing this fall because I took that stupid interview. I already had to ask Clara's mom if the girls could have a long playdate on Tuesday so Luke wasn't in a lurch when I left for Boston. He was probably wondering if he needed to line up more help, which he would if I took this job. What a mess.

"I'm sorry. I kinda messed up our ability to plan, huh?"

He kept his palm on one of my knees. "It's okay. You need to do what you need to do. We'll figure it out." His voice lacked its usual confidence. It made me feel sick to my stomach. "But I think it might make more sense to wait to tell Luna until things are more settled. Give you the space to make up your mind."

Make up my mind about what? Them? My mind was totally made up when it came to loving Luke and Luna and wanting to be part of their lives. Or maybe he meant make up my mind about my career?

I was about to ask what he meant when Luna's voice floated down the stairs. "Dad, are you coming?"

"Get some rest," Luke said to me. "You still good to take her tomorrow?"

"Yeah, we're getting mani-pedis."

"Oh, boy. Put it on my card. Yours, too." I opened my mouth but he cut me off. "C'mon, that's not an expense, that's a treat."

"Fine. Thank you." I smiled. He took my face between his rough hands and kissed me, running his tongue over my lip before nipping it playfully.

I hummed.

His lips stilled but lingered against mine, like it took effort for him to pull back. "Night, baby," he murmured, forehead pressed to mine.

"Night, Luke."

He squeezed my hand and turned to head upstairs.

Love you.

39

I looked out the bus window at the Cape Cod Canal, catching a glimpse of the boats passing by under the massive bridge that connected the Cape and Islands to mainland Massachusetts. The day was bright and clear, eighty degrees. Perfect.

I wish I was at the beach with Luna instead of on this bus.

I scrutinized the taupe nail polish on my fingernails. Luna and I had the best day yesterday. We got coffee for me and lemonade for her and walked in and out of the stores in town in the morning, spending the most time in the bookstore picking out some new books to read together at bedtime. Then we got our mani-pedis at a salon not far away. It felt a little like bribery, taking her to do something Luke would never want to do with her, but her unadulterated excitement made it worth it. We did the same purple color on our toes, but I went with a more conservative color on my fingernails because of this interview. I kind of hated it.

My conversation with Luke from the other night felt unfinished. *"Give you the space to make up your mind."* I still didn't fully understand what he meant. *He must mean career-wise.* He knew how I felt about him and Luna.

The bus zoomed up the highway as my mind raced in circles.

What if he didn't want me to take this job and only see them on the weekends for the most part? He said we'd figure it out, but did he mean it?

I pulled up the notes I took on my phone after speaking with the recruiter to prepare for this interview, but I couldn't focus on them. My head leaned against the cool glass of the window, and I watched, miserably, as the trees that lined the road blurred by. I felt like my heart was tethered to the island and the farther away I got, the stronger the rope tugged on my chest cavity, threatening to rip it right out.

I was jolted from my daze when my phone vibrated in my hand. The same bliss I felt every time Luke's name appeared on that screen rushed my system.

LUKE

Good luck today! I'm sure you'll get the job. They'd be crazy not to make an offer to such an intelligent, poised, experienced lawyer as you. I want you to know I support you either way. I want us to be together either way. We can make Boston to MV work. Make the decision that's right for you. I'm sorry we haven't had much of a chance to talk about it. I'm here if you need me.

The lump that formed in my throat as I read his words was so big I thought I might choke. I couldn't breathe. Tears formed silent streams down my cheeks.

I loved him so much it hurt.

I read it again, eyes straining through the bleariness. He was giving me permission to make my own choice, telling me I wouldn't lose him either way.

Make the decision that's right for you.

If only I knew what that was.

I didn't know what to say to Luke's text, but I needed to acknowledge it somehow, so I sent:

Thank you <3

As the bus pulled off the highway toward Boston's South Station, I dug in my bag for a tissue or a napkin to wipe off the streaks of mascara I knew stained the skin under my eyes. Instead of a napkin, I found several sheets of lined paper, folded like a letter, tucked securely into an interior pocket of the bag I'd taken with me everywhere this summer. The bag that usually held my laptop, headphones, and a notebook—my movable writing setup.

I knew what it was before I opened the pages, and another golf ball lodged in my throat. *Author Business Plan* was scrolled across the top of the page in Luke's handwriting. I read through the bullets for the tenth time since Luke and I made it together and felt a flicker of fire in my bones.

This! my heart shouted.

"South Station!" The bus driver called. I tucked the precious papers back into their pocket and disembarked.

I had over an hour to kill before the interview. I meandered across the bridge connecting downtown Boston to the Seaport neighborhood and sat on a bench facing the water. Lots of pedestrians, not so many boats. I'd rather be sitting on one of the benches in Edgartown Harbor, eating ice cream with Luna.

What am I doing here?

My edginess had steadily climbed since the moment Mimi dropped me off at the ferry terminal this morning, cortisol coursing through my bloodstream. She didn't say much while we were in the car. Her demeanor had never been one to influence or convince, but I found myself wondering what she thought. Did she think the summer had been restorative and I was ready to resume my career of negotiating contracts for demanding clients? Or did she feel like Luke and question why I would go back to something that wasn't good for me?

I scrolled my text messages. I didn't want to call Luke. Based on his text, I knew he'd wish me luck, give me a pep talk. He wouldn't want to throw me off before the interview. *He's probably at a site or something anyway.*

I stopped on Natalie's name.

Hey, are you free?

If she wasn't in a meeting or tied up working on something urgent, I'd hear from her within two minutes. When I didn't, I kept scrolling.

My eyes landed on my last text from Drew. I hadn't told him I had an interview today. Drew would tell me what he actually thought. Maybe it would help me sort my own scattered, unsure thoughts. If he said one thing, and I agreed with him, I'd feel relieved that the smartest person I knew agreed with me. If he recommended something else, and I disagreed deep down, I'd bristle. Like flipping a coin when you thought you were equally torn between two alternatives, you always knew in that millisecond before you looked at it what you were actually hoping the outcome would be. Content with my plan, I tapped the little phone symbol next to his name.

It rang twice before my brother's gruff voice answered, "Hey, Val. What's up?"

"Hey." My voice was throaty. I cleared it. "Hey, Drew."

"You okay?"

"Yeah, I'm fine."

"You sound...not okay."

I chuckled. "I've been better."

"What's going on?"

"I'm thinking about maybe going back to work. I got an interview at a firm in Boston that's looking to build up their private equity group and I figured, why not take it? I spent all this time and money and energy developing this high-earning skill, how could I just...not use it? So..." I sighed, not sure what else to add.

"I can see why you'd feel that way. It's a lot of earning potential to give up. But are you passionate about the work anymore?"

"I don't know." I closed my eyes and pictured it—the kickoffs, the diligence, the negotiations, winning points, closing deals, the press releases. It used to give me a little jolt of excitement to get assigned to a cool deal or prestigious client but now...it didn't. "Not really."

"So it's just a sunk cost. Who cares, ya know? You'll find something else you love." I pictured him sitting in his office, probably with his chair tipped back and his feet up on the corner of his big wooden desk.

"Luke mentioned sunk costs, too..."

"Smart man." After a moment he added, "But honestly, it isn't even *really* a sunk cost because you'll apply your skills in other ways. The problem-solving, the work ethic, your understanding of law and business—it will all benefit you no matter what you do. It's part of who you are."

I nodded to myself and felt a glimmer of relief. *Just because I don't want to do it anymore, doesn't mean it was all a waste.* "That all makes sense. Thanks, Drew."

"You don't sound so sure."

"I just... When people look at the background I have, won't they think it's silly for me to be a struggling, unemployed writer?"

"Is that what you want to do instead? Writing?"

Crap. I never told Drew about the writing. I said, "Yes," and held my breath for his reaction.

"Fiction?"

"Yeah."

"Oh, wow. That's cool as shit, Val. I wish I could write fiction. I'm not creative enough. Some of the chapters of these philosophy books I write bore even me."

I laughed. "Thanks."

"Have you started? What do you write about?"

I blew a breath through pursed lips. "Yeah, this summer I've been working on a novel. It's about a woman—she's a corporate M&A attorney."

"Naturally."

I smiled. "She has this big deal, and her boyfriend is a bit too interested in it. He sneaks into her home office and reads her documents and then makes a big trade in the company."

"Idiot."

"Ha! Yes, such an idiot. They're prosecuted for insider trading, drama ensues, but she forms this unlikely bond with the SEC investigator because...well, they don't get each other at first but then they do. And they meet again by happenstance later after thinking about each other nonstop." I was babbling. *I need to work on my pitch,* I thought with enthusiasm. If I wrote it down, practiced it, it would be easier to explain what I was writing on the occasions when people asked. "I guess you could say it started out being a story about betrayal, but it ended up being a story about love."

"That sounds really interesting, Val. O would love to read something like that," Drew said when I finally took a breath.

"Thanks. I'll have to tell her about it." Drew's wife was my other source of romance novel recommendations, in addition to Natalie.

"Can I say something without you getting upset?" My brother asked after a moment.

"Oh, boy. Yes." I pinched the bridge of my nose.

"You care too much what other people think."

I let the words wash over me, through me. He was right. Not because Drew was pretty much always right, and not because he was an intelligent professor—because in my heart and soul and mind, I agreed with him. And I was finally willing to admit it. Hadn't Luke and my therapist and my subconscious been trying to tell me the same thing all summer?

"Who cares if they don't get it?"

"You shouldn't worry more about disappointing others than you do about disappointing yourself."

"The best decisions I ever made in my life were when I ignored everyone else and listened to myself instead."

"What does success mean to you, personally?"

"They don't matter. They don't know you."

"I think you're right," I said to my brother, not a hint of bitterness in my concession.

"It's not just you—lots of people care too much what other people think. But like I've always said, fuck 'em, ya know?"

"Who?" I laughed. Of course he had to lob in some explicit tenet he held.

"I don't know, everyone. Everyone that's not you."

I laughed again, appreciating my brother's bluntness for once.

"Thanks, Drew. I needed that. You've always been better at that than me—self-confidence, not caring what other people think."

"Eh, it's because I'm a conceited bastard with poor people skills."

I guffawed.

"You've always been better with people than me," he went on. "And Val, you know, I had to learn my own lesson that being academically gifted and professionally successful aren't all that matters in life, either. I nearly lost the most important thing because of my horrendous social skills. And all the books I'd read and classes I'd aced didn't matter."

"I want to hear that whole story sometime."

"I'm sure O would love to tell you. You could write a book about it. What's that type of romance book she's always talking about...enemies to lovers?"

"I thought you guys were always friends?"

"Yeah," he said, his voice filled with irony. "Me too."

"Now I'm intrigued."

"Come visit us. We have a guest room. Bring Luke and the kid. I assume you're together now?"

I shook my head. For someone who claimed to be bad with people, he was sharply observant. "Yes," I replied.

"Nice. He seemed like a good guy. Is he treating you well?"

"Yeah." I tried to stop my mind from wandering to the strain between Luke and me the last few days. Ever since I mentioned this goddamn interview. "He's the best."

"When's this interview? You gonna cancel it and do what you actually wanna do?"

I moved the phone away from my ear to check the time. "It's in half an hour. And yeah, I think I am."

I get it now, I wanted to tell Wendy. There wasn't one objective definition of success. *Success is whatever I think it is.*

The only opinion of me that really matters is my own.

And I didn't look down on myself for making a change and leaving behind something I didn't love to pursue something that I do.

Alongside two people I love.

An overwhelming sense of peace and certainty settled in my gut as I typed out the email to the recruiter and the hiring contact for the firm apologizing, canceling my interview, and telling them I wasn't in a position to reschedule. I shoved my phone in my bag as soon as I pressed Send.

Silently thanking myself for wearing flats today instead of heels, I shot up from the bench and ran back across the bridge to the bus station.

The next bus to the Martha's Vineyard ferry terminal was departing in twenty minutes.

40

"Would it be alright with you if I kept living here, full-time?" I looked at Mimi as we drove down the beach road toward Edgartown. As soon as she picked me up from the boat, I'd told her about canceling the interview. "I'll take good care of the house," I promised.

She smiled. "I was wondering when you'd finally ask."

Relief settled at least some of my nerves. I sank into the passenger seat and texted my family and Natalie to tell them my decision was made: I'd be staying on Martha's Vineyard.

When we got back to Mimi's house, I changed as quickly as I could, anxious to go to Luke's and tell him my good news—that I was staying, that I'd somehow finally shaken off the insecurities that compelled me to take that interview in the first place. The excitement humming underneath my skin to finally start living life on my own terms was building to a crescendo.

When I pulled into Luke's driveway, the flickering, blueish light of the TV filtered through the living room window. I cut the engine and bounded up the front walkway. My hand stopped at the door handle. As far as Luke knew, I was spending the night at a hotel in Boston and returning tomorrow. I'd typed out several messages to him on the bus ride, but none of them quite conveyed what I wanted to say, so I never sent any of them. I couldn't just throw open the door. Even though it felt strange to knock on the front door of the house that had begun to feel like home, I did it anyway. Moments later, I heard the faint taps of bare feet on hardwood floors. Luna opened the door, Luke a few steps behind her.

"Val!" She wrapped her arms around my waist.

I hugged her back.

"Hey, Luna." I made eye contact with Luke over her head. Surprise was plain on his features.

"Clara loved my purple nails!" Luna wiggled her fingers at me.

"She has good taste."

"Yep!" Luna retreated to the couch, one of the books we bought yesterday open on the table. The Red Sox game was on TV, and Luke had a kitchen towel draped over his shoulder.

I opened my mouth to explain my presence to Luke at the same time that he asked, "What are you—um, did something happen?"

"I canceled the interview."

He inclined his head toward the kitchen, and I followed him.

"Why?" he asked, a line appearing between his eyebrows. I didn't blame him. I'd been all over the place lately.

"It's not what I want. I want to write. I want to implement that Author Business Plan we made. I want to stay here."

The thin line of his lips turned up in the corner and light entered his eyes. He was standing on the other side of the kitchen island from me. *Too far away.*

"Good."

That's it?

I glanced over my shoulder at Luna on the couch.

"Can we—" I started.

"Yeah. Luna, we're going out back for a minute."

"Okay," she said, unbothered. "Can I change the channel?"

"Sure."

He closed the slider, creating a sound barrier between us and Luna. We moved to the far side of the deck, out of view from the windows. Luke wrapped his strong arms around me, and I finally felt like I could breathe.

When he pulled back and looked at my face, his was knotted with concern.

I smiled at him. "I'm happy. I didn't really want to do it; I just thought I should. I let worrying about what other people think get the better of me. You were right, Luke. I'm happy here."

My fingers played with the ends of his hair, arms still wrapped around his neck. His hands flexed on my hips, compelling me to bring my lips to his. His kissed me back sweetly, tongue teasing but not delving. He was holding back. I felt it in my bones. Was it because Luna could walk outside at any moment?

I looked up at him. "Can we tell Luna now? It would be nice to be able to kiss and hold hands a little more, start having sleepovers again?" I raised my eyebrows and pursed my lips flirtatiously.

His gaze hardened. "Val," he said, dissent in his tone.

My stomach dropped like a brick through water. Something was wrong. My heart rate climbed, fast. Too fast. The tingling started.

Fuck. I need to sit down.

His eyes searched mine. He opened his mouth and closed it again. He took a step back from me, breaking my hold on his neck, and ran a hand down his face.

The cloudiness moved in at the base of my skull. Before it got any worse, I sat down on the wooden boards of the deck, bent my knees, and wrapped my arms around them. I sucked in a deep breath, not able to look at him for a second.

A moment later, he was kneeling in front of me, hands covering mine on my knees.

"I'm sor—" I started to say.

"What's happen—"

"I'm fine, I promise." My heaving chest proved I was lying. But I would be fine in a minute or two. The stoniness on his face moments ago was replaced entirely with concern.

I haven't felt a disconnect like this with him...ever. Something was off and my chest ached with worry. Did he change his mind? He texted me earlier that he wants us to be together either way.

I closed my eyes and took a deep breath, forming an O with my lips as I released it. *You're okay*, I told myself. *This panic doesn't control you. If Luke ends things right now, would you change any decision you've made?*

No.

My heart would shatter, but I'd survive. I knew myself better now.

The clouds in the back of my head retreated and my breathing leveled out. My internal pep talk made me brave enough to say, "Something's wrong. Can you please just tell me what it is?"

"Hey." He pushed my hair behind my ears. "Nothing is wrong. I am so happy for you, Val. You know I didn't want you to take that job, that I thought you'd be happier if you stayed here and kept doing what you were doing. But I didn't want to pressure you either way, that's why I texted you today."

"That meant a lot to me." I chewed my lip and studied him. His deep brown eyes were back to their normal, soft demeanor.

His mouth quirked up. "I'm glad."

My eyes continued searching his face, his posture, needing more of an explanation.

"I'm just processing. I didn't know you'd be back tonight. I'd prepared myself for both alternatives—that they'd woo you and convince you to take the job, and we'd need to figure out how to adjust our lives around it, or that maybe you'd decide not to take the job because you like writing and having freedom more. I spent all day trying not to get attached to either possibility, but I couldn't shake my selfish desire that you'd turn it down."

"It's not just writing, Luke. It's you. I want to be here with *you*. I don't want to move to Boston and only see you and Luna on the weekends. But if it makes you feel better, I would have chosen not to take the job whether I had you and Luna in my life or not."

He nodded and his shoulders dropped with relief. My hand clung to his, holding it against my leg. He lifted my legs and moved closer to me, placing my feet down on either side of his hips. His lips dropped to mine.

"I'm so happy you're staying," he said into my lips, brushing mine with each word.

"Me too." I smiled, finally. "It's like I didn't know what making the right decision would feel like until right now."

The smile on his perfect lips reached his eyes and calm washed over me. "Can we tell Luna? Please? Do you think she'll be happy or need a little time to adjust?" The stream of excited questions flowed from my lips in a burst.

The consternation I saw on his face earlier returned to his eyes. His mouth clamped shut.

Tears of confusion pooled behind my eyes, hot and frustrated. *I'm still missing something.* I didn't give him a chance to respond. "If there's a reason you want to wait a little longer, we can. I just..." I was at a loss for words; hurt penetrated all of my senses.

"I just want you to be sure," he whispered.

"Luke! I am sure. I have no doubts. I literally *ran* back to the bus station."

A smile broke through his serious expression. He pushed my hair back again. "We'll tell her soon, okay? I promise."

I nodded. I didn't like it, but I didn't have much fight left in me today. He must have his reasons for wanting to wait. It was natural he'd want to protect Luna, even though it hurt to think he'd feel the need to protect her from me. Was it because he wanted to make sure this relationship was serious enough before telling her?

But we are serious. We love each other.

Why did it feel like we were having two different conversations?

I tried not to let my swirling emotions show on my face.

"Are you hungry?" he asked me. "I have leftovers from dinner."

I looked down at my stomach. "Honestly, probably. I haven't eaten today besides a granola bar on the bus."

Luke stood up and pulled me up by my hands, no strain in his arms as he lifted me, like I was light as a pillow. "That's no good. You need food, you."

When his hand grasped the slider door, orange streaks reflecting in the glass, he turned. I paused one step behind him. "Hey, Val?" My gaze met his in the fading evening light. "I love you."

My eyes filled with tears of relief. "I love you, too."

He's Luna's dad. He has to do what he thinks is right. I kicked off the comforter, turned onto my back, and then flipped to my front again. The sheets on the bed in my room at Mimi's felt scratchy. I needed to buy new ones. This was insufferable.

"I just want you to be sure." Luke's low voice blew into my ears, carried on a breeze of worry.

What does that mean?

I was sure. I'd never been more sure of anything in my life. I meant what I said to him—I didn't know what the right decision would feel like until I'd actually made it. Not just the decision not to go back to BigLaw, but the decision to deliberately stop worrying what other people thought of me or my level of success.

I'm not a failure; I just changed my priorities. It took me all summer to believe it, but I did. The encompassing feeling of both elation and calm I felt the entire trip back to the island was unlike anything I'd felt in my adult life. *Right.*

I even bought a beer and mentally toasted myself on the boat ride back. It was such a difference from the insecure, unsure beer I bought on the boat ride in May. That felt like years ago, not months. I was a different person now, and I liked this version of myself so much better.

And I could not have gotten here without Luke. And Luna. Not telling her stopped me from embracing her and the life and the family I wanted more than air in my lungs. It hurt. But I was stronger now than I was before. I could wait, if that was what Luke needed. I'd keep telling him I was sure, that I was staying, that I loved them... I swallowed a new lump in my throat.

My phone buzzed. My heart hoped it was Luke, but we'd already exchanged "goodnight" texts, so I pushed down my expectations before lifting my phone. The name on the screen made me happy, nonetheless.

NATALIE

> Hi! I'm so sorry I missed your text earlier, today was so busy. How's it going? I'm free if you're still up!

I called her immediately. It'd been over a week since we'd caught up, so I skipped the pleasantries and told her all about the last week and a half. My first date with Luke, the week we spent together, sleeping at his house, saying I love you, agreeing to tell Luna.

She reacted with an appropriate amount of disgust and creative curse words when I told her what Edward Phelps said to me, adding "I won't be reading *his* books anymore." I snorted, and then I relayed the story about the interview, my trip to Boston, the clarity I finally reached to cancel the interview and rush home to Martha's Vineyard.

"I was expecting this fairy tale reunion, Nat. I would tell him I canceled the interview and that I was staying, and he'd pick me up and kiss me and we'd sit down and tell Luna we're together and everything would snap into place like the final piece of the puzzle. And he was happy for me, but he said he still wants to wait to tell her. He said, 'I just want you to be sure.' But I *am* sure, and I don't know if he's hiding the real reason or what. I'm sick over it, but I don't want to push him..."

"Hmmm," Natalie hummed, taking a moment to gather her thoughts.

I paced on the carpet, sweat making my PJs stick to my skin.

"Where'd you leave things?" she asked.

"After we talked alone on the deck, he said, 'I love you.' And when I left to drive home a little later, he asked if I was good to be there when Luna got home from her first day of school tomorrow."

Natalie hummed again. My bright friend, I needed her to collect her thoughts faster.

"I'm stumped, babe. It seems like the feelings are serious and mutual. You're staying on the island, in part for them. He knows how much you love Luna. I mean, you're obsessed. It's so cute. You're always sending me these pics of you guys together, texting me about her tennis matches. She's totally brought out this maternal side of you."

My body filled with warmth. I had no experience being a parent, but I agreed with Natalie. Spending time with Luna made me want to take care of someone, protect them, make their childhood fun and memorable. It also helped me appreciate the little joys of life more.

"He knows how much you love Luna."

"Hmm." My face scrunched.

"What?"

"Something you said. That he knows how much I love Luna. I mean, he must, right? I love reading with her and cried when she asked me to teach him how to do her braids because I didn't want to be replaced. I went to her tennis match and, and..."

I wracked my brain so hard my head hurt, trying to call up a memory of me saying the words to Luke. That I love Luna, not just him. That I don't see him having a daughter as an extra burden, but an enhancement. That I'm staying not just because I'm in love with Luke and want a new career, but because I literally cannot imagine missing any of Luna's firsts.

"Have you ever actually said it?" Natalie asked, reading my mind.

"I don't know." I took a deep breath. "I don't think so." I frowned, mentally kicking myself. I'd told Mimi and Natalie and myself, but not Luke. Not in so many words.

His ex asked if he ever seriously considered taking his parents up on taking Luna.

"*It's a lot.*"

"*We're a lot to sign up for.*"

"*Is it too much? Are we moving too fast?*"

"Oh, Luke," I murmured, more so to myself. I rubbed my sternum to ease the ache. "Do you think that's it? I mean, I know it's an insecurity of his, especially when it comes to dating."

"It would make sense."

It did make sense. And either way, I wanted him to know.

41

After tossing and turning all night, practicing the conversation I wanted to have with Luke in my head, I woke up sleep-deprived and bursting with the need to talk to him. He was taking Luna to school before work, and I'd get to his house by 2:30 when she got off the bus. *I should wait until Luna goes to bed to bring it up.*

But I couldn't. Twice as long on the treadmill as usual wasn't enough to ease my stomachache or cut through the nervous energy coursing through my veins.

I called him as soon as I got out of the shower.

He answered on the second ring. "Hey, Val. How's your day going?" His tone was cheerful, boyfriend-like.

"Hi. Um, good. What are you doing right now?"

"Putting together some quotes and timelines for a few new inquiries."

"You're at the office?"

"Yes," he drew out the word, a hint of suspicion in his tone.

"Are you alone?" I crossed my fingers. Jeremiah was often on site visits, and their administrative assistant worked from home a few days a week.

"Yes." Word drawn out longer, notable suspicion.

"Can I come by? I really want to talk to you, and I don't want to wait until later."

Please say yes.

"Yes, of course. Is everything okay? Should I be nervous?"

"No, I mean, yes." I took a breath. "Yes, everything is okay, and no, you shouldn't be nervous."

A low chuckle rumbled out of him. I took that as a good sign. "See you soon."

I took the stairs up to his office two at a time. When I opened the door, he was standing in front of his desk.

I closed the door behind me. "Can I take a guess why you want to wait to tell Luna we're together and you promise to tell me if I'm right?"

"Val," he said in the same tone as last night—warning, dissenting. "I didn't want this to be such a big deal."

"But it *is* a big deal, Luke. It's the biggest deal. I'm..." *sick over it, even though I know I could just wait like you asked.* I shook my head, took a deep breath, and steeled myself. I met his gaze. His deep brown eyes were a little confused, but mostly patient.

"I regret not saying this already so I'm going to say it anyway. I love Luna. So m—"

"I know, Val. I know you do," he said softly, kindly, but not in a way that convinced me he understood.

"No, you don't." I took another step forward, staring into his eyes, begging him to really hear me. "I. Love. Her. I love your daughter like she's mine. I don't just love her because I love you. And not just because she's the sweetest, spunkiest, most incredible eight-year-old. She's not a burden. She's not just part of a package deal I'm willing to take on so I can be with you. She's an enhancement. She's—she's..." I swallowed. "Crap." I was crying, and I wasn't done with my speech.

Luke's eyes filled, too. He looked up at the ceiling, pinching the bridge of his nose with his thumb and pointer finger. His tongue pushed into his cheek.

I closed the gap between us, inhaling another deep breath. I grabbed one of his hands, and he finally looked from the ceiling back down at me. "You know when I had that meltdown in the office, when Luna asked me to teach you how to braid her hair?"

He nodded, glassy eyes burning into me.

"It wasn't just because I didn't want to go back to my life in New York, or because I already had feelings for you and didn't want to leave you. I didn't want *anyone else* to know how to braid Luna's hair. I wanted to be the one to do it. Always. Please don't take this the wrong way, but I love her *just as much* as I love you. I know you think it's a lot for someone to sign up for, but I disagree. You two are the best package I could possibly imagine. I'm sure, Luke. I promise I'm sure. If I think about missing any of Luna's milestones, I feel sick.

"I know I can't make you believe I'm sure. You have to feel it too, but I already texted my mom and dad and Drew and Natalie and told them I'm moving here permanently and asked Mimi if I could keep living here indefinitely, and they're all happy for me, so I hope—"

His lips collided with mine. I didn't even feel him bend down. His rough hand pushed into my hair, holding my lips to his, pressing firmly before our tongues tangled sweetly. I wrapped my arms around his torso, leaning into him. I felt the tension leave his body. This kiss felt like the first one: unrestrained and passionate and *right*.

When our mouths separated, Luke dipped his head down to rest his forehead against mine. "I believe you, Val. I didn't know that's what I needed to hear. I just had this feeling like I needed to protect myself and Luna." His thumb traced my cheek. "Not that you'd ever do anything to hurt us. But if she got used to you being around every day and playing a different role in our lives, and then you left for a job... I'd hate it, but I could handle it—just weekends —but how would she feel?"

"I get it." And I did. I knew in my heart as soon as I stood up from that bench in Boston that I'd never entertain that possibility again. I didn't get to be half there for them. And I didn't want to be.

I never learned how to do anything halfway, anyway. But how could Luke be sure of that?

"Why didn't you say that?" I asked.

"What was I going to say? You've been through all this change, working all summer to find yourself again, recover from that fucking awful place you worked, doing therapy. I couldn't bring myself to lob in—hey, just a reminder what a massive literal and emotional responsibility it is to take on a parental role to an eight-year-old little girl who, oh yeah, already adores you as much as I do. It was too much, Val. I couldn't pressure or influence you into committing to that. What if it ended up pushing you away? I wanted it to feel natural, and I figured we just needed more time to get there."

Everything he said...it made perfect sense. My relief was a living, breathing thing inside of me. "I don't need more time."

"I know that now." He smirked, and I knew what he was thinking. This was all quite dramatic of me.

"Do you need more time?" I asked him.

He shook his head hard enough that my favorite dark lock fell across his forehead. Now that I was allowed to, I pushed it back. "No. I was already there, that morning before you told me about the interview, I wondered if I could make it through three hours in the car without telling her. But then when you mentioned the job I had to come to terms with the possibility of us not just rolling right into this family lifestyle I'd pictured...and finally allowed myself to want." He gave me an earnest look. "You're sure it's what you want? It's not easy, taking on a kid. I should know."

I nodded. My hands reached for his biceps, squeezing for emphasis. "Yes. I want to shower every latent maternal instinct I've ever had right on her. You know that feeling when you love someone so much you want to squeeze them so hard you fear you might hurt them, but the love has to release somehow? That's how I feel."

He laughed. A true, instinctual, infectious Luke laugh. I mirrored his joy and relief in my smile.

"I know that feeling. Come here." He pulled me into his chest, wrapping me up. "We'll tell her today, together, when she gets home from school, okay?"

A sob of relief ripped out of me, and I buried my face in his shirt. Pine and sawdust filled my nose, and that feeling like something was off, that there was some wedge between us, evaporated. "I'd like that," I said finally.

He guided us to the couch, placing me on the end, facing him and leaning on the armrest. He sat next to me, as close as possible, and lifted my legs to rest across his lap.

I ran my thumb over his cheek. He grabbed my hand and kissed my palm.

"I missed you," I murmured, not really sure what I meant. He hadn't gone anywhere. We hadn't spent more than twenty-four hours apart.

He reached his arm under my shoulder blades and lifted me onto his lap. I wrapped my arms behind his neck to hold myself up. Hands bracketing my face, he kissed my lips. "I missed you, too."

Maybe we'd been feeling the same thing—that longing to get back to the emotional and physical connection we'd had before we got off course. Before *I* got us off course.

"I'm sorry," I murmured into his lips, unable to meet his eyes as I said it.

"You have nothing to be sorry for, baby," Luke whispered, palms running down my back, pressing me into him. Using my hands to push myself up from his shoulders, I shifted one leg over his lap so I was straddling him, needing to look straight into my favorite brown eyes.

We studied each other, breaths mingling. I recognized the fire and longing flickering in those brown pools.

"Luke." It was a breath, a plea.

The hyperemotionality of everything we just discussed was quickly replaced with hyperawareness of how my inner thighs felt straddling his legs, and of everything we did on this couch the last time we were here. His large hands found my hips and pressed me into him.

When our lips met this time, it was frantic. I needed to be as close to him as possible, part of him. Our tongues savored, our hands explored—mine plunging into his hair, his raking down my bare back under my sundress. He used one hand to pull my head back slightly, moving his lips from my mouth to my collarbone, the skin where my shoulder sloped up to my neck, the sensitive area under my jaw. Featherlight kisses of his soft lips and brushes of coarse facial hair were followed by swipes of his tongue and grazes of his teeth. Desire filled my veins in an uncontrollable wave, drowning out everything that wasn't me and him and this moment. I loved how he knew exactly what these kisses would do to me—take my longing and amplify it tenfold so quickly my brain bordered on delirium.

His tongue swirled around mine in my mouth and a soft moan escaped me. I had no more thoughts except the taste of his tongue and the want building inside my body. I rolled my hips over his lap, needing the friction to start relieving the impossible ache in between my legs. He sucked in a breath through his teeth, and the hardness I felt pressing against the zipper of his shorts told me why. A few more needy, instinctual revolutions of my hips and I had to have more. It would never be enough. I'd never get sick of his calloused hands on my body, his strong arms around my back. I'd never tire of running my fingers through his thick, dark hair.

I need more, I thought again. More of him, less of the fabric separating us where our need pooled. My hands plunged down between us. I sat back on my heels to undo his belt, and then the button and zipper of his shorts.

His mouth claimed mine again, tongue delving so deep I whimpered, which only encouraged him more. His hands skated from my waist to the band of my underwear, giving it an aggressive tug. He pushed me up to stand in front of him and pulled them down to my ankles. Straddling but hovering over him, we worked his shorts and boxer briefs down enough to free his erection before I sank back down on him, rubbing my wet core over the length of his smooth, hard shaft. I nearly cried out, pressing my mouth into his shoulder to muffle the noise. It felt so good. The hisses and sharp breaths escaping Luke's perfect lips told me it felt good for him, too.

I covered his mouth with mine for a heady, breathless kiss as I slid against him carefully, his head hitting my clit in a bolt of ecstasy each time. But my heart longed for more.

"I need you inside me," I whispered into his ear, pulling the lobe between my lips. His hands squeezed my hips even harder. Hard enough to bruise me, and I lived for it, wanted my body marked by him as permanently as my soul.

"I want you so bad, baby, but I don't have anything here."

"I don't care," my body answered for me.

"I'm tested and clear," he said.

"Me too." I hadn't let Max near me without a condom, and I'd gotten tested after our breakup anyway to be sure.

Needing no more encouragement, he used those strong, addictive hands to lift me up, positioned himself at my entrance, and then pressed me back down over him, gliding himself inside.

We stared at each other as I moved myself up and down on top of him, mouths parted, our faces betraying the lust and ecstasy of our first joining like this—bare. I leaned back further, holding his gaze. His eyes were so dark they were almost black instead of brown, his dark hair tousled. Those sensual lips remained parted as he watched me. I was sure my desire mirrored his own as I braced myself on his knees while he shoved into me again and again. With one hand gripping my shoulder so I wouldn't fall back too far, the other lifted the skirt of my dress so his thumb could work circles over the most sensitive bundle of nerves between my legs.

"Luke," I whimpered, shifting forward again. Overwhelmed, I pushed a hand into his hair and kissed him like his mouth was sustenance and I hadn't eaten in weeks. His lips and tongue and teeth met mine with equal enthusiasm.

I relished that this was the first time we'd done this, been this close, nothing between us.

"I'm not on birth control," I felt the need to remind him. The chances it would matter were slim, but I didn't have the mental capacity to explain ovulation cycles while I was riding the edge of a shattering orgasm, and it felt like Luke was, too.

"I know," he rasped into my ear. "I don't care."

I pulled back to look at him.

"Do you want to stop, before...?" he asked. Our movements slowed. He stopped touching me for a moment, and my body screamed for his fingers to resume. His gaze was determined but questioning. He'd stop immediately if I asked.

"No."

Our next joining was forceful and deep and consuming. Our bodies picked up. I met each of his thrusts with a press of my hips and his godsent fingers reached between us again.

"Val, I'm going to—"

"Yes," I cried softly, because I loved it when he unraveled, and I was close to unraveling, too. One more adamant joining and he was there, panting into my neck, fingers still working me until I cried out too, moments later.

I began to lift off of his lap, but his hands held me in place by my hips. "Stay put," he all but growled. *Oh boy.* A bewildering amount of joy overtook me at the prospect we'd just discovered a new kink for Luke. For someone who'd spent her whole life trying *not* to get pregnant, I surprised myself with how much this thrilled me.

It's the commitment it symbolizes, you softie.

"I don't think it makes a difference," I murmured.

His dark brows knitted together. "Logically, it feels like it should. Let me have this." A satisfied sigh left his throat as he rested his head back on the couch, never loosening his grip on my hips.

I giggled and attacked his exposed neck with loving kisses before wrapping my arms around his back. Afternoon light snuck through the gaps in the blinds on the windows behind the couch. I'd forgotten what time of day it was, forgotten everything that wasn't assuaging Luke's doubts and reconnecting with him in every possible way. We held each other, the only sounds our breathing and the hum of cars and people outside, far away.

"What did I do to deserve you?" he whispered after a minute, or ten, I didn't know.

I pressed my lips into his cheek, just above his beard. "I've been asking myself the same thing about you."

42

When Luna got home, she went right to the kitchen and opened the pantry door. Luke followed her.

"So Luna, we have some news we want to share with you. Will you come sit with us?" Luke guided her toward the couches, where I was already seated, nerves humming beneath my skin.

"Can we have a snack first?" Luna pleaded.

I shrugged, making eye contact with Luke. I didn't mind if she wanted to have a snack first.

He kept guiding her into the living room. "News first, snack after. It will be quick, I promise."

"Okayyy," she whined. I fought my smile.

"So," Luke started, "I should have practiced this." He took a deep breath. "Val and I are together." Luna gave us no indication she knew what he meant. "As a couple. We love each other. We're boyfriend and girlfriend." He squinted at her. "Does that make sense?"

"You love each other?" Comprehension started to take over her features. "Like Nan and Pop? And Aunt Cesca and Uncle Jeremiah?"

"Yes, exactly like that," I answered.

"But, don't you have to leave and go back to New York some-day?" Luna asked, a hint of panic in her tone. Luke must have reminded her throughout the summer that I might not be there forever.

"No." I reached for her hand. "I'm staying here on Martha's Vineyard."

"Forever?" Her brown eyes widened.

I stole a glance at Luke. "That's the plan, yes."

Her wide-eyed gaze pivoted back and forth between me and Luke, like she was looking for her dad's confirmation before she got excited. When he nodded, a big smile plastered on his face, she jumped and gave him a hug. Then she quickly released and hugged me, too.

"Are you going to live here? Can we get our nails done every week? And make cookies?"

I laughed. I skipped her first question and said, "Maybe not every week, but we can certainly get our nails done and make cookies."

She beamed, and it filled my heart. When I pulled her in for another hug, I got choked up. My life looked so different now than it did six months ago, and I couldn't be happier. If anything, the feeling of peace and certainty I felt running back to South Station yesterday sunk deeper roots inside of me.

"And I can braid your hair whenever you want," I added, flip-ping a lock of her hair around in my hand. Her ponytail had all but fallen out at school.

"Yes!" She pulled back from me. "Can we have a snack now?"

She made her way into the kitchen, and Luke and I looked at each other, shaking our heads.

My heart released a breath. *Thank goodness she's happy.*

Later, I was teary-eyed in the kitchen. Luke was finishing up the dishes, and we'd poured fresh drinks. It felt like we were celebrating. "I'm so happy she's happy." I swallowed.

I couldn't help but watch Luna when we had dinner, searching for any signs she was uncomfortable. Luke grabbed my hand on the table at one point, and she didn't bat an eye. She pontificated happily about her trip to Hershey Park with her grandparents last week, adding that we should come next time—both of us. Some stress left my shoulders when she said that.

When she mentioned she wasn't sure which outfit to wear for her *second* day back at school, I told her I'd love to help her pick it out. She dragged me up to her room to decide right then and there.

"What'd you expect?" Luke asked, turning to look at me. I leaned against the counter next to him.

"I don't know. She's a kid. Kids don't always like change."

"That's true. But it's not really a change for her. You've been there for her all summer."

I smiled. Luke dried his hands and used his thumbs to wipe away my tears.

"They're happy tears, I promise," I said.

He kissed me. The soft press of his lips, his now familiar taste, felt like home.

When we settled on the couch, drinks in hand, baseball game on mute on the television, music playing at low volume from the speakers, my entire body relaxed.

This, my heart and my mind sang in unison, finally aligned.

Luke looked at me, suddenly pensive. "You look at her the way Monica used to. I'm sorry it took me so long to see it."

I reached for his hand. "You have nothing to apologize for."

"I think maybe she knew—my sister. She knew that someday I'd meet someone like you, and we'd have a family, that Luna would have a family that loved her. Is that strange?"

I loved that he was already thinking of us as a family.

"No. I kinda believe in the divine. But I also know you well enough by now to know your sister chose you because of who *you* are. Luna has had a family this entire time."

"Thanks, Val." His voice was soft and full of something deep. He said it like my words meant something to him. Maybe everything to him.

He pulled me closer, pressed his warm lips to my cheek, and said, "It just didn't feel complete until now."

EPILOGUE

Six Months Later

I'd neared the end of my Broadway musical playlist as I drove along the beach road toward Edgartown. The formidable wind whipped into the side of my car, and the bodies of salt water on either side of the road were covered in white-capped waves.

I drummed my fingers on the steering wheel, humming along. This car I bought with my dad last year had served me well. I finally let Luke start splitting my car payment and insurance with me. His argument was that I used it to pick Luna up and take her places, so it was a family expense. I liked it when he used the word family like that, even though we hadn't made it official yet.

I got my period a week after that day we threw caution to the wind in his office. I was ninety percent relieved, but shocking even myself, ten percent disappointed. We'd been more responsible since then. We talked about the future and the promise of more kids often enough that I knew we were still on the same page. *In time*, I told myself, not wanting to wish this time away, when we were a family of three.

My skin hummed with anticipation as I pulled up to my favorite weathered-shingle, cape-style house. The bushes and trees were bare, the lawn brown and thawing. It was still my favorite sight. Mid-March in Cape Cod felt like it was not quite winter, not quite spring. I was on my way home after spending a week visiting my parents in New Hampshire and then Natalie in New York. It was the longest I'd been away from Luke and Luna since August. Even when I was with the other people I loved, I missed them.

After Mimi returned to Florida at the end of September, Luke insisted I move in with them. "What's the point of you staying there less than once a week by yourself?" he'd said. "Just move your stuff in here. We'll go check on the house every few days and make sure it's fine." I didn't have any counter arguments.

My clothes now lived in his closet and one of his dressers, and my novels had started to accumulate in stacks around the house—the coffee table, the mantle above the fireplace, the corners of our bedroom.

Our bedroom.

Over the last six months, while Luke was at work and Luna was at school, I went to the gym and spent most of the rest of the day writing at the kitchen table or reading fiction and books about the craft of writing novels.

I was so close to finishing my first novel I could taste it. It was hard to even take a break from it while visiting my family and Natalie. I woke up early each morning, before anyone else, and was typing before my first cup of coffee had cooled enough to drink. I felt like I knew my characters—the disgraced but forgivable lawyer and the hard exterior, soft interior SEC investigator—in real life. As excited as I was to finish the manuscript, I was going to miss them. But they weren't leaving me yet. According to all the self-education I'd done, I had endless rounds of editing ahead of me. And Drew was right—my problem-solving skills and the confidence in my own ability to figure things out that I'd learned as a law firm associate had proved helpful as I worked through plot holes in my story and researched insider trading laws.

Francesca was right, too—I hadn't minded the Martha's Vineyard winter one bit. I'd even convinced Tyler and Erica and little Mina to take a trip here in the fall to check out the island in the offseason.

My legal skills hadn't laid completely fallow, either. I transferred my license from New York to Massachusetts, and I often read through contracts for Luke and Francesca. Reading and advising on contracts was second nature after so many years, and the event and contractor contracts were much shorter than the ones I was used to. It made me happy to help them and to use my degree in some small way, a way that didn't take me away from my true passion—writing. Luke insisted on paying me when I helped with contracts, so he'd somehow reduced my need to dip into my savings anyway, despite my objections.

I cut the engine as soon as my car was in park next to Luke's truck and bounded up the walkway, leaving my bags to collect from the trunk later. Luke opened the door for me before I got to the top step.

"Hi, baby." He wrapped his arms around me. I pressed my face into his soft hoodie, breathing in his pine and sawdust scent. *Home.*

"Hi. I missed you."

"I missed you, too." He kissed the top of my head. "We have a surprise for you." I pulled back and looked at him, then stood on my tiptoes to peer over his shoulder. Luna watched us from the living room, bouncing on the balls of her feet, a devilish grin on her face.

A reflexive smile spread on my lips. "What's going on?" My eyes roamed from her face to Luke's and then back. Their guilty, mischievous looks were so reminiscent of each other, it was like she inherited the gene from her uncle. He grabbed my hand, took two steps backward from the entry, and reached his other hand for the office door. When he opened it, the smell of fresh paint greeted us. Then he pulled me inside the room.

"What!?" I exclaimed, spinning in a circle, not believing my eyes.

The little room that had previously been filled with storage bins and boxes, the vacuum, and discarded mail had been cleared out. The entire back wall now boasted floor-to-ceiling, built-in bookshelves, all in bright white, complete with horizontal sconces above each case and a ladder attached to a runner along the top.

"Oh my gosh, a ladder!" My eyes were going to pop out of my head. I spun again and noticed for the first time a matching white-painted desk built into the wall just under the front-facing window. A camel-colored leather desk chair was tucked underneath. A bright throw rug and an oversized gray chair in the corner completed the room.

"This is incredible!"

Luna giggled from her spot near the door and I rushed over to hug her. Then I turned and threw my arms around Luke. "How did you do this in one week?"

"I'm pretty good at building things," he said, a smug grin on his handsome face. "And I had some help."

"Wow." I turned to look at it again, heart pounding with excitement.

"I figured you could use a space that's just yours. Somewhere you can go and write your future bestsellers. Somewhere besides the kitchen table where Luna and I end up distracting you when we get home."

"You guys don't distract me!"

Luke popped his shoulder up, like he knew they did but he wouldn't make me admit it. I did love the idea of having somewhere to go on those days when I just couldn't stop typing. He released me, nudging me toward the shelves. All the books I'd left around the house were already lined up, in order by author. I swept my hand along their bindings. My gaze caught on a little brass placard attached to the middle shelf. *Established* and the current year were etched into the metal. I ran my finger over it. "I love this."

"I'm hoping it's not the only thing we establish this year," Luke's low timbre sounded from behind me. When I turned around, he was on one knee, holding a velvet jewelry box open, a diamond ring glistening inside.

The sight stole my breath. A lump rose in my throat, and my eyes filled. "Luke," I murmured, taking a step toward him, closing the gap between us. I made to crouch down too, but he held up his pointer finger, imploring me to silence. I glanced toward the doorway, where Luna stood, brown eyes wide, pure hope and happiness plain on her face, Luke's phone in her hand. I shook my head slightly, overcome. *They planned this whole thing.*

"Valerie Leone," Luke said, drawing my gaze back to my favorite brown eyes. "You are the best thing that ever happened to me. I didn't know what I was waiting for until I found it, found you. You are a uniquely spectacular woman, and Luna and I are so lucky to have you in our lives. I love you. Will you marry me?"

Tears streamed down my face until they dripped off my chin. Luke's eyes were gleaming, too. I rushed into his arms, pulling him up. "Yes!" I squeaked, not caring as my voice cracked and tears continued to flow. He sealed our agreement with a quick, firm kiss, holding our lips together a moment longer before pulling back and taking my hand. He slid the ring onto my ring finger, his hand shaking slightly. A marquis center diamond was flanked by two, small oval diamonds. I loved it.

I looked over Luke's shoulder to where Luna was still patiently waiting by the door, a huge smile on her little face. "Come here, Luns," I said, extending an arm out.

She jogged over and launched herself at us. I caught her, giggling, smiling so wide my cheeks got sore. I squeezed her in tight, and Luke did, too.

We'd felt like a family for a while now, but this invitation from Luke to make it permanent, to put a ring and a label and a plan on our feelings for each other, felt like putting the final piece into a puzzle. A puzzle that was challenging and complicated and at one point didn't feel like it would ever be completed. A puzzle that I didn't realize for so long was missing its pieces. I found the right pieces here, on this island I'd loved since I was a child. Luke, Luna, and the version of myself that felt right and free. Free of that dangerous chip I had on my shoulder for so long. Free to love and do what I love.

We clutched each other for long enough that we had to release ourselves for air.

"I took some pictures," Luna whispered to her dad.

"Thanks, Luns."

I would have said yes no matter how or where he asked, but this—in the home that felt like home well before I moved in, in the writing office of my dreams built by the man I loved, with the little girl that stole my whole heart last year—was absolutely perfect.

After my first day writing in my new home office, I closed my laptop with a smile on my face. I turned off my music and removed my headphones from my ears. When I heard the clamp of the refrigerator closing, I left the idyllic room and strode into the kitchen.

"Hi," I said to Luke. He'd pulled some groceries out and put them on the kitchen island. A cutting board was already covered with chopped peppers, onions, and potatoes. Luna was at an after-school playdate, due home any minute.

"Hi, baby. How's the writing going? I poked my head in when I got home but you were in the zone."

The smile I had on my face when I shut my laptop reappeared. "I finished my draft."

"The whole thing?" His tone rose with excitement.

"The whole thing. First full draft, first novel. Done."

"Val! That's amazing!"

He rounded the island toward me and raised his hand for a high five, insisting I clap my hand into his before he pulled me into his warm, strong arms. Luke's hugs were an essential nutrient to me now. I wondered how I ever lived without them.

"I'm so proud of you," he said as he pulled back to look at me. "My fiancée, the novelist."

I felt my cheeks heating. My self-confidence had improved a lot over the past year, but I'd be lying if I said Luke's confidence in me didn't mean the world to me. He made me feel like I could do anything. I'd never felt this loved before. Ever. It made me wonder what I even thought love was before this. I had no clue.

"Thanks!" I bounced up on my toes and kissed him.

"So, what now? When do I get to read it?" He held me in place with his arms wrapped around my waist, swaying slightly.

"According to all the blogs I've read and podcasts I've listened to about the novel writing process, I need to step away from the story for a bit before I go back to edit it. So, for now, I take some time off from that manuscript."

Luke nodded, still focused on me, listening intently. I went on, "I was thinking, in the meantime, I'd start working on my next idea."

Luke's face lit up, mirroring my own. "Oh yeah? What's your next idea?"

"I want to write a book about last summer. About my burnout and how hard it was to change my life, and how it was so worth it in the end."

"Will I be in it?"

"Yeah, of course. You're the love interest." I smiled at him. "And the one that helps the main character find herself."

"Okay," he said, pushing a lock of my hair behind my ear. "I can work with that." A devilish grin spread across his face. It made me want to bite his lower lip. He shifted our bodies and caged me against the counter, leaning down to whisper in my ear, "You know that thing we do..." What he went on to describe instantly made my cheeks grow hot. "Let's keep that part out of the book."

"Okay, I promise," I murmured, taking my opportunity to nip his lip while he was so close. He returned it with a deep kiss, his tongue finding mine, savoring it. I pulled his body in tighter.

"Mmm." He pulled back, eyes glazed. He sighed. "We should start dinner before Luna gets home."

I'd be disappointed to stop our kiss before it led to more, but I was excited for Luna to get home, too. We'd have time to pick this up later.

He planted a wet kiss on my cheek, spun, and grabbed a frying pan out of the cabinet, his forearm flexing beneath his rolled-up sleeves. I watched him as he turned on the burner and added oil to the pan. It was so domestic. I loved it.

"Hey," Luke said as he grabbed the cutting board full of chopped vegetables from the counter, "you should name it Morning Glory Girl."

ALSO BY MARIA ANNE LENIHAN

BETTER OFF NOT KNOWING

COMING WINTER 2025/2026

The genetic testing mandate ruined her life.
She's going to get it overturned.

It's 2045, and it's been nearly ten years since New York's health agency passed the genetic sequencing mandate and Avery Preston received the test results that stole the future she wanted with her first love. After their breakup, she resigns herself to a solitary, straightforward life, saving money for her future and keeping her daydreams on lockdown. Until she finds out the rare genetic disease disclosed in her results has been cured, and it turns her worldview upside down.

Avery is furious the government's mandate forced her to learn her genetics without her consent. After she discovers other states are planning to enact similar laws, she hires Charlie—a handsome plaintiff's attorney known for winning unwinnable cases—to take on her state government and change the law.

Over the yearlong litigation full of late nights in conference rooms and multiday business trips, Avery and Charlie become close in a way that neither of them can deny, but with their case long from over, mixing business and personal could be disastrous. And the further they get in the litigation, the more things they discover that simply don't add up. Like the overly involved director of public health whose hostility toward them grows with each stage, and reported disease rates that are way outside the norm. All the while, time is running out for their case to make a difference in those other states.

To succeed both in and outside the courtroom, Avery will need to expose parts of herself she normally keeps hidden, or else risk sabotaging not only the case that now means everything to her, but also her second chance at happiness.

Told in a dual timeline, the reader gets to know Avery both before and after she receives her genetic test results. Equal parts steamy and heady, this futuristic tale will have you wondering, *What if?*

***

Subscribe to Maria Anne Lenihan's Newsletter to stay informed about the release of *Better Off Not Knowing*.

https://www.marialenihanauthor.com/newslettersignup

ACKNOWLEDGMENTS

It is surreal to be writing the acknowledgments for my debut novel. *Morning Glory Girl* is a story that came together piece by piece, and then all at once when I decided to take a break from my corporate legal career last summer and finish writing the coming-of-thirties summer romance that had lived in my head for a long time. *Morning Glory Girl* embodies a message and a healing journey that is so important to me because a lot of what Val experiences is based on what I have experienced, and what I know so many people—including (but not limited to) millennial working women—have gone through. The expectations we put on ourselves—always striving, always doing what we're supposed to do, and never having time to reflect. My *aha* moment came when I finally asked myself: What would I do if I cared more about disappointing myself than I did about disappointing everyone else? My answer was: write the stories that have lived in my head, and in notebooks, and in unfinished documents on old laptops, for as long as I could remember. What's yours?

Now to thank everyone that has helped me make this dream a reality!

My amazing beta readers and friends (Carol, Margaret, Ashley, Allie, Colleen, Maria, Peter, Sara B, Katie, Dolly, Caitlin, and Sara S): thank you for reading and believing in this story from day one. Your time, support, and enthusiasm mean the world to me.

To my team of talented editors (Victoria, Allie, and Sara): thank you for helping *Morning Glory Girl* reach its fullest potential. I am so proud of it!

Sam: thank you so much for the stunning cover. Courtney and Patrycja: thank you for the incredible character art bringing Luke & Val to life.

Hayley, Maude, Shay, and the Hayling Bookstorm team: thank you for seeing my vision, helping me hone my brand, and getting *Morning Glory Girl* noticed by so many readers. I can't wait to work with you on future releases!

To every friend and family member that has asked how my writing is going, told me they can't wait to read my book, liked every single one of my Instagram posts, and generally showed so much enthusiasm about this book: thank you, thank you, thank you. It all counts for more than you know.

To my Lenihan family: thank you for your support of my reading, writing, and bookstore habit. I'm fortunate to be part of such an enthusiastic and loving family.

To my parents: thank you for believing in me for my entire life and always supporting me in my endeavors, even as I continue to change my mind. I wouldn't be where I am today without you both. Mom: thank you for talking to me for hundreds of hours about my book ideas and being there for me through all the ups and downs. I'm lucky my mom is also one of my best friends. Dad: I hope this is the only section of the book you read. Thank you for being the best dad a daughter could ask for and inspiring the unconditional love between fathers and daughters shown in *Morning Glory Girl*.

Dan: I'll never forget the conversation we had around Christmas of 2023. It was a Saturday afternoon, the day before Christmas Eve. We'd been home for several days—a rare event for adult siblings who don't live near each other anymore—and I spent the entire time at that tiny desk in my bedroom, hopping on and off phone calls and working around the clock on a deal. We finally got a break, and you'd all been waiting hours for me to go to our favorite brewery. I shut my laptop, but by the time we got there half an hour later, I'd gotten another twenty emails on my phone. I wanted to cry. I wanted to quit. I told you all about my book ideas that day, and how, if I could, that was what I would rather do. You said, "It sounds like you have a calling. I think it's time you pick up the phone." Six months later, I finally did. Maybe it's strange to say I look up to my little brother, but I do. Thank you for your service, for being an inspiration, and for inspiring others, including your big sister. You and Analía are so supportive, and I am so grateful.

Kyle and Katie: your enthusiastic support of this book and this dream mean so much to me. Thank you for being my go-to psychologists for bouncing ideas and checking that the therapy sessions I write are accurate. I'm so lucky to have the best siblings and siblings-in-law. I'd want to be friends even if we weren't related. I can't wait to celebrate your marriage next year!

Mimi and Poppy: thank you for introducing me to Martha's Vineyard. It is a magical place and I never would have been there if not for you. I'm so lucky to have spent at least a portion of my summer on the island for over thirty years. I have the fondest memories. Mimi: thank you for your love and support my whole life—it's no secret everyone's favorite side character is based on you!

To my readers: thank you for picking up a book by a new author and taking the time to read it. There are so many amazing novels out there, and I'm honored you chose mine. I hope you enjoyed Val's story—whether because you could relate to her journey or because you fell in love with Martha's Vineyard and Luke and Luna, too. Or ideally, both!

Finally, Patrick: this book is dedicated to you because it wouldn't exist without you. Thanks for being my balance and showing me that there is more to life than the corporate climb. I think loving and being loved by you is the reason I've been able to become a more authentic version of myself. I'm scared to think where I'd be without you. I definitely wouldn't be sitting at my desk in our condo writing the acknowledgments for my first novel.

ABOUT THE AUTHOR

Maria Anne Lenihan is the author of *Morning Glory Girl*, a coming-of-thirties contemporary romance novel set on Martha's Vineyard. She grew up spending summers on Martha's Vineyard with her own grandmother and cannot wait to share the magic of the island with readers. As a corporate intellectual property attorney, her passion for creativity and innovation extends to the laws that protect creators and innovators. When she's not writing novels featuring lawyer main characters with a heavy dose of romance, she enjoys hiking, skiing, and visiting breweries with her husband.

Let's be friends on social media — booksbymaria.a.lenihan.

instagram.com/booksbymaria.a.lenihan
tiktok.com/@booksbymaria.a.lenihan